I0682087

Memoirs of Jesus

as told to

David Kurtz

New Brevet Publications
Minneapolis, MN
www.newbrevet.com

Memoirs of Jesus as told to David Kurtz

ISBN-13: 978-0-578-67924-2

New Brevet Publications
2nd Publication July 2022

Book Cover Design by ebooklaunch.com

CONTENTS

Prologue

Deep in sleep, and troubled, I arose from the depths toward consciousness as I felt a gentle nudge somewhere, likely on my shoulder. Thoughts swirled around me before another nudge came, definitely on the shoulder, followed by one of even greater intensity, along with a sharply whispered, "David. David! Wake up!"

Groggily I cracked open my eyes, sore with sleep, and slowly, awkwardly rose into a half-sitting position, propped up by one elbow. Who was talking? My wife? One of the children? It definitely wasn't any of them, though the voice seemed oddly familiar. I struggled to place it and couldn't. Should I be more worried? I rubbed my eyes one at a time and blinked toward the source of the sound, just off the side of my bed where there was also light (even though the bedroom windows were on the opposite side, off of my wife's side of the bed). Cracking them open a bit more, I expected daylight, but my bleary eyes came across something less intense. Was I dreaming?

He knelt by my bed and smiled at me, the one who had nudged me. Illuminated from somewhere, I saw his face clearly, but I don't know how. In the deeply shadowed room I couldn't detect the source of light. A strand of fear ran suddenly through me, but I kept breathing to remain calm. In all honesty though, I was close to freaking out. What time was it, anyway?

The man was dressed in some kind of robe or sheet, white with an off-white or maybe tan section slung over one shoulder. I could see he had long dark hair and a beard, but his eyes were wide and the whites of them very bright. His skin looked nearly brown, his eyes a matching color, or maybe darker. His teeth were bright, too, for he smiled broadly.

"Don't be afraid! Do you know me?" he asked quietly. I thought I did. Maybe I really was freaking out? Thoughts and questions coursed through my mind. Was I dreaming? What time was it? Wait, I had asked myself those already. New thoughts swirled and coalesced: Was I dead? Could I excuse myself to go to the bathroom without seeming to be inappropriate?

It felt like hours that I sat there staring, but was likely just a second or two. Through all the strange variety of thoughts I had, the biggest one of all was: Is this really him? I mean, HIM him?

"It is I," he said as he knelt there, and then I knew for sure it was him (something about the proper grammar of that phrase, maybe). He smiled at me again, and that definitely helped. As my eyes cleared from sleep but watered for I wasn't sure what reason, I caught a glimpse of his hands and wrists as they rested on the edge of my bed. They looked like they had fresh wounds in them. I wanted to run away, but the covers kept me close. My eyes teared up some more as I tried to look away. Finally, I whimpered and reached over to wake my wife.

"No, no!" he said quietly but urgently, placing a quick hand on my arm, gentle and firm. "Let your wife sleep. She's tired."

"And I'm not?" I said aloud, turning back quickly to him. I could've kicked myself. Those were my first words to Jesus?

"Yes," he said, laughing off (what I would indulgently call) my faux pas. "Only, I have a job for you to do, so let her sleep."

"Oh," I said, a little calmer now but still confused. "Right." This made no sense to me at all. That is, nothing made any sense to me at all. Was I sure I wasn't dead? I don't think I'd had an answer to that one yet.

"You're plenty alive," Jesus whispered. He beckoned to me as he stood up straight, his robe cascading silently to the tops of his feet, where my eyes lingered a moment, while that strange glow continued to pervade the air all around him. "Come, get out of bed."

"Right," I said again, pushing aside the covers and awkwardly standing up. Reaching out quickly, he caught hold of one of my flailing arms and he steadied me. When I felt stable I looked at him. He was taller than I was, and he didn't look away or even blink in embarrassment as I eventually did. As I looked around, I screamed at myself to get my brain in order. "Right," I said again, but it was for the final time. Looking in his general direction once more, I emended it to: "Yes, Lord."

"Ah!" he said, smiling generously. "Now you're getting with it. Get your Bible and a notebook. Let's go downstairs. Oh, feel free to use the bathroom first."

After a quick break (but a thorough washing of hands), I found him waiting patiently in the upstairs hallway, just outside my open bedroom door, with a serene smile on his face, still lit up somehow. Maybe there was a full moon and it reached through a window to shine on his face? Except, of course, there wasn't a window in my upstairs hallway, and I thought the full moon had been a week ago.

Forcing myself to breathe, I quickly reviewed in my mind what Jesus had listed: Bible, notebook, downstairs. Right. I spied my Bible in the shadows by my bedside table and it made me momentarily ecstatic that it was just a step away from me and not farther afield. I kept a small notebook around somewhere and found that partially under the bed without making too much noise. After grabbing the two items, I stepped fully out into the hallway and held them up in a little gesture of triumph. He gave me a "thumbs up". He turned and I followed him downstairs, his footfalls quiet, but still hitting the one step that never failed to creak. My step made it two in a row.

He turned on the lights of the kitchen, pulled out one of the chairs (my son's, I noted, to the right of my spot) and sat down at the table. I put the books on the table roughly (accidentally), knocking them into the fruit bowl that always sat in the middle of our table, and then I simply stood there. He reached out nonchalantly and steadied the fruit bowl. I wondered if I was supposed to sit? Or maybe to kneel? I really wasn't prepared for this situation. For a moment longer he simply looked at me, and I at him. In the light of the kitchen I could see him more clearly (or maybe this was because I was waking up). No extra illumination remained visible to me. His skin—where uncovered—I now called a glossy, olive-brown. His hair and beard were dark; I'd probably say it was a deep brown, but being a little color-blind left me at odds how to describe it, for it was shiny and multiple colors seemed to reflect off of it. (Could that have something to do with the conditioner he used? What was I thinking?) Anyway, it was a decent length, and bound simply in the back, keeping it out of his way. The beard was neatly trimmed and framed his face well. Everything focused one's vision toward his eyes, deep, soft and quiet.

"David," he said after that pause, gesturing smoothly with one hand to my chair, "sit down."

I sat. His eyes locked on me, piercing me. I didn't like to think of the word "pierce". What was he going to say to me, what? Not knowing what else to do, I nodded at him.

"Do you know I'm going to visit you for forty nights?" His solemn look continued, with rare blinks, and he even leaned forward slightly, but with a slender smile. I couldn't believe he had sat down at my son's spot at the table and rested his arms on a shiny placemat listing all the presidents of the United States (except the most recent two). I feared for how sticky that placemat might be and made a mental note to stick it in a drawer somewhere soon. His eyes widened even farther—if possible—and he seemed to be waiting for something, and this told me that a response of some kind was expected at this juncture.

"Why?" I asked. I didn't know what else to say. Maybe I should have stuck to nodding.

Jesus smiled and sat back. The chair groaned slightly, old and heavily abused by my progeny's leanings. I worried mightily about it giving way and sweated out Jesus' movements.

"I like that you answered me with a question, David, and I'm going to respond back with another question. You'll learn about me doing that soon enough. Why would I visit you for forty nights? Do you know what I want people to do?"

I shook my head.

"Are people confused about me, at all? What's in the way of them coming to me? What if they don't read the Bible, or don't understand it if they do? What then will they do? In their despair? In their pride? In their monotony?"

The way he asked these things—a rapid-fire spread of questions—made it obvious that they were not for me to answer, so I didn't insult him by trying but remained silent. I hoped he took it as respectful.

"I want to encourage people who love me, show myself to seekers looking for me and give the skeptics a chance to rethink their current positions. I want to save a life, but I also want to change a life. This is how we're going to do it: Each night I'll have you read some of the Gospels."

"The Gospels?" I squeaked.

"Sure," he said, leaning back even a little more now. "You know: Matthew, Mark, Luke—"

"Oh! And John!"

"There you go," he said with a big smile. He reached over and clapped me on the shoulder. The part of me that was waking up felt like an idiot. While I was recovering from this latest shock, he pulled the fruit bowl toward him.

"You read," he said as he took out an orange.

"Out loud?" I asked.

He nodded and started peeling the orange. "Out loud. That's the best way."

"Okay." I watched him peel the orange. He was quick.

"Every so often, I'll stop you and talk about stuff. It won't usually be long. But you just do your best to write down what I say. I love these things," he added as he stuffed an orange wedge into his mouth.

"Sure, Lord. Of course. Um, what stuff?"

"Oh, memories, thoughts, reflections, glimpses behind the scenes, so to speak. A whole range of things, really. Then, as I said, you write down those parts."

"Okay," I said, warily looking down at the notebook in front of me on the table.

"Problem?" Jesus asked me, one eyebrow of his arching mightily.

"Oh, no! Just wondering . . . can I use my laptop instead?"

"You can do that at the end. You'll get a good feel for the words as you form them with your hand."

"Ah. So . . . notebook," I said with an enthusiasm I didn't quite feel, holding it up for him to see.

"Very good," he said, nodding, feeding himself more orange wedges. "So, you'll write it down in your notebook. When we're done, you can type it all up and arrange it how you think best."

"You really want me to do all that?"

"Yep, I do. Problem?"

"No . . . it's just . . . well, why me?"

"Why not you? I think you're probably a good one for this job. Don't you want to do it?"

"Well, yes, Lord. Of course! I just . . . just . . . I'm not. . . ."

"What? Worthy?" He cast wide eyes my way, tilting his head in a slightly teasing manner.

"Well, yeah!" I said, feeling the protest weaken as I said it.

"You let me worry about that part, David. You just do this part."

"Okay. Um, anything else? Uh, Lord."

"Yes. Along the way I'll let you ask me . . . say . . . twenty questions. I won't count these first few groggy ones. Sound good?"

I nodded, dumfounded.

"Good!" he said and smiled. He leaned back a little bit again. "Now, what translation of the Bible do you have there? New International Version? Okay, that's fine. We could use others but that one will do."

I had the feeling he was teasing me a little bit again, but it made me feel more like his friend than anything. His smile was the most reassuring thing I'd ever seen.

"Crack open that Bible and start reading, David."

* * *

I did as he told me. Right away, he interjected his thoughts. I mean, I started at Matthew chapter 1, verse 1, and he stopped me right there (he raised a finger, smiling and not even looking at me). Fumbling between open Bible and closed notebook, I got the latter opened and realized I didn't have a pen. I jumped up to the counter and grabbed a pen from the kitchen pen jar, nearly knocking it over and sending a dozen pens and pencils (and one pair of scissors) flying. I thought—bizarrely, and also incorrectly as I sheepishly returned to my spot, now ready to roll—that maybe he had chosen me because we had a kitchen pen jar. He seemed to sense my thoughts because I thought I caught a nearly imperceptible shake of his head. Oh well. With a deep breath, I was ready to go.

*   *   *

After I had read the first two chapters of Matthew, and he had given me four of his memories and I had written those down, he stopped us, rose from the table and bade me good night. My hand felt a little cramped, but not bad. He motioned me to go upstairs and he told me that he'd turn off the lights. Also, he said that he'd see me tomorrow night. I went upstairs dutifully, noticed the downstairs darken silently and went back to my bedroom, closing the door and climbing back into bed beside my wife's deep, rhythmic breathing. I lay there wide-eyed for a moment, briefly supposing I would be up all night, but immediately after that I must have fallen asleep.

In the morning, things looked normal in the kitchen. My wife asked me if I was feeling okay; I must have walked around with a stupefied look on my face. She then told me she thought I hadn't slept well.

"Why do you say that?" I asked, wide-eyed, wondering what to tell her.

"Well there's an orange missing from the fruit bowl and the skin's in the garbage. Didn't you get up and eat an orange? You always have such terrible acid reflux if you eat late at night."

I shook my head. "No. I slept well." I had, too. I felt quite refreshed. All day at work I contemplated telling my wife about the visitation. All day I kept trying to figure out the right opening. When I got home, each time I came close to saying something, even opening my mouth, my wife would jump in and say something instead, like: "The kids' toilet is clogged again." After a comment like that, I felt unable to say anything about Jesus giving me homework. I just went and plunged the kids' toilet. I'd have to wait to tell her. It seemed like there needed to be a "right moment" for that.

All evening long I thought about him coming to see me. I looked at my notebook forty times at least. Several pages were filled in. More than that, I found my bookmark in my Bible where we had left off. It didn't seem to be a dream. I wasn't on medication, nor had I ever been subject to somnambulism. Was that proof? Did I need proof? Did I care about proving it to the world, or to myself? What would happen tonight?

I prepared for bed systematically, remembering to brush my teeth only by rote, my eyes constantly looking to the sides of the mirror as I went through all the regular stuff. My wife said she was very tired and that if I had the light on to read it wouldn't bother her. She leaned over for a quick kiss, said good night and was soon breathing evenly.

I sat there, excited and nervous. Jesus was coming to see me that night! Was Jesus really going to come and wake me up again? I didn't think I would be able to fall asleep waiting to see him. I felt like a kid anticipating Santa Claus on Christmas Eve, telling myself to go to sleep while feeling wide-eyed and energetic. The light was still on and I looked over at my Bible on my bedside table. I didn't read it a lot on my own, I just kept it there. Maybe I should look at a chapter or two, at least skim over them, then turn out the light. Maybe then I would sleep . . . but what if I slept through the whole night and Jesus didn't wake me up a second time?

True to his word, though, he did wake me up again that night. I had read a little bit, those first couple chapters of Matthew again, thinking about what Jesus had had me write the previous night as I read to him, and then I had turned off the light. My thoughts had swirled, but at some point, I know I simply dropped off, because he shook me awake like the first night.

"David! Wake up! Are you ready?"

No grogginess this time. Ecstatic and overjoyed at my good fortune at having Jesus wake me in the middle of the night again, I smiled a big goofball smile and swung my legs out from under the covers and out of bed. He appeared the same as the previous night, except this time he wore a cloth covering on his head, but slightly back so it did not shroud his eyes which easily bore into me.

I followed him out the door and again we went silently downstairs (well, except for that one creaky step). He picked another orange out of the fruit bowl, briefly fingering a large pineapple before choosing the smaller fruit. With that we got settled. (Was I dreaming, or this time did another orange appear in its place? Was he going to eat forty oranges?) As he started peeling, he nodded to me to continue reading. (The orange rind just seemed to fall away for him. I always had such trouble getting a clean peel that orange-eating was a messy business for me, but he didn't even need a napkin. Wow, it was truly impressive! What would he do with a pineapple?)

On the third night, just after the first time he stopped me to offer me a memory or thought, I pondered the actual writing down bit, the job I was doing, and I couldn't help but wonder about the very Gospels I was reading aloud to him. He'd smile as I'd read, often sitting upright, or look far-off, sometimes leaning back in the chair, or even tear up a bit. I wondered what he wanted from me, writing down his thoughts. Was this going to be another Gospel?

"Is this 'Inspiration'?" I asked him, feeling inspired.

"No, it's dictation," he said, and reached into the fruit bowl for another orange as visions of *The Gospel According to David* evaporated from my mind's eye. "I love these things," he said again, and started peeling.

When we were done, he threw away his orange peels and pushed in his kitchen chair. "I'll get the lights," he said as he had the previous two nights. "Good night!"

*　　　*　　　*

That's pretty much how it went for forty straight nights (except he sometimes had grapes or an apple, but usually it was an orange). I knew I was missing sleep, but I must've slept more deeply after his visits, because I always felt great in the morning. He really was very peaceful to be around.

My notebook filled up, and I started wondering more and more about his mandate that I would type it all up and arrange it. That "arranging" bit had me for a while. What did he mean? I could see that most nights he stopped me three times. Some nights it was four or five, and sometimes only two. He had done a lot in Matthew, like he couldn't contain himself to talk about so many stories, so much so that I doubted we would get through all four books in forty days (until it seemed his pace quickened in Mark). What did it all mean?

I started going through his words, reading the Gospels again and again. Each time I thought I understood them better, and each time I saw more and more things I hadn't seen before.

Then I started to put his different memories together in my mind, and I realized that I might indeed have to re-arrange everything he said to me. We were reading the four Gospels straight through, as they were listed in the Bible. First Matthew, then Mark, then Luke and finally John. He had different things to say in each of them, and sometimes wouldn't say anything about a story in one of the books that he'd commented on earlier, and others he commented on the story each time it came up. I could type this up and keep it in the order he told me, but then his comments on the crucifixion, for example, would be in four different places. I don't think people would want to read his memoirs that way, though. I could see that that was fine for the different Gospels; I hadn't ever read them straight through, all four of them at once. No, I'd read one on one occasion, then another at some other time (admittedly, most of that was long ago, until this recent revival). So, a rearrangement to something close to chronological began to seem essential to me as we went along. It might make following along in the Gospels tough, but they'd be easier to go through at the end, having read the memoirs once, first.

Well, the forty nights passed, and on the last one we finished the Gospel of John. After he had said his piece on John 21:25, he was done. He said nothing new about the arrangement of the whole material. He just pushed in his chair, threw away his orange peels and said his familiar refrain of: "I'll get the lights. Good night!"

The next day seemed full of trivialities that tugged me in multiple directions, all without any satisfaction or sense of purpose that my nights had had. I could tell my wife was unhappy with my short responses and the heavy, cold shoulder I showed her. Tossing and turning for hours that night, I wrestled with the endlessly circling thoughts: Was it over? Would Jesus come for me again? Is it really over? At some point, after nearly despairing of sleep, I went under, sleeping without interruption for what little remained of the night.

A few more days and nights passed like this, though with less bitterness and a bit more sleep. With Jesus a no-show for nearly a week after those forty straight amazing nights, I started to realize how selfishly I was reacting. A part of me felt such massive disappointment, like I was owed something more than I had gotten. It was a terrible, tempting thought that I had lost something special that could never return.

That's when I started laughing.

"What's so funny?" my wife asked as she came into the room with me sitting on the bed, paging through my Bible, smiling like I hadn't in days. I thought about all Jesus had told me, and how it seemed he really was going to leave the rest of the job up to me, to put all his stories and vignettes together the best way I could and present it to the world. It was a fantastically bad idea trusting me with this, and that rang a clear bell with things Jesus had told me about one of his best friends. That's what made me laugh.

I also realized something else that was amiss.

"Sit down, Honey. I have to tell you something awesome!"

Yes, as my wife listened to the incredible tale I had to tell her, I felt sure I'd screw up the job Jesus had given me, but at the same time I also felt very peaceful, with a stillness from deep inside me, a marked difference from earlier that week, like a new day with a bright sunrise. His promise to me that he'd worry about whether I'm worthy or not echoed in my mind. With the addition of my wife's love and support, I decided to trust Jesus' words and forge ahead.

So, here's what I did:

1. I noted the section of Scripture he stopped at, adding a quick summary of the context (if it seemed warranted) and quoting one or more Key Verses each time he stopped me. He didn't tell me to do that, exactly, but it seemed right.

2. I also noted what night and what entry that night it was that he said each particular memory or teaching. That way, the whole commentary could be mostly reconstructed based on how I received it. There were a few entries in which, with his comments on the same story from different Gospels, or for some other reason, I placed them together. Those will have multiple nights listed (and multiple Key Verses quoted). Most likely though, you'll ignore the "Night" and "Entry" listings.

3. I set down his words, but the punctuation is mine. If my comma placements prove incorrect or I misheard him or (as sometimes I think happened) he talked too fast and I missed something . . . mea culpa.

4. Like the punctuation, the title is mine. He never suggested one. Ditto the chapter headings (and using Roman numerals . . . I almost regret that; numbers like "87" are cumbersome).

5. (*Any commentary of my own throughout that I added—apart from the Prologue, certain obvious parts of the Epilogue, Glossary and any context summaries—I put in italics and parentheses, like this.*)

*   *   *

Oh, and the rest of the 20 questions he let me ask? That's the Epilogue. He had a wry sense of humor when it came to those. That's why I say "the rest of" them. A few nights into the forty, I brought up the subject, because he hadn't returned to it. There weren't a lot of opportunities for me to interject comments, but I found them here and there. I said, "Those 20 questions . . . it sounds like a game. Do they have to be 'yes or no' type questions?"

"No," he said.

"Why 20?" I asked.

"It's a nice, round number. Seventeen questions left," he said.

"Wait, did we start already?"

"Yes, when you asked if this was inspiration."

"Can we go back to the beginning? Let me rephrase that! That's not a question!"

"Too late. The answer is no. Down to fifteen."

That's when I shut up for the time being. For all those parables he told, he could be a concrete thinker when it suited him.

I - NAME

Night: 1
Entry: 1

Matthew 1:1-17

Key Verse

¹This is the genealogy of Jesus the Messiah the son of David, the Son of Abraham[.]

Night: 1
Entry: 2

Matthew 1:18-25

Key Verse

²³"The virgin will conceive and give birth to a son, and they will call him Immanuel" (which means "God with us").

Call me Immanuel.

That's not a very good opening, is it? It's not all that funny, either.

Actually, what's funny about it is almost no one ever calls me Immanuel, except sometimes on formal occasions. One cousin called me "Manny", but that was it. It was fine; I'm humble enough to answer to pretty much anything, as long as I know it's me who's wanted, and I can usually tell.

I mean, "Jesus" is the Greek form of my human name, or rather, it's the transliterated English of the Greek of my name. The English of my name is Joshua. In this alphabet I would spell my original name Yeshua, or even more fully, Yehoshua, which itself basically means "God's salvation". Pretty cool, huh? However, why don't we agree on simply using "Jesus". I'm fond of that one.

Almost everyone has heard that form of my name, even if it's only as an expletive.

And if it is used as an expletive? Don't assume you know my feelings on the usages of my name. I'm quite familiar with all of them. You should also not assume that I don't listen. What I mean is, if you say my name and aren't intending prayer but a swear word, I often listen to the words above what you think is the intention. For example, someone said to me the other day: "Jesus, how did I get here?" What do you think? Was that a prayer, or an expletive? If you can tell me that, then maybe you can also tell me how I responded? For you see, I always answer and I'm always seeking to go deeper.

* * *

So, who am I? Jesus the Messiah the son of David, the son of Abraham. "Son" is the right name for me. I am the Son of God. I am God. One with the Father and Holy Spirit; one God, three Persons, existent always, but then, about 2,000 years ago, born fully as a human. What do we do with that, huh?

That time on earth is called my "incarnate" time and before that "pre-incarnate" (perhaps obviously). Now, I'm not going to review my pre-incarnate memories, except briefly where it's necessary. We'll focus on my earthly life, on my humanity, all right? As to my divinity, well, that will never be separate. Like a person with parents of two different ethnicities, I have two halves, except they aren't halves at all, but wholes. I can't say: "Hi, my name is Jesus. I'm half-Jewish, half-deity." No, for me it's always dealing in whole numbers. You might think it violates simple math, me trying to state $1+1=1$. When you say you are half one thing and half another, you arrive at $\frac{1}{2} + \frac{1}{2} = 1$ (or, if you break down your nationalities or ethnicities further, you have additional pieces all equal to 1). You think you're whole, then, maybe especially so if you say you're "100%" one thing. I have to tell you that you're wrong, on multiple fronts.

First, while tracking your various nationalities is endearing, and may help you learn your family history and give you some interesting insights, there is only 1 to show for each of you. I'm not 1 Jewish and 1 deity, I'm 1 human and 1 deity. You are 1 human, too. On that side, you can't be less.

Second, it's not 1+1 for me. No, personhood is—like all relationships—multiplication against something. Only "one" other thing is also a 1. All else falls short of the glory of God.

Maybe that sounds strange coming from me. If you understand what I'm telling you, and some of the things I will be telling you throughout our look at my life, you'll realize I'm staking my claim as what you would call a "relationship expert". Some of you might think that's a big risk, taking relationship advice from a guy who's never been married. In a spiritual sense, I'm a bridge-groom, but skeptics would tell me that's a technicality.

So what?

Many of my fondest memories are around the relationships I formed while I walked the earth the first time. I had family relationships and deep friendships. Then, as now, I understood all about marriage and dating and sexuality. I was—and am—even in touch with my feminine side (that's how you might describe it). Oh, and I had hormones back then, too. I did. Can be nasty, but I think they're necessary.

In addition to how I view relationships with others, I want you to see the trials and risks that formed me and informed my message. Woven throughout will be a picture of God's power structure, something that many of you will doubt as I present it, and I will give you a small, partial view of life as I see it, filled with both freedom and foreknowledge. Also—and I don't want to sound too prideful here—you'll get a picture of my true humility.

I'll scope out my basic chronology in a moment, but as far as thrillers go, I'll assume you either know enough not to mind that there are spoilers, or you can find what you need at one of my local churches. Yes, that's what they're there for (among other things).

* * *

3

So, here we are, walking through the Gospels together. I know some of you want to put this right down, thinking a variety of thoughts ranging from boredom to rage. Others of you can't wait to get started. To the former let me say just give this a chance. To the latter I say don't make assumptions.

Actually, to both groups I would say don't make assumptions. Most people in both groups would make one (or many) assumptions, just different ones from each other.

While this is not going to be a full-fledged autobiography, we will touch on many of the events of my life on earth. You may or may not be aware of them, so let's start off with a brief sketch: There's my birth in Bethlehem, of course, to my human mother Mary (Joseph was there, too; I guess you'd call him my "step-father"), and I'll touch on circumcision, school-days and growing up in Nazareth. As a young man I worked in construction, then left one day to be a rabbi (that's a Jewish teacher and preacher). I got baptized in the Jordan River by John the Baptist, called disciples to be in community with me, to become my followers, protégés and more. There were Twelve who were closest to me. We traveled throughout Judea, Samaria and especially Galilee. I would go up to Jerusalem for the major festivals of the Jewish year.

Telling parables and preaching sermons, I would train up my disciples and fill the hearts and minds of the people while also healing people and performing other miracles, always with a purpose. While this thrilled people, it scared them too, and antagonized the powerful factions of the day: the Pharisees, Sadducees and even the ruling Romans. Eventually I went to Jerusalem one final time. There I would see my darkest challenge and, ultimately, my greatest triumph. I would get nailed to a cross, die horribly, but rise on the first Easter Sunday, surprising everybody from that time until now. (Of course I rose, how else could I be dictating this to David?)

If you read the Gospels you won't come across such stories as games I played with schoolmates or the village girls who liked me, and I'm not going to dwell on those here, either. Those are nice memories, but I didn't let those relationships develop personally for me, for I had other goals in mind. If you're familiar with my story, I hope to shed some additional light on you—I mean, my story—and encourage you to read it again. The Gospels are purpose-driven books, not biographies. They are a major part of the grand narrative of God's whole story, from creation to the final redemption of His people, and I'm not intending to separate them from the rest of the Bible. My purpose here will be seen by talking through my life presented in the Gospels. Again, not a full-fledged biography here. I don't think I need one of those, anyway.

Like I said, if you're familiar with my story and love it, then I hope to encourage you further. If you're familiar with my story and don't love it (hate it, try to ignore it, scoff at it, etc.), I hope you'll give it another look. If you don't know my story at all, I pray that you follow along with this narrative. For everyone, I ask that you get a Bible, read each account and then tell me what you think. All responses are welcome, but not all will be eternally valid. Fair warning.

Maybe someday I'll tell someone to put down an accurate, modern biography of me. I don't see how that would help anyone right now, though. Let's just see how this turns out first, shall we?

II - BIRTH

Night: 23
Entry: 1

Luke 2:1-20; 35

Context Summary

Mary and Joseph travel to Bethlehem to register for the census, and there Mary goes into labor.

Key Verse

[7][A]nd she gave birth to her firstborn, a son. She wrapped him in cloths and placed him in a manger, because there was no guest room available for them.

In many ways, apart from theological ones, the circumstances of my birth mattered little to me. Had I been born in a palace I basically wouldn't have known it. I have no human memories of this time. Like how you started out, I had massive, unexplainable sensory data; barely able to see, but knowing my mother's voice (and Joseph's), and being comforted by her touch, to nurse and soon to sleep. I was content, except of course when most everything else made me cry. It was, after all, my only true means of communication for a while.

What else did I need that was not provided in that manger scene? So there was no room at the inn, so to speak, so what? A local woman came late to midwife, but she helped find new straw for the manger, then the shepherds arrived. Really, apart from theological concerns, it was for their benefit that I was born in Bethlehem. Had I been born in a palace, they wouldn't have been let in to see me (not to mention the occupant of the palace wouldn't have rejoiced like the shepherds did . . . in fact, the irony speaks volumes about the realities of humility and pride and how you live in or out of them).

I was not sentimental over my birth date or the surrounding circumstances, but do you want to know what date it actually is? Well, it doesn't matter, not really, and I don't want to mess up your Christmas celebrations. I will tell you that birthday celebrations were not usually a big deal in my culture 2,000 years ago. When my followers first thought about it, in the 2nd and 3rd centuries, it was only incidental to my crucifixion and resurrection.

See, they believed that my Spirit came to earth and left again on the same date. That is, conception was the same date as crucifixion, which they reckoned to be March 25th. Add nine months and they got December 25th as a birth date. About some things, many things, they weren't wrong.

Anyway, Mary too did not need to publicly recall this time, her being so young and soon in charge of a house full of little ones. She took most of her life to process these things: the angels, the shepherds, the words concerning me. When Luke came to her, interviewing her as an old woman, she would rightly describe the glory in the humility, hidden in her heart.

III - CIRCUMCISION

Night: 23
Entry: 2

Luke 2:21-24

Key Verse

²¹On the eighth day, when it was time to circumcise the child, he was named Jesus, the name the angel had given him before he was conceived.

Here's something I don't remember from my earthly life. Good thing, too, don't you think? Do you ever doubt the mercy of God? Well, you needn't. I won't say you shouldn't, because it doesn't matter all that much that you shouldn't. It matters a little, but if you have doubted the mercy of God it's probably because you think you have a really good reason to do so. I don't mind the doubts and the wavering, but I can confidently speak of the ever-present mercy of God. The doubts and wavering usually lead to good questions. It is the good questions that sometimes lead to the good listening, and in the good listening comes the understanding of that ever-present mercy. New life follows that.

The eight-day-old baby will feel pain—though sometimes the rabbis like to say they don't, they just scream coincidentally at the same time as the cut—but will have no memory of it. Why not rather never feel the pain, you might argue? What? And miss out on this? The circumcision wasn't a rite of passage, it was admission into the largest family on earth, the people of God! It was the starting point in a very real way of a relationship, told in the best book in the world, written for a time and for all time, and written in our hearts, as well.

No, I have no human memory of my eighth day, but I received a foundation that would carry me through to the end of my earthly mission. Foundational pieces are certainly worth a little pain.

IV – THE MAGI

Night: 1
Entry: 3

Matthew 2:1-12ff

Context Summary

An astrological sign announcing the birth of Jesus is seen by wise men in the east. They travel to Jerusalem to ask King Herod where they can find the new king. They're told by the old king to go to Bethlehem. They bring gifts of gold, frankincense and myrrh.

Key Verse

[1]After Jesus was born in Bethlehem in Judea, during the time of King Herod, Magi from the east came to Jerusalem[.]

This has become a rather famous moment from my earthly life due to Christmas pageants and the like. You may know that the visit of the Magi at my birth is an anachronism, but if not, well . . . surprise! The shepherds came on the night of my birth, but I was nearly four months old when the Magi rolled into town. Trust me on this one (I say that phrase a lot; it's sort of an "in joke" between my disciples and me), but my first couple of years were pretty weird. I have a lot of sympathy for anyone who had to move often as a child. Born on the road, an early move to Egypt (and several places down there, first Alexandria, then smaller towns on the outskirts), then back to Judea after Herod the Great's death, to Nazareth.

I really don't have any stories to tell about these guys, though, the "wise men". Their traveling party was large—replete with retainers and bodyguards—and caused quite a stir in Bethlehem, but Joseph had us out of there before morning. They brought gifts, they worshiped me, that kind of thing, you know.

I know about this event in the fullness of my divinity now—post-Easter, post-resurrection—but it was too early on for me to have a human memory of it. Let me try and give an explanation to that conundrum. In order to become fully human a couple of millennia ago, I was given the brain development of a normal child. The divinity couldn't add to it, though it was always there. How was this possible? Theologians try to catalog it and name it the "hypostatic union"; isn't that a mouthful? It doesn't quite cover it, so don't worry about it (unless you are a theologian).

Suffice to say that in some ways I was so like you, alive at conception, but generally unaware of things for a few weeks, until Mary's presence was assured to my little heart. It's a blessing all around not to remember being born or teething. That's not the only reason our brains develop slowly like this (some would say boys' brains develop even slower than girls', too), but it's certainly one of them. There's this whole other model of dependence thing that I'm really after with you, though. That I got to live it out like you was simply one of the factors that made me the Son.

The upshot is, however, that I don't have an earthly memory of the Magi. Mary and Joseph tried to keep their gifts, but in the end, they sold the gold and the myrrh to pay for our travels to and from Egypt (of which I only have a few impressions and memories, and that mostly the return journey when I was two). They put the rest of it into establishing Joseph's construction business once we ended up in Nazareth. The frankincense was stolen, two weeks after the Magi left, while we traveled, if you can believe that.

V - NAZARETH

Night: 1
Entry: 4

Matthew 2:19-23

Key Verse

23a[A]nd he went and lived in a town called Nazareth.

Nazareth was a small village, never much more than 300 or so people while I lived there. Joseph was actually related to most of the inhabitants. You might use the term "clannish" to describe it. The relationship was perhaps what you might call weak or tenuous; a lot of sixth cousins, that sort of thing. That was still pretty important back in the day.

We settled there when I was nearly three. It's not very picturesque, but it was hilly and so some of the views were quite good. That made it marvelous for hiking, too. When my chores were done, I could go out walking and climbing, and sometimes I would get a whole afternoon of communing with my Father this way. Sometimes other boys would follow, sometimes a brother or two would tag along, but mostly I had very enjoyable times by myself.

I would often go to the precipice of the hill on which the village rested. Peering over it, I would contemplate the height and depth and length of God's love as I viewed the height and depth and length of that hill, a dangerous drop but with the best of the views offered by the village. Directly laid out in the valley below were the many olive orchards of the village, surrounded by tracts for grape vines, while farther away sat the heavily tilled arable land, ploughed and planted with barley and wheat, the crops of the local farmers. Behind were other hills, and while there weren't many areas covered by woods, one could find little nooks and crannies in the earth, just out of sight of everyone else, a perfect place to sit and inhale the various smells of the harvest cycle carried up from the valley, the fecund planting and luscious harvesting, to feel the grass and the warm sunshine and there pray.

I at times longed for alone-time, so those little hideouts were lovely. Those times brought my energy level up and made me feel rested, which makes sense because of my human personality trait. I mean, you may be surprised or perplexed by this, but I am an introvert.

Now, I'm not shy. That's not what I mean, at all. I mean, the more I interacted with folks down here, the more tired I became, emotionally (and—introverts, back me up here—it could eventually feel like physical exhaustion). I needed to spend some time alone with just my Father. I knew when I was older I wouldn't get many chances to be alone. I would be faced with the choice of demanding to be left alone or humbling myself to accept exhaustion as I kept meeting with people. (Yes, I chose that, it just was never a choice that came without cost.)

My mother understood my need for time alone. When I was still quite young, I would see in her eyes her inner struggles, her desire to keep me close versus the understanding of my obvious desire for flight to the hills.

"Yeshua," she would call out, and I would turn at the threshold.

Crossing over to me, she would place a gentle hand on my shoulder, sometimes having to shift a small sibling to rest more on one hip and look down at me. "Are you finished eating? Are you sure you've had enough?"

"Yes, Mother," I would invariably assure her, and she would force a smile, pat the shoulder one last time and nod, final permission to go be outside, roam freely for a time and then maybe wait at the edge of town for Joseph.

Now Joseph was in his mid-forties by the time we settled in Nazareth. His relations welcomed him, but not overly warmly. The stories about my conception followed him wherever he went (and I don't mean the accurate ones, but the gossipy ones, the ones that questioned his morality as well as Mary's), but he trusted in God's goodness to be his shield as he took sarcastic comments and dirty looks in stride, biting back what most would retort. It wasn't easy to set up shop there for other reasons, as well. He had acquired some tools and a small stockpile of materials in Egypt, but he had left those behind, or lost them on the travels back to Judea and Galilee. Tall and lean, with bony elbows and a receding hairline, Joseph was a serious, sober man who always went to synagogue service and made the study of all of God's teachings, His Torah, a priority for his children (*see "Torah" in the Glossary*). Though his face was dry and almost leathery, and his beard sported touches of gray, his eyes caught everything, and he would remonstrate with my younger siblings without even turning his head. That never ceased to amaze them.

"James and Judas," he would say, not harshly, but with a certain amount of rush, getting out two names in the span of one. "Put back my tools. They are not toys." And those two brothers—completely out of the line of sight behind their father, and on silent tip-toes—would freeze and stare, mouths agape.

"Joses! Simon! You two knocked over the goat's milk, you clean it up." The young boys would try to point at our sisters, shaking their heads, but that was one thing Joseph apparently couldn't ever see.

At no point, let me assure you, did my step-father ever tell any of his children: "Why can't you be more like Yeshua?" It would only be relevant later on in life.

Now Joseph himself formed a good business reputation in Nazareth. Hard work, long hours and generous terms formed the basis of his work ethic, and these ideas were infused into every lesson he taught my brothers and me about his trade. Neighbors and clients trusted him because he never changed the price on them, even when the job got larger. I can't say that didn't frustrate Mary.

He worked mainly in stone. You may have heard he was a "carpenter", but that's not a great translation. He was a "builder", and while he was decent at woodworking, that's not what he mainly did. I mean, there simply wasn't much wood around us. We mostly had stone quarries, and he taught me early on to shape and build with stone. I learned to use tools under him and grew strong lifting heavy loads (though I think you'd say I was somewhat wiry, as well). My brothers did the same. James got to be quite stout.

We stayed busy in Nazareth because it was a fine walk away from a larger town called Sepphoris, where there were many ongoing building projects. Joseph worked there regularly, and often I went along with him as an apprentice. This one time when I was quite young, one of my first weeks working there, on site at what would be a large private dwelling, Joseph brought his hammer down hard, missing the stone but not his thumb. He dropped the hammer and sucked in a huge breath, then slowly turned his head and spied me carrying another stone, ready for him to put into place. My eyes wide and mouth agape, I waited for what would come out of his mouth. His eyes watered ever so slightly as his gaze held me, while his lips quivered and he seemed to cycle through a number of responses in his head, discarding each of them until the pain was too much and he let out a quiet, "Shoot!" (Well, the Aramaic equivalent, anyway.)

The other workers, some our neighbors, but mostly people living within Sepphoris itself, told stories and sang songs all through the workday. Yes, sometimes the stories and language were vulgar (Joseph couldn't keep that away from my ears forever). I minded their talk on one level, and didn't mind it on another— the people were mostly poor and not well educated, and they were generally more genuine than the finer speakers who were to inhabit the buildings they constructed.

We would talk about most anything, but I was always able to bring the conversation around to Torah and God working amidst His people. Most of those we worked with who were also Jewish were steeped in Scripture, and often alluded to it, sometimes accurately, even those who hadn't gone far in school. However, they also felt themselves very far away from the temple in Jerusalem (not just physically, but spiritually) and quickly did much of life without thinking very positively of God at all.

"Yeshua," one might say to me, "why does He beat down on us?" They didn't refer to the sun despite the heat, or not the heat itself, but the combination with work and thirst and what they felt was a pittance wage.

"Do you ascribe greatness to your need, friend?" I might respond, hefting a hammer or other tool. "What of the poor merchant who will reside in this hall we're building him? He's without the Scriptures!"

"He doesn't know what he's missing then," they'd say flatly, surveying the vastness of the hall for the incoming Roman. I knew they were oftentimes sarcastic.

By themselves, the other workers wouldn't have related everything back to God the way I did. If they thought me a wet blanket it was rare, because we had established a good relationship, and they knew I asked honest questions for them to ponder and answer, asking back their own. They just didn't always buy my premise that God was interested in them.

"Why?" they kept repeating. It's a fine question to ask, as long as one is willing to wait for an answer.

It's tempting to think what would have happened had I started producing miracles back then, as a youth. Honestly, it wouldn't have altered things too much. When a heart wants to move toward God, it doesn't usually need a miracle first. The miracles confirm the message, not the other way around.

There was one other thing about Nazareth you should know, or rather, one other thing about the people of Nazareth, the Nazarenes. Now, Nazareth itself wasn't mentioned specifically in what you call the Old Testament by the prophets, but "Nazarene" is actually a pun . . . or as close to a pun as the Old Testament prophets got. There was a term they used that was nearly a homophone, a word which meant "Branch".

Branch, if you don't know, was a highly meaningful word for the prophets, a word given to them by the Spirit of God to mean the coming Messiah who would be a descendant of David (the great Jewish king, not my friend here taking notes). A "branch" of the family. That was what made it a pun. Well, for them, anyway.

See, there were many true, spiritual things written and spoken between Malachi and John the Baptist (the last two prophets who came before me, but separated by over 400 years), many things, just not complete things. I mean, the Spirit was speaking many things, to many people, in the years leading up to my incarnation, but it couldn't be complete until I came with the message. It was a bit of a "broadband" declaration, so to speak, in those last, waiting years. The inspired texts that had come centuries earlier had some specifics, of course (an amazing amount, my followers would eventually see), but between Malachi and John, God just started to get really excited about what was soon to happen. God was preparing the earth, so He spoke to the whole earth, but always with a voice that was quiet, the smallest voice He could use (for otherwise He would shatter the whole world). Whoever had ears, they heard.

Now, upon hearing, what did they do with it? If they didn't sit still, pray and fast, they were never going to be able to hear all that the voice said. So did any of them do that?

Well, that really depended on who did the hearing. The Gentiles—people who weren't Jewish—who heard either ignored it or ran with a partially deciphered message, adding some value and messing up other things. For example, they heard that God was about to reveal His great "mystery", but they focused on the concept of mystery and started up a slew of "mystery cults" where they searched for secret knowledge instead of divine revelation (and if those two seem like the same thing to you, the difference was that, for them, secret knowledge made them special, while revelation always humbles one, as a human realizes in awe that it has come from outside their mind and even outside their total human experience). Some folks in Persia turned it into this whole system of "angelology" (a study of angels and demons not found in the Old Testament), some of which they heard correctly and some they made up.

Ironically (you might think), a group that came out of Israel's history, of my people's captivity in Babylon, called the Pharisees, got the most and did the most with it. If you know about some of my struggles with these guys in the last year or so before Good Friday, that may surprise you that anything good came from the

Pharisees, but actually quite a bit did. They knew that study of Torah—the study of God's Word—was an act of worship. The more they studied, the more they could discover, in alignment with God's Spirit whispering to them.

Well, they got some stuff wrong, too. That's what got me so upset, in that last year. They were so close in so many areas! They were waiting for the Messiah, they were being prepped for it by God. "How will we know when the Messiah comes?" they would ask themselves. "There will be certain signs! There must be! God will confirm it! The Messiah will perform signs no one else can! Therefore, we must be ready to verify these signs."

So that's actually what you'll see happen. The Pharisees come to me, they watch and listen. Then they question me. All of it should have been done in order to verify what they were expecting.

Guess what? They were expecting me. What I did should have confirmed to them that I was the Messiah.

Unfortunately, they fell from strict studying of God's Word, and being ready for what God was doing, to trying to be in control themselves and fighting everyone and everything that messed with their version of the status quo. The questions moved from ones of searching for and confirming the identity of the Messiah to laying traps to try and destroy a burgeoning movement of God.

Anyway, as far as the various sects of Judaism at the time—and there were many, but I'm primarily talking about the top two, the Pharisees and the Sadducees—I had a lot more in common with the Pharisees than the other guys. I loved the teachings of Hillel and other great Pharisee teachers. Some would say I learned from them, and in my humanity I did, but the sparks of truth they spoke had initially come from me, so to speak. Still, the Pharisees had some greatness to them. They all should have flocked to me. Some did during my lifetime on earth, and many did after my resurrection, but obviously others did not.

With all that God was whispering to the world in the years leading up to my incarnation, if people who heard thought it was God at all, they usually thought the partial message they heard or understood was actually a complete thought instead. Sometimes they believed it was a thought originating from themselves and never followed up on it. Slowly, however, certain things about what was coming began to be believed. Others of these ideas were disseminated by people. Some of them were actually correct, or very close. So the people (often the Jews, sometimes not) had some true expectations of the Messiah not explicitly recorded in the Old Testament. "Hey, he's going to grow up in Nazareth" was just one of them. Nobody believed it more than the people of that village themselves. Their saying was: "The Messiah will be one of us." The rest of the country didn't like that interpretation too much, and it made the people of Nazareth almost outcasts in the eyes of the wider Judean world, and what the Spirit had said about Nazareth fell into disrepute. As you start to see where we're going in this journey of my story, don't let the irony get too much for you. It's a significant piece about me being Messiah.

I hope you've heard that word before, "Messiah", I mean. It's a beautiful word. The literal meaning is "anointed one", but it's good to think of it as meaning "savior". There are not that many words that embody hope more than "Messiah", except maybe "hope" itself. Hardly a day went by in Nazareth when someone didn't mention the word "Messiah" to me (though they weren't directing it at me, not at the time of my youth). They just couldn't stop talking about it. While it made for a lively village, I feared that they weren't taking this calling from God seriously.

VI – As a Boy at the Temple

Night: 23
Entry: 3

Luke 2:41-52

Context Summary

Twelve-year old Jesus and his parents are in Jerusalem for the Festival of Passover. When the family starts off for home, Jesus stays behind, unbeknownst to Mary and Joseph, so they have to go back and look for him.

Key Verse

[46]After three days they found him in the temple courts, sitting among the teachers, listening to them and asking them questions.

There aren't a lot of stories from my childhood in the Gospels. From my boyhood, there is only this one. Luke heard it from Mary. I think Mary told it because it really tweaked her nose at the time. I'm pleased it was told, because it's one of my favorite childhood memories. As far as anyone being lost goes, if properly considered, it was Joseph and Mary who had gone astray. But back to the narrative.

This was my first time traveling to Jerusalem since I had been an infant. My family had gone, taking my younger siblings to the temple, as they had done for me. Joseph and Mary went each year, and Joseph would also go as often as he was able to the other main feasts, and sometimes some of the lesser ones. (*See "Festivals" in the Glossary.*) In the coming decade, we all would go for the Passover, at least, every year.

I had longed to go back to Jerusalem and see it.

Along with a huge number of pilgrims, we were feted by the crowds already there as we went from the gates of the city to the temple. Then we joined the massive throngs in welcoming still more. "Hosanna!" we'd say. "Blessed are they who come in the name of the Lord!"

My heart nearly burst going up to the temple. The temple. It was a long climb up to it, actually. The road rose slowly from the outer city gates up to the temple complex. Inside the temple, in the heart of it, sat the Most Holy Place, situated at the top of one of the foundational mountains of the city, Mount Moriah, the altar a rock outcropping at the old, flattened summit, now completely covered. Old King Herod—the one from whom my family had fled in my earliest months on earth—had greatly expanded the complex surrounding the temple, building up the walls and the outer courts. We would enter that complex by climbing extensive sets of stairs, long enough to allow hundreds to ascend at once. Passing through the gates in the temple complex walls, I could reach out to touch each giant stone, a massive cousin to the stones I had formed under Joseph's tutelage. The solidity of the rock remained despite its smoothness (roughness rubbed away by the many millions of hands that had swiped over them). All smells of humanity mingled in the complex, funneled by air currents to the entryways. The coolness of the short tunnelway through the walls ended in the renewed splendor of daylight as we got our first unfettered look at the temple, the copy of Solomon's original rebuilt by Zerubbabel and Ezra five hundred years earlier. Rising sixteen stories higher than the complex grounds, absolutely the tallest thing around, above the storehouses and courtyards, even above the Antonia Fortress, the temple told the people of Israel that this was God's house. First into the Court of Women, past the last gate where any Gentiles would have to leave off, into the courtyard where the Jewish women and children could go no farther, crossing through one last gate to where the sacrifices were performed, a short few steps away from the sanctuary itself. Two tall pillars, columns whitewashed and reaching up to heaven, guarded the entrance. Three more steps before entering where only the priests could go, into the heart of the holy place, to the Most Holy Place, shrouded by a very heavy curtain through which the High Priest entered once a year only. God's house on earth. I wanted desperately to be there and to stay there, not for what it was, but for what it could be, into which it would one day transform. I was living in something of a separateness from my Father, and being there was the closest I would get to Him until my public ministry started, when I would be baptized. It was sort of like I was a deployed soldier, and now I had a chance to call home. Many former and current military personnel know the feeling.

After the Passover festival, I found the old men, hearts devoted to God, gathering back near the temple, under the porticoes, talking and asking each other questions. So I missed the caravan as it started out for home, so what? It was far too exciting being with those who wanted to discuss what I wanted to discuss all day long. This was different than school. My teachers and schoolmates would have been flabbergasted at my questions here. They knew me as a mediocre student. I had not come to be a scholar, but here I allowed my joy of the Word of God, of Torah, the Law, the Prophets and the Writings—even the beginning stages of being the full and correct interpretation of them—to run free. I lost track of time as I listened to the teachers. When I questioned them, it was in the rabbinic style, showing my understanding through the asking of penetrating questions in response to their questions. I stayed late each night until an old teacher named Shezzel took me to his home, questioning me all the way. We'd go back again to the temple as early as we could arrive. It was a truly phenomenal time, the best!

At his house the second night, Shezzel sat with a cloak, old and stained like the man, draped over his thin shoulders, his beard tucked in it while he alternately blew on and drank some broth. He asked me, "Yeshua, what does humility before God look like?"

I responded as soon as my cup of broth was downed. "Rabbi, why would God ask Abraham to sacrifice his long-promised son?"

Shezzel appeared startled at this, bringing up the story of Abraham called on to bind his son Isaac and kill him, before a sheep was substituted at the very last (*see Genesis 22:1-18*). "Abraham was indeed humble, my son, but are there not more appropriate examples you know?"

"Rabbi, why do you ask about Abraham when the son was obedient?"

"My son, by your own words is not Abraham the father of humility?"

"Rabbi, was not Abraham an old man, and was not Isaac in the vigor of youth?"

The old man's eyes went wide and he stared at me, shaking his head slowly, in disbelief (though I don't mean that literally). He had not considered such a line of thinking before, but got a faraway look in his eyes and began saying over and over phrases like: "The son obedient unto death, the son obedient!"

Then, laughing with a dry, throaty rasp, he clapped me hard on the back before offering me more food. Smiling and enjoying the time together, a new line of questioning quickly followed. Such fun evenings together!

I suppose it should have occurred to one of us that there was the matter of my mother and step-father missing. I wasn't panicking and I was distressed that they had. The more important thing to take away from this time was the simple joy of a deep and profound conversation. I miss talking like this!

Do you ever get the feeling that, when you pray (I don't say "if" because everyone has said a prayer), there is an "answer" given in the spirit by God, but that it comes across as a question?

VII – LIFE UP TO THE START OF MINISTRY

Night: 24
Entry: 1

Luke 3:23ff

Key Verse

23Now Jesus himself was about thirty years old when he began his ministry. He was the son, so it was thought, of Joseph, the son of Heli[.]

So . . . what were you doing when you were in your early thirties? I love asking that. People in their thirties and forties get so frustrated and defensive! Some people accuse me of all sorts of nefarious purposes. Maybe you just need your nose tweaked, have you ever thought of that? People need that sometimes. It cuts down on the false pride and helps us have a more honest conversation.

Many folks will argue, saying that maybe they didn't do all the ministry I did, but they still did okay. Others will point to all the volunteering they did in their twenties, and what was I doing then, huh?

It's funny, maybe a little sad, too. The reaction I'm looking for is one of humility. I can spot the false humility stuff a mile away. *(He then gave me a few examples of when I had exhibited such false humility. His examples had an amazing amount of clarity and details, much of which I had conveniently forgotten, though the truth of what he was saying came flooding back to me. Thankfully, for all our sakes, he said not to add them to this entry.)*

I can work with all sorts of reactions, but humility is the easiest and false humility is only slightly less difficult than indifference. Yes, I smile when your reaction is humble. I don't want you humble so as to clamp down on you, not at all. It's actually so that I can lift you up. You say you've been kicked to the floor in this big, bad world? Well, that is not my definition of humility, but that is where I go. I go low. That's basically where I spend all of my time.

As for my twenties on earth, I did a lot of volunteering myself, actually, only we didn't call it that. We called it work where we weren't getting paid. My step-father Joseph died when I was 23. My brothers and I took over his construction contracts. As the eldest, I took the lead. It was hard, demanding work. Most of the jobs were in the neighboring town of Sepphoris, where a lot of stone buildings were being erected.

I've mentioned Sepphoris before. It was about four miles away from Nazareth, where I grew up. Nazareth was small, but Sepphoris was a regional capital of Herod Antipas (for a short time, anyway). He authorized all sorts of new buildings and first Joseph, and then me and then also my brothers, were hired to work on some of those. My first job was sitting and shaping blocks of stone. The blocks were crudely taken out of quarries and delivered to young men like me. There would be many of us situated in a line, taking deliveries of large blocks, sitting under the sun with our outer cloaks off (and usually under us for some padding), sometimes keeping our inner cloaks on as protection, sometimes wearing only our loincloths, our brown skin glistening in the sun. I took my place among them speedily. Carefully turning a block and taking off chip after chip after chip with tools Joseph gave me, the stone eventually formed to its purpose and fit precisely into its place.

Sitting in the hot sun, sweating from the heat and the work, rarely shaded as we needed the light to observe our progression, the stone stayed warm as it morphed before our eyes. We talked to the stones as if they were alive, or coming alive. They would sing to us as the flecks of stone flew off and each side smoothed itself, giving glory to God as they reached their intended fullness and purpose. Each one we finished we blessed—using a variety of different words amongst us—and looked upon it in satisfaction as it left us. The breather was quick, however, and a new "birth stone" (as I came to call them), was quickly delivered.

Sepphoris was a large town of great activity. As we shaped rocks, or hauled them or lifted them into place, the multitudes of people chattering away in Greek, Latin and Aramaic made it seem like the meeting-place of the earth, the very center of everything. Of course, I knew even then that it was in reality just a small place, a dot really. Its level of importance became both of those things to me, a central area in my early life, plus a comparative for bigger jobs ahead.

We had long walks there and back again. On the way home, our arms would throb from the labors of the day, but we didn't complain about it. The work was good. Sometimes we'd get back to Nazareth and a neighbor needed something repaired. Those were the free jobs, done not on the weekend (we only had a one-day weekend, and we weren't allowed to work at all on that day) but done right then, regardless of how tired we were.

Sometimes some of the family resented that, doing the jobs for the neighbors for free. I didn't mind, because Joseph had always done it that way. He was a brave, godly man. They said in town that he died poor. Don't you believe a word of it.

VIII – BAPTISM: ANTICIPATION

Night: 2
Entry: 1

Matthew 3:13-17

Context Summary

Jesus abruptly leaves Nazareth to become a rabbi. He travels to the Jordan River where John the Baptist has been preaching a message of repentance and baptizing people.

Key Verse

[13]Then Jesus came from Galilee to the Jordan to be baptized by John.

So this is the starting point, in some respects. Of course birth can be seen as a starting point, and certainly conception; but my baptism was a sure demarcation line. I was under starter's orders, so to speak. The Gospels are nearly silent on my childhood (and totally silent on my twenties), and for good reason. No, not because those decades were either boring or salacious (far from it). That time was perfectly lovely. Stories from then simply didn't matter for the theological purposes of each of the four Gospel writers.

I mean, Luke told that one vignette of me at twelve (*see chapter VI*), but he didn't really need to include it. Its theological merit is fairly lightweight. He had interviewed my mother Mary when she was in her seventies. She really liked that one (by that time in her life; earlier she had been a bit upset about it), so Luke included it. That was a good one; I'm glad Luke wrote it down. (I will tell you one of my favorite memories from early boyhood, though it might make you a little sick: The first time I could read Torah by myself. Wonderful! However, I always took so much time reading, forming the words so slowly, reverently, I'm afraid the rabbi thought I was a bit slow.)

My brothers told Matthew some stories about me, but they weren't needed for the New Testament as they were mostly about working or going to school. I didn't walk on ponds or raise any puppies from the dead or anything like that. I went to school, worked for Joseph, spent hours walking the hillsides reciting Scripture to myself. I laughed and I played some games and was teased about being a typically gawky teenager. People thought I had little respect as I showed no attention span. I was in a state of anticipation almost constantly, from my earliest human memories.

I was anticipating, awaiting this moment, my baptism. It wasn't nerves, per se, but I wasn't calm about it, either. All four of the Gospel writers included my baptism; John's reference is oblique, but Mark basically starts with it. He could talk to you for hours about why that's the true starting point. That all four Gospel writers have this moment shows its importance to me (and them, and hopefully to you, too).

Why is my baptism so important? I left Nazareth to become a rabbi, to preach and teach (and so much more). Throughout the Scriptures, the Old Testament, three figures were called and anointed: prophets, priests and kings. Prophets spoke the words of God; priests brought people to God; kings led in righteousness (or were supposed to). Rarely did someone have more than one of those roles; only the Messiah would combine all three. It wouldn't be exactly how the people expected it, perhaps, but three-in-one makes a lot of sense to me. My baptism would be an announcement and an anointment, the start of my mission, the beginning of showing myself as the Messiah, a line to cross from which I could not—would not—draw back. Soon after, I would bring the message of the kingdom of heaven almost continuously until I handed the ball off to my disciples.

IX – Baptism: Invasion

Night: 15
Entry: 1

Mark 1:9-11

Key Verse

[10]Just as Jesus was coming up out of the water, he saw heaven being torn open and the Spirit descending on him like a dove.

You know those days you have that you remember all your life? The days that define you, focus you, even keep you going in hard times? It might be a wedding or a birth, a graduation or a promotion. I don't have time to enumerate all the possibilities to include each of yours (read: I actually have the time, but David here doesn't).

My baptism was one of those days for me. I was born to go and do what needed to be done, but this time was a time of preparation for the road ahead. This was my first public pronouncement: It would be about death and resurrection.

You may have a hard time associating baptism with death. Baptism today can mean different things, even to people who have gone to church their whole lives, much more so to people who haven't. In my culture growing up, before or apart from John the Baptist, we had baptism as a purification ritual, a cleansing of the body symbolically before starting something new. John the Baptist turned it into a spiritual cleansing, for turning away from sin. The seeds of rebirth were all right there.

Some people have always wondered why I was baptized, since John's baptism was a baptism of repentance, which is something I never needed to do. In other words, in some people's minds, I didn't deserve to be associated with repentance. While it's true that I didn't need to repent, I can't help but find it odd that the same people who wonder why I would undergo the baptism of repentance have no problem understanding that I underwent crucifixion, even though I didn't deserve that, either.

Anyway, you may have a mental picture of water being sprinkled on an infant or maybe a dunking in a little pool, maybe even a lake. Hah! You should've seen the Baptist in action. There's been no one else like him. His zeal shone through his eyes, framed as they were by his wild, grizzled hair and beard, bare arms hard and gnarly like tree branches in winter, his skin interwoven with dry cracks looking like fault-lines. Reaching out alternately to heaven and for the next head to bless as he stood in the Jordan River, he moved in a rhythm he alone shared with God, frightening and compelling to those around him, his grip adrenaline-filled. When he put me under the water, I stayed there.

My heartbeat pounded in my ears. My lungs burned. I could feel consciousness slipping from me. Actual death was not that far away. I could either fight the Baptist or trust in God's plan.

When he raised me up and I broke the surface of the water gulping in air, I was gifted with this sight, what Mark describes here. God tore open heaven—a violent shattering of what the natural order had been up until then, a signal that earth was not safe from Him. What had always been planned had reached a key point. What I had always been was ready for a public reveal. In this moment, God invaded the earth; I was the weapon.

You can dislike that metaphor if you want.

X – Tempted by the Devil

Night: 2
Entry: 2

Matthew 4:1-11

Context Summary

After being baptized, Jesus is tempted by Satan in the wilderness to turn stones into bread, to throw himself from the highest point of the temple and to bow down to Satan. All of this he rejects.

Key Verse

¹Then Jesus was led by the Spirit into the wilderness to be tempted by the devil.

Night: 24
Entry: 2

Luke 4:1-13

Key Verse

⁹The devil led him to Jerusalem and had him stand on the highest point of the temple. "If you are the Son of God," he said, "throw yourself down from here."

People have all sorts of crazy ideas about the devil. I'm the only one about whom people have crazier ideas.

The riskiest thing ever done by God is giving freedom (and I say "is" intentionally, for it's ongoing). Do you know the phrase: "Go big or go home"? That's a godly phrase, really. Granting freedom is "going big". Creation is possible without it, but it's pretty sad. Most people have seen that in anything they cage and control. It doesn't fulfill God's will. No one can ever love or serve willingly if there's no freedom. Why would God's will be different from that?

So, risk rebellion in order to have relationship with His creation.

30

First came spiritual creatures. Among them, Lucifer, now known as Satan. He went bad. He fell. It was really sad and I don't like remembering that time.

When this happened, the tempting in the wilderness, I was battered by hunger and thirst, weakened intentionally, for I had been out there for weeks. That was preparation for the test the devil would bring. It's easy to pass on cake when you've already had a slice of pie ala mode (well, easier than when you haven't had one, anyway). This, however, was about passing a test that was difficult. There was no doubt I'd pass it, though. No doubt on my end, anyway. I really don't think he understood that, the devil, Satan. I'm not sure he really knew me then. He didn't look. He tried to command from on high, but I was already down to earth. This was the closest I came to being bored, truth be told, going from one temptation to the next, at least the first couple. I would face worse trials, much worse, many of which you might not recognize as trials for me. These ones just made me stronger in resisting him.

When he came, it was with power and almost-glory. What he looks like shifts for different people, but is generally a mask of something that moves you: beauty, strength, spiritualism, materialism; it can vary significantly. Get one peek behind the mask, though, and all that's there is smoke; the light being from mirrors. To me he wore the garb of a priest with a body like Samson's. Light and dark played all over his skin and clothes (mere figments as they were on him), like a thunderstorm brewed inside him. "Tell this stone to become bread! If you worship me, it will all be yours." His voice thundered toward me as he puffed himself up to eight feet in height, though had anyone else been there they probably would not have seen or heard much; they may have felt fear and not known why.

Anyway, he tempted me about food and he tempted me about power. No worries. Then he took me to the temple in Jerusalem.

"Throw yourself down from here."

You hear these messages all the time, like this one to jump, but they are never really what they appear to be. It may as well have been a TV advertisement or a story on the internet you really want to believe. This point on the temple where I stood, it overlooked the Kidron Valley. Green and brown terraced hills, the gardens and the tombs, with the land dropping away, almost sliding into the horizon. The view was breathtaking at nearly fifteen stories up. Below me was the spot where the priests of the temple proclaimed the morning and evening sacrifices. Many said that the Messiah would appear suddenly in the temple. Ironic I was there without their knowledge, huh?

Was it a temptation to jump? Oh yes; for the briefest of moments, anyway. Lured to jump to one's seeming destruction, believing oneself to be above the consequences. I didn't need to know events unfolding in order to be wary of these sly words; no, I felt them burn in my core. My heart beat wildly in my chest: "Announce my presence like this!" Avoid the work, the speaking, the walking, the healing, the day-to-day with normal people of small towns and hamlets and big cities. Be proclaimed Messiah and never face a friend's betrayal to the cross!

In other words: Take the easy way out. That message came so often to me (and, I suspect, I'm not the only one to ever hear it). The road is long, but it can be walked. Not alone, but it can be walked together.

Standing on that point on the temple, poised high above Jerusalem, with the wind sweeping up and swirling around me, I thought many things. One thought actually dominated as I stood there: Will anyone look up?

Yes, they were temptations, but in the end, they were easy for me to turn down. I was ready for the next step. I was ready to start preaching, ready to start gaining followers.

XI – An Auspicious Start

Night: 33
Entry: 1

John 1:35-39ff

Key Verse

[38]Turning around, Jesus saw them following and asked, "What do you want?"

They said, "Rabbi" (which means "Teacher"), "where are you staying?"

As I walked along, I pondered all the ways that the message I was bringing would and could grow. The plan was simple and elegant and filled with risk: Find some willing hearts, teach them, release them to the world and have them teach others; repeat the process. It would be a bit of a tight-rope walk, but I knew it wouldn't fail (though we might disagree on what success looks like). Wherever I stopped, I started to preach, and then I'd move on some more. I was on the lookout for people to call, to be my disciples. That's when Andrew and John appeared. Did they find me or had I found them? Perhaps it's not necessary to state the answer outright.

I had seen them with John the Baptist; they were his disciples. That is to say, I could see in them that they had been prepared by John the Baptist, and so were looking to become my disciples. Andrew appeared behind me, tall and wiry, a bit fairer than most of us, and beside him John (not the Baptist), barely fourteen with merely the tiniest wisp of down on his chin. Coming up only to Andrew's shoulder, his small head belied his deep intellect and spiritual curiosity. He sported scrape-marks on both arms and both knees, effects of his ceaseless scrabbling over rocks and boats and anything in his way. I felt protective over him immediately, as my own small sibling whom I would drive to incredible depths.

Both of them were younger brothers. Anyone would have guessed it. Though they had come to the Jordan River where their older brothers had not gone, a potential problem persisted, for they had come always looking over their shoulders. I knew when I saw them that I wanted them for my disciples, but some sort of hesitancy lingered in their hearts. Instinctively they looked to their older brothers (I know the look well), but not being around, they followed like puppies. I would have to teach them to follow like men.

When I turned, I asked them a question. As much as anything else, this was a starting point to relationship, practically an invitation. The sub-culture of a rabbi within Judaism was still in its infancy, not to be codified until after the year 70 AD, but as these young boys well knew, if one went after a rabbi, expect a question.

Does it seem mundane? If you had two young men—boys really—following you, I daresay you might say something like: "What do you want?" It could have all sorts of tones and inflections. Most likely it would have an undercurrent of authority, a façade of fear about what two youths might be up to. However, my question was sincere, not so much curious as the opening remark to a long conversation. One could even say that it was a bit of a start to an interview for being disciples. I knew even then many would want to follow, but who would want to become like me?

You yourself might say, "But, you're Jesus," and while of course that's true, I was mostly unknown at that moment. John the Baptist had known, though. He had seen. The authority that the young men had seen in the Baptist had been directly transferred by him to me. They instinctively trusted it.

"We don't want anything." They could have said that, in answer to my question. Colloquially in your time now that answer might have been: "Nothin'." Had it been, I would have nodded my head, turned around and kept walking. I would have to see them later.

Instead, they answered as they had long learned. To a question from a rabbi, answer with a question. This signaled they wanted more. So we ended up at the little house in the village where I was staying, kept by a widow named Esther. I rarely stayed in such a small house (because most of the places were complexes, built for multigenerational families), but this venue was perfect for the moment. Soon Andrew went and told his older brother, convinced in the exuberance of young faith (which is wonderful) that they had found someone to follow. John then did the same.

But what can I say? I did not call them yet, none of the brothers. When I call people, I am decisive. I want them to follow me. Yet I am patient, for I know the human heart. What entrapments won't it fall for? As we sat in the house and talked and went around—this is over the course of many days—and I studied the young men, Andrew and John and then others who came to me, and I looked at their faces, I pondered (not for the first time, not for the last) what it would cost these young men when I did call them?

I know what will happen for some. This is how it went, and this is how it still goes. Some came when I called and thought I was pretty cool for a while, but then they moved on. They said I was part of "their process". (*He actually used air quotes here.*) It happens every day. If they leave, who will come back? Do you know the phrase: "If you love someone, set them free; if they love you, they will return"?

Plenty of people say I do it all wrong. I have to grab them then and there, get their attention, manipulate them into commitment! Go after the weak and the stupid and, if you keep them quiet enough, the elite will nod and wink and let you get on with having your little group. Get too big, though, and they'll come after you, trying to destroy it all.

So I know some who hear a calling will leave, but in this growing group of young men, I'm seeing the potential in them to be in an inner group of close disciples. Their preparation had been started by John the Baptist, but this was still an incubation period, of sorts. Andrew and his brother Simon Peter, John and his older brother James, they were like a pot being put on a flame. I am the flame. I am patient for the boiling point and don't need to watch for it. Not hearing the call they expected and longed for, they slowly departed, confused, unsure what the experience with me had taught them. They didn't think they would ever see me again.

I will ask like I did here, when Andrew and John first showed up: What do you want? Do you know? The young men I addressed were nervous and expectant. Those open hearts made them so vulnerable; they could be so easily manipulated by untrustworthy teachers. The world has its share of them, certainly. We talked and got to know one another. Then they thought it was over, but I knew it was but a start, and an auspicious one at that.

XII – FISHERS OF MEN

Night: 2
Entry: 3

Matthew 4:18-22

Key Verse

¹⁸As Jesus was walking beside the Sea of Galilee, he saw two brothers, Simon called Peter and his brother Andrew. They were casting a net into the lake, for they were fishermen.

Funny story, true story. . . . (Do I really have to say that? Yes, I suppose I do.) This was early in the morning, though actually toward the end of the best fishing time. It had been several weeks since I had seen these young men in the home of the widow Esther. I went down to the lakeshore to find them, sensing (so to speak) that the time was now ripe.

Simon and Andrew had been out for hours. Brothers and friendly rivals it was easy to tell, even if I had never seen them before. Simon Peter was obviously the older brother. While a bit shorter and stockier than Andrew, every mannerism he had (around Andrew at any rate) was authoritative. His thick black hair stood up in the wind, while Andrew often shrugged his lanky shoulders at his brother's gestures and shouts as they both moved about the boat during its run to the shore. They had a decent haul, but they were arguing. You know the phrase "bickering like an old married couple"? It would have originated here if Matthew would've included that part of the conversation. A lot of "I mended the nets last time, you do it this time" and "No you didn't, I did" going on.

They reached the shore and stared at me as I spoke to them. It was time. I called them. Young fishermen though they were, they recognized what I had just done. They knew more than that a rabbi liked to ask and get asked questions, they knew what a call meant: to join a new type of community. Rabbis and their followers were known to them; the goal of forming a fellowship was obvious and understood by them, by all Jews in that day and age. To have a child called by a rabbi was a goal of most of the parents in this area, so it had been instilled in Simon and Andrew from birth to want this, though it had seemed unlikely while growing up, and at this point in their lives they thought of it as impossible, an absurd dream. They had been especially disheartened when they had previously seen me and then thought I would never call them.

I talk to you now, through this medium, meeting you halfway, so to speak. I want to give you a picture of what it was like back then for me, as well as let you know I have never left, that I understand you and your world. My context back then was ancient Jewish, and though some would appreciate me if I spoke only that way to you, other ways of processing thought and context are also valid to me now. Not to other ways of belief or validating other so-called gods, and not denigrating or violating the call that I make. In many ways, it is about returning to that meaning, the original meaning. The call from me is for you (in the plural sense) to form a community with me. That's what Simon and Andrew understood.

"Come, follow me."

Simple. Direct. A light just clicked for them. That old dream, that first dream, of being called by a rabbi, being called by me, had miraculously come true for them. They scrambled out of the boat, tripping over themselves and screaming to each other "I heard him first!" and "No, I did!"

It's kind of endearing, but it can quickly become irritating as a behavior, their sibling rivalry. It's probably for the best that we left that out of the Gospel text. I mean, that might make it into a more modern biography, but that wasn't the purpose of Matthew and the other three writers. It didn't help any of Matthew's theological points, not at all.

One can only find the spiritual value of "Yes I did" and "No you didn't" arguments in seeing the value of not behaving that way at all. I'd like to tell you that the reason it's not there in the Gospel is for how obvious of a lesson it is, but that's not true of every generation. It's a tricky thing, having a book be written that's good for all time. I think you'll understand what my opinion of the success of it has been as we go along.

Back to this point in time, by the Sea of Galilee. I mean, it's a lake, right? It's a decent sized one, though, over twelve miles across at its widest. Overall, Judea was a pretty dry place much of the time. But the valleys could be beautiful, and this lake, as well. It's a very low point on the surface of the earth; almost metaphorically low. While I myself delight in the water, most Jews didn't like it much. They associated it with the abyss of the devil and stayed off it as much as they could.

I loved being around the water and that was one of the main reasons for basing my ministry in Capernaum, on the shores in the north. It was a large community for that area, in easy reach of many other villages, flush with people seeking daily to be filled, farmers and fishermen. Loving the water, it would be most helpful to have friends with access to a boat. It was, therefore, almost a foregone conclusion I'd have some fishermen join me.

With Simon Peter and Andrew in tow, we came to John and his older brother James. James was over twenty, a bit younger than Simon Peter, a quiet, introspective man, an unlikely future leader, perhaps, but God used his taciturn nature as a bulwark for the work to which I would propel him. He kept his beard short, for it never grew in fully, the brown of that framing the bottom of a tall, thin face. His younger brother John delighted to be around him, being junior by seven years.

These two left their boat as well when I called. Their hearts were ready for the call, but they were still fishermen. I would need time with them to mold their hearts and make them my "fishers of men". I felt very good about the prospects.

XIII – NATHANAEL

Night: 33
Entry: 2

John 1:47-50

Context Summary

After Jesus calls Simon Peter and the other fishermen, plus several more men from various pathways, he also calls Philip. Philip in turn tells his friend Nathanael about Jesus, and tells him to come and see Jesus.

Key Verses

[47]When Jesus saw Nathanael approaching, he said of him, "Here truly is an Israelite in whom there is no deceit."
[48a]"How do you know me?" Nathanael asked.

I love this guy. He was my comic relief, if you can believe that. The Gospel writers didn't do much in the way of humor (though there are a couple of my quips recorded which were real doozies back in the day); otherwise, we'd have had a little more of Nathanael's antics.

Humor is good. It can be awful, even hurtful, depending on how it's directed, but I enjoyed a good joke and a well-meaning tease. One sister loved to jest with me until she was scolded by Mary back to her chores. She was much younger than me, and we'd make faces at each other to get each other to laugh.

Nathanael was more like my schoolmate Matthias (*see chapter XCV*), subtle, witty, sometimes sarcastic and sometimes downright sardonic. Like here, this very day John describes. I played a little joke on him, knowing him somewhat supernaturally and lavishing some praise on him. I mean, sardonic wit, maybe, but he still had a kind and honest heart.

How does he respond after I've called him the most honest man in Israel? Not, "Aw, shucks," but, "How did you know?" He said it with a twinkle in his eye, as he had seen the twinkle in mine. The start of a beautiful friendship. He was very honest. It's sometimes hard to see when a man might open up his heart. For Nathanael, it was immediate.

XIV – MATTHEW

Night: 5
Entry: 3

Matthew 11:1

Key Verse

[1]After Jesus had finished instructing his twelve disciples, he went on from there to teach and preach in the towns of Galilee.

Let me tell you something about Matthew. He was chosen to write this Gospel for a reason, for many reasons, in fact, but one of them was not due to his sense of humor. He loved punning and irony, but was not very good at either thing. Too subtle, possibly, though not for me.

Take this verse, for instance. He said "finished" quite intentionally. He thought he was being funny. Thomas couldn't stand it when Matthew tried to make a joke and, frankly, I don't think the other disciples understood him most of the time. I like puns myself, well, some of them, but I "get" people with an obtuse sense of humor. James (the other one) would tell him to, "Stop, just stop!" but not much could deter Matthew.

Anyway, by "finished", Matthew meant that a current round of teaching was complete . . . and, at the same time, that I may never "finish" teaching them.

"I've arrived!" he'd say, or one of a dozen variants to the theme, whenever we'd enter a new town or village. He'd look at me and wink, like we were the only two in creation in on a grand joke: Yes, we've completed our current physical journey and have arrived at our destination, and we're pretending that his own spiritual journey is also accomplished.

All the while, Matt knew that he was about the least of the group. Having been a tax collector, a position reviled in many ages, but definitely in an age when that means one is working for an occupying force, it took Matthew some time to feel like he could speak up. He let others speak first, but eventually found his voice. I liked that about him, too.

He stayed close as I went from town to town, sometimes asking about my sermons during the journey, sometimes getting Simon to ask about them. Once there, wherever we were headed, he went away or to the back as quietly as a mouse. He didn't want to be noticed, I think, in case someone recognized him from before, when he had been in the tax business.

More than that, though, he knew he had his time with me. He wanted all the new people to get what they needed. That doesn't make it much of a surprise anymore that he was chosen to write for me, does it?

XV – The Twelve Disciples

Night: 5
Entry: 1

Matthew 10:2-4

Context Summary

This section is one of the lists of Jesus' twelve main disciples (later known as apostles). Simon Peter is always listed first, while Judas Iscariot is always listed last. The disciples are sometimes known by their Greek names and sometimes by their Hebrew names. I added their other name in the Key Verses if Jesus ever used that.

Key Verses

²These are the names of the twelve apostles: first, Simon (who is called Peter) and his brother Andrew; James son of Zebedee, and his brother John; ³Philip and Bartholomew (*Nathanael*); Thomas and Matthew the tax collector; James son of Alphaeus *(he's the "other James")*, and Thaddeus *(the "other Judas")*; ⁴Simon the Zealot and Judas Iscariot, who betrayed him.

These were a great group of guys, all twelve of them. Yes, I mean all twelve. The Twelve. When I saw them, I could see so much potential in them! Of course, I see potential everywhere. They weren't unique in that respect. To be honest, most of them were pretty smelly, especially the fishermen (the first four that are mentioned). That odor was baked in; it did not dissipate quickly.

Simon Peter, he was a natural born leader. He was excitable and extroverted, a classic big brother, as I've said. He could be brash and he could be easily embarrassed, too. He wasn't just older than Andrew, he was the oldest of my disciples (he was almost twenty-three and was married).

Before I called him, Andrew had been flitting between the fishing business and listening to John the Baptist. He had a real spiritual bent from the beginning. Their father wanted at least one of his boys to become a rabbi; it was his sincerest wish. He had sort of given up on Simon, but he still thought Andrew might make it, despite rather poor results in beth midrash (*see Glossary*), because he spent time with John the Baptist.

When they left their boats to join me, raucous and excited, both of them, their father watched from a distance shouting for joy. Dancing and screaming to heaven until his wife scolded him, asking him how he was going to tend to the boats by himself without his sons, he said he would "hire new sons." Well, Simon and Andrew came back fairly frequently, either during my ministry in and around Capernaum on the Sea of Galilee, or when I sent them back for a period of time and told them to join up with me again later when we were farther afield.

James and John were the other set of brothers I've mentioned. Their father Zebedee wasn't quite as happy as Simon and Andrew's father Jonah (often called John). He was pragmatic and took it matter-of-factly, stroking his beard as he sat in a boat, thinking. He wasn't sure if his family was being blessed or cursed. From an earthly point of view, it's an understandable conundrum. All my life people would feel that way about others hearing a call, being chosen.

I could've chosen others, too, for my inner circle, but I went with my gut. When I saw that they were ready to be called, I called them. There was faith there, desire to follow, but everything else was included, too, I knew.

What specifically did I know? Is this a question about predestination? What do you think? Why do you think the Scriptures support such an idea as predestination as well as true freedom of action?

I will emphasize to you that, at this time, some things were hidden from me. I knew, and I had foreboding, and I had suspended and hidden my omniscience, all at once. In my humanity, I came to understand that Judas Iscariot would betray me, but it took some time. In my divinity, I knew it all along. Suffice to say I saw tremendous potential in him. In the end, of course, someone was going to betray me.

People like to say that time heals all wounds. That's an imprecise saying, since God created time, and did it for many reasons (not least of which was for the healing properties of the heart implicated by the passage of time). For me, it's different. Many have betrayed me, not just Judas. I hold all of those in sadness in my heart. Not to depress you or anything, but thinking about the beginning of my ministry and the potential a guy like Judas Iscariot had is still a very sad memory for me.

XVI – WEDDING AT CANA

Night: 33
Entry: 3

John 2:1-10

Context Summary

Soon after calling his twelve disciples, they all are invited to a wedding. The wine runs out and Jesus' mother asks him to do something about it. He tells the servants to fill the jars with water, but when it is drawn out, it is the best tasting wine of the whole feast.

Key Verse

[4]"Woman, why do you involve me?" Jesus replied. "My hour has not yet come."

M y growing group and I made the short trek to the town of Cana, still in Galilee. Well, I say short, but it was a little over twenty miles. A good walk back in the day, a good time to have some of the first of our many deep discussions.

We approached from the east and saw the village as we crested a hill. It rested on the next rise, smaller than the one on which we trod, a green hill with dozens of dingy white stone homes standing like a choir waiting to sing, each one or two story house set a bit higher up the hill than the last. We descended before climbing again, passing small copses of stubby trees and a scattering of low, flowering shrubs, moving between competing flocks of sheep the same dirty color as the houses.

Entering the village, we were greeted variously by excited people running in every direction. Immediately we were invited to this wedding, where everyone was either going, or quickly returning to after some random errand. The groom was actually a distant cousin whose mother had been close to my mother; she had been in the village for several weeks. We were invited just because we were in town, though; the whole village had been invited.

When my mother saw me and asked me to interpose, rest assured my response to her was respectful. "Woman" sounds a bit derisive here in English. "Dear lady" is closer to the point, but seems antiquated in this time period. I never said "Mom" after a certain age, though not for any theological reason.

Anyway, I was having a nice time at the wedding festivities. Most of the talk around me was idle and inane, of course, but people were happy as we sang and clapped our way through the many dances of the wedding and the blessings upon the couple. We ate well there, too. The family had fattened up an old cow for the feast (all the guests spoke of it as the "fatted calf") and I often had to prod my disciples away from extra helpings of not just the roasted meat, well-seasoned as it was, but also the cucumbers and chard with lentils, the sweet figs in pear compote and many, many dates. The smell of the meat mixed with cumin and saffron and dill, along with the bread and honey and olive oil, pulled us in to the colorful spread more than once. The meal filled our senses as well as our bellies! Soon, enough was well enough, and so we sat on the outer edges, Andrew and Simon nibbling their last bits, sipped our wine (the one thing that didn't seem to be there in abundance) and talked, starting naturally with the wedding in progress. Things were still quite new between my disciples and me—I mean, we were new as a group and still getting used to the group dynamics. It was my intention to continue having a nice time through to the end of the celebration, gradually bringing more and more topics to my disciples' attention.

Most of the people around did not know me yet (some even knew me only vaguely as "that one of Mary's" as harsh rumors die a harsh death), and so they let us be, though some wondered at the cluster of young men around me. Nathanael they knew, as he was one of their neighbors, but most of the others were unfamiliar to them. They thought we were friends or a clique. The observant would have known I was the leader, likely, but all basically missed that I was a rabbi, as I stayed out of the limelight. There were only subtle hints of the typical rabbi behavior that were so obvious in other circumstances, and I was not teaching publicly (which would have been the big give-away).

When my mother intervened and asked me to take care of the wine problem, a thought considered once arose, a line of action and reaction crystalized, and I decided what I would do. What did Mary expect of me? She acted on trust alone. I had never performed a miracle before her. A part of her thought I could get wine from Nathanael's house maybe, but another part considered something, something she had pondered in her heart my entire earthly life.

XVII – EARLY DAYS OF TEACHING

Night: 24
Entry: 3

Luke 4:15

Context Summary

After the wedding at Cana, Jesus and his disciples travel around the country. He begins his ministry, preaching and healing.

Key Verse

¹⁵He was teaching in their synagogues, and everyone praised him.

They love you as long as you don't offend them, am I right?

Honestly, though, I had a feeling the good times wouldn't last long. At some point, I'm going to offend them. Hey, if I don't, how will they ever grow?

I'm not trying to confuse you. The people I'm meeting with at this point in my life loved what I said, how I said it and everything I did along with it. They loved my preaching. They expected to hear about God their protector, God their defender, God the merciful Who heard them and would bless them. This was my message. "The time has come," I'd say. "The kingdom of God has come near." But there was more to it, much more. They needed to go beyond simple truths, to get into the heart and confront their doubts in order to grow their faith. How does that happen?

When I was younger, living and working in Nazareth and Sepphoris, I watched the people carefully. They lived in a rough environment, always on the edge of war, clinging hardily to their culture. This doesn't always sharpen the senses; it can actually lead to a numbness. The people I saw who loved what I was bringing needed to be woken up from their doldrums. It's easy to walk through a life, even eighty years or more, even one filled with hardships. What I mean is, it can seem like you just blink and it's all passed you by. That blinking is the type of doldrums I'm talking about: Where there actually is enough time, but lassitude, like a gravity of the norms, takes hold and covers one's eyes.

It was there in Nazareth and Sepphoris, and when I started traveling and preaching I still saw it. Many could get excited by healings I performed, but so few were willing to have their lives changed, their inner hearts touched (they had whole metaphorical walls thrown up trying to protect that place, much like you do). When you get right down to it, sometimes brokenness ends up being a good thing, in the long run.

How to achieve this? There's no other way except to keep telling God's truth. It's offensive to this world, and the people will hear that. They love me now, but it's not going to last. I'm counting on it. I've got to get beyond the surface level.

My viewpoint is that I am the appropriate one to be allowed entry in to that inner sanctum of the heart, to see what you don't show the rest of the world and sometimes never admit openly to yourselves. It doesn't scare me; it won't ever scare me.

I think of those synagogues that I visited as I started my public ministry. There was one in every town in Judea and Galilee. They were built to face Jerusalem, the main room a generous rectangle with a dais in the middle from which Torah would be read, benches along the outside and pillars in the inner corners. Some were completely open to the sky, others had a canvas covering; a few of the larger ones had a full roof, but raised in the middle to admit more air and light, a type now called a clerestory. Basically everyone in town went there for services. That was normal. That was why I went there. The small-town synagogues depended on traveling rabbis to reach them, spend some time with them, teaching, instructing, training. When one came it was cause for a minor village festival. The rabbi was expected to go into the synagogue. A good word was anticipated. The townsfolk weren't callous; they wanted to be the people of God.

As a young man in Nazareth, one haggard housewife said to me as one of these parties was winding down with the traveling rabbi moving on: "We're the people of God. Now we still have to get supper on the table."

What do you do when you run into something as unmovable as supper and the work needed to get it on the table? More than that, what do you do when someone comes around to interrupt your day-to-day routine? That routine can be sacred, and any change is therefore a threat. Even if it's from someone who loves you, who isn't trying to get you to vote for something, it might still be perceived as a danger! What do you do?

At that point, it's fight or flight, and the teachings and healings no longer matter. It's time to stop flattering the teacher and praising the healer; curse him or get out of there. That day was coming quickly for me, when the crowds would turn. At this particular moment, however, all the headlines were still good.

XVIII – HEALING A LEPER

Night: 15
Entry: 3

Mark 1:40-45

Context Summary

A man with leprosy comes to Jesus and begs him to heal him, if Jesus is willing.

Key Verse

41aJesus was indignant.

Night: 4
Entry: 1

Matthew 8:1-4

Key Verse

3Jesus reached out his hand and touched the man. "I am willing," he said. "Be clean!" Immediately he was cleansed of his leprosy.

There weren't a lot of lepers in Nazareth when I was growing up. With the population we had, it was not possible. At the same time, some did get sick, some with actual leprosy, some with other afflictions. We had no doctors in our town, no modern medicines, only herbal lore that had been gleaned over the generations, some oils and healing prayer. It wasn't much, perhaps, in comparison to what you might see in a hospital today, and not because there weren't smart people around.

No, the hillsides fed the sheep and produced vines and olive trees. We had our wild plants and flowers, but there was no Amazon basin around filled with exotic plants to be tried. Many who got sick withered and died. Some were sent off so as not to afflict others, but I didn't like that. I knew in my heart that the compassion of God in a fallen world was preached in terms of clean and unclean, for a people meant to prepare the world for the Messiah, and within that context some of the masses were therefore kept as healthy as possible. It still made me angry. I had the power to heal them when I was a boy and when I was a young man, but I had to wait. While I waited, some died.

Some of you reading this will scoff at me because I didn't heal them then, as if I didn't care. That's crying out at the sky because the universe is unfair (for those who don't believe in God). It's all right to be angry about people suffering; in many ways, I encourage that stance. However, if you don't understand the wait, then you can't ever understand the miracles.

You yourself might say, "If I had the chance to," and really think you mean it, but I wouldn't phrase it that way. Imagine trying to bring the message of the Good News that God has come to redeem people from their sin when a boy of six can heal afflictions and diseases of all types. That doesn't fan the flames of faith. If it doesn't, you grow old and die anyway, don't you? Even if all the diseases are healed.

By the way, back when I was six and fifteen and twenty-two, and people died, is it enough that when they did, I wept?

I was indignant at this moment, in front of the man with leprosy. I even said that—a little later—to Simon: "I'm indignant!" It's kind of a pun in Aramaic, since it sounds a lot like "I'm compassionate!" They were both true at that moment. Anyway, Simon and I kind of made it a saying between us, naming things that made us indignant, sometimes seriously, sometimes sarcastically, as good friends do.

I felt it seriously at that moment. I wasn't indignant at the man. Other rabbis would have been since he was breaking rules and mores. I can't explain it fully to you—there isn't even a great parable to get us close (I'm trying to stay away from adding many new parables, for your sake)—but I've seen and understand heaven and eternity, and so I know what they mean, but I also see with earthly eyes, knowing they see mortality and decay, with false pride in human strength and shadows over human weaknesses.

Perhaps it's easier for me to trust long-term, when I've seen both those things, but perhaps not. I could have told Niehum (that was the man's name) to be of good cheer, his leprosy (and it wasn't always genuine leprosy I ran into, but this one actually was) would kill him in a few years, that his suffering would therefore soon be over and he could then be in paradise. That's what will happen for many. However, my compassion rose up, and it was so powerful my heart overflowed, spilling over almost into anger at the fallen world and what it does to people, showing no favoritism at all, in the end.

"If you are willing, you can make me clean."

When Niehum knelt down, that thin face and those hollow cheeks, marked and lined by time and irregular diet, so humble, so aware of his need, I simply hated sickness and disease. Am I willing? Of course I am willing! I was willing to do that for Niehum.

Guess how I feel about you?

XIX – WOMAN AT THE WELL

Night: 34
Entry: 1

John 4:4-30

Context Summary

Jesus and his disciples head back to Galilee, passing through the region of Samaria. While the disciples run an errand, Jesus sits down at a well because he is tired. He asks a local woman for a drink, which surprises her, since Jews normally wouldn't talk to Samaritans. Jesus tells her he's the Messiah, and proves it by telling her all about her past.

Key Verse

[7]When a Samaritan woman came to draw water, Jesus said to her, "Will you give me a drink?"

All days we wake up with a purpose. The purpose may be mighty or mundane, pursued with passion or overtaken by other matters as they arise. It cannot be avoided that it is there, purpose placed within us intentionally.

This day's purpose was to travel, as so many were in my time of ministry. We had traveled away from Cana and all of Galilee, and needed to head back. I knew there was someone to meet along the way.

"Where are we going, Master?" young John asked me.

"We are going into Samaria," I told him, though there were other ways back to Galilee.

Do you know that, had I taken one of those other ways, there was someone else I could have met along the way? Most of my disciples would have preferred it, too. Samaria was the wrong side of the tracks, even for those from Galilee, which was the boondocks of Jewish territory (in the opinion of people from Jerusalem, anyway).

Walking through the seemingly endless hills, past clusters of cultivation and suspicious locals in remote homes, we strained our eyes toward the outskirts of a village and a watering place. Was it for my disciples that I cut through the worn, dusty tracks? To place them where they were uncomfortable and superior, all at once? Or was it for this woman, who should have been numb and simply living, having gone from man to man for years, her thoughts as shrouded from her neighbors as her face? What little peeked out from her coverings showed that years were on the verge of piling up. Men would have called her pretty in her youth, and still would in less sunlight. A wisp of hair splayed out from her headdress, and the sunlight bounced off her eyes as she looked at me, still dazed that a Jewish man had spoken to her.

Some women—maybe many in that area—would have simply turned away, never engaging with me. What was it that spurred her to respond? Miraculously, she clung to hope and jumped at the chance for real life faster than almost anyone else I've ever met. How different life would be today had I not taken that road and walked hard without stopping to get provisions. I was exhausted, truly. I asked for some water quite honestly. She left without actually drawing any for me. That's how it goes sometimes.

XX – RETURN TO NAZARETH

Night: 6
Entry: 4

Matthew 13:53-58

Key Verse

[54]Coming to his hometown, he began teaching the people in their synagogue, and they were amazed. "Where did this man get this wisdom and these miraculous powers?" they asked.

Night: 18
Entry: 1

Mark 6:1-6a

Key Verses

[5]He could not do any miracles there, except lay his hands on a few sick people and heal them. [6a]He was amazed at their lack of faith.

Night: 24
Entry: 4

Luke 4:16-30

Key Verses

[24]"Truly I tell you," he continued," no prophet is accepted in his hometown. . . ."
[28]All the people in the synagogue were furious when they heard this. [29]They got up, drove him out of the town, and took him to the brow of the hill on which the town was built, in order to throw him off the cliff. [30]But he walked right through the crowd and went on his way.

I was astounded when I went back to Nazareth. It was a good place filled with people I loved. The friends, neighbors and relatives perhaps thought I hadn't left on good terms. During those days—I mean after Joseph died and before I left to teach—if they thought about me at all, it was probably to cluck their tongues a little bit at the fact that I was not married (though it wasn't all that unusual for a man to wait until he had built up his income a bit before taking a wife), or that I didn't drive a hard-enough bargain for stonework or woodwork. "There's something unnatural to it," they would say. I heard, but I didn't care. (Based on a technicality, perhaps, they were correct.) I worked hard but it wasn't my job to grow the family business. We never lacked for food and I never provided outside of earning through my physical labor.

Of course, sometimes when someone couldn't pay or couldn't pay without difficulty, I might not care to collect, and other times when someone could easily pay, they sometimes felt so happy with the work they voluntarily gave a bonus. Maybe you consider that miraculous? Well, suffice to say I did work hard and we didn't starve.

One day, though, it was time. I woke up in the morning, had a light breakfast and said good-bye to my mother and brothers and sisters. Nobody said a word until Mary ran after me when I was just out of the door. I think they all at first thought I was just leaving for another day of work, perhaps to go get a tool fixed or to see how Elieazer's pillar was holding up. My mother sensed something else was afoot (of course; she's a mother and they are specially gifted). Stopping me and grabbing my arm, she looked up into my face when I turned to her. She stared at me with her eyes watering a bit, then let go of me.

"What will you do?" she asked me.

"I am a rabbi. Do you not know I must preach the good news of God's kingdom?"

Though this must have been a shock to her, she merely said, "Where will you go?"

"Where will my Father not send me? I will go throughout the land," I said, and even gave a little shrug. I knew she wanted some details. I wasn't being smart-alecky; these were the simple and bold truths of the matter.

"Will I see you again?"

That was her big question, of course. Her eyes glistened as she took tentative steps toward me. The years that I had seen her in our simple home in Nazareth passed through my mind, memories of her as a young mother, cooking and washing, singing at synagogue and watching Joseph go off to work. Those eyes of hers were dark and mysterious, though caked with lines where once youth had reigned. I knew she pondered many things she never spoke. She trusted when told things, but feared emptiness. Would she see me again? I smiled and nodded, knowing that would be enough for her, then turned and walked away.

I headed east and a little south, to the Jordan River and John the Baptist. Now I was at my first time back; it hadn't been all that long, just a few months. Knowing people, it must have been quite the hullabaloo when I left and didn't come back that night or within the week. My brothers took up the work and built up the business, but there must have been a lot of "Where did that brother of yours get to?" type of questions asked; really, it was a small village. Anyway, when I came back, there was a mixture of awe and skepticism among the people, resentment and incredulity.

On the one hand, I could understand some of their skepticism. After all, they knew me as the rather plain boy Yeshua. They thought I was simply Joseph's son. I had gone to bet sefer (*see Glossary*) with them or their children. I did all that was asked of me, but showed no outward promise of becoming a rabbi (except one time, and then not to them).

On the other hand, I had such hopes for the Nazarenes. I wanted them all to be healed, because I loved them. I wanted them to praise God because the good news was being preached! Why isn't that enough? Why don't some people see it? I was very difficult to astound back then, and while I can't be surprised as such today, I find myself getting more and more frustrated over these questions.

If I had showed myself to be a super-genius as a child, sailed through beth midrash and had a rabbi come and call me to follow him at fifteen to train under him, if I had done all that was expected of me by the society of that time and reached my worldly potential the way they might have expected, would they have approved?

Why isn't it enough to believe me that I did the will of my Father?

So when I came back there, these people who knew me as a child and as a young man when I labored among them, doing work for which I had been trained by Joseph, they were one of my toughest crowds. Not much of the "Local Boy Makes Good" headlines, not unless I really were the Messiah, their kind of Messiah. If not, they would have rather I had stayed and kept laying stone. I had laid that work aside, of course. If I were only a human, perhaps their jealousy and hard-heartedness would be warranted. Perhaps.

Why not listen to the message first? God has often called deeply flawed people to be his messengers; indeed, they are all that; by definition deeply flawed (myself excluded—modesty forbids bragging but also demands truth-telling).

What should I tell people who knew the ten-year-old Yeshua? The twenty-two-year-old one? "You're a good person, have no fear"? We all know that when you justify your lack of repentance with phrases like "I'm a good person" (which I hear a lot of), it is simply a façade, a desperate bluster to cover up your feelings of inadequacy. But why? Why cover it up? This is actually something the Holy Spirit placed in you, to convince you that you need a savior! You're close when you do this, but also close to pushing away. Don't do that! It kills faith! I was still powerful enough to heal in Nazareth that day, but faith reaching out . . . that's a key component in our relationship. Amazing.

The visit to Nazareth was difficult for me. I looked upon faces I had known my whole life, but they were blank stares, frowns, simple puzzlement up to and including both disgust and amazement. Some of them were ashamed to say they knew me. Some were eager to see me as the Messiah (with caveats). Some few had just been healed. I could see them whisper to each other. When I walked into the synagogue, there were many casual smiles and a few gasps of recognition, people who hadn't yet seen me that day. Then, when I moved to speak, there were more gasps, more whispers. The stares were the worst. The kind where their mouths were agape and their brows were furrowed. Stand-up comics know what I'm talking about, right? Every one of them has had a gig like that. Not even sympathy laughter from the home crowd.

What should I tell you if you were in my hometown? "The kingdom of heaven is like a rock show. The band came out to play their new album, but the crowd booed because they only wanted to hear the old hits they'd known all their lives." That parable works; the converse of the parable works, too (*see chapter XXXVII*).

Let me tell you something else about going home to Nazareth. Remember I said that the people from Nazareth had a saying: "The Messiah will be one of us." I wasn't coming back as a visitor, exactly, not to Nazareth.

See, you have to understand some things about growing up there. I'm not trying to put everything I say during these 40 nights in the light of my Jewish upbringing. There are scholars around and books and websites and whatnot to help you learn more of that, if you so wish. Some of that is important—incredibly important—and I hope you get that. Other events and circumstances, while important, are not as necessary, so I'm not going to emphasize all those aspects. My thoughts on these subjects, and what I hope you do with them, are not limited to these words, just as my words were not limited to the people of Nazareth, or Capernaum, or Jerusalem. There was one truth I was presenting, but many ways to express portions of it, in order to paint the picture of it, or even just to start painting it.

In Nazareth, the people thought "Crazy Yeshua" when they discovered me gone, but when they heard about the healings and the miracles, they wondered aloud to each other if I was the Messiah. It actually made some sense to them, because it was so rare for anyone to strike out on one's own; the entire culture was against it because life had to be lived in community. But a crazy person would do that, or maybe, just maybe, the Messiah might do that.

I hadn't cut all my ties to Nazareth, though, at the time that I first left to go preach. I had been a member of their synagogue, and, well in advance, I was on schedule to be the Torah reader for this particular service. Would I come back and do that duty? Yes. That's what this trip home was about. Elsewhere I would be a guest speaker, but in Nazareth I was already appointed.

We would do it this way, generally speaking: The attendants would go to the ark of the scrolls, placed along the side of the synagogue, for the scroll of the Law (as "Torah" is often rendered—somewhat poorly—in English), or one of the chests for one of the other scrolls. When a scroll of the Torah would be carried out, each about two feet tall, twenty to twenty-five feet of parchment sheepskin rolled up, weighing close to thirty pounds, we'd dance and sing and weep for joy around it; a special, sweet time, for coming amongst us were the very words of God. The one designated to read would read from the Law, then maybe read from one of the other scrolls (in my case, from Isaiah the prophet). This is how it went that day, after we had all gone in to worship and the scrolls were brought out, and I read both of them.

Then—see, this is where it gets really interesting—I sat down.

You might read that as I was done. I was merely done reading. They all understood that sitting was the position for teaching. It was time for a short sermon, so I gave mine. Most of those types of synagogue sermons (I use "sermon" for lack of a better word in English) would be maybe five minutes long. That's not long at all. Mine, however, was six words in the Aramaic that I spoke to them. After reading from Isaiah 61:1-2a, a prophecy concerning me, that I was to "proclaim the year of the Lord's favor", my sermon in English is (eight words): "Today this scripture is fulfilled in your hearing."

Everybody stared when I said that. Their curiosity and amazement at all they were seeing and hearing had, at least temporarily, held at bay their anger and disgust. Were they genuinely willing to give me a shot to prove my Messiah-ship? Waiting for me to begin teaching on the sermon, the reading and my sermon on it had heightened their expectations.

It had begun so well. Why not leave it at that? Leave them laughing, exit on a high note?

I had to explain it to them, though, and they weren't going to like it. It's like being on a date (so I've noticed) and the other person seems into you, only there's something they don't know about you. When they find out, it's probably going to end the blossoming relationship (or so you fear). Say it now or string them along? I've been accused of stringing some people along, but that's not a very objective analysis.

Do you understand what I told them? What it was that got them so upset they wanted to push me off a cliff? I said the Messiah only comes for those who have faith.

See, they didn't just have a saying about the Messiah coming from among them, they felt that gave them a head-start, an "in" with the new ruler. It wasn't about believing in God, it was about being the right person, having the right pedigree, being better than everybody else. They had this even though the rest of the country looked down on them. Who cares what everybody else thought? Why would they have to have any faith in God or dependence on Him? They were from Nazareth!

And so they became a small but angry mob. Another time and I would have let them have their way.

People are passionate, especially when they feel they have been misled. They "double-down" almost instantly, for they sense at least subconsciously that they are in the wrong. That wrongness is a sore spot; when exposed, it causes pain and pain is to be avoided (that's the fallen-nature thought all people have). Lash out, kill the messenger, blame the victim, call the one pointing out the problem the problem. Only the humble repent, go through the pain and find healing. The rest work themselves into a frenzy, continuing to justify themselves in order to escape blame . . . which cannot be escaped, in the end.

I was there—on earth, at that time—to be torn to pieces. I was not avoiding the physical pain this would have caused, only God's plan was not yet fully ready to be enacted. Preparing my disciples and laying more groundwork would take time. My death could not happen here, this way, so I walked out on it. Was it cheating? You have that phrase "cheating death", but I wasn't, I was merely working to align things completely to the intended scenario. When that came about, then the crowds could call for my death, and some of those on that hill in Nazareth would be there that day. It would happen in Jerusalem; it would happen by crucifixion. That was not an accident.

There was a curse, you see, written in Deuteronomy. The rabbis of the day all taught that the Roman capital punishment of crucifixion was a manifestation of this curse. "Cursed be anyone who hangs by a tree!" they said, paraphrasing the fifth book of Torah (*Deuteronomy 21:23*). In the end, that's why those who connived for my destruction didn't try to stone me, their traditional form of capital punishment. If they got the Romans to execute me, then they looked innocent in the proceedings, and all the rabbis and teachers would proclaim that since I had been crucified, I was under God's curse. How political is that? In some ways, it's kind of deviously genius (or should I say "devilishly clever"?).

Cleverer than that, however, was that it was intentional. When someone sets a trap for me, generally speaking I walk into it with eyes open and I spring it. I was born to become a curse, taking that on from you. The crowd in Nazareth didn't get that; even my disciples didn't get that, for a while, anyway. Many today would have fit in quite well in Nazareth 2000 years ago.

When I had vanished mysteriously from them—I mean, when I had stopped construction work, left it in the hands of my brothers and cousins, and left Nazareth quietly to be a rabbi—they put me from their minds. "Crazy Yeshua," some said. Returning, they had to revise their opinions, but based on what? I wanted them to admire me because they knew me anew, but for some rumors. So I told them true things. They got angry. This was a small mob that tried to attack me. Eventually, as I said, some of them would join a bigger mob.

XXI – CAPERNAUM

Night: 16
Entry: 1

Mark 2:1-12

Key Verse

[1]A few days later, when Jesus again entered Capernaum, the people heard that he had come home.

C apernaum became my hometown somewhat by default. Prophesied by Isaiah and all, but it was a good center for ministry, a place to teach and preach. I was planning on using it and Nazareth both, but eventually it was difficult to go back to Nazareth; their hearts were too hard.

The village lay on the northwest corner of the Sea of Galilee, only a few miles from where the Jordan River entered the lake. The residences were laid out in neat rows around the center square with its wells and marketplace and synagogue, with well-worn pathways leading down to the lakeside. Short piers, nearly a dozen of them, overlooked a squat masonry seawall where dozens of young men and servants worked or kept watch. Quaint and busy, I had high hopes for it. It would be my base of operations for the next two-plus years, though the amount of time I would spend there was much less than that. While a number of wonderful people came from there, it too disappointed as a headquarters, eventually.

Capernaum wasn't my home like you might think of a home. I came to a house in the town where I spent the most time sleeping of any town after I became a rabbi. Some nights I stayed elsewhere in Capernaum, but most nights I stayed at this place. Now, I didn't own the house (from the perspective of earthly ownership and title). It was a small complex, as many homes at that time in that region were (some are still like that today). A modest place in comparison to some of the structures around it, stone of course, it was a single story high, but long, with a flat roof typical of the area, where people could go and get some fresh air and think. The stairs up to it were on the side of the house and the rooms on the back opened up to a small garden area. It was built for a large family (you would probably say it was made for an extended family, or a multi-generational one), ready to be occupied.

The family that had been there was down to a widow and her niece. When I first entered the town, there wasn't as much fanfare as there would be later, like in this incident where crowds gathered. Walking into town that first time, nobody knew me.

I met the widow and her niece in the center of town, on their way home from one of the town wells with jars of water. I had asked a few of the boys and men hanging around there who might have rooms available, and they pointed out the woman Anna and the girl, the niece (also named Anna; I called her Ina).

"Who are you?" Anna asked me cautiously when I approached her and asked if she lived nearby. I told her I was a rabbi and needed room for about a dozen or so, maybe up to twenty.

Her eyes widened in amazement. She stared at me, staggered. She was thinking, "A rabbi is talking to me? Have I done something wrong?" She was sure this was against someone's rules, and it was, but not my rules.

"Where are the dozen?" she asked me, looking to either side of me, knowing I was alone, wondering if perhaps I wasn't a little bit "touched". "Where are the twenty? Where are even two?"

"When I call, will not people come?" I told her. This satisfied her. She smiled and nodded and had me follow her home. We got to be good friends. Anna and Ina stayed in Capernaum for the rest of their lives, but that doesn't mean they didn't end up following me. Anna never asked me for any remuneration. She was, however, well taken care of. As the crowds started to swell, and my disciples were along, she told me her home became more raucous than it had been since her childhood spent with five younger brothers. It made her smile, for a while, until some of the noise gave her a headache.

XXII – THE LAME MAN LOWERED
THROUGH THE ROOF

Night: 25
Entry: 1

Luke 5:17-25

Context Summary

While Jesus is teaching in a house, four men carry their paralyzed friend to see him, but when they can't get through the throng, they go up to the roof and make a hole in it.

Key Verse

[19]When they could not find a way to do this because of the crowd, they went up on the roof and lowered him on his mat through the tiles into the middle of the crowd, right in front of Jesus.

This was a good day, oh yes! There were a number of good days like this. All days are good in their way; all days are days in which you can give thanks to God. What I mean by saying that this was a good day particularly is that certain days held more promise than others, because of which people were involved; hearts ready to find God. I so wanted to stir up the faith of the people coming to listen to me.

Faith sometimes comes from the least likely of places. In my idiom of the time, I said to my disciples, usually as we traveled: "Why do your eyes look down when you walk along the road? Who can see the future by looking at the ground?" They would look up then, thinking that I was hinting at declaring something apocalyptic, but I had said this a moment before it started to rain, and they all looked up and got pelted. We all had a good laugh together then.

But this day the crowd surrounded me again, as happened when I taught, though this time they wanted to hear what I said and were not predisposed to see limitations. Other crowds had not been that generous. It's not such a great thing to be pressed in like that, though. I quickly felt desperate for some air, and I knew I would need some alone time soon, to refresh and recharge.

Everyone was there for a reason. It sometimes was nearly intolerable to face all those looks, like masks readied beforehand, like the poet said (*I could be wrong, but I think he was alluding to T.S. Elliot's "Love Song of J. Alfred Prufrock": "there will be time/To prepare a face to meet the faces that you meet"*). While I had mercy for them, too, I was ecstatic when the dust and small bits of plaster began falling all about me. The crowd gasped and gaped. My hostess Anna let out a particularly loud shriek. The sun broke through the expanding hole in the roof and blinded all who first looked up, for the room had been much darker than daylight.

A nearly hopeless man lowered on a litter by four nearly hopeless friends. It's a close-run thing, sometimes, hope. Humans must have hope, and some recognize it right before despair. I love when they reach out, responding to the summons of faith! It makes for a really good day.

XXIII – GOING TO SYNAGOGUE

Night: 6
Entry: 1

Matthew 12:9-14

Key Verse

⁹Going on from that place, he went into their synagogue[.]

This was one of my favorite parts. Going to synagogue was always special to me. Once I reached the age of twelve, we went to Jerusalem as often as we could for the Festivals, the Feasts, but it wasn't as often as we all would have liked. It was especially tough after Joseph died, but he was a good man who wanted to do right by his God for his family, so we made a number of the pilgrimages through the year when he was still around. Work didn't always allow for it, especially when he was working in Sepphoris on some of Herod Antipas' projects, or for Roman or Greek retainers building houses there. Some of the ones who employed us were knowledgeable about our customs and wouldn't begrudge a week away or so to get to Jerusalem, but that wasn't the norm.

Going weekly to synagogue in Nazareth was sacrosanct, though. It was one of the newer buildings in town, not as generous in size as ones I would see in Capernaum and elsewhere, but it still had room for basically all of the adults in town, and when we squeezed, all the children, too. As kids we would be there daily for school, or to meet up and play. The giant Torah scroll called to me (not literally). I loved to hear the reader read. More than just that, I loved when they brought it out and unrolled it. There was a little gesture of love in it. We'd dance and sing around the scroll joyfully, tearfully, as they brought it out, for these were the very words of God, given only to this small nation, but for purpose, amazing purpose. We celebrated Torah in synagogue services, and we celebrated being this one family.

We had one creepy guy there, though. He didn't love the ritual for what it meant, for the reality behind the ritual. No, he loved it because without him the ritual didn't happen. People could only go in when he said so, it only started on his word, then he would open the doors and we went in lines down three entrance steps and across the threshold. Each week he'd make the boys line up according to height and put his hand on both their shoulders, one at a time, lingering too long, a most uncomfortable situation, until one time he came to me and looked in my eyes. I stared at him until he sheepishly took away his hands. He stopped doing it to all the boys after that, and the people entered their synagogue more freely, though I must say with less precision.

We called him the "Wolf", for he snarled if we were able to get him in trouble with any of the teachers. Fortunately, he had no real bite; he was still part of the family. There's someone like him in every synagogue and church, ones who harm, even if the authorities don't label it as abuse; it's still not good enough. I'm not here to apologize for the "Wolf" around you, if you have one, only to say I'm not done with either of you. As to any worse offenders who may have hurt you, I'd like to deal with that with you as you need it over a very long talk.

XXIV – Healing a Hand in Front of Pharisees

Night: 16
Entry: 2

Mark 3:1-6

Context Summary

Jesus goes into a synagogue and finds a man with a withered hand. The Pharisees are there watching to see if Jesus will heal the man on the Sabbath.

Key Verse

[5]He looked around at them in anger and, deeply distressed at their stubborn hearts, said to the man, "Stretch out your hand." He stretched it out, and his hand was completely restored.

The kingdom of heaven is like introducing the iPhone to a crowd in 1973 and having that crowd yawn.

Listen: I was at synagogue! I loved being at synagogue. The Word of God is spoken there! I had gone weekly to synagogue in Nazareth growing up, always (perhaps obviously) without incident (not counting that time I stared down the "Wolf"). Now it was a trial. Not to me, to my abilities and attitude, but of me. My presence brought in the crowds. That would be true of my church today, I think. The Spirit is there, but if I just showed up for a weekend service like at this synagogue, the church would be packed; but with how many regular attenders and how many strangers, hmm?

Why was this man—the one with the shriveled hand—there that day? Was he a regular attender, a member? Was he planted by the Pharisees? Stacking the deck to get me to break one of their made-up rules? Could he have been their test to determine if I could be the Messiah? Or had he come of his own volition, having heard of the healings taking place?

What do you think?

Oh, the tension in that packed room! Bodies pressed in together so that it became difficult to move around, yet directly surrounding me people pulled away, strangely, as if to leave a space in which I could perform. The air was electric. Truth and rumor about me had run rampant. It had gotten the attention of the Pharisees. Were the things attributed to me accurate? Was I a force with which to be reckoned? They were starting to grow curious, skeptical and nervous. Their talk ran through the crowd and added to the pressure in that synagogue.

The women, mixed in all around usually, had gathered together in groups and they whispered and pointed. The men were at once fearful and expectant. Everybody wanted me to heal that man, each for his or her own reasons.

I wasn't healing for healing's sake. There is such small purpose to that. I was willing to heal him, and them, but it broke my heart to cure someone of cancer and have them die years later of something else with a heart still hard toward God. How I wanted them to believe! How I still want people to believe!

XXV – AN EARLY MORNING

Night: 15
Entry: 2

Mark 1:35-39

Key Verse

[35]Very early in the morning, while it was still dark, Jesus got up, left the house and went off to a solitary place, where he prayed.

I love people. I mean, there's loving people so much that I was willing to die on the cross to pay for their sins (and when I say "their" feel free to substitute "your"). That of course is true for me. Here, what I mean is that I do enjoy being with people. I'm not shy at all—I'll talk to anybody, anytime, anywhere, about anything. I talk to people that my mother warned me about.

I can talk, and I also know how to listen. I can laugh and joke around, and I can also respect a meaningful silence. I discuss things deeply with people, and I cut through their ("your") lies and façades and stories to reach their ("your") hearts and what's really going on with them ("you" . . . okay, you get the idea). Sometimes that happens quickly, but oftentimes it happens over an extended period of time, both then and still today.

But . . . well, don't take this the wrong way, but back then sometimes I needed to be alone and away from people. The time alone was hard to come by when there were so many wanting me to perform more and more miracles. You might use the term "stalking" here and it might be somewhat apt. What's wrong with people wanting to be healed? What's the point of the healing if they don't listen to the message about the medicine? Is it healing only to die later? I didn't mind the people coming, but they thought the healings were the horse, while the message was the cart, and it got tiring trying to persuade the people that the opposite was true.

I sometimes stayed up late to get that precious hour or two to recharge, and some mornings—like this one that Mark recorded pretty early on in my ministry career—I roused myself while it was still dark. The disciples and I were bedded down in the main room of this house, which belonged to Simon's extended family. We were staying there while our normal residence underwent some repairs to the roof. There were no servants at Simon's, but had there been they would've been asleep, too. With bleary eyes and no hope of brewed coffee, and so nothing external to waken the senses, not caffeine, not the heavy smell of the grounds (those blessings would be uncovered much later), I forced my head up from my simple rolled up cloak (my standard pillow) and looked around, finding not even the earliest cracks of dawn through the closed shutters. Yet it was time.

Did I have an "internal alarm clock"? Maybe. That's an okay description. When your soul needs to be alone with God, it can wake you up and propel you to tip-toe around some ex-fishermen. My stomach growled and I had to wipe the sleep from my eyes. Most people would roll over and push the feeling aside—the one that wants to get up and pray—and go back to sleep. It was very tempting for me, too. However, I've found that people willingly sacrifice even good things for necessary things, or for something they want more than what they've got in hand.

I wanted to maintain connection with my Father, and I needed internal energy back, after having spent so much time and vitality on crowds, large and small. They were coming for me again, soon, too. It was now or never for some time alone. I know about 30% of the people reading this will understand. I have a sympathetic ear when they're in similar circumstances. I know that feeling just a little bit more intimately than not; it's the introvert in me.

XXVI – NICODEMUS AT NIGHT

Night: 33
Entry: 4

John 3:1-21

Context Summary

A Pharisee named Nicodemus comes to Jesus at night. Jesus tells him that he must be born again, and this greatly confuses Nicodemus. Jesus goes on to talk about the eternal life that comes from this.

Key Verses

[16]For God so loved the world that he gave his one and only Son, that whoever believes in him shall not perish but have eternal life. [17]For God did not send his Son into the world to condemn the world, but to save the world through him. [18]Whoever believes in him is not condemned, but whoever does not believe stands condemned already because they have not believed in the name of God's one and only Son.

There's this verse in the Bible, the one that every sports fan knows about. You also know the one I'm talking about, of course, since we're in John chapter 3. People hold up these signs that say "John 3:16" and sometimes someone even goes to look at a Bible to see what it says. Then, sometimes after that happens, they look at what comes right after it, which I've always thought is just as important a message to shout out to the rest of the sporting community as John 3:16.

How about three friends behind a goal post hold up three signs that say "John 3:16" and "John 3:17" and "John 3:18"?

That'd be a little different.

I like those people who hold up those signs. Some critics say that they're just a bunch of hypocrites, to which there's only one response: Well, of course they are! However, I'm the only objective one capable of determining how much hypocrisy there really is; many are being faithful to me the best they know how. I know an awful lot of people who are hypocrites, believers and non-believers. I'm not excusing my followers for their hypocrisy (forgiveness is much more vital), and I'd like to see them work on reducing it (spiritual growth is a necessity). What is the cost of encouraging several million people to read (or re-read) one solitary verse in the Bible? I want it read. Where my followers are hypocritical, I'll deal with them as I see fit.

So maybe someday three friends do sit in a row behind a goalpost. Even if someone goes to read three whole verses in a Bible, there will still be another worry: Will anyone read John 3:1-15?

It happened back then on occasion, but some Pharisees (generally recognizable by their own hypocritical tendencies and unwillingness to accept that description) actually did come to see me, curious or willing to look into their own hearts. So came Nicodemus, and he came at night to see me.

I sat by a fire in the front courtyard where my disciples and I were staying, warming myself from the cool night air. Young John stoked the flames lazily as he listened to Simon and me discussing the day. Some of the disciples on the outer edges stirred suddenly as a newcomer entered through the open gates. Nicodemus approached the light of the fire cautiously, and a small pathway cleared for him.

He was an average man in so many respects: of average height for our time, an average age for an active Pharisee of the Sanhedrin, from a family of average wealth for the area. His robes were a standard display, his nose a nondescript standard shape. Well, he had an old scar on his forehead, an accident in his youth that had knocked him out and could have been even more serious had a neighbor girl not helped immediately to stem the bleeding. After that, a very standard life for a rising Pharisee.

Did he come to me afraid and trembling, fearful of being seen by his friends? What if they knew? What would they do to him? That wasn't his main fear, actually. He may not have actively discussed visiting me with his compatriots, but he didn't come cowering. A man with a question, he came directly.

"Rabbi," he said, bowing to me slightly as he launched into his prepared speech. I smiled as I looked right through him; I even laughed a little bit to myself.

What's funny about his visit is that he never got out the question he really had. He started hinting around at it, calling me a teacher from God, acknowledging the signs and wonders that had happened. Expecting the conversation to go a certain way—such as me thanking him and asking him what I could do for him—I instead told him he needed to be born again.

If you read the Gospels closely, you'll notice on occasion the trouble I had with both disciples and opponents in taking what I felt were obvious spiritual truths that I had spoken and processing them as strictly literal statements. I told people that Abraham rejoiced at the thought of seeing my day and they thought I meant that I was thousands of years old (as a mere human being). (See chapter *LXXI*.) After hearing that my friend Lazarus was deathly ill, I told my disciples that he had fallen asleep and that I needed to go wake him up, and they were dumbstruck because they figured I should just let him sleep in, not realizing I meant "sleep" euphemistically (see chapter *LXXVII*).

So too, Nicodemus. "How can someone be born when they are old?" he asked, his eyes wide, the reflection of the flames dancing in them. "Surely they cannot enter a second time into their mother's womb to be born!" he cried.

Silly Nicodemus.

Look, there's a problem with speaking metaphorically and there's a problem with speaking literally, and oftentimes they are the same problem: People misunderstand and people willingly misunderstand. Some just want to be told to do certain steps, and if you want there to be certain steps to following me, they can be listed out: Repent, believe, obey. That's really it, and it's really liberating when you look to me to do the work you just can't do. Other people just want to argue about the minutiae: What do you mean, Jesus? Do you mean I should be born from my mother's womb again?

Duh-hey. No, Nic, I don't.

See, I didn't have a problem with Nicodemus being a Pharisee and coming to see me. I didn't have a problem with Nicodemus coming to me when his friends couldn't see him. I didn't even really have a problem with his literal thinking (the misunderstandings were something of a pet peeve during my time on earth). Night is a great time to study, think and ask questions. Nicodemus and I and all the Pharisees even had all been raised in that culture with that viewpoint (this is perhaps a partial reason why I've been seeing David at night these weeks). Getting away from other teachers and teachings to come to me is always a good thing. I give people what they need, and Nicodemus needed to be taken in a whole other direction from where he meant to go.

Do you want to know what he was intending to ask me? You won't be impressed or inspired. He was going to ask me if I intended to become the high priest of the Sanhedrin. Maybe he wanted to get in good with the up-and-coming. Advancing in years and advancing in hierarchy, Nicodemus thought he had arrived (or at least was close to the finish line). Is it any wonder I told him he had to start all over? Is it any greater wonder that I also told him why?

For God so loved the world. . . .

XXVII – QUESTIONED BY PHARISEES

Night: 25
Entry: 2

Luke 5:29-32

Context Summary

Jesus is at a banquet held by Levi (Matthew) which is also being attended by many other tax collectors. The Pharisees complain that Jesus is eating with the wrong people.

Key Verses

[31]Jesus answered them, "It is not the healthy who need a doctor, but the sick. [32]I have not come to call the righteous, but sinners to repentance."

Q uick question: In this group of Pharisees, teachers and a former tax collector and his friends, who were the sick and who the healthy, who the sinners and who the righteous? What I said to the Pharisees when they asked me why I ate with "tax collectors and sinners" begs that question, doesn't it?

I ask questions like this a lot in various different guises. Some people know the answer right away, some people discover it after painful searching, but most tend to think I'm trying to trick them, assuming I've assumed things about them that aren't true.

The Pharisees really were becoming my foil at this time, many of them, anyway. They weren't wholly evil or anything like that. Some things they had right. Some things they taught I had long admired. They had had a job to do for the people for generations, building up a wall, a defense, that said they were the Chosen People of God, only they went further than that and said that they themselves were the Chosen People of the Chosen People of God; everyone else was disqualified automatically. I came to tell them that about the only automatic disqualification was instituting automatic disqualifications.

Who were the sick? The Pharisees assumed the non-Pharisees were. They were right, too. I called them. Getting called by a rabbi when all their lives they had been kicked out of the temple system (or threatened with it, at any rate) was a blessing to which the rest of the people responded. They rushed in to repentance . . . and quickly backed out again; many of them, anyway, though certainly not all.

Who were the righteous? After I spoke, the Pharisees' eyes narrowed and shot darts my way. Their heads bent and twisted back and forth while they whispered in harsh sibilance with each other, but always those eyes stared at me. They might be angry with me that I had called them "righteous" (they sensed sarcasm), but really, in order to be called "the sick" they just had to say they were sick. Nothing much has changed.

XXVIII – A Healing at the Pool of Bethesda

Night: 34
Entry: 2

John 5:1-9

Context Summary

Jesus goes up to Jerusalem for one of the festivals and finds a man who has been paralyzed for thirty-eight years at one of the ritual pools who wants to get in, but can't.

Key Verse

[6]When Jesus saw him lying there and learned that he had been in this condition for a long time, he asked him, "Do you want to get well?"

I loved going to Jerusalem for the Feasts, Passover and Pentecost, and also the Feast of Tabernacles. I loved it and it hurt a bit. They weren't what they were supposed to be.

On this journey—just a quick visit, really—I had traveled in from the northeast; this was my first stop in Jerusalem, even before reaching the temple. I was there, believe it or not, to stir up trouble. I chose that spot for several reasons, least of which was my own little joke, of a kind I enjoy now and again.

See, at this pool, called Bethesda, there was a superstition that the water would be "stirred up" by an angel from time to time, and the first ill person who then got into the water would be healed. The pool was fed by natural springs, so sometimes it would bubble. They had no promise from God on this; they were just desperate. It's a kind of faith; small and fragile, perhaps, but it is something with which I can work. It is also an affliction for which I have a certain amount of compassion.

So where the springs "stirred up" the water, I came to "stir up" people's lives. It's not a great pun, perhaps, and it's about the same in English as in Greek. It wasn't understood as a pun by anyone other than me, but sometimes a private little joke—even a tiny one—is a lovely way to stay focused.

Anyway, I saw this man, gray-bearded, bilious, legs so thin and deprived of vigor that the sight of them made my own legs ache. I could tell he had been there a long time, had been unwell for a very long time.

"Do you see that man?" I asked to those near the pool. I gauged their reactions in my rabbinical way, some scowling and turning away, not wanting to know, others suddenly curious, expecting someone special being pointed out before casting a questioning eye back to me. "He has been ill quite a long time, hasn't he?"

"Well, yes, of course," they all variously answered. "Why wouldn't he be?"

"He's been here a long time."

"Thirty-eight years, I heard," a woman said, nodding with a knowing smile. She gasped as I stepped toward the man on his mat and knelt beside him. Yes, his present circumstances were easily discerned by all, but two equally clear paths for his future arose in my mind's eye. I did not see a decrepit, useless man at all, of course. He would work for me, and choose to give his heart up, or not. Invalided for thirty-eight years does not keep the heart from pride.

"Do you want to get well?" I asked him, and of course he did, my question one of engagement rather than seeking approval. His eyes reached out to me slowly, not comprehending at first, while daggers flew from the eyes of watching Pharisees in the shadows.

Oh, I was happy to heal him, but it was time to poke the bears who couldn't even rejoice over the healing.

XXIX – WALKING WITH PHARISEES

Night: 25
Entry: 3

Luke 6:1-5

Key Verses

¹One Sabbath Jesus was going through the grainfields, and his disciples began to pick some heads of grain, rub them in their hands and eat the kernels. ²Some of the Pharisees asked, "Why are you doing what is unlawful on the Sabbath?"

It's almost as if I'm intentional about creating these conflicts with the Pharisees, isn't it? (*Here he winked at me.*)

This was a beautiful Sabbath day, not too hot with a light breeze. I remembered the day and gave thanks for it. It was here for me, so we walked. The road went off in the wrong direction, so we headed into cultivated fields. The gold of the sky matched that of the ground. The wheat fields smelled fresh and clean, and though we stayed mostly on the small pathways of the farmers, it was easy to reach out and touch the growing grain.

It might be odd for you to walk through a wheat field and harvest some of the grain that didn't belong to you, but we lived a communal life, and God's law permitted such gleaning by the lowly traveler. In fact, it was not just permitted, but expected.

However, it looked like work to the Pharisees, and that violated their own special definitions of keeping the Sabbath. I pitied them. There was no purpose to their definition except to control people, and—even more irrationally—to protect God from offenders. So they said no one can walk more than 2,000 paces on a Sabbath day, otherwise that is considered work, and working is against "Remember the Sabbath day and keep it holy". They would have loved the Fit-Bit back then. Anyway, I interpreted that law—correctly, I might add—as I would correctly interpret "Thou shalt not commit adultery" to include looking on another lustfully in your heart.

"What gives?" you might argue. "That one was done intentionally to control us! You're a no-good Pharisee yourself!" Okay, if that's what you want to think. It would take a miracle to change your mind. I know. Though to be clear, it was not about control, but the offer of grace. If you think you're without sin, you're not just wrong, you can't accept grace.

So the Pharisees told everyone that on the Sabbath 2,000 paces was it. I was on the move however and, sadly for them, they had to keep up. One of them took the rules so seriously that after we had gone what he felt was 2,000 paces, he stopped and sat down (he was close, he had gone 2,014). Middle of the wheat field, but he wouldn't go any farther. He had to wait until sundown to move again and hurry home. At least he felt obligated to obey those customs himself.

I answered their concerns but they kept at it. "You are violating the traditions!" the other Pharisees shouted at me as I kept moving.

"Oh, are you counting for all of us?"

They snarled as they recognized the rebuke. "We need to keep an eye on you!"

Boy were they right.

XXX – SAYINGS

Night: 3
Entry: 1

Matthew 5:1-12

Context Summary

During Night 3, I read through the Sermon on the Mount section of Matthew. Jesus spent most of this night talking about ideas for his sayings and sermons, so I grouped several of the entries together.

Key Verse

[8]"Blessed are the pure in heart, for they will see God."

Night: 3
Entries: 3 and 4

Matthew 7:1-29

Key Verses

[2]"For in the same way you judge others, you will be judged, and with the measure you use, it will be measured to you. . . ."
[28]When Jesus had finished saying these things, the crowds were amazed at his teaching, [29]because he taught as one who had authority, and not as their teachers of the law.

People ask me, "Where do you get your teachings from?" They ask similar things of writers and musicians and comedians; all creative people.

Well, I am creative. Teaching can certainly be creative, and I, of course, had to be creative when bringing a new or more complete understanding of God to the people. What I mean is, I've been in heaven, seen it, then came down to earth to try and explain it. Guess what?

It's not explainable.

I suppose I had the option of not trying, but that's hard-hearted, and I'm not. I'm actually pure in heart myself. That may strike some as egotistical, but when it's true and not said for personal gain it isn't.

I've seen heaven. It makes sense to me. On earth, it is understandable to a degree. There are not exact words for it, though. I had to think about how to come close.

The rabbis understood this, as much or more so than anyone. There were two types of rabbis, the Torah teachers (or "teachers of the law")—of which there were hundreds during my day, including the rabbi who came to Nazareth when I was a boy and taught at the school there, Rabbi Ben Shimon (Nice man, smart, bit of a lisp. It made his Aramaic difficult to understand for some, but I listened long enough to him to understand him just fine.)—and also the ones seen to have godly authority, the Masters of Tanakh (that means what you call the Old Testament). I, having learned (maybe "re-learned" is the right term?) the whole of your Old Testament and been authorized by heaven to teach, was a rabbi unlike good old Ben Shimon. In his own small way, he helped prepare me, though he never knew exactly how good of a student I could be. I did much of my work on my own, in the hills and quarries of Nazareth. Still, some important parts were done in the daily work at the school, asking questions back and forth in the rabbinic style, discussing merrily, vociferously, even argumentatively (it was, and remains to this day, a typical way to learn in Judaism). Rabbi Ben Shimon sometimes broached the subject of heaven, asking things to get his students thinking.

The questions we would ask one another were deep, intense and fun. While the rabbi knew that apparent paradoxes can help expose truth, he still couldn't fully explain how to see heaven. He knew it required purity, and so he focused his questions on the laundry our mothers would do. Washing is purity, in one sense, but there are others.

*　　　*　　　*

So, where did I get my sermon ideas? Is it a cop-out to say I was inspired? Or that they all simply are original to me?

Okay.

On the human side of the equation, my inspirations include the Law, the Prophets and the Writings (i.e. the Old Testament), the teachers and preachers of the day, and, perhaps obviously, the people and places around me.

As a construction worker, Joseph was a big believer in the measuring stick. "Measure twice, cut once" is an exceptionally old adage. Wood was expensive and was not to be wasted. Even when cutting stone one wouldn't cut foolishly and risk squandering it.

When we'd walk from Nazareth to Sepphoris for a job, he would talk to me about the goodness of God seen in a twice-measured line. There are ways to be generous, he would say, and ways to be stringent, but when a beam needed to be an exact length, it helped no one to add or subtract an inch.

He had many nice things to say like that. I liked him a lot—well, I still do, in fact. It was hard on my brothers after he passed, and I, being the eldest, did not grow the family construction business as was expected of me. When the moment came, I left it and proclaimed myself a rabbi, a teacher (and more, of course).

I hate being taken out of context, but I do see this saying, the one about judging others (*Matthew 7:2*), as memorializing Joseph in a small way. He gets it.

Now, as to authority in teaching, it all boils down to this (argumentatively, anyway). It was the same back in the day as it is now. It's about power and control. As they asked me about where I had gotten my authority, they were asking where and how had I become a Master of Tanakh.

Back in the day, a rabbi had godly authority when two already recognized as having godly authority laid their hands on the rabbi and transferred that authority. This happened only rarely. In a way, John the Baptist did that to me at my baptism (though he was only one; the other was God Himself when the Spirit descended upon me), but it was also a microcosm of the reality.

I remember these crowds, those who listened to my sermons. They were sheep, almost literally. They acted like sheep, followed where the leaders went, stopped when they were told to stop, spoke when they were commanded to speak and kept quiet when they were told to keep quiet. While various eyes shone forth, there were few sets of good clothes among them; some quite dirty, others washed regularly by redoubtable mothers, some of whom were also there. Crowded together, one could only think of a sheepdog turning a whole flock one way or the other. This wasn't everything about them, certainly, but it was a disproportionately large part. They were created for so much more! At the least, they recognized that I had godly authority, and that was exciting to them, but it didn't automatically mean they believed I was their Messiah. It was okay for them to be sheep—to start out that way, I mean. One part of that metaphor will always stay: that I will be your Good Shepherd, and when you are mine, you will listen to my voice. At the same time, the metaphor, like all metaphors, is limited. You're a sheep now, but you're not supposed to stay a sheep. It's tough to grow from being a sheep to being a disciple. Sheep follow, but they don't transform into their shepherd. Being a sheep is a great start, just not a great ending point.

Like people from many places and ages, as sheep they were simply bullied. They had not had a good shepherd. The teachers and leaders would nip at their heels like herding dogs, and the people would bend. It was the path of least resistance for them. Far worse was the fact that the people ended up not only doing what the teachers and leaders said, but believing them, as well. The teachers were supposed to be the ones who could correctly train the people in the ways of faith. Corruption came upon this system swiftly, so that hearts and minds were not won, they were simply leashed. In other words, the people didn't know what they were doing or why. It is easy to judge bad teachers, but not so easy to judge their students.

Later, in Jerusalem, it would take most of the week for those dogs to turn the herd of sheep cheering me in the other direction. This day—me turning them—wouldn't be instantaneous, either.

Hearts and minds were meant to be freed, and freed ones were meant to choose a shepherd to whom to shackle themselves, a loving one or a controlling one. One or the other is always chosen.

What's the difference between a sheep who comes in willingly to a shepherd's pen and one who is harassed and bullied into submission? You're a sheep either way, aren't you? You're shackled to someone or something, so why does it matter?

I was talking earlier about some of the sources for my teaching. While there were germinations from all over, even from the rabbi of my school-days, there was nothing to attribute to him or any other human. The leaders ascribed everything to an earlier rabbi (especially the stuff they made up). When I didn't do the same, they didn't like it, not the leaders and not even the crowds. The crowds were used to attribution, and the leaders soon convinced many that I was a fool.

Still, some ended up following me. Rabbi Ben Shimon liked to say that people in numbers were like sheep, but alone they were like a cat, but he would never explain himself. So, I didn't use that one.

XXXI – PARABLES

Night: 17
Entry: 1

Mark 4:33-34

Key Verse

[34]He did not say anything to them without using a parable. But when he was alone with his own disciples, he explained everything.

W here do you get your ideas from?" Let me continue with this subject, as it's still such a big question, as much for my parables as for my sermons. It's hard for any teacher or artist or writer or comic to explain, because ideas often develop and connect subconsciously, linking to something half-similar tucked away in some far corner of memory, or laid as a foundation for another long-pondered idea to be constructed higher with the mortar of yet another word or natural form, so it's difficult for most people to know all the antecedents. That's the core point, isn't it? Every idea expressed by people has roots from other ideas of humanity, unless they came from God first.

My parables have deep roots, and took several standard forms. The true parables (the kind with a full story), the metaphor or epigram parables ("faith like a mustard seed", that sort of thing) or the similitudes (like: "If one has a hundred sheep and one goes astray, will he not go after it?"). The teachers—and even the students—of the day called all of those things parables. But from where did they come? Many roots came out of the Old Testament—my Torah; my Law, Prophets and Writings. Others had similarities to other rabbinic traditions and teachings. Still others, of course, were based on some experiences I'd had, or seen, growing up.

The crowds loved parables. They were used to them and expected them from the traveling rabbis. Many of mine really stuck with them. My disciples heard them often, or several variations of them, so were soon able to commit them to memory, along with many of my other sayings.

The thing is, the parables weren't always light and easy teachings. The people in the crowds could most often relate to the parables, but that wasn't their primary purpose. The parables could leave the people confused, and I admit that the ambiguity involved was intentional. The purpose of the parables was to reveal truth about God, not just to relate to others, and truth about God sometimes is learned through holding two complete ideas in balance. If you really understood the parable well, you might then think that the teachings were hard. You might just have to give me some sort of response.

The people who came to hear me were amazed whenever I took on the Pharisees or other teachers, because they didn't always stop to think about what was actually being said. They saw the point when I had to kick in the façade of the Pharisees' own teachings. That was David versus Goliath for them. (I played the role of David, in case you wondered. If you don't know what that means, you can look it up, or just consider that I was the underdog against the well-funded political elite, endorsed by the media.)

Of course, had the crowds heard all the application of the teaching I set down to my disciples, more would have surprised them, because they weren't prepared for what I was essentially saying.

"He's taking on the big bad guys! Go, Jesus! Go! Wait, what? He wants me to get involved personally and change?"

That's how the crowds would have reacted. While many people are that way, I am buoyed by so many others: Young men and women with fire in their hearts and zeal in their mouths; quiet, faithful couples in their 70s and 80s, devoted to me all their lives, never with any headlines, still finding small ways to live and grow by remaining humble before God; little children who love to sing songs about me. They don't all understand the change I want to bring to their lives, but they all trust that God has a plan for them.

XXXII – PRACTICING RIGHTEOUSNESS

Night: 3
Entry: 2

Matthew 6:1-4

Key Verse

[1]"Be careful not to practice your righteousness in front of others to be seen by them. If you do, you will have no reward from your Father in heaven."

When I was growing up in Nazareth, this was quite tricky, the bit about others not seeing things. Nazareth was a small town, agrarian, but with most of the dwellings clustered fairly close together between the hills and on top of the main precipice. Small and large plots surrounded the terraced hills and down into the lower valley where the villagers who farmed argued with the shepherds who overlooked pastures. It was a town where everyone knew everyone else, like small towns everywhere. Knew each other? Most of us were related, though in a clan-like way. If someone did something nice, within the hour everyone probably knew; some praising too effusively, some too sarcastic in their infantile jealousies.

"Hmph, that Yeshua thinks he's so good carrying little Hisarael after he fell, we should probably just all bow down to him now, huh?"

It wasn't crowdedness that made it difficult to practice righteousness privately, but familiarity. The mothers and eldest sisters worked together keeping an eye on everyone, especially the young boys. Despite the societal dangers, I looked for ways to do some nice things for these mothers or their daughters without their knowledge. Very tricky.

One time, one of the neighbor girls had several large jars to fill, each about two feet high, with water from the small well in the center of the village. She carried the empty ones there two at a time, then filled them all and began hauling them back, but one at a time as they were quite heavy, around thirty pounds each. When no one was looking, I hefted one to her mother's door—taking a bit of a circuitous route, dodging by windows and around the curious toddlers shooed out of the houses—then calmly went about my business.

It's not that I minded carrying the jar, but it was a patriarchal society and this was a job the girls did. Even though this girl—her name was Rachel, she was almost ten and hadn't hit her growth spurt yet—needed a break, she never would have asked for anyone to help her. It's part of the human condition that this work ethic can be both a virtue and a vice, prideful when it ventures too far one way. She had her job and wouldn't want to appear weak for anything, though how she would get everything done, she didn't know. She found herself strangely one jar ahead and was actually too tired to find it remarkable.

Of course, if the other boys had seen me, they would have teased me mercilessly. "Are you doing girl's work, Yeshua?" I could have handled that just fine. However, before I had gotten too far away from Rachel's house, her mother stuck her nose out the door, saw the jar and only me nearby . . . and she told me off! She never thought I had toted the jar to its place; no, she assumed I was up to no good, maybe getting ready to throw pebbles at Rachel and the other girls as they returned carrying their jars (and admittedly some boys did this with a certain amount of frequency).

From this day forward, I'm sorry to report, I had a rather poor reputation in my hometown.

XXXIII – Faith of the Centurion

Night: 26
Entry: 1

Luke 7:1-10

Context Summary

In Capernaum, a centurion has a sick servant, and so he asks some Jewish elders to go to Jesus and beg Jesus to heal the servant. Jesus says he will come to the house, but when the centurion is told, he protests, sending a further message that Jesus should only "say the word" and his servant would be healed.

Key Verse

[9]When Jesus heard this, he was amazed at him, and turning to the crowd following him, he said, "I tell you, I have not found such great faith even in Israel."

I am very hard to amaze. In fact, now, nothing surprises me. Nothing. People are awesome sometimes, people are horrible sometimes. Great things happen and terrible things happen. Ridiculous acts of kindness and loyalty are performed every moment around the world between people, and at the same moment, others are inventing new ways of being evil. Still, I'm not amazed. I'm heartened or saddened, moved to tears of joy or grief. As I am now, though, I cannot be shocked.

See, this day that Luke records though, I still could be amazed and I was. Why I could be was wrapped up in my role as the Son of God, in the full humility I embodied. Entering Capernaum from the south, enjoying the breeze off the lake and laughing at the gaggle of cries from the cormorants and warblers circling over us or heading to the waters, a group of seven men reacted to a boy runner. He had spied us out on the road and had raced ahead of us to tell his news. So the men approached us quickly, forming behind the leader like an arrow-head.

"Rabbi!" the leader called to me, the oldest man among the group, dressed his best, but still simply, his arms outstretched to me in supplication. "Please help!"

"What is it you want me to do for you?"

"There is a friend of the people. His servant lies low," the leader said. "He has heard of you and has asked us to go to you on his behalf."

"Indeed," I breathed, intrigued. "But why should I attend to him?"

"This man deserves to have you do this, because he loves our nation and has built our synagogue."

"I will go with you," I said simply and they bowed to each other and smiled, rejoicing. Turning as a group, the leader offered me his arm while another sent the runner boy on ahead. As we walked, I contemplated the swell around me. Their words to me surged with the sheer improbability of a Roman centurion filled with faith.

I could see faith in people, see it in bunches or as a small seed planted in their hearts. I could tell if one had willingly choked it off or desperately sought to nurture it. I could not see this Roman centurion; I was not yet at his house. Having others call for me showed me the possibility of faith in him, of course, but I could not physically set eyes on him. This was a hardened soldier, an officer who had spilled blood in his day and was ready to do so again if ordered. How much faith could he have, really?

After he had been posted to Judea, he had—though skeptically at the start—listened to the locals talking about their synagogue, their Law, their prophets, their one God. Though monotheism was a difficult concept for him, having grown up in a deeply polytheistic culture, he listened in. He got caught up in the narrative of creation and calling, the Exodus and the judges and the kings. He heard the mighty words of God through the prophets and wondered at this people who would even defy the might of Rome to worship their single God, yet in their past had forsaken Him and been divorced by Him and sent into exile through the power of a mighty army.

That should have been the end of them, he thought. He had been part of armies coming in, burning down opposing cities, carting off the best of the remnants and salting the earth so no enemies could remain behind. Rome had been doing it for many years. No one talked about being a Carthaginian anymore. If the Babylonians 600 years earlier had been anything like the Romans—and they were—this centurion knew that no Jews should have survived to his day. That they had was evidence that their story was true, their Book was true, their God was true.

He was moved and began to believe, even though he still had many questions. He wasn't interested in becoming a Jew (especially once he heard about circumcision), but, he began to do what so many Pharisees didn't. He protected the weak around him, built a new synagogue out of his own funds, listened to God's word to try and do it. Like only a small percentage of the Romans in Judea, he made friends with the Jews around him. They in turn liked him, though they wouldn't have dinner with him because of the rules that seemed against it. All this became clear as we walked through Capernaum.

The runner boy, with three other men—retainers or friends of the centurion—met us on the street and bowed low. "Lord, don't trouble yourself!" they begged me. Then they gave me his message. "Say the word, and my servant will be healed."

This centurion had power, he had authority, but it turned out that even more he had faith, and it was activated by true humility. I admit, I didn't see this one coming.

XXXIV – JOHN THE BAPTIST'S QUESTION

Night: 26
Entry: 2

Luke 7:18-23

Context Summary

John the Baptist has been imprisoned, and he sends two of his own disciples to Jesus with a question. This is not long before the Baptist is beheaded.

Key Verse

[19][H]e sent them to the Lord to ask, "Are you the one who is to come, or should we expect someone else?"

Night: 5
Entry: 4

Matthew 11:2-15

Key Verse

[7]As John's disciples were leaving, Jesus began to speak to the crowd about John: "What did you go out into the wilderness to see? A reed swayed by the wind?"

I had an interesting relationship with John the Baptist. On my mother's side, he was a second cousin once-removed. That's not the interesting part nor the relationship I meant. Of course, I meant our interactions.

We never saw each other as children. We had only a few, very brief conversations as adults. The respect I had for him was boundless. Most of you would not have liked him at all. Most people of his time didn't like him all that much. I mean, even for a pretty smelly age, he had a terrific odor. Standing in the Jordan

River all day never seemed to do much to help that; it was part of the reason he smelled so much, really.

I kid a little bit about that, but he was extremely brash, forthright and had the fire of real, puritanical devotion in him. People were drawn and repelled at once. You, too, would have gone out to see him, or almost all of you would have. Would you have been baptized by him? Would you have gone and done what he said?

He called for repentance and there was no hypocrisy in him. That made him frightening to others. God's power on him was undeniable, though, and the people were drawn to it. They came from all walks of life, out from the cities and small towns and villages, down to the Jordan River. There were huge lines to come and get baptized by him or by one of his disciples. All throughout the lines there was tension; true desire to show God repentance and be made right with Him, versus the desire to bolt and leave the exposure of bright light and crawl away to be hidden in the darkness, not for what the public would think of as a great sin, but just for some little ones, to hide and avoid, as if God had not created the very stones under whose shadows one tried to cower.

Even I stayed away from him for a while (no, not because of his pungency, though truly it wasn't pleasant). It was not possible to stay away for long. Yes, people came to see him, many even left their metaphorical shelters and braved the light. Even Pharisees came to see him. They had to at least listen. It was "must see", or rather, "must hear" kind of stuff.

I had a lot of emotion when John's disciples came to me later with a question from him. There's a lot to our expectations, aren't there? People let their expectations rule them, no doubt. Who hasn't been disappointed in a politician, a job, an ex? People run ahead with their expectations and end up disillusioned when it turns out differently; but whose fault is that if the expected one has only ever told you the truth?

John the Baptist was gifted, spiritually gifted, and he had expectations of me, even though it had already been confirmed to him on three separate occasions that I was the one he longed to behold (though, to be fair, one of those times was in utero). Perhaps he expected a little more "winnowing fork" and "unquenchable fire" (*see Matthew 3:12*), like maybe he thought I was too soft, but that really isn't it.

What happened? Now he's doubting me? Am I the one who is to come, the one for whom he's been waiting? This from the same man who had cried out, "Behold, the Lamb of God!"? That's how strong these assumptions can be, especially the ones you keep close, guarded and secret, the ones around which you build walls. There is rarely true vision through the lens of expectation.

His disciples were in a bind. One of them—you can almost imagine them doing a sort of "rock, paper, scissors" type of mini-contest to avoid this—he eventually got deputized to be the spokesperson, and he passed on the question from John. They loved John, they would do whatever he asked, but they didn't have the same question. It was easy to see they were conflicted. Following close to me, they had seen more miracles than John had, but though the miracles confirmed the message, John still needed to get over that wall his expectations had built.

Those walls were tall and powerful. The disciples of John were humble, and so had fewer inner walls, or lower ones. They were being won over just by the message. They all became my followers. When presented with my message, some people—both then and now—walk away, saying they need miracles in order to believe, but I'm not so sure that's really the case. Plenty have seen miracles and dismissed them.

It was hard to let John just go to prison; harder still to hear about his death a little while later. Even sadder still, to me, was what happened to the people. John prepared them to hear from me. What was the response? I still view humanity as having been prepared. It's perfectly reasonable to want to be prepared some more, to want there to be yet more time until you have to make a decision about who I really am. We aren't always ready for the final act. Sometimes, a person gets a whole lifetime to prepare.

Sometimes.

XXXV – YOKES

Night: 5
Entry: 5

Matthew 11:25-30

Key Verse

[29]"Take my yoke upon you and learn from me, for I am gentle and humble in heart, and you will find rest for your souls."

Most of you don't know what a yoke is, do you? The more agrarian society of my day knew—it was common knowledge. (I told you Matthew was a jokester, but at no point did he ever say, "The yoke's on you!" It's only a bad pun in English, really. Had it been one in Aramaic or even Greek, I shudder to think.)

Your society still talks of yokes, but almost solely in metaphorical terms connoting oppression. Is that why so many of you have hardened your hearts against me? A yoke is a tool that helps bind one to another so that the one bound can be most useful, and can benefit from the strength of the leader.

You've seen miracles done in your towns and you've rejected them so completely you don't even know or admit miracles were even done there! The only advantage the people of my time had over you right now is that they had a much better understanding of the word "yoke"!

I looked on those people—as I look on you now—and the main thing that I saw, the thing I see most clearly, most in the forefront, was their (and your) longing for God. So many don't believe it. That there is longing is self-evident, and as I wanted for them, so I want for you, to look deeply into your heart, to consider what I state as the truth, that the longing is actually for God. But in looking and finding, even glimpsing what I know is inevitably there, most of you feel so much fear you'll do anything to beat down that

101

desire rather than admit its existence. For in the admission, you know you have a need you can't fill, or can't get anyone to fill by dint of your own will.

It's true they saw me, the people of that day. They physically saw me. It's also true that they saw some pretty cool natural-law-defying matters (hey, healing the lame or turning water into wine is very cool), but you have much more.

Well, you have the possibility of having much more. In admitting your desire for God—if you do—and your need for a savior, far above and away anything you can do about it, you can have the needed salvation, yes, but look at what you have that they didn't have: You have the full Bible, you have your local church, you can have the Holy Spirit, you have two thousand years of written and (more lately) recorded teachings. You just need a deeper understanding that a yoke would align you with me, so you could actually lean on me for support.

The people back then got that part, but everything else, well, they just had no idea.

XXXVI – A Woman Anoints Jesus

Night: 26
Entry: 3

Luke 7:36-50

<u>Context Summary</u>

Jesus is having dinner at a Pharisee's house, and a woman with a poor local reputation comes to him, weeps at his feet, pours perfume on them, wipes them with her hair and kisses them.

<u>Key Verse</u>

[48]Then Jesus said to her, "Your sins are forgiven."

You might read about me and wonder many things. For example, many read this story and start wondering how often I got invited to dinner, why would I accept an invitation from a Pharisee and maybe even what that woman was doing there, all while glossing over that I have seen her faith and forgiven her sins. The theologians would read this story and wonder how I could forgive her sins when this was before the crucifixion and resurrection, wouldn't they? I find the whole dinner concept most interesting to discuss, however.

I myself had no money at this time, not the human way of possessing money. I had handled money for Joseph on occasion, but it always seemed to "slip through my fingers" (as Joseph put it, some of it always landing in a hungry neighbor's hands). As a rabbi I charged nothing for my teaching. That was the way of rabbis. They would work at other trades to support themselves, or would have followers support them, but the teaching was free. For me, mostly some devoted followers paid for my food and lodging, as well as that of my disciples. Invitations flowed in plentifully, as well. These occurred more often than not.

The Simon who gave this dinner didn't believe. I mean, not at the time he didn't. That is to say, he believed there was a God, he even believed God would send His Messiah, but he didn't yet believe he was talking to him. This Simon had heard what I said to the woman and he would contemplate the power of forgiveness for the rest of his life. Splendid little man; he didn't push away the idea.

As one of the more important people in town, he prided himself on his dinner parties. I was certainly a story, whether he believed in me at the time or not. It was socially unheard of not to throw a dinner party for a traveling celebrity (a status I tried hard to duck, though it's not a word that connotes well with the times in which I lived back then; however, we'll go with it for now).

The custom of the time, which I did like, allowed anyone to come into the compound, be by the walls or hang out by the windows, in order to listen to the conversation at the main tables. While only the invited guests were supposed to be at the tables and eat, this arrangement made for a perfect opportunity to teach a larger audience about God.

The woman's face had started out stolid and unmoving. She was a nondescript piece of the background to the Pharisees, with the rough, standard cut of her robes soiled from many years, mended multiple times and drawn close to her face as the only shield left to her. They neither knew nor cared she was named Mary (like so many of that time). As she contemplated drawing near to me, emotions played about what showed of her face. Was it fear or steeliness in her eyes I saw in her last hesitation? By abandoning the walls, though, the woman had committed a fairly major breach of etiquette. She moved to me in a quick, staccato pace once her decision had been made; what this woman did scandalized Simon indeed.

Leaning against the low table at the front of the banquet, his knees tucked toward him to help prop him up a bit (being shorter than the other Pharisees reclining with him), Simon's close eyes narrowed even more as he surveyed the scene, full beard and moustache mostly covering a slowly spreading scowl. She poured her tears and her perfume over my feet. "Lucky" for me (*He used air quotes here.*), my feet aren't very ticklish at all. This Pharisee at first looked down on me even more when I didn't recoil in horror at being touched by this woman.

"Simon," I said to him at that moment, "I have something to tell you."

He listened with the false eagerness of a polished host, until my parable about the two people with different debts dumbstruck him, and my rebuke at his true lack of hosting skills cut him to the quick. As he tried to look away, I caught his eyes flicker to the woman's face before lowering, recognizing something of equal, bitter humanity in her.

Her story was a long and sad one, and you've heard it many times. She always carried this jar around her neck, her one prized possession. She willingly gave it up, and who doesn't give up something good for something even better?

Actually, I know the answer to that.

XXXVII – TOURING

Night: 27
Entry: 1

Luke 8:1-3

Key Verse

[1]After this, Jesus traveled about from one town and village to another, proclaiming the good news of the kingdom of God. The Twelve were with him[.]

The traveling I did was a bit like being a rock group on tour, supporting a brand-new album. Maybe not with superstar status, perhaps, at least at the start, but it was more like that than an old-time circus. I am not trying to intimate that the women who helped me in my ministry were "groupies" (you should be ashamed if that's where your mind went); they were more like the band's management, though even in the little towns and villages, there were temptations to be had, girls who thought (or had been taught) that being close sexually to someone they saw as important would equate to filling that hole in their hearts they all had (I would insist they learn it differently). The Twelve . . . that would be the "band", of course, the musicians, leaving me to be the star or front-man or lead singer or what-have-you. Of course, the "band" were all supposed to become lead singers sooner or later.

People's focus was on me when I came into town during those days. Word of mouth ran faster than anything. Some people came out just to "hear the show". For others, the "music" would transform their lives. It was new and brilliant. Then as we went on tour again and again, I often "played the hits", maybe tailored a bit for a local flavor (though not changing any of the essentials of the spiritual message), e.g. the Beatitudes, or certain parables involving seeds and sowers.

Most loved it (unless they thought I was talking about them . . . and usually I was). If they had had lighters back then . . . well!

106

We didn't stay in hotels and trash them, but were usually invited into local homes and were always good guests. It was a big deal for these folks to have a rabbi in town. This wasn't the local band made up of kids from the high school playing at Joe's Bar, but an act with a major album and hit singles deciding to play in small venues and be close to the crowds. It would be a great show and then the tour would move on in the morning, leaving the townsfolk to talk, consider and hopefully have a new favorite.

XXXVIII – FAMILY

Night: 16
Entry: 3

Mark 3:20-34

Context Summary

Jesus enters another house with his disciples, but there is such a big crowd that they can't even eat. While Pharisees accuse him of being in league with demons, Jesus' family comes, fearing for his sanity.

Key Verse

[21]When his family heard about this, they went to take charge of him, for they said, "He is out of his mind."

Ever have days with your family like this? My family heard that I wasn't eating right or taking care of myself. (How about that ever happening to anybody?) Stories abounded making them think I was a religious fanatic. From their point of view, I was. That's not how I describe myself.

Now, I wasn't about to let my family take me back to Nazareth and keep me in the house where I wouldn't be a danger to myself, but neither am I right now giving carte blanche to ignore what your family says without any context. I think I've been pretty clear that I ask people to follow me. It doesn't mean "Honor thy father and thy mother" is abrogated. Sometimes, however, it means that family will listen to rumor and believe things about you that either aren't true or truly aren't important.

This was a busy, crowded house. It was full of people laughing, talking and singing. I loved it! People who had been coughing and moaning, blistered and ulcerous, had suddenly been healed, and everything was humming along nicely . . . until the Pharisees felt jealous of the attention focused on me and tried to deflate it.

"He is possessed!" a barrel-chested member of their order yelled as he advanced on me.

"By the prince of demons he is driving out demons!" another said, snarling and coming up immediately behind him. Still others of them directed similar words throughout the crowds.

I cocked one eyebrow at them and slowly folded my arms. How patently absurd. Looking past them to the crowd around, I took in all those looks: some downcast, some hesitant, some afraid, afraid of the Pharisees and being caught there, but others more afraid they were right.

"A kingdom divided against itself cannot stand," I said calmly, as I utterly rejected their false claims. As I spoke, I could see the effect on the various faces, the anger of some crumpling into rage, while others of fear rising into something more liberating.

My mother and brothers arrived on the scene about then, but they didn't make it into the house (they would have said they couldn't make it through the crowds, but perhaps "wouldn't" would be closer to the mark). I could picture them, though: My mother nervous-looking, like she hadn't slept well in a long time, my brothers sullen behind her, refusing eye contact with my disciples, unsure of what they were supposed to do.

I came with purpose and, after I started ministry, I was not going to play a standard role in a family. That wasn't my objective, though it remains at least part of the plan for most folks.

Has your family ever doubted you? Questioned you? Thought you were insane? Regardless of the circumstances surrounding all of that, I know the feeling. It can be quite lonesome.

However, being in that crowded house, so full of people desperate to follow God and honor Him, invigorated me. I couldn't—and wouldn't—leave it. The people there called themselves children of Abraham. I didn't call myself son of Joseph and Mary, or even just son of Mary. I called myself Son of Man. All these people could become my brothers and sisters. They would be called children of God.

XXXIX – SEEDS

Night: 6
Entry: 2

Matthew 13:24-30

Key Verse

24Jesus told them another parable: "The kingdom of heaven is like a man who sowed good seed in his field."

Returning to the theme of a more agrarian society, many things I said did not need explanation for my audiences. Like my neighbors and relatives where I grew up, they knew all about planting seeds; even we did, despite being builders. There were enough farmers right around us and in our family to make us aware. Some of us would have to help each spring and fall harvest, at least, and sometimes during the planting sessions, as well. Indeed, we had our own rather substantial garden, one section of a terrace on a nearby hill.

Planting the seed ends up being the easiest job in the whole cycle of producing fruit. Preparing the soil? Labor intensive. Harvesting the fruit or grain? Again, labor intensive. Separating out the weeds? Agonizingly slow and laborious. Compared to those, planting was almost a breeze.

My parables struck a common chord. Like this one, the "Parable of the Seeds" as I called it, the sower planting his seeds in a well-prepared field, with an enemy coming behind him and scattering weeds everywhere, so that the harvest was choked with the weeds growing with the good wheat. Now, I say that I called this the Parable of the Seeds, but my disciples strangely called it the "Parable of the Weeds in the Field". Most of the people there did. Maybe they didn't have enemies intentionally sowing weeds in their fields, but they fully understood the gravity of such a crime. It brought home to them what they needed in order to understand

God. It was of course the first reason why I chose to speak such parables to the crowds. I mean, I didn't do it lightly. This was teaching for posterity! Do you think that's easy? I spent many long afternoons alone, praying, watching, anticipating, readying myself for this coming teaching time.

Seeing the planters go around and the harvesters come after was not dulling in its repetition, it was reinforcement of its importance. The work all those people did is all but forgotten. The farmers rarely had time to spend thinking of what heaven was like. They looked to teachers; they had to, and they instinctively trusted them. They were people who needed truth. To them, it was self-evident when I spoke that a parable wasn't a literal statement. It was a vehicle in which to convey truth, as much truth as can be conveyed sometimes.

The crowd that heard this parable that day didn't need any footnotes, but maybe you do. Most Bibles come with them, though you might need to delve even deeper than those, at times.

XL – PLAN A

Night: 6
Entry: 3

Matthew 13:36-43

Key Verse

³⁶Then he left the crowd and went into the house. His disciples came to him and said, "Explain to us the parable of the weeds in the field."

D id I say that you might need footnotes? Oh, how I loved my guys. They talked like I couldn't hear them. I mean, they talked like kids do, thinking parents can't overhear them when they're really being quite loud and obvious. Nothing divine needed to divine their thoughts. Starting with whispers to each other, each one hoped one of the others felt confident of the answer to the question: "What did the teacher mean?" Then the panic would build in them as they tried more and more loudly to get one another to ask the question of me and save themselves the embarrassment of admitting they needed some help:

"You ask him!"

"No, you ask him!"

"No, I asked him last time!"

And so on.

Very human; endearing even, to a degree. However, as I sat in what I was hoping to have been the quietude of the house, I contemplated how I would train up these "boys"—overall they really were quite young—to become the men of God I needed them to be. Crowds drained me back then, you see. I loved them, but it was always important to get some time alone with my Father. Some quiet time then would have been nice.

However, since there was a need, I happily met it. They had to become leaders. Because I had chosen this as my plan, I needed to use them to change the world. They were Plan A and there wasn't a Plan B. I loved their passion for God. That was necessary—yes, it was necessary—but they needed to learn and grow and be grounded, too. When they grew abundantly in one area, another area would be exposed for its shallowness. Twelve boys from Galilee and its environs. The tall and lanky Andrew, to the shorter John with the simple smile, to James and James, the stocky one and the one with the overbite, and all the others. They would never be alone, but a lot was still riding on them. One had to concentrate over the "Not me, you do it!" comments and the "Get Simon to do it!" cries to see the bigger vision and play the long game with them.

We still had a little bit of time. That house was nice, very airy. The breeze flitted in, growing and dying, then growing again, as I briefly closed my eyes and drank it in, letting it cool the sweat on my brow. It was fine that the disciples followed in right after me and needed answers, but would they really listen to me? Plan A depended on it.

XLI – CALMING THE STORM

Night: 4
Entry: 2

Matthew 8:23-27

Context Summary

Having finished another long round of teaching, Jesus and his disciples climb into a boat to go across the Sea of Galilee. While Jesus sleeps, a storm comes up. When the disciples wake Jesus, he tells the storm to abate, leaving the disciples in awe.

Key Verse

[24]Suddenly a furious storm came up on the lake, so that the waves swept over the boat. But Jesus was sleeping.

I was tired, all right? My life was—certainly in many respects—like your own. I needed to eat and sleep and all the other accompanying facts of life. Well, most of them.

Anyway, I was exhausted and fast asleep. Maybe you think I was only pretending to sleep in order to test the faith of my disciples, but that wasn't it. Not that everything isn't a test—I didn't say it wasn't. How would you react if I told you that everything is a test? Would you rightly consider what is meant by a testing?

The Hellenes—the Greek-speaking Gentiles of my day—had more than one word for testing. One of them meant a testing to pass into improvement, like an exam to move up a grade or get a license for something. The other meant a testing to one's ruin and destruction, more a trial or temptation than an exam. So, if this were being written in Koine (that's the Greek of my day), you would know immediately which type of test I meant. I hope you can guess which kind of testing God gives.

Anyway, I was tired. I had moved among a large throng of people, teaching and healing them, letting all of them be fed while I went without. I entered the boat at dusk, and we cast off almost immediately.

"Here, Master," Philip said, beckoning me to the back as he spread out his cloak on a plank. "Lie down here and rest."

I readily agreed. The air was crisp, cooler by ten degrees or more than on shore; refreshing. The boat started out rocking so nicely. It was like an angel's lullaby. . . . Sorry. It's not like that at all. That's a sort of heavenly "in joke" since angels are basically unlike the lullaby-singing paradigm, being pretty loud and brash about God and His truth, though humble before Him at the same time.

No, I was simply put to sleep by the rhythms of the water before the storm. It soothed my mind and activated my vestibular system, lulling me right to sleep. Then I started dreaming. All of a sudden, Simon is shaking me vigorously and Nathanael's shouting in my ear! They ruined a lovely little dream, but I didn't hold it against them.

Of what was I dreaming, you might ask? I dreamt of gardening. Surprised?

XLII – At the Tombs

Night: 17
Entry: 2

Mark 5:1-20

Context Summary

Jesus and his disciples cross the lake and reach a region on the southeastern side where they encounter a demon-possessed man. Jesus sends the demons into a herd of pigs (which run into the lake and drown), but the man is healed, leaving the local populace amazed and frightened.

Key Verse

¹⁷Then the people began to plead with Jesus to leave their region.

I had just gotten there, too.

This place was about as wrong for a Jewish rabbi as a place could be! Let me set the scene: I'm outside of Judea, the Jewish homeland, in a land filled with some Jews but was majority Gentiles, that is, non-Jewish people, the single touch of any one of them would make one ritually unclean (something most every Jew cared desperately about). An angry, naked, crazy man is running toward me, looking like he's going to tackle me (so, that point about a single touch can be underlined in triple, especially since he's coming from some tombs and—guess what—touching those would make me ritually unclean, too). That kind of stuff wasn't my main concern with this man, and it won't be my main concern with you, either. I am not bound to rules that recognize such ritual, but it was going to affect the people in Judea, for whether they listened to me or not.

This place, with its tombs, was a lonely, desolate spot. As we sailed from Capernaum, the land across seemed dark, fuzzy, impenetrable. Most of the lake was surrounded by rolling green hills, with small villages tucked into the edges and mountains in the backdrop. A few spots were barren and brown, and my companions reacted differently to each direction we took. As we approached this particular section, where a mixture of Jews and Gentiles lived in often disturbed peace, the sights may have clarified, but I could sense the nervous energy of my disciples ratchet up. The sun beat down on this location harshly, and the sand crept too far inland from the lakeshore. A large hill with a rugged cliff peered over us. Early on it had been designated as the local site for burials, and the somber mood engendered by such a place palpably penetrated us, even when we were still offshore.

The disciples who had managed the boat had been perplexed at my instructions to set down there. When I pointed out this place, Simon said, "The town is over there," nodding to a spot farther on. I just kept pointing where I had been, so they adjusted the rudder appropriately, if reluctantly.

"We'll have to pull the boat onto the sand," Andrew muttered, though he had done such things his whole life.

"Where are we supposed to get food?" James whispered, forgetting he was a fisherman on a lake.

The others murmured similar things.

They'd get over it. I wasn't worried about them (at least not right then; they caused me plenty of worry overall). As the boat struck the shore, I jumped right out, splashing into a foot or so of water before climbing the rock and sand.

We all heard him immediately. Everything that could be wrong with this man was wrong: He was demon-possessed; he was mentally ill; he was unfit for society; he was unkempt and full of rage. Oh, and the smell. Apart from never bathing, his own feces were spread about the grounds, and likely on his own feet and legs, too. No one took care of him apart from setting out some food at a distance; no one in that area could take care of him. Today he would be locked up in a hospital and probably heavily sedated, a ward of the state, lost in the system.

Then suddenly I heal him, and he and I are having a quiet chat. He cried and found words difficult early on, for it was the first time he could think clearly in many years, and he had so many things to say at once. Eventually, he just said, "Thank you!" and we went on from there.

That's not all that happened, though. See, there's a cost to everything. This one cost a couple thousand pigs.

I was not unaware of the economic damage here. The pigs together belonged to several local farmers who would be unhappy but nowhere near destitute, Jewish owners who employed Gentile herders and sold to other Gentiles (thus keeping themselves clean of the unclean animals, never touching anything but the money). When the crowd came, I wanted to tell them a parable about a shepherd leaving ninety-nine sheep to go after one lost one. Instead, I left behind one witness, a sort of living parable.

XLIII – THE SUFFERING WOMAN

Night: 4
Entry: 3

Matthew 9:18-26

Context Summary

Jesus is asked by a man named Jairus to come heal his daughter, but on the way a woman interrupts Jesus with a need. Also see Luke 8:40-56 for additional context.

Key Verse

[20]Just then a woman who had been subject to bleeding for twelve years came up behind him and touched the edge of his cloak.

Night: 17
Entry: 3

Mark 5:21-34ff

Key Verse

[26]She had suffered a great deal under the care of many doctors and had spent all she had, yet instead of getting better she grew worse.

H ave you ever had one of those days with nothing but interruptions? Matthew doesn't tell the half of it (he didn't need to). This is far from a complaint. Many days my waking plan was specifically to be interrupted. That's different than most folks' normal plans (well, excepting most mothers').

It helps having a plan to be interrupted. I know it helps. Now, I didn't "channel" heavenly patience; that's not what I mean. What I mean is, having been above and beyond time once, and then getting anchored in it, I could look at the lives of the interrupters— like this poor woman, named Sarah—and allow my day to slow down, opening up to the people and their needs.

A man named Jairus, who was the custodian of the local synagogue, fell at my feet. He was completely distraught and barely understandable. The lines of worry on his face had been etched deeply over the preceding hours and days. When our eyes met, I felt the anguish so visible in his face. His friends tried to pull him up, pull him away. They all kept talking at once. His only daughter was dying. No, another said, she was already dead. Jairus himself just kept pleading with me to come with him.

"Come!" he shouted through tears and phlegm and violent shaking, his arms open, as if wishing to surround me. "Lay your hands!"

He knelt face down, and the friends started to use force to tug Jairus off my feet. The crowd began pressing in, some embarrassed at Jairus, some wanting to join him in mourning, mostly out of compassion. Into this turmoil came another person with great need, just as I started toward Jairus' house.

Some might say that the man whose daughter had died or was dying should not have been interrupted, but what was his wait, his pain, compared to hers? What if this woman Sarah had tried to see me when I first taught and healed? Or if she had come from Nazareth and not Capernaum? I would have seen her first suffering, twelve years earlier in Nazareth, witnessed her be outcast from her husband and family, her sole dream of children dying slowly with her body, and watched her pour out her few resources on doctors unable to help her. Increasingly desperate and destitute, she risked breaking taboo.

Risked? Risked what exactly?

The taboo against a woman in her condition touching a male, especially a rabbi, was severe in those days. She was ritually unclean, which made her unwelcome in synagogue and most everywhere else. For touching me, the rules could have been bent ever so slightly into a penalty of stoning. She touched a lot of people getting to me, all of whom would hate her if they knew. The "cures" the doctors had come up with for her were nothing short of superstitious (terrible things involving corn kernels plucked from donkey dung; I kid you not). I wasn't there to turn the medical profession on its head, to announce words like "obstetric fistula" and "meno-metrorrhagia". I didn't need to heal Sarah. Had she not been healed and not been captured for posterity by the Gospel writers, you would never have imagined she once existed on earth. So I ask again, what was she actually risking?

She had nothing left to lose except her life, and that was still dear to her. Into her hopelessness, God had planted an audacity to believe. She could have buried that in the broken promises of the doctors of her time and stayed at home that day. Instead, she came and touched my cloak, a kind called a "tallit", with tassels on the corners called "tzitzit", which were affectionately referred to as "wings". She believed that healing came from the Messiah and that this touching fulfilled a prophecy from Malachi. She believed that in the act of touching something would happen.

It was not the touching at all that provided the healing, but the faith. The faith grabbed hold of the power of God and wrested its need to be met. Still, for her, she needed to do an action, touch the cloak, as if because the cloak had touched me it was holy. Just think if you actually had the cup I used at my Last Supper around. Was it weak faith to think touching my cloak would heal her? Or was it strong faith?

If that seems like a spurious set of questions to you, I'd beg to differ, and tell you the contemplation of such could lead you to much spiritual insight. It's well worth the effort.

Let me tell you another thing about this encounter. Desperate people do desperate things. Yet even in desperation, there can be a recognition of salvation, like what the woman Sarah had. Maybe you recognize her desperation. Maybe you've lived it or are living it now. Maybe you try everything to hand and it just seems to get worse. In that time, who reaches out to God? Sarah did—literally. Desperate people do desperate things, and reaching out to God when all else seems hopeless is a desperate act. Glorious, but desperate.

The rules still apply to desperate people . . . but not the institutions she faced that said she was "unclean" and therefore worthless. No one reaching out to me in such circumstances could be turned away, because she had faith. I wasn't looking to heal her. Being human my eyes could not be everywhere. That actually worked well to activate a desperate woman's faith.

Faith is a gift, and it has been given liberally. It requires nurturing to blossom or it can grow cold and even die. I'm fond of the word "covenant", a word you've mostly lost. All my covenants start with the activity of God, a gift given, awaiting then the proper and mandated response from the gifted. And so Sarah was gifted. What will she do with it? Sarah did not consciously know she was acting in faith, responding in a covenantal relationship, but her faith activated when she dared to hope that God would help her.

This story is told and remembered to bring you hope. Many similar things happened during my days on earth, but like it did for the Gospel writers, this one was one of those that stood out for me. Death and sickness. They matter, even as short and small as they actually are. I always love seeing desperate faith in action.

XLIV – JAIRUS' DAUGHTER

Night: 27
Entry: 2

Luke 8:40-42; 49-56

Context Summary

After being interrupted, Jesus continues on to the man Jairus' house. Servants come to confirm his daughter's death, but Jesus tells him not to be afraid, to believe and she will be healed. Then they arrive at Jairus' house.

Key Verses

[52]Meanwhile, all the people were wailing and mourning for her. "Stop wailing," Jesus said. "She is not dead but asleep."
[53]They laughed at him, knowing that she was dead.

A house in which there has been a death is so full of emotions, a strange mixture of the earthly and the divine. When I came into this house, the professionals had already taken over and were wailing away. That may surprise some of you, but it was the standard custom to hire a group of mourners, to have them on hand during an illness in order to begin wailing as soon as the death was announced. They would do loud, over-the-top cries, making a big spectacle for the entire household and neighborhood. It was only their occupation, and so if they heard something they considered ridiculous, it would be no big deal to turn off the water-works and have a good laugh. A professional lapse, maybe, but easy.

Not that there weren't a few in the household genuinely moved by the girl's death. The mother was too numb to do anything but follow me up the stairs when I had come in and said what the mourners called my "macabre joke". The little girl's cousin—Jairus' niece—had taken charge below, but I could tell she had been crying, and was trying to stop (and she was nearly successful at it).

When you read this story, you may have a voice-over in your head on how I said, "She is not dead but asleep" in a calm monotone, but it wasn't like that at all. I was not immune to thoughts of mortality and death, of loss and suffering. I just view death differently, then as well as now.

It is a different state than when you say you're "alive", but to me it is not a polar opposite. The body ceases functioning and will decay, but the spirit remains alive. It leaves the body and goes away, awaiting to be called. It is not a ghost, though people have always thought that, it is not anything other than your soul, created by God at conception, breathed with His breath, never to die or be out of existence afterward, never not to be you. It's not karmic, not neo-platonic, not any of the thousands of false notions of which humans let themselves suffer.

So, I said she wasn't dead, only sleeping. Was that literally true or even metaphorically true? I told them to stop wailing. I wanted to get their attention. Oh, I got it all right.

My voice was sharp, like a whip crack, stopping the nonsensical babbling immediately. They stared at me and yes, they were embarrassed, and yes, they laughed at me. Not the parents, however, nor the niece.

In the marketplace, when he received confirmation of his daughter's death just after Sarah had been healed, the man Jairus broke down completely, until I told him not to be afraid. He rose slowly and nodded, steeling himself while grief continued painting his eyes and the corners of his mouth. He stayed silent and kept his eyes on me as the servant led us back to the house. Just outside it was the girl's mother, shocked and numb, as I said. She looked from her husband to me, but only had the strength to go to her husband's side and stay there without words.

In the house, they continued to follow me, despite what all the mourners and family attendants said and did, despite all the evidence of their eyes. Do not be afraid, only believe.

Oh, faith like that can move mountains! Sometimes immediately, sometimes one tiny atom at a time, but moved nevertheless. We entered the little girl's room. Sallow-cheeked and ashen, with dry, cracked lips that spoke of her silent suffering over the previous days, she lay still, her hands clasped on her chest (arranged, perhaps). When I spoke to her, it was a gentle whisper: "My child, get up!"

I will be saying it again.

XLV – More Touring

Night: 18
Entry: 2

Mark 6:6b

Key Verse

⁶ᵇThen Jesus went around teaching from village to village.

Every time I stayed in one place for a while, often coming back to my home base in Capernaum after a round of preaching, I soon started to get the itch to go out on "tour" again. There were many to meet with and preach to in Capernaum, of course, but I had seeds to scatter throughout the region. I couldn't give a sermon on cable, or connect live to multiple churches and an internet audience all at once. I had to wait a long time to come to preach, but I couldn't wait around for you to develop all that stuff! Therefore, I had to get out there and go around from village to village.

Walking to each place, to tiny hamlets that didn't even have a name or a synagogue, to villages and small towns like Bethany and Bethsaida and cities like Jerusalem and Jericho, I spread my message. Over and over I called to the people, telling them my parables and riddles, healing and amazing before moving on, to be followed out of town by small boys and dogs for a while only, then—rarely—someone would want to stay with me.

A routine day involved waking up early, as a visitor in someone's house or under the wilderness sky when we were between towns. After ablutions and morning prayers, a quick breakfast, followed by an encouraging word to my disciples to get moving. I usually roused Simon and James first, and they would get their brothers going, then the rest of those who were with me. Sometimes all of the Twelve were with me (plus others) and sometimes a group of them would be off traveling or tending to home. Once in a great while I was alone, but most often there was a significant group.

They would wait for me to choose the direction and to set the stride. I always began with a song and set a steady pace. Andrew liked to whistle, and sometimes he would walk up front with me and we'd whistle a little tune together.

After a time—and we had settled into a good pace—someone would have a question, a single question. I would take that and use it to teach the nearest the rest of the way to the next village. They might ask about the Sabbath, or about the temple, or any number of topics. Not all could hear all of it, so they would switch positions and share what they heard back and forth.

During the early days of ministry, I could arrive in a town with little to no fanfare. From the way I spoke to people as we entered, to the size and make-up of the company I kept, I was quickly identified as something special. Recognition would blossom in the eyes of a few locals. Quickly they'd whisper to some children or teenagers, who immediately started running and shouting, "A rabbi! A rabbi has come to the village!"

Word spread throughout the whole countryside this way, and in these smaller towns, this was a big deal. If it were near the end of the week, the villagers had every expectation that I would stay for the Sabbath and speak in their synagogue, but if it were early in the week they were sure they would miss out.

The first healings came without crowds. Usually we would be invited to stay in someone's house, an invitation we readily accepted, blessing the household as we entered. If someone in the household was sick, I would go into a small room where they were lying, speak a few words with them and they would come out, feeling much better. I didn't have to advertise, for the healed people were so overjoyed they spread the news far and wide.

Sometimes they weren't supposed to speak. I would ask them to keep it secret. The next day I would be preaching publicly, either in the synagogue or just outside the town on a hillside or in a field. What is the impact of the word, of the message, when people are interested merely in a show?

Soon a routine day did involve healing people. The mortality rates around Judea and Samaria and Galilee plummeted in my wake. They did not stop, and after this phase of my public ministry had come to a close, they returned to approximately normal. All this was done, however, not just to show compassion to people, but to let them know the news, the message, of the approach of the kingdom of God. Many people—most even—stayed to hear the sermons, at least while the good times lasted.

The Twelve heard my sermons so often they had them memorized, though I would alter certain aspects of the teaching to fit the local flavor (without changing the core truth, of course), and I could send them out to do some teaching on their own. Those were the good times. They were never without struggle, but that doesn't mean they weren't good, weren't joyful. It was mostly joy! More joy would follow, after suffering. This, too, the disciples had to learn to appreciate, just like our traveling in those days.

Sometimes they were annoyed at our peripatetic journey, for to them it seemed to have no end. "Why go to another hamlet to speak to these who don't follow you?" they would say, or, "There's not enough people here to make a difference, Lord. Let's keep going to a larger town." Even, "We've been here before, not long ago, why not go somewhere else?"

Good questions, but I still say for every ninety-nine I leave behind, I find one I can take along who wants to go. It's a terrible campaign strategy, isn't it? I'll hold to my dying day (that's a funny expression for me), that it's the most worthwhile thing I do.

XLVI – Unseen Blessings

Night: 28
Entry: 1

Luke 10:17-24

Context Summary

Jesus sends out seventy-two of his followers in groups of two to villages ahead of him. They return ecstatic at the reception they had and the miracles God worked through them.

Key Verses

[23]Then he turned to his disciples and said privately, "Blessed are the eyes that see what you see. [24]For I tell you that many prophets and kings wanted to see what you see but did not see it, and to hear what you hear but did not hear it."

I was almost manic that day. It was a day of highs and lows (as you might imagine from my "almost manic" comment). I enjoyed some rare time without any of my closest disciples around. After I sent them out on this short-term missionary trip, I spent my time variously, teaching my female disciples who remained and talking with passing locals, while also getting in some much-desired prayer and fasting.

When my other disciples came back, their cloaks flying behind them, dragging in the dirt as they laughed and shouted, pointing their hands to the sky and praising God raucously, they reported what they termed "success". Describing it to me, they talked over one another, shouted out details, loudly agreed with their compatriots, all while grabbing food prepared by some of the women, dribbling bits of bread and olive paste all over.

"Nothing," one said, glowing, "no, not a thing can stop us!"

"Demons couldn't stop us!" another added with a raised fist.

"Surely the Romans can't do it, either!" a third concluded, and that brought a rousing cheer from the rest.

I smiled at them, but it was a bit forced. Their mission was fine, and their report, but my definition of success is a bit different from what theirs was back then. I worried immediately about the pride they exhibited. Power is so easily misused. While they listened to me, they didn't yet understand. Their own not-so-latent desire for a military coup and subsequent dictatorship over the land was ever-present during those days. It would take a miracle to get them to truly drop it and embrace a different sort of revolution.

Yet in them I continued to see faith that could lead to true success, success as I defined it; the future in which most of them would humble themselves and embrace a new model, God's model, and then be murdered because of it.

I thought about the nearly infinite number of circumstances God had helped will to bring them here. All their spiritual forebears wanted to *be* them, but my disciples just didn't know it. Even Luke, having heard about and recorded this vignette, born one lousy generation too late (though just right for God to use him) was almost inordinately jealous of them all.

XLVII – MARTHA

Night: 28
Entry: 2

Luke 10:38-42

Key Verses

[38]As Jesus and his disciples were on their way, he came to a village where a woman named Martha opened her home to him. [39]She had a sister called Mary, who sat at the Lord's feet listening to what he said. [40]But Martha was distracted by all the preparations that had to be made. She came to him and asked, "Lord, don't you care that my sister has left me to do the work by myself? Tell her to help me!"

We came to Bethany, a whole group of us. Some were with me specifically, others had joined the group as a traveling party on the way, still others were simply arriving in Bethany at the same time. We were all headed to Jerusalem for the Passover Festival. As there was never enough room at the inn (story of my life), many of us would be welcomed into the homes of people in the surrounding villages. It was as if everyone in America in the days leading up to Thanksgiving all drove to the exact same town. If everyone's grandma lived in Des Moines, some of the travelers would just have to stay in Ankeny.

I enjoyed getting to know Martha. In another situation, she would have been lighthearted and free, but as the eldest daughter whose parents had died when she was only fifteen, she had become more pragmatic. It showed in the furrowed line of her forehead, etched deep due to frowning and squinting in the lower light of evening as she worked on her mending. She was of average height but seemed taller due to how erect she held her head, proud of her forebears and home, but not so much that she didn't know the truth about her deteriorating situation, with the edges of the house crumbling and no funds to pay for their repair. Her dark skin and high cheek bones framed her eyes magnificently, but helped hide her thoughts from her remaining family. Though she didn't joke around much, she appreciated a chance to laugh in private. Her voice rang clear when she laughed unencumbered.

I also enjoyed getting to know Martha's sister Miriam (I should say Mary). I would become good friends with their brother Lazarus, too, and end up staying often at their house. It was technically Lazarus who made the official offer of hospitality, though we could all see it was Martha who made the decision and prodded him along. She would be the hostess. The irony of the situation that day was that Martha was so serious about being a good hostess she got distracted, while I had quite a bit on my mind at the time, too. It was tempting to want to be away from the crowds, to pray and be with just a few disciples. Soon I would need that time even more.

However, it wasn't every day I had the chance to teach in the home of a friendly family. We stayed in many, many homes, but only sometimes was it such an honest invitation as Martha's. Their parents had been wealthy, and they had a large home to accommodate us, but they weren't nearly as prosperous in those later days. Housing us would be a burden, more so to Martha who ran the household than the others, yet she made the invitation gladly. This was not a banquet at a Pharisee's house, or someone wanting to say: "Jesus slept here." When I taught in her house, more women dared to sit and be taught as Mary did than at those other places.

And so I reclined at the table—empty as it was, starting out— and spoke to Mary and Lazarus and their friends. "How blessed are the poor in spirit," I said, holding each set of eyes like a parent holding a child's hand. I didn't even look around for the missing sister, though.

Somewhere in the day-to-day, Martha lost sight of the joy she had had in making the invitation. It's understandable, and also understandable that she'd want her sister to help her.

"How blessed are they who mourn," I continued, and tears and a smile both illuminated Mary's face, while dishes clattered in another room.

Perhaps even more so is it understandable that Martha would look to my moral authority as both rabbi and visitor to goad Mary into helping with preparations. I wouldn't ask Mary to leave and go serve, as good of a task as that might be.

"How blessed are the meek."

Nor would I absolutely tell Martha she should sit. I've said that to people so often, I know they really have to want it, like my friend Mary did. There were other preparations to be made, not just those for a meal, and both Mary and Martha would need to let in the message of the kingdom of God, so they could see me as more than rabbi. They would sorely need that when I returned there later. A meal can wait a bit for the soul to be fed.

"How blessed are the ones who hunger and thirst for righteousness."

Martha heard. She wept bitterly in the other room. Surveying the half-prepared dishes and so many other menial chores piling up, she felt weak in her bones. How would the food ever get served if she should choose the same as her younger sister? Trust me when I say, knowing my disciple Andrew's appetite, he would eventually forget that the society said it was not the visitor and not the man who should get the food on the table.

"And how blessed are the pure in heart."

As I continued teaching, the sounds of plates and cups from the other room quieted. Sneaking a glance that way, I saw Martha peeking around the corner, but low, on her knees, listening as tears streamed down her face. She was the older sister, used to taking care of things, but burdened. She knelt, while Andrew got fidgety and kept looking around.

I was hungry, too, but I love making new disciples more than a good meal.

XLVIII – A Tower in Siloam

Night: 29
Entry: 1

Luke 13:1-5

Context Summary

Jesus speaks to a group in Jerusalem, emphasizing that they are all in peril without repentance.

Key Verse

⁴"Or those eighteen who died when the tower in Siloam fell on them—do you think they were more guilty than all the others living in Jerusalem?"

I'll tell you about that tower. It was old, only four stories, but the construction had been shoddy. No one really wanted the expense of the upkeep. Some people worried, as they do, but when one isn't a direct owner, it's easy to push off the worry to another day or to another person. I don't say that as emotional blackmail of any sort, simply as true to the fallen nature of people.

Some of those eighteen who died worked in and around the tower; they had a good chance of being there when it came down. A couple were there occasionally, and the rest were simply passing by. What do you make of that? Other towers have fallen, or been taken down. You might care about those, but what about the tower in Siloam? What if it had come down as I had walked beneath it? Interesting speculation, perhaps, but I'm worried you're not taking the right lesson from these events.

I hear from many who feel that God should intervene and make sure towers never fall, or at least never fall on people or with people inside them. Well, if you build no towers, I will comply.

Seriously, though, first you have to think about all the towers people build, both real and metaphorical. Should they never fall?

Stop screaming at me that people who die in falling towers are innocent and should be spared. You say that that's what you'd do were you God. There's not much I can do with that statement. It's ephemeral when you have to start understanding the eternal.

That day, when I was doing this teaching, the lives of the eighteen were already in God's hands, while all who listened still hung in the balance, like the many odors of the city, ripe with sweat, baking bread and a nearby fish market. The day was bright and sunny. Some thought the days would all be like that.

XLIX – Healing a Woman at the Synagogue

Night: 29
Entry: 2

Luke 13:10-17

Context Summary

Jesus is teaching in a synagogue when he sees an infirm woman and heals her, to the consternation of the synagogue leader.

Key Verse

[13]Then he put his hands on her, and immediately she straightened up and praised God.

My love can sometimes burn in my heart. Teaching in the synagogues was easy and fun. Yes, I said fun. For a short time, I could open up Torah, read and give proper interpretation. To anyone who wanted to know more of God's word, there was nothing but delight.

Yet, all around was a minefield. I had to tread carefully in order to ensure I made it all the way to Jerusalem and wasn't assassinated by insensate Pharisees too soon. How and when I died was as important as that I died. Still, some things burned in me.

I ached that no one cared what happened to her, this woman, beyond her dwindling extended family members. I saw her, bent and humbled, her threadbare head covering the only thing people saw when they looked down on her. Not just advanced osteoporosis, but she had a spiritual illness bonded to her, as well (as most afflictions have). Her tears had been poured out to God for years, but lately silence had reigned in her life.

Slow and hobbling along, she had come to the synagogue to hear me, but also with a small dose of hope that she hid away as well as she could, stuffed down in her heart in order to avoid disappointment. Word of healings had reached even her ears, however, and it was this that spurred her to struggle to get to synagogue on time. She was not dead to hope, not yet.

She said not a word to me as I stood up and bounded from the dais. Bending my knees and beckoning to her, the crowd gasped as she made her lonely solo walk three more steps to me. It was so hard for her to look up, she only stared at my feet.

"Woman, you are set free from your infirmity!" Not seeing my hands shoot out, one on her head, on that old cloth, the other on a stooped shoulder, she jerked up in surprise, fear and delight, body movements unknown to her for decades.

"Praise to God my savior!" she shouted, back straight and head up, her sight fixed on heaven. A moment later she looked around at wide eyes surrounding her, wondering why no one joined her.

I could have healed her the next day and kept the Pharisees' Sabbath, but I was keeping mine instead. The woman didn't have to wait one more night in pain for them. I have compassion on whom I will have compassion, and also when. I had come that she might be set free!

In addition to the timing, I could have healed her without touching her, without breaking another one of their no-nos. I didn't have a compulsion to break all of the mores of that day and age; the point wasn't to break them for the sake of breaking them. That isn't what makes a rebel like me. Instead, it was that I knew things about this woman. I knew her name, Reheboah, and I knew she desired a single touch to show her her value to God.

There's a time and a place for rules. Some things are inviolate, but the Spirit led me here.

L – HIGHLIGHTS

Night: 4
Entry: 4

Matthew 9:35-38

<u>Key Verses</u>

35Jesus went through all the towns and villages, teaching in their synagogues, proclaiming the good news of the kingdom and healing every disease and sickness. 36When he saw the crowds, he had compassion on them, because they were harassed and helpless, like sheep without a shepherd.

These were some good days. I used to dream about preaching and healing when I was a boy as I helped Joseph with his work, sometimes cutting stone, sometimes hauling it. As I've mentioned, he often had jobs in nearby Sepphoris. I and sometimes my brothers would accompany him and help out.

My mother always said it took me away from my studies, that it was the reason I only went to bet sefer and was not asked to continue on to beth midrash. She was incorrect.

It was the wrong time and place. Progressing in school with top marks could have led me to a very different path in life. I knew the Scriptures, and I could hold my own with the great minds of the day, as I showed once (*see chapter VI*). I knew, however, that the crowds were out there. The dust on the road from Nazareth to Sepphoris gathered on my feet day by day. As I walked there, carrying whatever load was needed, I thought about the people I would see when other roads were walked, those from village to village, synagogue to synagogue. The people. The people!

Harassed and harried, desperate for God, desperate to be valued, willing to believe but needing some truth and grace first. They might live in community already, technically, but they still felt alone inwardly. So grateful for a touch of grace they'd willingly wash my dusty feet with their tears (although that's primarily a metaphor; I only allowed that to physically happen a couple of times).

Yes, very good days indeed. There are seasons of work and warfare. This was spring, when armies go to war. In a fallen way, armies throughout history have only mimicked what God does, what I did in the springtime of my ministry.

There were trials and tests throughout these years, of course. The good days like these wouldn't last. So many were thrilling to the message, the miracles were (in many senses) simply an extension of the message. All that energy laid out in those days. Amazing stuff, great stuff! How many people had hearts changed for good in those days, though?

Very sadly, it was surprisingly few. In Jerusalem, right before Easter, it would be down to bare bones.

LI – PEACE ON EARTH?

Night: 5
Entry: 2

Matthew 10:34-36

Context Summary

Jesus is teaching his disciples before sending them out for a short time to go preach on their own. See all of Matthew chapter 10 for complete context.

Key Verse

³⁴"Do not suppose that I have come to bring peace to the earth. I did not come to bring peace, but a sword."

I know, I know. Where's the "Peace on earth and mercy mild"? Can I say I was misquoted? *(He winked here.)*

See, you may want what you think you want, but you're usually wrong. I know. If there's anyone who could possibly know humanity, it's me. Peace is great. I bless the peacemakers. I call you to be peacemakers. The problem is, how many of you have already charged away to go and be peacemakers before sitting down and being taught what peace looks like?

I could see it all around and feel it in all the towns and villages, a seething anger, wanting to burst out and start fighting. There had been many wars in Judea and many more would follow, including a big one just a few decades after I left. That fighting, those wars, is neither my sword, nor the absence of it my peace.

What is the key to what I said back then? What's the most important word, the most important phrase? Is it possibly the first three words?

As I sat and taught the Twelve, they looked shocked by my words. They had heard me say similar things before, but this time, with just them, they felt the weight of responsibility.

"Proclaim this message," I told them, and Simon Peter looked at me, slack-jawed.

"Heal the sick," I commanded, and James and John glanced at one another.

"Raise the dead," I said, and Nathanael's eyebrows shot up.

"Freely you have received; freely give," I taught, and Philip looked like he wanted to ask something, but bit his tongue.

Then, as I buried them in instruction, I also said, "Do not suppose."

All the people, even my disciples, needed this new teaching, without their own suppositions. They had school, they had Torah lessons, all of them, all of my people Israel. They even had other rabbis who preached amazing sermons. What they didn't have was a clear picture of heaven, or even of earth.

Yes, peace on earth, and yes a sword and not peace. What kind of peace will you have? Go ahead and work for your own kind of peace. It's nice, I'm sure. It's fine. It just might not be worth anything in the end.

"Do not suppose," is a lesson to the humble and a warning to the proud.

LII – JOHN THE BAPTIST'S DEATH

Night: 7
Entry: 1

Matthew 14:1-14

Context Summary

John the Baptist condemns Herod Antipas for marrying his half-brother's wife Herodias, so Herod imprisons John. During a drunken feast, Herod promises anything to Herodias' daughter after she luridly dances for his guests and him. Herodias has her daughter ask for John the Baptist's head, and it is duly delivered.

Key Verse

[13]When Jesus heard what had happened, he withdrew by boat privately to a solitary place. Hearing of this, the crowds followed him on foot from the towns.

I find water soothing. It's a substance that can mimic moods and is never absolutely the same way twice. It absorbs tears, disperses strong emotion, calms with its touch.

I was saddened to hear about poor John the Baptist's cruel death. My human view of death was of course informed by my divine view of eternity. John the Baptist shared the view of Paul who would later write: "To live is Christ and to die is gain." (*See Philippians 1:21.*) When people share that outlook, the world looks remarkably different from their former views.

Still, in a way, my human experience gave me a deep perspective. Sadness and grief were never strangers to me, but I now also hated losing people like people had always hated losing their friends and family.

Was I depressed? A psychiatrist might have a lot to say on that subject (and I might have a lot to say back). Regardless, I took to the water. There's a lonely sound to water, when it's not quite still but not rushing either. "The Spirit of God was hovering over the waters." (*See Genesis 1:2.*) I was thinking of that verse, over and over, as I sat in the prow of the boat and leaned my face over to peer into the lake, before the boat was really moving.

Matthew said I went "privately", and I did, in terms of not being public, but I was not alone. My disciples took me out (it wasn't my boat, per se, and needed several handlers). I sat alone, up front, thinking truly privately, grieving, gulping in large lungfuls of fresh air. The sounds were sharp and resilient out on the lake: the wind billowing out the sails, the water cresting off the boat, sudden creaks of any number of pieces of wood on the craft, the low tones of conversation half-taken by the wind.

When we came ashore, with the crowds already gathered, I was tempted to want to dismiss them. Someone had spied me leaving and had run through the nearby villages, bringing everyone before I was ready to face them. Didn't they know someone important to me had just been killed? Didn't they know it was a step closer to my own death, a testing of which I was still unsure?

Yet I saw them as little children, with needs to be met. Some of the people were from the local villages, and would have seen me probably the next day. Others had just reached the lakeside towns, arriving coincidentally (so many thought), having come from miles away in their desperation. With the crowds around, the water was no longer quiescent. I smiled sadly at it and climbed out of the boat, my feet splashing into six inches of water. Turning to the gathering, I set aside my grief.

Do I regret taking care of their needs before mine? Does any good parent?

LIII – SHEEP WITHOUT A SHEPHERD

Night: 18
Entry: 3

Mark 6:30-44

Context Summary

Jesus mourns John the Baptist by going across the lake. This will culminate in the "Feeding of the Five Thousand", but Jesus sees an even more immediate need.

Key Verse

[34]When Jesus landed and saw a large crowd, he had compassion on them, because they were like sheep without a shepherd. So he began teaching them many things.

More needs to be said about this crowd. I said to Simon and Andrew about them, "They look like sheep without a shepherd."

"Yes, Lord, you're right."

"You guys ever seen sheep without a shepherd?"

They both shook their heads. I knew they hadn't; they were fishermen.

"They say sheep are dumb, and while as pack animals that's not exactly true, domesticated sheep without a shepherd can sure act like it. One thing they know above all else: They are supper for any carnivore who happens along. That's not a very comforting thought for them, is it?"

Wide-eyed, they slowly shook their heads.

There were lots of times when, going through towns, people did not respond the way I wanted. They hesitated at real change. Still, curiosity and excitement compelled them. Once a small crowd formed it could quickly swell to become an immense gathering. Then they would pursue me. Like this day, I could even get in a boat and set out to another spot on the lake, even wanting to be alone, and the people would walk and even run along the shore, gauging my destination and getting there when I did or sometimes even a little before! I'm not saying I minded it (much), but it's ironic how often they found me like then, when I started out craving some alone time, or time with just my disciples. That feeling always fell by the wayside—as it did for me then—as the people converged on me.

"Where did they all come from, Lord?" my disciples asked me.

My disciples might have always wondered, but I knew some of these people had come from miles away. That's a clear signal. Nothing moves me more—or more quickly—than people betting on me.

What I mean is these people couldn't leave their homes on a whim, travel ten or twenty miles and return home later, either easily or without cost. How many family members stayed at home, shaking their heads and calling their departing friends and family "crazy"? There were many costs to be paid. Soon they would be hungry and quickly their stomachs might make them forget their reasons for coming to me in the first place. My compassion for them would extend to that, too, but I remember looking at them. No offense to you as fellow human beings, but the people in this crowd not only acted like sheep, but they had many blank looks like sheep can have, too. They had big needs, and I set out to fill them. I'm a teacher, so I taught them.

LIV – WALKING ON WATER

Night: 7
Entry: 2

Matthew 14:22-32

Context Summary

At the end of a long day of teaching and miraculously feeding the people, Jesus sends away his disciples on the boat in which they had come, heading out after them later on his own.

Key Verse

^{25}Shortly before dawn Jesus went out to them, walking on the lake.

So I mentioned about liking the water, right? Perspective on this, because most people tend to forget this: When I sent my disciples away, I was still—what's your phrase? (*"Bummed out?" I offered. He nodded and pointed at me.*)—" bummed out" over John the Baptist's death.

I had met the needs of the people, feeding almost twenty thousand (don't let that "Feeding of the Five Thousand" title fool you; it was about five thousand men, a few thousand children and a whole lot of women, too many to easily estimate) and healing all those who had needed it. I was tired. My head throbbed and my shoulders ached, while my stomach caved in on itself as my legs kept me upright only unsteadily. It was maybe not physical exhaustion, but it was getting there. It wasn't from performing the miracles themselves, but I needed food and rest. It had been a long day.

Alone I climbed the hillside and prayed, before sitting down and eating a little something left over. I got my "second wind", so to speak. I stood up and walked to the shoreline. Thin waves lapped the shore, coming out of darkness to brush against the beach, as a stiff wind met my chin, whipping my outer cloak like a flag on a flagpole. Curling it up closer to me, thoughts of John the Baptist swelled in my head. My heart ached, then I gave a little cry as sympathetic pains shot through my hands and feet.

I missed my disciples. "This is the hour for fishing," I said softly, blinking back tears and smiling in spite of my thoughts. Then I had a little tongue-in-cheek conversation with myself: "Well, you're tired and far from home, Jesus. Good thing you sent the boat away."

I pulled first one leg up and then the other, taking off my sandals, looping them onto one finger. Striding forward simply, my feet struck the water. As I walked, the coolness soothed my soles. The wind and water swells died down slightly, letting me think while leaving me plenty of traction. I breathed deeply and rhythmically, thinking about all my friends.

Reciting a praise psalm as I walked, mourning faded as morning approached. There was a hint of light out on the water, the earliest stages of the brightening of the sky, before darkness died in the dawn. Ahead I spied my disciples' boat.

I know people have said a lot of things about this episode through the years, trying out some ridiculous theories to explain it without the use of the supernatural, including that I found sand bars out to the middle of the lake (at night?!?), or simply disbelieving. Somewhere in those thoughts lies the position of my disciples' mindsets. What hadn't they seen already in order to prepare them for a meeting like this? They didn't even realize they should've been home hours earlier, but the wind and the waves kept pushing them back or circling them around. ("Coincidence?" *He asked this as an aside as he winked at me.*)

Simon came out briefly, stepping out of the boat and walking a few steps on the water as the wind picked up again, lashing us. Taking his eyes off me, he started to sink.

"Lord, save me!" he cried out in fear.

That's a real thing that Simon Peter went through. It's also a metaphor for your struggles.

Look, I don't care if you have an issue with this story, with me walking on water. If you don't want to believe I walked on water, or if you want to misrepresent why, go ahead. There are much bigger miracles happening and available. Will you believe those?

LV – The Argument

Night: 35
Entry: 4

John 10:22-39

Context Summary

Jesus travels to Jerusalem for the Festival now known as Hanukkah. As he walks through the temple courts, his opponents want clear declarations from him so they can get rid of him.

Key Verses

[24]The Jews who were there gathered around him, saying, "How long will you keep us in suspense? If you are the Messiah, tell us plainly."
[25a]Jesus answered, "I did tell you, but you did not believe."

There is an argument that goes around in heaven. I should maybe say "debate". It starts: "The problem with people is that they're human." It is argued eloquently and forcefully (but does not quite convince) that humans don't want what they say they want, instead they distort the definition of what they want all the time to be something they don't have at hand.

They want the Messiah, I am the Messiah, they don't want me to be the Messiah.

I say people still want the Messiah—they want a savior—they just don't want to surrender to him. That means change. They don't want that part because it is hard, it can hurt, it can require time and effort when so many other false gods bring such immediate palliation to their minds and hearts . . . no matter how temporary. Even my followers tend to forget that the transformation God wants them to make cannot be made on their own effort, they need me to do it for them. That's why I say having a savior means having to surrender. That's true change.

The hardness of the change, the fluctuation of their feelings, the commitment to something other than that in which they are currently entrenched, all scares off most people. The group around me at this point was not so unique—this same type of group two millennia later would spin dreidels and be too busy Hanukkah shopping to mind me.

"Tell us plainly!" they said over and over again. It wasn't a plea; it was dismissive. These never even chose to be disciples, unlike others.

They knew that the miracles I had performed testified to my being the Messiah; they totally knew. It was as if I had filed paperwork to run for President, established a PAC and run a bunch of advertisements where I said, "I am Jesus, and I approve this Good News." Then, a group of reporters came up and said, "Jesus, are you running for President?"

The debate in heaven I mentioned earlier gains more ground when it adds this: "Sometimes people just want to pick a fight." True enough, in my experience, at least that day. It doesn't mean God accepts the argument, even then.

LVI – Many Disciples Stop Following

Night: 34
Entry: 3

John 6:41-66

Context Summary

Jesus tells a large group of followers (disciples, but not to be confused with his inner-circle of Twelve) that he is from heaven, and that he will give them his own flesh to eat, but a large number find this difficult to accept.

Key Verse

66From this time many of his disciples turned back and no longer followed him.

There's both a knowing what will happen on a certain day, plus a cloud of the future, where each one's reaction may take one down a different path. There could be trillions upon trillions of different circumstances, combinations and possibilities that make up one's day, but in fact there are really only a few that matter. These choices arise at unexpected moments.

People like to come up with phrases such as "Be prepared" or "Expect the unexpected", but these are gamesmanship, at best. Preparation is wonderful, in its own way. Reaction is necessary.

During my circuitous journeys around Galilee, or between there and Jerusalem, I sometimes felt I was in the middle of a storm on the lake. A wave would swell, gathering height, maybe even with a whitecap, only to come crashing down, very quickly to be replaced with the energy of another building wave

This was the embodiment of the struggle of my people as I called them to follow and obey. Harkening and rejoicing, they flocked to the call of a rabbi and prophet. The impelling heights of anticipation that he could be the long-awaited Messiah churned and broiled the people, clashing with their hopes and expectations.

They followed, some even calling me "Master" and themselves "disciples". Suddenly and with great force, pulled back by the gravity of their preconceptions, or breaking upon the rocks of their traditions or their leaders, a wave of people would scatter in rejection, some of them irrevocably, some of them trailing after, ready to join the swell again. Over and over I would ride the waves, back and forth from Capernaum in Galilee to Jerusalem, or back and forth across the Sea of Galilee. Over and over I would ride the waves, not because I needed to reach the heights, nor survive the storm, but simply because it was the only way to reach as many as possible then, to scatter seeds and, in some hearts at least, to ride out the storm and calm it.

This came out even in my sayings. I would tell the people plainly who I was, using titles and references they clearly understood. When pressed by them, I might say no sign would be given them, and I was like a wave crashing down on them, on hard-heartedness. They had had signs; they had all they required. Where their purposes were impure, a cleansing wave was rightly needed. All this could leave my Twelve disciples hanging on for dear life, a bit seasick but hopeful of reaching the shore.

I sat in the synagogue in Capernaum this day, the one John's talking about, teaching a crowd comprised mostly of people calling themselves my disciples. The synagogue was impressive for its time. It had been paid for by that centurion who had amazed me (*see chapter XXXIII*). Black basalt blocks in a basic rectangle, roughly fifty feet wide and seventy feet deep, if one accounts for some antechambers. The interior plaster was white-washed in order to reflect more light. The benches alongside all four walls were filled with people looking to each side of each of the numerous pillars, one near each corner, plus a few others along the sides; that meant a capacity crowd indeed. The men stuck nearly together with beards bouncing up and down as they called for me to speak. A political leader giving a victory speech on election night to a crowd of supporters should expect favorable responses. Like those events now, this was a partisan group if there ever was one. Only, something happened.

It wasn't having to be in the synagogue. There was a cool, steady breeze filtering through that refreshed everybody, while the canopy roof sheltered us from the direct sunlight. All the doors and windows were open. I sat in the center. The crowd hummed and swayed; claustrophobic for some, though I'd be in more densely packed houses in the days to come. No, it wasn't the heat or the compactness; the people turned on me as soon as I said something they didn't like. How's that for devotion?

"I am the bread of life," I said and eagerly offered them my future flesh.

They reacted quickly. I saw some of them cringe and look away. The looking away bit was the guilt they felt, for they had decided to abandon me then and there.

Let's face it, they were offended. They didn't want to admit to what really offended them. The worst type of blame-laying involves a lie. So many times I've then seen that covered up with a question, designed to look innocuous or even innocent. See, sometimes people ask questions to gain information. Other times their questions are rhetorical. Still other times they can be genuine and heartfelt, asked of God and directed to what they fear is a lonely sky, to be surprised by an answer, if they listen well enough. Then these times, a question asked defensively, looking to vacate a once-cherished position. These questions are subversive, intentional, the work of an apostate. Listen to them and you'll hear how they've already left me in spirit.

"This is a hard teaching," they said, the older men stroking their beards, now swaying in nervous shakes of the head.

"Who can accept it?" they asked, while the women among the group whispered to each other.

Behind those words is the intention to say it is the teacher's fault for teaching things they don't like. The teacher who hears from God and then changes the lesson to fit the popular culture is as unworthy as the one who promulgates lies for the sake of his or her own power.

Go ahead and leave, if you need some salve for your wounded pride of place. To be taught requires humility. Humility involves kneeling, and when you're down on the hard earth, kneeling can hurt. Congratulations to the few who are honest about why they're leaving, though in the end that's worth as much as a prize in a Cracker Jack box. I know it happens all around my churches today, too, this exact same way. It's all fun and games when sins are being forgiven, but then I say that I want a person to grow and I want to forgive the actual, specific sins you're committing, not some vague, general bad feelings, and many people walk out.

For a group dynamic like this, like that day in the synagogue, there's eventually just a few self-designated who lead, who themselves pick out a single spokesperson for a group, and it came down to a man named Moishe, nearly six feet tall but not burly, a natural leader with a propensity to speak his mind quickly (in some respects reminding me of Simon Peter). He and the other leaders who stood directly behind him spoke against the literal meaning of my words, about "my flesh, which I will give for the life of the world," ignoring the significance of it, saying it was hard.

That was a cheap out. We had those back then, just as you have them today. They tried to pretend that they were giving an expected response to a rabbi, like the game-show "Jeopardy", because it had been in the form of a question. I had given them a simple but powerful challenge. What they meant by their response was that they didn't want to be changed by my words, by my message. They didn't want their hearts, their secret places, to be touched; a strange, foolish sort of pride. It was terrible to see.

I told them then, as I tell you now, that the words I speak are full of the Spirit and life. To their question I asked my own: "Does this offend you?"

One big challenge for people is always to deal with their status quo.

LVII – The Disciples Who Remained

Night: 7
Entry: 3

Matthew 15:1-20

Key Verse

[16]"Are you still so dull?" Jesus asked them (*the disciples*).

This one makes me laugh, even to this day. We still say this to each other. (*I think he meant in heaven, maybe?*) It's a kind of "in joke" between us. We can be talking about anything and one of the guys will just drop an "I'm still so dull!" into the mix and we all have a good laugh together.

Not to lose the context of what was going on at this point, back in Judea two thousand years ago.

Pharisees came and tested me. I've already said something about "Everything is a test", right? It's a fairly true statement. I mean it to apply to my time on earth as well as yours. Those who have only a basic working knowledge of the Gospels think about the devil tempting me as my only time of testing, but in reality, pretty much everything was a test. This wasn't the first time the Pharisees had tested me and it would be far from the last. It would also be far from the last time I insulted them.

"Why do your disciples break the tradition of the elders?" they asked tauntingly, smugly.

"And why do you break the command of God?" I answered. "You hypocrites!"

The disciples said to me later, "Do you know the Pharisees were offended" when I told them off?

Did I know? I was counting on it, actually.

Look, the people "drinking the Kool-Aid" (*He used air quotes here.*) are on one side and maybe—just maybe—if they get super-offended they'll question themselves and their preconceptions and end up taking off their blinders. Otherwise, they have no intention of listening to the message or questioning themselves. Then, they're literally hopeless.

On the other side sit my disciples, the ones who remained. They're getting there—to that place of humility and faith where I want them—slowly, but they need some cajoling (they could've used a good, swift kick, too . . . just a quick one, mind you), because I need them. Without them, the whole plan falls apart, the "Plan A" I've talked about. I need my disciples, and not just the original Twelve. Would it clarify it at all if I called it "Plan Z" instead?

"Leave them," I said about the Pharisees to my disciples; "they are blind guides." As the parable stupefied them, they asked me to explain. That's when I dropped the "Are you still so dull?" on them. My plan called for them to be sharpened.

This pointed plan was for me to change the world by using disciples to announce God's love and the forgiveness of sins that was going to become available to anyone desperate enough to say they needed to be forgiven, after the first Easter. I wasn't going to be doing all the announcing. Mostly, I was going to be doing the preparatory work of training up the announcers. With those Twelve, as well as the few others who chose to follow me back then, it was a simple start, but necessary.

There were so many others around, though, listening. I needed them, too, but how many would I get?

It doesn't take much to start out, just a bended knee of some sort and a quick word addressed to me (any way you like; remember, I always listen).

LVIII – A DESPERATE WOMAN

Night: 7
Entry: 4

Matthew 15:21-28

Context Summary

Jesus departs Capernaum and heads to Tyre and Sidon (northwest of Galilee) where he meets up with a Canaanite woman. She has heard of him and cries out to him, asking him to heal her daughter of demon possession. Jesus tells her that he has been sent to the Jews, but she kneels before him and begs him again to help her.

Key Verse

[26]He replied, "It is not right to take the children's bread and toss it to the dogs."

I'm not sure if people notice what's happening at this stage. You have to realize that, at this time, there were certain portions of omniscience I willingly set aside. There were lots of things as a child that were veiled for me in my humanity that I've already mentioned, like simply being born. Some things, as an adult, also. I didn't know at this point when I'd come back to take my followers from the earth. I had no idea. I didn't really get the unbelief of the people of my hometown, and the faith of that centurion was almost a complete (though lovely) shock to the system. Me not knowing those things doesn't mean a lack of divinity or sovereignty, but actually means a complete embracing of my role as the Son; it is a manifestation of my humility, my foremost character trait.

This, however, was not one of those times where something was hidden. I knew all about this woman, knew all of her past. I knew she had faith (I could see it buried deep within her), a lovely faith covered over by years of ridicule and self-denigration. Faith is a gift, and the intent is that it is nurtured, together, but it can instead be quashed alone, reduced, even killed—the truest form of suicide—though not easily. It can survive many long winters of the soul, as if in hibernation. Her faith remained, for she desperately wanted to be accepted by God. Sometimes she knew it was God for whom she longed in the night, sometimes she didn't even know that. Still I could see her faith, sense it, almost sniff it, for faith embraced—or at least held onto—is a fragrant praise to God. Needing a little push, a small challenge, her faith had the possibility of bursting forth from its long dormancy. A push or a test could accomplish that.

I didn't say absolutely everything was a test, did I? No, but many things are, and whatever challenges I set you are for your benefit, and whether a testing or not, I can find something of value to bring out of the current circumstance. Just like for this woman.

Let me tell you about her. Her name was Shurah, and she lived in a small village on the road to the old city of Tyre, in a small place in the back that used to be a storage barn, now home to her, her daughter and three aging goats, only one of which still gave milk. We were on the main road to Tyre, descending, on course for the sea, encountering all the signs that it was near: new winds, palm trees and sea birds, with the slightest tang of salt in the breeze beginning to be tasted. She came out to us while we paused in the hamlet to get water and to eat, our mere presence in their midst stirring up the villagers, disturbing their day. She came out toward us with purpose, dropping her own jars for water which needed filling. Reaching only to my shoulders, when younger she had been considered a local beauty; it had certainly not all faded. Her dark eyes could flash or play with her changing emotions, and this day things started out bleak indeed, the whole morning spent desperately trying to stop her daughter thrashing around, smashing a remaining plate or two, screaming wildly.

Learning of me from stories told by passing caravans over the previous months, she silently kept hope through many rough days as she watched her young daughter suffer, unable to stop the fits, unable to help her at all apart from what comfort there was in a mother's touch and some goat's milk. Then suddenly this strange man always in the back of her mind appears in her village, but culture says to turn away, reject, do not speak.

She had long been silent. Why keep quiet now? Though she wasn't Jewish, she had heard of Judaism and had always thought it strange, incomprehensible, alien. Yet she could never forget what she had heard about God, that He cared for His people, that they would bring a light to all the Gentiles. She lived about as far away from Jerusalem as I ever went, and I went there to meet her. She couldn't have known that, nor ever expected what the caravan leaders called a "Jewish holy man" to travel to Tyre and Sidon, for Jews despised the Gentiles from here (from all over, but definitely from those cities).

"Lord, Son of David, have mercy on me!"

I heard that call and my heart leapt, though for the testing I kept a stony façade and responded with what seemed an insult. My people called her people "dogs" (I suppose you might call that "anti-canaanitism" or something, but it was the source of my intentional pun). Along with her big need, she had a small picture of grace in her heart. She was scared to let that vision blossom by trusting that God would ever listen to her.

Do you get what I'm doing? She has a small type of faith, small but potentially potent, and it's just waiting to explode! God has listened to her! He has even reached out to her! She needs only not to turn away, then to respond somehow, almost in any way. That anchors faith! It bursts it into growth, like a seed planted deeply and securely blossoms with warmth and nutrients, water and light! Oh, Shurah, you have the faith, will you show the humility for God to grow it and make it last?

I knew she could answer this when I told her that the dogs shouldn't get the children's bread: "Even the dogs eat the crumbs that fall from their master's table." She said it, and it was beautiful to behold.

How does one make a diamond? Add some pressure. Who will believe that's a good thing in the moment?

LIX – MYSTERY

Night: 19
Entry: 1

Mark 7:31-37

Context Summary

After Jesus leaves Tyre and Sidon, he travels to the area of the Decapolis where he heals a deaf man. The crowd is greatly amazed.

Key Verse

[36]Jesus commanded them not to tell anyone. But the more he did so, the more they kept talking about it.

This was both an exciting time of ministry and a frustrating one. I was excited to see fulfillment come, despite how I knew it would be fully accomplished. What was most exciting was seeing the crowds grow. More and more people were arriving and staying for days. Some of them were actually listening to me, too!

Many of these people had gone out to see John the Baptist, before my ministry started, and had made a public confession of their sins. Most had fallen back into them, and not just the big ones, as you define them (take gossiping, for instance; it's bigger than you imagine and causes vast misery). Returning to follow another man of God was difficult for some of them, but the stories of healing and feedings were a brilliant allure. The old "word of mouth" PR campaign, I guess. Thus the frustrating part: Everyone wanted a free meal and to tell the doctor their troubles.

Didn't I know that's why so many of them were there, why so many had come back (in a manner of speaking)? Of course. Should I have stopped giving to them? That was not a choice. I gave though none deserved it. I healed them though they turned right around and sinned.

You can say it doesn't matter, but I feel it very deeply. It is painful to me, quite literally. I persevered because not everyone chose that way, or when they sinned they did not choose to justify it all away (in their minds). Some even asked me to do more. For these, I had to keep going. At the same time, they needed to shut up about some of the ridiculous things they were saying about me. Besides, the really good stuff was yet to come.

"He has done everything well," they said, and that sounds right, sounds good. In actuality it takes away from the true revelation of God's plan in an oversimplification that allows people to leave.

See, I am not some cheap magician doing tricks. I'm not fully defined as merely a wise teacher, a prophet or a good man. That's not who I was then and is not who I am today. I never told anyone to think of me in that way. I was a rabbi, a teacher, yes, but so much more than that. I deserved to be known for better than just those things. The message I preached warranted all the attention. When they treated me like a circus act, I pleaded for them to stop. If you can't promote the correct idea, then you need to keep quiet, too. The mystery will be fully revealed in the last pages of the Gospels.

"Mystery" was a buzz word in those days. The Spirit had been whispering to many, many people (not just Jews, mind you) in the days leading up to my coming to earth that "the mystery" would be revealed. Some took those words and went off in massive tangents creating "mystery cults", others shrugged off the pervasive sense of awe in their spirits and went on with their daily lives, not wanting to take off their blinders, while a few brave souls went searching for that meaning, and so heard more from God. They waited eagerly for their Messiah. Some of them came and found me, and some were bitterly disappointed in what they discovered. A few of them, however—overall a sadly small number relative to the whole—were humble and accepted what God had sent them; they even rejoiced! I did not ask them to be quiet. Instead, I blessed them and told them to tell people all that God had done for them.

The ones who went on shouting weren't always the ones I wanted talking. The bigger crowds who heard of me second-hand therefore ended up hearing disparate and often fallacious things about me, despite the truth that was out there that could be known or sought out. In this respect, things have not changed all that much.

LX – SIGNS AND FRUSTRATION

Night: 19
Entry: 2

Mark 8:11-13

Context Summary

After Jesus feeds another large crowd (the "Feeding of the Four Thousand"), the Pharisees come and demand that he perform a miracle.

Key Verse

[12]He sighed deeply and said, "Why does this generation ask for a sign? Truly I tell you, no sign will be given to it."

Frustration isn't a sin. Maybe you thought it was. What manifests from it out of the heart and what actions are chosen in response can lead to sin. Anger can boil up and it can be selfish or it can be righteous. Righteous anger can lead to righteous actions. Here, I walked away. I had ministry to do there, too, but the Pharisees had to come and test me, asking for a sign.

I was frustrated here. In the same vein, I'm frustrated with many people today. How many people want a sign today? How many want to test me (and what kind of test)? How many have missed all the signs I've given them up to this point?

They think of it like a little "freebie". (*He used air quotes again here.*) "If he provides this little sign, this little miracle, then I'm willing to consider what he says." Except they aren't. This group of Pharisees wasn't going to concede anything, for they had already made up their minds and solidified their stance, which is another way of saying they had hardened their hearts against me. They didn't want to join my movement; instead, they wanted to destroy it. What kind of sign were they seeking?

Most of you know when someone is asking you a loaded question, one they can twist for their own purposes. The kingdom of heaven is not like a lawyer in a courtroom cross-examining an innocent defendant. No, the kingdom of heaven is like the innocent defendant being cross-examined by a lawyer in a court of law, treating him as a hostile witness. (Okay, there's another parable for you. That's the "freebie".)

This group didn't want a sign. There's almost nobody who screams for a sign or a miracle who actually wants that! They react in horror and rage if they get it! No, they didn't want a sign, they weren't going to consider my message. They wanted only to see something they could then attack, for any quickly made-up reason. They poke and they prod and they question, question, question, but never for information, never seeking the knowledge of God, never once wondering or considering if any of their values—so dear to them—could be mistaken.

I can reach people who are very far away from me, sometimes even with the coldest hearts imaginable, because sometimes something so hard and cold can surprisingly be broken apart and softened. The toughest cases end up being the ones loudly proclaiming their zeal for God, when they truly don't even know Him. Pride gets in the way again, and is even more desperate and offensive in a group mentality.

This group would be there, in Jerusalem, on the night before I was executed, plotting, and on the following morning, leading people astray, celebrating their victory.

Today, wouldn't a similar group ask me leading questions? Wouldn't they make demands for power and for control? Wouldn't they trot out all those they clamor for who have an accusation to bring against me? What should I say to them, and how should I respond? I'm not afraid in the slightest, but what answer do they need that is not in the Word of God? I did not come each of these nights to answer everyone's individual grievance. It's not an apology in either the classic or modern sense. I'm here to proclaim what should be obvious to anyone reading the Gospels: I am here to seek and save the lost.

And you've had enough signs, too! Very frustrating.

LXI – WHO DO YOU SAY I AM?

Night: 27
Entry: 3

Luke 9:18-20

Key Verse

[18]Once when Jesus was praying in private and his disciples were with him, he asked them, "Who do the crowds say I am?"

This was an important question. I sat on an old, woven mat in the room of the house where we stayed on the road. The sun slipped low while shadows lengthened. Around me the disciples did quiet chores, but quickly settled as I looked up from my prayers. Almost everywhere I went, including most times I tried to get some alone time, crowds of people flocked to see me, hear me, get something from me. Who were they coming out to see? So many wanted a show. So many were excited for the miracles. What I needed was a gauge on both the crowd and with my followers. What would they think?

People thought many things about me; they still do. I've said some of this before, but it bears repeating. These are some of the things they thought about me, some of the things they called me: I was a good man, a wise teacher, a prophet, crazy, a magician, a hustler, a charlatan, impostor or pretender. Does any of that sound familiar? Some even thought I was the Messiah, God's savior, but that begged the question of what kind of Messiah? They overwhelmingly wanted one who would just kick out the Romans from Judea. Too small of a thought.

I asked my disciples a question and, as the start of a rabbinic dialog, it was a leading question (but without deceit). What the crowds were saying was important to know, vital to notice, and even my disciples' perceptions of the crowds were important. As stories ran rampant, it showed how the people's knowledge of the

Scriptures was in a sorry state. Even if they knew them, they couldn't properly interpret the message. They didn't have the Bible in their homes (apart from a few verses kept in their lintel or tied to themselves). There were teachers everywhere, but what would they teach and what would people learn? What tools could they use to check against the teachings? Who do they say I am?

So the question was not innocuous. I asked in order to gauge the current state of affairs, but within the rabbinic context to continue teaching them also. I returned again and again to certain topics—as you're even seeing in this work—because of the importance of them. The questions had to be asked. The answers would inform how I proceeded with my ministry. I was ready for the big gambles of God's plan. I was ready to push people. Decisions had to be made. Life is short, until it's eternal. Basic training would be over someday.

Who do you say I am?

LXII – THE ROCK

Night: 8
Entry: 1

Matthew 16:13-20

Context Summary

Jesus leads his disciples north of Galilee to Caesarea Philippi and asks them who the crowds say he is, and then who they say he is. Peter proclaims that Jesus is the Messiah, the Son of God. Jesus blesses Simon Peter for his answer.

Key Verse

[18]"And I tell you that you are Peter, and on this rock I will build my church, and the gates of Hades will not overcome it."

What a day this was. If I could take you back to Caesarea Philippi, I would (that's just a figure of speech; I'm not here to address time-travel or teleportation). To be clear, Caesarea Philippi was not a nice place. That's not why I'd bring you there, to experience such a nasty environment. No, it was because of the importance of that day.

I went there with purpose, and will continue to go places with purpose, nice or not. Try to understand: the sights, the sounds, the smells, the crowds. Apart from my small group, nobody there claimed to love God. This was a pagan place (and I mean that literally): A river flowing out of a cave in a cliff, with Greek temples for idol worship all around, the base essence of the fallen world—people looking desperately for something to fill in the hole in their hearts. This place was named the "Gates of Hades". Really. That was its name. Well-known throughout the Mediterranean world of the time. Well-loved by some, well-despised by Jews and some others, it was almost as far from Jerusalem as I went in my ministry days. My disciples were not comfortable there.

We came over a hill to look down at that sight. The opposing cave in the cliff looked like a monstrous open maw. The surrounding niches carved for the pagan gods gave it the appearance of many outlandish orifices, multiple eyes, ears, mouths. Oozing out of the cave, the water appeared heavy, a dark gray-green glass, almost slate. It moved, but ponderously, weighed down by the disillusionment it was forced to flow past.

My disciples didn't want to look, but I turned their attention that way, not to contaminate them with images that shocked them, but to show them a bigger picture of the world that God wanted to save. Some people were down at the base temples worshiping Pan or Zeus; many were there to engage the temple prostitutes. Dancing in intoxicated frenzy, enlivened by the drugs of the day, their soiled robes and torn togas trailed their movements in silent witness to their lack of hope, trying to force a feeling strong enough to be a spiritual meeting of some kind, all as I walked nearby.

Some people screamed. Some people laughed. Acrid smoke from dozens of ritual fires and scores more of cooking ones assailed our senses, a mixture of the savory and the unsavory hitting our nostrils in volume. All our eyes watered. No one paid any attention at that moment to the rabbi with the twelve young Jewish men with him. Maybe, apart from the river flowing out of the cave, the scene would not be so out of place in any downtown today. What was supposed to happen here? How were my disciples supposed to respond?

Yes, this too was a test. As I've said, put something under pressure and it might explode in destruction, or it might turn into a diamond (an uncut one, mind). Only the wisest know what the right amount of pressure is (except in hindsight; even fools know that).

"Who do you say I am?" I asked them and Peter answered.

Peter—I usually call him Simon, of course, but there was a pun to be had in both Aramaic and Greek on the word "rock". It's like I nicknamed him "Rocky" in English: "You are Rocky, and on this rock I will build my church."

It's a tricky thing, perhaps, interpreting this verse in the Bible. What did I mean? Did I mean that Peter was the head of my future church organization, that whatever leader followed him was the top guy? Or did I mean that his confession of faith was the firm foundation of the church I was establishing? Or did I mean that the physical bedrock upon which we gazed (the manifested "Gates of Hades") was going to be replaced by something better?

That's a lot to interpret out of one verse.

There is an old Jewish saying that the family of faith—meaning specifically the progenitors of the Hebrew family, Abraham and Sarah—had been quarried by God, and were rocks He formed. Peter was another of those now, and so were the other disciples who would make the same declaration; so were all my future followers. Their confession down through the years would be a firm foundation of faith. Looking down at the sordid views of the pagan temples in Caesarea Philippi, I knew it wouldn't be long before it was supplanted.

"Who do you say I am?"

Peter spoke up, spoke for the group. "You are the Messiah, the Son of the living God." Now he had it! This was new for him, an acceptance both humble and glorious! It didn't fit his preconceptions! That was a starting point. Still, he had been—was even still part-time—a fisherman. His emotions could be all over the board some days. He's not what the world would call a "safe bet" for leading a radical movement. None of those boys were. It was an enormous gamble, choosing Simon Peter. Could I have started with a more unstable "rock"?

Do you even know me yet???

LXIII – Transfiguration: Up the Mountain

Night: 8
Entry: 2

Matthew 17:1-13

Key Verse

¹After six days Jesus took with him Peter, James and John the brother of James, and led them up a high mountain by themselves.

Then, as Matthew says, I was "transfigured". Well, Mark said it, too, and even wrote it first, but Matthew sure seemed to enjoy the big word. Luke toned it down. John, having been there, didn't write about it directly, but, being humbled by it, spoke of it in awe: "We have seen his glory. . . ." (*See John 1:14.*)

That's very nice of them, to write about this the way they did. It was a good day. It can certainly be remembered as the "Transfiguration". My humanity was momentarily paused, one might say, overshadowed by divinity. When one breaks down the word, it's as accurate as human language can get using a single term.

Well, I could suggest another word, if the theologians in the crowd could handle the (perhaps) crudity. One word: vacation!

Seriously. It was my version of going to the beach, putting on sandals and breathing deeply (I mean this metaphorically since I always wore sandals, regularly walked in sand and, except in and around Jerusalem—or in too close of proximity to certain fishermen—the air was always fresh). To use such a word as "vacation" may be, for the puritan, "coming down the mountain", but I needed rest. Climbing the mountain was nothing. It was a goodly hike, maybe nothing compared to the Rockies or the Himalayas or the Alps—that would've been somewhat awkward, to take my disciples to those places at that time—but still, not for the faint of heart nor the out-of-shape. I was like the parent on the last leg of the drive to the hotel: Ignore the screaming kids in the backseat and just keep going until we get there!

John acted the brat that day; fairly unusual for him actually. James said something to him early on and John turned morose, sniping back at his brother and sulking the whole way there. While he didn't ask, "How many more miles?" since he could see the top of the mountain, he may as well have. His comments contained that tone of voice. He felt ashamed when I revealed what I revealed, thinking later that he should have been able to suffer in silence for good seats to that. I can't say I disagree.

"After six days," the verse says . . . well, well. Could that be a coincidence to something said in Genesis? (*See Genesis 2:2.*) The week—the one we had just come off of, leaving Caesarea Philippi and heading toward Jerusalem—had been like a tough work week with many stressors. It was definitely time for an end to that week, and none too soon. That's kind of the reason why a week is seven days long and not ten or anything else.

LXIV – TRANSFIGURATION: DOWN THE MOUNTAIN

Night: 20
Entry: 1

Mark 9:2-13

Context Summary

At the top of the mountain, Jesus is transfigured, shining brilliantly and appearing with Elijah and Moses. Then a cloud conceals them and the three disciples with Jesus hear a voice saying that Jesus is the Son and they need to listen to him. The cloud and the brilliance then vanish; it is obviously time to return home.

Key Verse

[9]As they were coming down the mountain, Jesus gave them orders not to tell anyone what they had seen until the Son of Man had risen from the dead.

This was a long, slow march. I set the pace.

If I called going up the mountain and being up on the mountain "vacation", then this was coming back from one. Many of you know the odd mixture of feelings, of regret that work was ahead and not all one set out to accomplish had been achieved, mingled with simple excitement at getting home, back to the families, even the routine. A good vacation refreshes and energizes one for new, hard work. Those receiving the benefit of that new work will be getting the very best effort.

Still, the experience, though it lingered somewhat, faded away with each step downhill, both for me and my disciples. We passed rocks and bushes and culverts that we had seen on our ascent. It wasn't as memorable as the sights on the way up, like at the beginning of a modern road trip might be, perhaps, but they were still metaphorical milestones.

I was with Simon, James and John. They were among my closest friends and I wanted them for big things later in life. I picked them out from the rest of the Twelve to see this great wonder. It wasn't about what the other nine didn't get; the focus was elsewhere.

Simon Peter—what a great guy, but totally lost without me. Had he been a man of the modern era he would assuredly have taken to culture, or at least culture's "answers" to all of life's problems. He wanted to be good, he wanted to be right, he wanted to be acceptable to others. He had seen, but he didn't yet understand. He kept trying to cover this up with inane chatter. I kind of wanted him to stop.

James was still thinking through—still processing—the responsibility he had, both what he had taken on as a disciple and what he had left behind in Capernaum. I knew his deepest fear, that he would flee from his new responsibility, for he blamed himself still for (what he termed) "running away" from his old responsibilities. If he stood firm, he would be the first of them to die for my sake (not including Judas Iscariot, who would die for his own sake). James seemed to sense this, so he stayed very quiet.

John smiled foolishly and charmingly all the way down the mountain. He smiled at Simon chattering away about nothing. He smiled at his older brother brooding. He didn't know what to say about what he had seen on top of that mountain. Pondering it for almost seventy years, he would finally put it into words: "We have seen his glory, the glory of the one and only Son, who came from the Father, full of grace and truth."

Indubitably.

LXV – HELP FOR UNBELIEF

Night: 20
Entry: 2

Mark 9:14-29

Context Summary

As Jesus returns from the Transfiguration to the rest of his disciples, he finds a large crowd arguing. A man has asked the remaining disciples to drive a demon out of his son, but they cannot do it, and they wonder why. Meanwhile, Jesus asks them to bring the boy to him.

Key Verses

[21]Jesus asked the boy's father, "How long has he been like this?"

"From childhood," he answered. [22]"It has often thrown him into fire or water to kill him. But if you can do anything, take pity on us and help us."

[23]"'If you can'?" said Jesus. "Everything is possible for one who believes."

[24]Immediately the boy's father exclaimed, "I do believe; help me overcome my unbelief!"

Who needed to be healed here? I came down the mountain and found a tumultuous scene. At the edges of the crowd, some of the stragglers recognized me and started shouting my name. I could see the disciples I had left behind in a couple of clusters, with Pharisees and their allies yelling and gesticulating at them. The crowds followed the volleys and formed groups of their own, supporting one side or the other, sometimes switching sides frantically.

People screamed at me as I came up, some running directly at me, some away. "Son of David! Son of David!" others called as my disciples tried to break from their opponents and get to me. Dust swirled as people kicked it up all over.

A man from the middle of one of those clusters broke through all the others, pushing disciples and teachers of the law aside roughly, swerving through the rest of the people to reach me before any of the others, even as I stepped toward him, two fast-approaching trains on the same track.

"I brought you my son!" the man said, his tone a curious mixture of pleading and accusation, as if he were in a courtroom and on both sides of a trial.

I looked at him as he explained about his son being possessed and my disciples being unable to help. Nearby Pharisees had jumped at the chance to descry their mission, their zeal, their leader. A large circle formed spontaneously around me, and all over people shouted and hollered, "Heal him! Heal him!" or "You can't! You simply can't!"

Everything felt so heavy. My body wasn't ready for this yet, so soon after the mountain. I cried out, rebuking the crowd, and it quieted them at a cost to my heart. The man motioned and the crowd parted, letting a family member bring his son into view.

The boy leapt away from the gentle handling of his relative. He fell on the dirt before me, the circle of onlookers widening immediately as they all gasped and shouted some more. Rolling around without control, the boy drooled, screamed and frothed at the mouth.

It seemed pitiless, but I looked away to the father and addressed him.

"How long has he been like this?"

I was not asking for information here. There were some blank spots, some holes. I mean, I could run into something hidden from me in my humanity, due to me embracing my role and living out God's Plan as Son. Did I know how long the boy had been like this? Does it matter? The issue as I saw it was not the boy—I loved him deeply and his pain would be gone in but a moment—but what about the father? What about my disciples?

I looked at the father. My question to him was as a rabbi and more. Would he engage? Or did he want to walk away? What do you think? I am showing God's compassion here, from my rebuking the crowds to my turning to the father. Is this difficult to believe? Is it more difficult to believe than asking me "if I can" heal a child?

What did this father have to do, except to ask? Didn't he have to willingly give up the power and control he imagined he had in his family (a very real thing to him)? Didn't he have to sacrifice his preconceived notions of how the world worked?

He wanted to, yet he was humble enough to know it wasn't possible, not on his own at any rate. As I looked at him, his face dark and cracked, wind-shorn from a rugged life of outdoor labor, his world up to that point as small as his eyes: God, family, work; but in a blind acceptance of humdrum and daily routine, until one only was threatened, revealing to him how fragile his world really was.

Certain illnesses—certain possessions—are connected within and between people. What affects the child affects the parent, and vice-versa. This confused my disciples, who had grown used to simply doing things in my name. "Why?" they asked me as we huddled inside our lodgings later, after most of the crowd had gone home happy. "Why couldn't we drive out that demon?" I told them the truth, that it could only come out with prayer. Didn't you hear it? Didn't you hear the father's pure heart crying out? "I do believe; help me overcome my unbelief!"

Who needed to be healed that day, anyway? The boy, yes, of course the boy. But the world and how you think it works starts to flip over when you pray a prayer like the father did.

LXVI – The First Shall Be Last

Night: 20
Entry: 3

Mark 9:35

<u>Key Verse</u>

³⁵ Sitting down, Jesus called the Twelve and said, "Anyone who wants to be first must be the very last, and the servant of all."

I said it many times over my preaching career, many times. (Go ahead and read them, David.)

(Matthew 19:30 "But many who are first will be last, and many who are last will be first."

Matthew 20:16 "So the last will be first, and the first will be last."

Mark 9:35 Sitting down, Jesus called the Twelve and said, "Anyone who wants to be first must be the very last, and the servant of all."

Mark 10:31 "But many who are first will be last, and the last first."

Luke 13:30 "Indeed there are those who are last who will be first, and first who will be last.")

That doesn't even include the "greatest shall be least" variation (another good one). Context shifted how I used this phrase and why I used it, for it is a good phrase, a winning phrase, a spiritual phrase. It's as true today as it was then, and for just as many reasons; it just sounds a little trite now. I don't think that's my fault, though.

What does it mean, the first shall be last? I keep getting asked that question, and many explanations in addition to what is in the Gospels have been posited by people. Many of those answers have an element of truth to them; some expound very clearly what I meant in one context or another. Some are way off base; a few are intentionally misleading.

It would take a long time to walk through all the instances of when I said it and especially the why I said it. Primarily—and very, very succinctly—I said it to get the attention of my listeners (whose minds wandered so quickly) and shake up their preconceptions and give them a huge dose of truth. The world is not the way it looks. Not in the end, not when it matters. During the course of the day, the world works for the powerful, is ordered and controlled by money. If life ended at death, my advice would be to go that route. If being nice or doing good could get you into heaven, I would say to still live it out using power and money (just adding some good causes, especially if they're felt passionately and argued over vehemently) and then I'd see you there.

Fortunately, that's not how things really end up. The rich and powerful still die, and are never really in control. At some point, you have to trust me on this, and—have I mentioned this before?—it takes a humble person to trust. The first one to die will be the last one who'll be able to convince you of the truth of my statement, because they can't come back and tell you about it. Only I can.

Look, in some instances, "the first will be last" sounds like a threat. If you're "first" in this world, you'll be "last" in the life to come. It may be terrifying to hear that, but also pretty easy to gloss over and get on with your life (that's terrifying to me, but sadly so because of your self-inflicted hard-heartedness). What I mean is, this interpretation is saying if you're rich and powerful here, you won't get into heaven. However, it's not a threat (though it is a warning).

I sat with my disciples in Simon's house, with his extended family surrounding us, listening in. So I said it again. "Anyone who wants to be first must be the very last, and the servant of all." They looked alternately concerned and contemplative as the kids walked among us, untroubled.

One of the things my phrase meant was actually a promise and a calling. To my followers, the "first" are the ones who have become the most Christ-like. In this world they will be the last for everything here, willingly, in order to serve those coming after them, especially so that there will continue to be more and more who come after them. They willingly do it not because they will get rewarded later (which they will), but precisely because they're not worried with that aspect at all. They're concerned about doing what I would do.

My humility has been on display since the very beginning of the book. If you've been paying attention, that won't be news to you. My dependence on God, modeled for you, has been evident, concomitant to humility as it is. Despite the many wonderful moments I've had with people, it has of necessity all been a trial, and the trial phase is about to ramp up.

LXVII – ARISING

Night: 8
Entry: 3

Matthew 17:22-23

Context Summary

Jesus predicts his coming death and resurrection to his disciples.

Key Verse

23"They will kill him, and on the third day he will be raised to life."
And the disciples were filled with grief.

If you think about it, I had good reason to be exasperated
with my chosen Twelve. Indeed, one would betray me,
one would deny me, one would doubt me; the rest would run away,
at least for the weekend, anyway. Really though, when you get right
down to it, they all would deny and doubt.

These were my disciples. In Hebrew they were my "talmidim".
I called them, they came willingly. Their goal was to become like
me. They expected to get sermons, they expected to get advice on
how to live and work and worship. They may not have thought at
the beginning that they were going to see miracles, but that quickly
became their focus, which actually meant that they lost the focus I
wanted them to have.

To them, the miracles meant God's power was on display.
True. What were they forgetting, though? They were hearing the
message, memorizing it even, but they were as yet unable to apply
it to themselves and let it change them. So, instead of wanting the
message more, they only wanted miracles more. They never got
tired of seeing me heal or produce something not natural to their
prior experience. They wanted the miracles and they got them. I
couldn't stop healing.

That wasn't the end-game for me and it wasn't for them, either. I wanted to reach people's hearts and win them for God, while at this time my disciples were much more interested in restoring an independent kingdom of Israel; God's power would kick out the Romans. I would be king and they would be my chief ministers. That's what they called the "Kingdom of Heaven", but that was not what I came to bring. I sometimes looked at these young men and saw them as not much different at all from the people in the crowds. They were sick and needed a miracle, or were passionate for a moment about hearing a teaching, but then were hungry. What does it take to look upon me as savior?

As frustrating as it was dealing with people who refused to commit, I continued to have compassion on them, I mean both my disciples and the crowds. It isn't easy living on earth, unable to see heaven. Would that make it easier if you could? See heaven, I mean? I tell you, the peoples of that day saw many miracles. How many days went by that the Twelve didn't witness one? Simply put, for some people, nothing is ever good enough. To see the miracles as an attestation to the Good News, but to fail to see the message as applying to them in their innermost places due to a technicality (in their own minds)? It's criminal! Pain upon pain will be borne by me! Here I was, telling my group serious news, but ending with foreknowledge of my resurrection, something that absolutely, positively, 100% was going to happen. After dying, I was going to rise, to be raised. What do I get? Not cheers. Bitter tears. On the road to Capernaum, seeing familiar sights, they wept unashamedly, grasping onto each other, creating a bit of distance from me. Out of context it sure sounds like they want me dead!

It wasn't true of them, of course; they just couldn't focus on the truths after the news about the killing. They loved me, they didn't like hearing news about me dying. The mind normally rebels against a message of life after death (for others, anyway; for oneself it can be a different contemplation). Why wouldn't they immediately rejoice, though? They had seen Jairus' daughter be raised by me. I had commanded them to raise the dead on their own missionary journeys! Did they think I was speaking metaphorically then?

No, it was so much simpler than that, of course. They didn't hear the real message, did they? They only heard I would die and me dying defeated their dream of being power-brokers.

What do you want? What did they want? A Jesus who just preaches and even does healings is pretty cool. He can be viewed like going to a summer blockbuster movie; you go home again after seeing the movie happy, but with hearts soon empty again. A Jesus that rises from the dead, however, that's a scary proposition. Everything he says must be true, and must apply to you.

The way some people act and speak about me nowadays, one would think they'd want me to have stayed in the grave. How does that one song go? "You can't always get what you want." Seems appropriate here somehow.

LXVIII – THE GREATEST

Night: 9
Entry: 1

Matthew 18:1-5

<u>Key Verse</u>

[1]At that time the disciples came to Jesus and asked, "Who, then, is the greatest in the kingdom of heaven?"

The people of that time were very much like the people of today. I saw it growing up and as a young man. At every stage, there was someone in control, or seemingly so. Even in Nazareth, a very small village, people defined themselves (but not always consciously) based on a hierarchy.

There was a rich farmer in Nazareth; well, the richest one in that community, anyway. He had numerous tenant farmers. Every harvest he would make the rounds, one farm to the next, with great fanfare. He would clap and call loudly, making sure anyone nearby would hear him. A group from the village, like a deputized community, gathered at his back, following but keeping a respectful couple of steps behind. At each stop, the farmer expected his share of what had been produced. When the baskets were brought out for him, he always scolded, expecting more, and only grudgingly left the tenants enough to live on (if they thanked him profusely enough). He was a bit of a bad character out of a Disney movie, really.

There's no doubting that he got the most attention in town, though. He could be outshone if a traveling rabbi came through (this was after Rabbi Ben Shimon who had taught in our synagogue for a while had left us), or a rare appearance by a member of the Sanhedrin (in reality it would always be an official tied to one of the seventy members of the Sanhedrin, the Jewish court that met in Jerusalem). They in turn could be upstaged if a Roman centurion came through. (They did, at times. We boys would line the lane and they'd call us to carry their shields for a mile. I would go with them until they'd make me stop and go back home, generally not more than three miles.)

They had power, but there was always someone higher who had more. It pushed down on them, so they in turn pushed down on others. That was their only view of the world, even when God was brought into the equation. That wasn't, however, God's view of things. I had come to speak truth, to show people God's way, God's power structure. This was one of the beginnings of that teaching, when my disciples asked me about being the greatest and wanting to know if it would be one of them.

LXIX – SETTING FORTH

Night: 27
Entry: 4

Luke 9:51-56

Key Verses

⁵¹As the time approached for him to be taken up to heaven, Jesus resolutely set out for Jerusalem. ⁵²And he sent messengers on ahead, who went into a Samaritan village to get things ready for him; ⁵³but the people there did not welcome him, because he was heading for Jerusalem. ⁵⁴When the disciples James and John saw this, they asked, "Lord, do you want us to call fire down from heaven to destroy them?" ⁵⁵But Jesus turned and rebuked them. ⁵⁶Then he and his disciples went to another village.

You think you have problems—and I hope you can hear how I mean this, not sarcastically, but seriously. I could say it sarcastically as I'm headed for torture and death at that time, but that's not how I need to speak to you right now. What I mean is, you think in your day and age that problems exist and they are unlike problems have ever been, but I say I know and understand your world better than you think I do (at least as most of you think I do).

Hatreds, jealousies, racial tensions; we had it all. Many Samaritans had heard of me, had come to hear me teach, and many had also been healed. However, many also could not look past the fact that I was a Jew. My disciples would not look past the fact that the people of Samaria were, in fact, Samaritans.

Had they had DNA testing to show them all their genetic similarities, it wouldn't have mattered. These things I listed above are not physical sins, but deeply buried spiritual ones. They can be healed. Trying really hard will never conquer these sins. Legislation will never eliminate them. Rage will never overwhelm them. Revenge will never undo them. A heart opened up to the Gospel will heal it all.

John himself—my disciple—desired his own form of retribution that day, but one day in his future he would be sent to preach in that same village and see miraculous things, especially a new church with both Jews and Samaritans in it. Getting along even. More than that, loving one another.

It happens still, but all of it is dependent on the resoluteness I felt that day in setting out for Jerusalem. I was "resolute" in my setting out, but please don't confuse that for "directness". There was purpose in all my travels, but there was a change when I set my eyes to Jerusalem. I would yet wander, even making it into the city itself, like a brief reconnoiter, before walking some final paths in its outer environs. I would go with an even greater focus, as if circling my opponent, waiting for the proper moment to move in for the final scene. So an early moment of this final phase was passing through this Samaritan village. Otherwise, if John never sees it, then he never goes back, that church never starts, a similar pattern for you is never formed.

LXX – ENCOUNTER WITH A GROUP OF TEN LEPERS

Night: 30
Entry: 1

Luke 17:11-19

Key Verse

[11]Now on his way to Jerusalem, Jesus traveled along the border between Samaria and Galilee.

L ike the environs of Caesarea Philippi, this was not a nice place to be, in many respects. Oh, I didn't fear for my safety, particularly (it was a lot safer for me than being alone in a crowd of Pharisees), but many people avoided this road if they could. "Road", hah. An oversized path, mostly dry and dusty and rocky. Keep traveling east and one would hit the southern route to Jerusalem. Beyond was the Jordan River.

It had been a quiet morning for me. I strode a bit ahead of my disciples, softly singing a psalm of praise. As we approached a cluster of small homes scattered about as if reluctant to be seen together, a group of ten men and women stood like a welcoming committee just outside the tiny village, as if they had long expected us. They cried out a warning to us as they did to all, "Unclean! Unclean!" Those words died out and quickly changed to, "Jesus, Master, have mercy on us." Such a lonely little village. These cries from the group of lepers in that sad spot might have been surprising, but it seemed right on time.

Yes, it was a lonely place, but where else should outcasts be?

Every time one of my disciples would ask me, "Lord, why are we going this way?" or, "Why are we stopping now?" we'd usually meet up with someone. Seeing with eyes of faith, it's neither unexpected nor coincidental. It's just being ready and willing.

Those poor lepers. Some of them had been ostracized for Hansen's disease, but others for a mold infection and one even for psoriasis. With long years of close contact with each other, all now had some form of leprosy, caught from a more virulent strain among them. These men and women were sick and diseased; only a few could really move well, and they helped the others along. There were a few left in their colony in even better shape than some of those who came out. A couple of them who called to me had an arm missing, or most of a nose gone, worn down from the disease. Bandages were on all, circled on arm stubs or over hands or feet with blood showing through. If you're not surprised that they were out there near that small village on that wild path, or that they had found me, were waiting for me, are you surprised that, even in their isolation, they had even heard of me and believed I could help them?

Someone I had healed earlier had spread the news, and it had arrived even at their small colony, from a family member or friend bringing food, maybe shouting it from a distance. There were more than ten of them in their community, but only ten came out, the nearly hopeless. I like nearly hopeless people; they still have hope and are willing to concentrate it on God, for the things of this world have utterly failed them and they admit it. Hope is a solid thing, though, not easy to destroy, especially when directed to me. Maybe it seems like I talk about this kind of hope a lot; maybe it's to help you see the kind of hope God dispenses to you?

LXXI – Walking Away

Night: 34
Entry: 4

John 8:31-59

Context Summary

Jesus speaks to a crowd of Jews who had believed in him, but then they can't accept what he next tells them, that they can be set free from their sins. They claim they are descendants of Abraham, and therefore aren't enslaved to anyone or anything. They can't accept what Jesus says about their ancestor.

Key Verses

[58]"Very truly I tell you," Jesus answered, "before Abraham was born, I am!" [59]At this, they picked up stones to stone him, but Jesus hid himself, slipping away from the temple grounds.

Sometimes it's right to be happy with people agreeing with you, or at least to be happy when people aren't against you. A world full of politicians, however, is a truly frightening thought. Yet how different from reality is it? Wisdom is needed to know when people agreeing with you is not enough, to know when people need to be pushed.

I had made it to Jerusalem, but I would not be there long. I stood in the very shadow of the temple. Had I merely gone in to worship, you might have passed me by. I looked a lot like my fellow Jews of that day, with my flowing outer tunic with its tassels, secured by a very simple belt. You might have stared had I come into your church or business or home in your day and age, but for my day I was in many ways nondescript. It wasn't my clothes that told people right away I was a rabbi, but my words and actions, my teaching posture and my disciples. I think also it was my peaceful spirit I brought with me everywhere.

This was a beautiful day to preach, though. It wasn't to be wasted. The crowd around me liked what I said. So many of them were ignored by the religious powers of the day, the leaders and teachers, that they came readily to hear me. They liked it. It was new, it was radical, it opened up amazing pictures in their minds about what could be true for them, that instead of being cut off from God that God actually cared about them. Amazing, but was it too good to be true?

The swelling of crowds happened again, always cresting in Jerusalem before receding, ready to grow again later. How many would stay until the end? I could see their hearts. It was plain to see most of them wouldn't be easily touched; they remained as black as a thundercloud, and just as ready to erupt. I wouldn't coddle them, though. What's the point of that? I'm not looking for votes. I don't have to pander to be popular. It's not on my agenda. They had believed me, but up to a certain point only. I did what was necessary; I gave a gentle nudge.

"If you hold to my teaching, you are really my disciples."

"Abraham is our father," they cried to me, trying to tell me more than the simple fact that they were fellow Jews. They may as well have shouted out, "We don't like you telling us we're not okay on our own." It didn't intimidate me so they changed tactics and said, "The only Father we have is God himself."

I didn't shrug then, but I could have. These were all adults who had been taught at least some of the Torah; most had been taught a lot. I mean, a lot. A lot a lot. Many had whole books of the Bible memorized. What had they been taught, though, about how to interpret what they read and how to apply it to their lives? To whom had they listened? I know the fault of their teachers who couldn't see (or wouldn't see) what the Messiah would really be like. Had you been in their shoes, would you have done better?

I'm not worried about those who believe now without seeing. There's great, wonderful faith there! The skepticism of your age isn't new, however, and it needs to be addressed. Look at what these people chose. Look and think carefully. All the black hearts in the crowd turned from me irrevocably when I told them I was

God (because I did; I told them openly I was God; some of you need to know that). I needed a little divine power to escape them, but actually not that much. I mostly just walked away, because I was unafraid of them, and had plenty of other things to do, hidden in plain sight as I became.

LXXII – A Man Born Blind: Sight

Night: 35
Entry: 1

John 9:1-12

Key Verses

[1]As he went along, he saw a man blind from birth. [2]His disciples asked him, "Rabbi, who sinned, this man or his parents, that he was born blind?"

[3]"Neither this man nor his parents sinned," said Jesus, "but this happened so that the works of God might be displayed in him."

The day was hot and oppressive. People milled around listlessly, in part due to the weather and in part because of the Sabbath rules of the Pharisees, which excoriated them for too much effort on this day. It's good for the body to rest, but after all, it's hard work to follow in such a way. Someone else sat around, a blind man, himself listless, a small clay cup between his legs with two copper coins in it.

I spit and made a little mud from the dirt and put it on this blind man's eyelids. I could have healed him in a dozen different ways, such as simply saying, "See!" but I wanted them (my disciples and even more so the rules-makers) to "see" how little physical exertion was involved on their Sabbath.

Let's be clear. It wasn't going to matter to them that: a.) bending down; b.) spitting; c.) rubbing the dirt and spit a little bit to make some mud; d.) putting that mud on the man's eyelids; and e.) telling him to go and wash, did not constitute an amount of "work" that broke their rules. That is, if I had done those physical actions and the man had stayed blind, I wouldn't have been accused of "working" on the Sabbath. Of course, he was healed, and so it was going to break their rules even if they had to make up a new one ex post facto. They could quantify the physical effort, but not the spiritual effort. So, they assumed it was enormous, or at least enough to qualify as too much work, simply because they lacked the faith to do it or believe it was from God and therefore a gift, which never counts as effort.

Of course, there was more going on here. It was important to them, the Pharisees. They had been waiting for it, but then they intentionally disregarded it.

Imagine if you knew someone born blind—I mean, you were 100% convinced they had always been blind—and then you saw that person healed like I had done here and so you were further 100% convinced that a man had put a little bit of dirt on that person's eyes and then immediately that person could really see. You would have to start thinking a lot about God.

For this time, this culture, there were actually healings that had taken place, where God had worked miracles through other rabbis, devout men of the previous decades, not just me (though they would each do only one or two or three, so not nearly as often as me). The reason for this was to establish not just God's compassionate nature, but to show the people of Israel exactly and immediately who the Messiah was. This was done because there were only so many types of healings those rabbis could do (read: were gifted to do). In fact, there were four specific types of healings they couldn't do and hadn't ever done. If the Pharisees ever saw one of the four, they knew—100% convinced—that only the Messiah could perform such a feat.

One was to heal leprosy. They knew that since the Law of Moses had been given, no Jew had ever been healed of leprosy. One Jew was healed before the Law of Moses was completely given (it wasn't exactly leprosy, either), and one non-Jew after (which really was leprosy), but that was it. There's a whole large section of Leviticus given over to the cleansing rite for after a healing from leprosy, and they had that section memorized, but for no practical purpose. They didn't believe leprosy could ever be healed. Yes, I had done that; they had seen it.

Another was to heal someone who was mute, who couldn't speak. They believed that a demon controlled the muteness, and if they knew the demon's name then they could control the demon and cast it out. As the demon had to speak through the human it was controlling to give its name, this was self-defeating for the rabbis. So it was known that no one could heal someone mute. Yes, I did this kind of healing, too, and it wasn't just because I already knew the demon's name.

The final one was raising the dead, especially after four days, which was coming, but the third type of healing was that of a person born blind. If the Pharisees were smart, and they were, they would thoroughly investigate such a healing, to make sure the man had literally been born blind. If so, the conclusion any smart but humble person would make was that the healing had been done by the Messiah.

It's funny (and I really mean sad) how there can be only one conclusion to something, yet people still find a way to choose a different course, no matter how illogical. They so wanted to be wise, but instead they became the fools they deplored. Little children believed in me, not these grown men, and I always thanked God that it was like that.

"Go," I told the man, "wash in the Pool of Siloam."

How beautiful it was that he went and washed! It was the simplest action of faith. It caused an immediate stir and a message was sent up the chain of command, and of course the rulers said they would investigate this healing of the blind man. Let them, because even before getting to the skeptics investigating this healing, I had to deal with my disciples.

People thought all sorts of strange, incorrect things back then (sound familiar?), and what people would take away from my words (and later, my disciples' words) caused me much sadness. Like, there is a correlation between sin and sickness, but not one you see without deep wisdom and much prayer. A man is born blind and they assumed he or his parents' sin caused it. Today someone comes down with a disease and they assume their sin or someone else's has zero to do with it.

People like directness. It doesn't take any effort to understand, whether today or back then. I tried to show something in opposition to that, which requires a little energy, at least. I want people engaged, don't you know.

Come this way. Look and see! That man believed he had deserved not only to be blind, but to stay blind; yet he was also willing to be wrong about that. Good for him!

LXXIII – A MAN BORN BLIND: UNDERSTANDING

Night: 35
Entry: 2

John 9:13-38

Context Summary

The man Jesus had healed of blindness is hauled before the Pharisees. They hear from the man's parents that he was born blind, but the Pharisees don't accept that Jesus has healed him. When the man proclaims his own astonishment at the Pharisees' attitude, they kick him out.

Key Verse

[35]Jesus heard that they had thrown him out, and when he found him, he said, "Do you believe in the Son of Man?"

I'm not unfeeling toward those who are maligned after encountering me. I'm well aware that this man born blind didn't ask me to heal him (he didn't say no or ask me to re-blind him, or any such nonsense, either). It happens today, all around the world. Families can be split, ostracism or worse can ensue (just ask any former Muslim who has met me personally). The blind man who could see would rise above that with which they tried to burden him.

Jerusalem was a big city with a small-town charm: That meant that most everyone knew immediately all that was going on. Gossip is as old a sin as almost anything. A string of servants passed the news of the religious leaders—their meeting with the man I had healed of his blindness—to people on the street and to my disciples. It wasn't wrong to tell me he had been thrown out of a leading Pharisee's house. These leaders were supposed to investigate honestly and discover that Messiah had come, but they wouldn't even listen to a man healed of blindness. What a day for that man. Imagine: First day seeing, first day seeing the leading Pharisees, first day seeing their boots. Some day!

This man, whose name was Hezekiel, had had a big day for anybody. I could have let him be. He wasn't looking for more confrontation. It is a lightness of heart signaling the possibility of deep faith to laugh off such an encounter with the powers that be as he did. I don't mean he was creating faith ex nihilo, but he wasn't running out on what God had given him. Those times come at odd moments, sometimes when you are least prepared, but even a small choice, even one in what looks like failure, can be the response to the gift of God that starts a new life growing. It wasn't for nothing that I preached first to a mostly agrarian society that knew all about planting and sowing and reaping. Some of those tasks one plans for, but sometimes a storm comes or a season turns early and one of the tasks needs to happen unexpectedly.

Hezekiel would get just a little bit more that day. Many people who I had healed went on their merry ways, praising God sometimes, but often soon returning to their everyday lives. Some turned to follow me for a while or for good, but I didn't often see them again, face to face, like I did Hezekiel later that day.

I saw him on his way home. While he knew the way there by steps and memory, sight actually slowed him down his first few times. So he stepped slowly, his arms akimbo and moving hastily back and forth, not so much to feel for walls he could now see, but for balance.

People made room for him as he looked a little crazy, whipping his head around often, but I stepped into his path with wide arms. "Peace, brother," I greeted him, and he stopped and goggled at me.

"I've been looking for you," I said with a smile. "I hear they threw you out."

Recognition slowly lit up his face. While I knew the answer already, I purposely asked him, "Do you believe in the Son of Man?"

LXXIV – The Good Shepherd

Night: 35
Entry: 3

John 10:1-18

Context Summary

Jesus speaks to the Pharisees about their own spiritual blindness in numerous sayings about sheep, shepherds and the gate for the sheep-pen.

Key Verse

[11]"I am the good shepherd. The good shepherd lays down his life for the sheep."

As you read the Gospels—if you read them, and I hope you do—you might notice more than a few references to shepherds and sheep and lambs. Shepherds were my first visitors. That didn't imprint on me or set the stage or anything like that. That's the cart before the horse, I'd say.

Shepherds represent something, of course. John even said it in this chapter: I spoke of sheep and shepherding things as a figure of speech. Had I been born in Bethlehem, PA in, say, the 1990s or something, I wouldn't be using shepherds as my metaphor. Steel workers, maybe?

Obviously I was born into an agricultural society where there were lots of shepherds and sheep about. I was around them in my youth, of course. The hierarchy assumed and imposed by the housewives and the working (and even non-working) men in and around Nazareth always amazed me. The shepherds were looked down on by the villagers—even the farmers—possibly due to their smell, but mostly because other people looked down on them, especially people from larger towns, especially meaning Jerusalem.

"Shepherds are smelly and dirty," one old man in Nazareth said, and he being one of the smelliest men ever (I mean this literally). But he grew crops, so that was better.

I would go out to the fields, some ways outside the village, or meet the shepherds back at the pens—low stone wall enclosures where they all slept at night—some of them on the sides of the hills just outside the village houses, counting their sheep at the sheep gate, the single entrance/exit as they brought their flocks in for the night. We talked sometimes. Sometimes they were nice. At other times some of them could be downright jerks. Most of them were lonely most of the time. They would've loved having the internet back then, but I'm not sure that would have helped them. How many of them wanted a good shepherd of their own?

LXXV – MUTTERING

Night: 29
Entry: 3

Luke 15:1-7

Context Summary

In front of a mixed crowd of people listening to Jesus and grumbling against him, he tells a parable about one-hundred sheep, with one getting lost and the shepherd who goes after it.

Key Verses

[1]Now the tax collectors and sinners were all gathering around to hear Jesus. [2]But the Pharisees and the teachers of the law muttered, "This man welcomes sinners and eats with them."

I hate the muttering. I hated it then and nothing has changed about it.

This day had been another busy one, only the meal at the end of the day was given by one of the women supporting me, not by an outside notable, and so she asked me to host. She invited the whole village, though not everyone came. While they were outnumbered in a literal sense, the Pharisees and their allies would have easily dominated the room had I not been there, like a small clique of "cool kids" intimidating a whole cafeteria full of "nerds". (*He used air quotes both times.*)

Long, low tables lined the inner courtyard of the house, open to the sky apart from a cloth covering over a section of it. I reclined at the head of the table, my disciples scattered about, mostly on lower tables, while Pharisees fought for position.

"Suppose one of you has a hundred sheep," I said, launching into one of my favorite parables, "and loses one of them." Ears perked up everywhere, some with smiling heads, others that refused direct eye contact.

I loved times like this, actually, with tension as ripe as the harvest fruit. The "sinners" (by which I mean those the Pharisees called sinners, since everyone else there was one already) were easy for that group to daunt. They—the Pharisees—had almost all the power, at least on the religious side of things, and that was incredibly important in that day and age. As a matter of routine, they could and would exclude people from the temple and even the local synagogues, and those were the only ways the people felt they could meet with God. To have it be taken away from them confirmed in their own hearts the opinions of the Pharisees themselves.

It's tough to look on God's children who want to participate in that life and do what is necessary, but are ostracized due to some group's twisted rules. It's not so hard to watch those who don't want to be a part of that life; it's sad, yes, but they've had their "No" that they've said to God, and God listens. The former group want something different, at least initially, but they're in danger of disregarding all God's attempts to reach out to them as they cement the current position of their hearts created mainly by others.

Maybe it was a little easier to see that day, since I was physically there. Looking solemnly at each packet of people as I spoke, some still muttering, they all well understood who were the "ninety-nine" and who the "one". Since that day, almost everyone else besides the Pharisees has believed they're the "one", too. Sometimes they're right.

LXXVI – A Pharisee for a Host

Night: 28
Entry: 3

Luke 11:37-54

Context Summary

Jesus receives an invitation from a Pharisee to eat at his house. Jesus accepts, but shocks the Pharisee by not going through the ceremonial washing beforehand. Jesus answers this reaction with a number of words against the Pharisees and the teachers of the law, pointing out their hypocrisy and greatly angering them before he leaves.

Key Verses

45One of the experts in the law answered him, "Teacher, when you say these things, you insult us also."

46Jesus replied, "And you experts in the law, woe to you, because you load people down with burdens they can hardly carry, and you yourselves will not lift one finger to help them."

Well, it was time for lunch, and I had to eat anyway. . . .
Seriously though, even without my divine nature, I could tell how this meal was going to go down. In between going in to eat and coming out again, I said a few things. Polite society would call the things I said to the Pharisees rude, but I had had it with these fakers and it was time to make some noise. They needed some hard truth. What names hadn't they called me? What had I done that they didn't look askance at? How they longed to twist my words, just as surely as people do today. I had tweaked their noses some, but it was time to get serious with them.

My host on this occasion was a simple legalist who didn't understand any other way of doing things. He had been taught there was no other way. Who was to blame for that worldview? The man himself or the teachers who had taught him? Does it matter when only the man has to live out the life he has? That may sound rhetorical, but it only is for me, not for anyone else.

My host needed a jolt to show him the molehills against which he struggled, thinking they were mountains, were actually molehills! His house was filled with power-brokers, with a vested interest in the status-quo. Would it matter if they were pushed hard?

This started innocently enough: I didn't wash my hands. What I mean is, I walked up to the house, stopped at the entrance and gave my blessing, offering my peace. Then, as if not seeing them, I stepped past the four giant pottery jars filled to the brim with water. I continued right to the tables, sitting down on the floor before stretching out my legs, my shoulder near the table as we did it back then.

That was the jolt. See, they had this delicate ceremony of draping water over each elbow until it dribbled down over the hands that took care of no bacteria; a symbolic cleansing, taken especially to make sure they were ritually clean just in case somebody who didn't fit may have accidentally touched them in the marketplace that morning. If one did it to honor God, the ceremony could become valid (though unnecessary), but as it was built up on human customs and twisted the words of God, it really was the height of the ridiculous.

I wouldn't do my host's rituals at his house, and I shocked him more with my response as I judged them harshly. "You foolish people!" I cried, trying to wake them up. "Woe to you!" I shouted, six times at least.

Sadly, I'm not sure it made a dent, as they all looked at me, wondering how their dinner plans had gone so cockeyed. My host had his hand over his heart (I think it was indigestion), and a hard look on his face. His lack of repentance saddened me. All the Pharisees and teachers of the law there, with their lack of brokenness and mourning over their sin, appalled me. Where was the desire for the true things of God?

So they warned me that I was insulting them. Oh really? I hadn't even reached my peak yet.

LXXVII – In Bethany: Lazarus and Family

Night: 36
Entry: 1

John 11:1-16

Context Summary

Jesus receives word that his friend Lazarus is sick (and in fact will be dead before he and his disciples get there). He delays starting his journey two days before setting out for Bethany to see Martha and Mary, the sisters of Lazarus. His disciples are afraid for Jesus to return so close to Jerusalem, but Jesus brushes aside that concern. He tells his disciples about Lazarus, but they have a hard time understanding him.

Key Verse

[11]After he had said this, he went on to tell them, "Our friend Lazarus has fallen asleep; but I am going there to wake him up."

I had met Lazarus and his sisters numerous times during the course of my travels. I stayed with them whenever possible, which was most every time I went up to Jerusalem. Lazarus had gone out to hear John the Baptist and had been baptized. He told me about the long lines, the hushed whispers all the way to the river's edge, finally being pointed to by John as he stood waist deep in the Jordan. The prophet's hand was clean from being in the water, but when it pointed right at him, Lazarus said he felt like it was a bolt of lightning. John's eyes had been fierce, the pupils so dark as to be almost wholly black, but so wide as to be like rocks in the river as the waters broke over them in ragged waves. While compelling, Lazarus said he thought he would never know peace in his heart, and prior to meeting me he had only ever confessed this to his eldest sister Martha (though she then told Mary).

His sister Martha had heard a neighbor tell about me, and when I had come through town the first time, she had wanted to invite me to stay at their house. Then she thought it would be more appropriate if her brother "formally" (her word) made the invitation. So, she made sure Lazarus did this. He was altogether a shy person, and the whole village was watching him (and while it was a small village by itself, there were always people from Jerusalem there, swelling the daytime population three-fold). It was lovable but rather comical: Martha stood right behind him, her head bowed down, but she whispered to him fiercely. Every few words addressed to me he'd pause and almost look back and I'd see Martha's head bob again. Then, after a loud clearing of his throat, with his Adam's Apple bobbing like it was reverberating, Lazarus would find his voice and his courage once more. Eventually, he got out all the words. Of course I accepted. When alone after dinner, not shy with a newly trusted friend, he and I talked into the wee hours of the night, and he made sure I knew I had a standing invitation.

Martha and her sister Mary were kind. They each had deep spiritual insights, like Martha understanding that, while John the Baptist had been a prophet of God, I was something altogether more, and that her brother (as well as her sister and herself) needed to know me. Martha and Mary took care of their brother, but they each wished to be married and be mothers of many children. Over the course of their later lives, they would be spiritual mothers to hundreds, and they would ultimately embrace that role, but marriage in this world ended up not being for them.

Lazarus wasn't the smartest of men, according to this world. Our records in school were actually fairly similar, and it would have been remarked upon, had we both grown up in the same village at the same time. He was also on the heavy side, though in his youth he had been slim and very fast, kicking up dust as he ran from one end of the village to the other just for fun. It was long since he had run and played games. While he dearly loved his sisters, he wasn't eager for them to follow their dreams, though he didn't think he stood in their way. I loved his sense of humor and self-effacing manner. His humility allowed his faith to shine and dig deep roots.

He used to grimace and dig both hands into his beard, scratching desperately. "My beard itches!" he would cry. It was so funny to look at him doing it, and he knew it. He wasn't perfect, and he knew that well enough, too. When I was desperate for a few minutes alone to pray, he would nod and escort me quickly to his room or the garden, then spend his time warding off everyone else, including my disciples (who were indignant at his: "I don't know where Jesus is!" statements; or his: "He's busy right now!" excuses).

He would have been one of my Twelve disciples if he could have been, but he was old for the job and he had already been singled out for this task, to die wondering where I was. He passed about an hour after the messengers left Bethany to search for me. I would bring glory to God this way, but it also would have been wonderful to heal him beforehand.

LXXVIII – In Bethany: Martha

Night: 36
Entry: 2

John 11:17-27

Key Verse

25Jesus said to her, "I am the resurrection and the life. The one who believes in me will live, even though they die[.]"

We passed by a large olive grove and some vineyards on the way to the village of Bethany, all of them ready for the growing season to begin. The path leading up a small hill toward the village itself was lined with low stone walls. Even before the village proper the farmland stopped and houses rose up, a clear line of demarcation, for Bethany had grown outskirts. The walls continued, outlining each courtyard, the largest ones enclosing a family's own well, storage chambers and main house, some with children playing, running back and forth, others with servants and young men carrying loads or leading donkeys, or women grinding grain or gathering vegetables.

We coursed toward the main street like soldiers returning from a long stretch of duty, not quite recognizing their old home due to some distinct difference. A convoluted accumulation of people scurried into and out of Bethany, passing us by in both directions. As we approached closer to town, numerous people confirmed my friend Lazarus' death as they strode by us on errands of their own.

The bustle of others can be so sad and dispiriting in the midst of our own sorrow, an unwanted reminder of how life continues uninterrupted, even though it will never be the same for the sufferer. At the very edge of the village, I made eye contact with a young girl who I knew sometimes ran errands for Martha as she waited nearby, and I watched her scamper away. She found Martha who ran straight to me, even pushing other people out of her way, some she knew as neighbors and distant relations, and others who were in from Jerusalem, having heard of her brother's death.

Martha came up to me and looked at me, her face stolid, her eyes steely, though there was some puffiness, evidence that this was her brave face she showed me.

"Lord, if you had been here, my brother would not have died," she said. By itself, those words stung. Her heart was crystal clear, however. Her mourning was not over, far from it. The controlled emotion she presented me, something she so evidently didn't feel, was both sad and courageous. Martha's world was disintegrating, and she worried desperately about Mary and hers future. That kind of fear can be lethal to unrooted faith. It searches around the heart and will, seeking safe harbor. Finding none, it begins to wither, and is meanwhile strangled by the very fear that, rooted, it can fight.

Her moist eyes reached out to me. "But I know that even now God will give you whatever you ask."

Martha hadn't cast away her hopes fruitlessly; no, she saved them for my arrival, to cast them in my direction. She had been prepared for this very time, as full of pain and effort as it was. Something inside her had insisted on waiting in the house, even outside the house, waiting not for the word of her servant, but even the sight of the girl running back toward the house. That set her course straight toward me. All four days since her brother's death, she and her sister had talked ceaselessly—when alone—of me, and what would have happened had I been there in time. That's faith, and is beautiful to me.

Yet even greater faith was available, ready to be planted and to grow. She humbled herself to it, surrendered to it. She had known I was more than wise or good, more than a teacher or a prophet. At the same time, she hadn't ever needed me to be bigger than what her eyes or her experience could tell her. So I told her: "I am the resurrection and the life. The one who believes in me will live, even though they die."

Her heart, mind and soul were ready. How I loved that family!

LXXIX – In Bethany: Mary

Night: 36
Entry: 3

John 11:28-37

Key Verse

[33]When Jesus saw her weeping, and the Jews who had come along with her also weeping, he was deeply moved in spirit and troubled.

So then Mary came up to me, after her sister had called her. To those two I was not only "Rabbi" or "Teacher", but "the Rabbi", "the Teacher". Both of them, but Mary especially, because she liked to talk about it with other women, took plenty of abuse for that. They called me the Teacher and I called them my daughters, my friends, my disciples. It was a patriarchal society, of course, but I found it unbearable that no other rabbi would teach women, take them on as disciples. They could be in synagogue but would never be called to follow, or even to sit and learn. All the other women knew this, accepted this, lived this, and scolded Mary for her pride in assuming an intimacy with me—a rabbi—they felt she couldn't, or at least shouldn't, have had.

It wasn't pride in her, of course, but joy. She wasn't thinking of these things then, but was instead consumed with grief. She knelt before me and said the same words as Martha (a phrase they must have mutually repeated a hundred times or more, thinking of me in desperation): "Lord, if you had been here, my brother would not have died."

Mary loved freely and gave her heart gladly. Society didn't see her as the prettiest girl or the best, but still the men missed out on her. I liked her honest smile; it was beautiful to me. There wasn't much for dentistry in those days, and she had a few crooked teeth. So what. When she sat down to learn from me, she never thought about that nor ever cared about how her scraggly hair came out from her head covering.

The cost to wearing her heart on her sleeve as she did was great. It was so sad to see her that day. She trusted in me at least as much as her sister and sometimes more. Mary had thought my love for her and her family would preclude anything like a sickness and quick death happening to them. The sudden revelation that she had gotten it wrong could have fractured a fragile heart and quashed her growing faith.

I thought about all these things and more as she led me to the tomb, just a short walk away immediately outside the village. God gave the human heart resiliency. Combined with the faith to which she clung had her holding out hope even four days after Lazarus' death, when all the other rabbis would say Lazarus' spirit had departed. Perhaps if they had deigned to teach her she would have believed them and become hard-hearted.

How much skepticism and unbelief are the fault of a bad teacher? I've been asking you to consider that, but it is difficult to answer. Society's rules benefitted Mary here. Her rabbi was different. Her rabbi did love her. The things that moved her, moved me, too. In great sorrow and joy, I wept.

LXXX – IN BETHANY: RAISING LAZARUS

Night: 36
Entry: 4

John 11:38-45

<u>Key Verses</u>

[38]Jesus, once more deeply moved, came to the tomb. It was a cave with a stone laid across the entrance. [39a]"Take away the stone," he said.

Like everyone there, my emotions ran hot, but I knew I saw things differently than everyone else there. I saw death as you see it, and I mourned, but I also saw things divinely, things you can't see without great faith, mature faith, where God's power raises and where all will eventually rise. God alone can bring dead things back to life.

Things look differently now than they did, even to me, on that side of my own death. Lazarus' death had certainly brought my own coming one into sharper focus in my mind. That's quite human, isn't it? Thinking of one's own death at a funeral? The thoughts quickly faded, though, because I knew what my job was.

I looked at the tomb, cut into a hill, barren of even weeds around it. It was the newest one, with the older ones set farther back at various heights. Lazarus' tomb and a few others nearest the road had been white-washed, to help travelers avoid them. We gathered there intentionally, and people understood the mourning, even though some felt it was time for the sisters to stop.

When they rolled away the stone, three men heaving against the roughly carved circle set in a rougher trench, I ignored the many incredulous stares. They only did roll away the stone out of their indoctrination of respect for rabbis (though had I been a normal one, this would have been the last time they would do anything I personally told them). Only a few believed at this point, and they were unsure why their hearts felt so expectant; the sisters of course, but almost no one else. The rest were merely indulging the grieving family and the rabbi with the mixed reviews.

"Lazarus, come out!" I called, and there was the most dramatic pause imaginable—it was a moment made for a movie, truly—before he appeared. The body that had started to decompose and smell was restored. He appeared, my friend, staggered and staggering. People shrieked and gasped all around. People want the miracles, but the miracles scare them, too. It's about feeling like they don't have any control (which is ironic since they don't). Breaking through that feeling establishes truth and can launch faith.

Lazarus came forth in small steps, ambling like a monster from a black and white movie, while people continued screaming. His legs were still partially bound, as were his arms. He struggled to free them, which only amplified the connection to those later suspense films. It was actually his belly most people recognized first. Seeing that in profile and hearing me tell them to get him free of the grave clothes finally got people moving. Martha and Mary ran to him and latched onto him like two magnets onto a pole. They cried and he cried; there were no words to describe it for their experience lacked context until that moment. Lazarus finally looked up and, blinking away tears, found me. We just regarded each other and shared a little smile. His faded as he realized something, and I turned to go.

I was so happy to see my friend again, but I left quickly, letting him be in the care of his sisters. I would be back soon, and we would break bread together again, but only once more.

LXXXI – BREATHER IN EPHRAIM

Night: 36
Entry: 5

John 11:46-57

Context Summary

After the raising of Lazarus, the Pharisees meet to consider what to do about Jesus. High priest Caiaphas prophesies that Jesus should die for the nation so that the Romans don't destroy the temple, thinking the Jews are rebelling by following Jesus. The Pharisees then begin to conspire to get Jesus killed.

Key Verse

[54]Therefore Jesus no longer moved about publicly among the people of Judea. Instead he withdrew to a region near the wilderness, to a village called Ephraim, where he stayed with his disciples.

Upon leaving Bethany, I had to be careful. I had a plan for my life, as most of you do for yours. My Father formulated the plan, and I would carry it out. I was supposed to die and the Pharisees wanted to kill me. After the raising of Lazarus, this friction only intensified. So what's the problem? Was it just about timing? I'm coming back in a blaze of glory, too (not like this intermediate diversion, here at this kitchen table), so why not let them kill me right then?

Well, what happens if you leave something unfinished?

The Pharisees could have killed me before what is now known as "Good Friday". That's a hard truth to accept, and for different reasons for different folks. I had to be careful at times, be deliberate, even hide or escape, thus why I removed myself at this time to Ephraim, moving away from Jerusalem just as I had gotten close to it again.

At the same time, God's plans are assured, and I would certainly make it back for my appointment with Good Friday. That's another tough concept for many, that both are true at the same time, especially for people with a more "Western" mindset. This is where I had an advantage in growing up Jewish in the Middle East, and have an even bigger advantage in no longer being purely of that background. I mean, that background is still me, but I can divinely include others. In this way, I can understand anyone, though if I'm down here talking to someone like David, I can only show so many facets at once.

Anyway, I hid out in Ephraim. It was another in a line of rather small villages, very much the same size as Nazareth. It bordered wilderness area and was several miles away from the main roads north out of Jerusalem. The villagers there, basically one extended clan, herded sheep and scratched a living out of the sparse soil. None of the lush green and silver of an olive tree grove or the fertile valleys. Many of the young men would go out into the wilderness areas in small gangs, looking to waylay travelers. They called it "taxation", but they never had much success; hardly anyone went where they could catch them, and those that did were either too big a group for them to set upon—like us—or were as poor as they were—also like us. Besides which, the undulating hills of the area were small, lonely—beautiful in their own way—but usually allowed ample warning of brigands for those tramping through that region, set apart from the road as they were.

We found welcome there, but it was a little guarded. Jacob, the patriarch of the clan, with a hard face, brown and wrinkly, and bulbous nose that distracted from his otherwise lively eyes, listened with other men of his extended family patiently, if at first skeptically. They had heard of me even in Ephraim, but discounted it as news out of Jerusalem, which they thought either all bad or lies (that was a local saying of disbelief, to describe anything as "news out of Jerusalem"). When Simon told Jacob that people in Jerusalem were looking for me, and hinted at the danger, he smiled and welcomed us in. We slept in several different homes, but met each morning in their dilapidated synagogue. Hiding out until my appointed time didn't mean an end to teaching my disciples. That had to continue.

These relationships were important to me. My time was running out. It felt precious. Ephraim was a quiet, little place. The accommodations were simple, but we were all grateful for them. We ate simply there, too, mainly coarse barley bread, small amounts of ewe's milk, lentils, dates and a few salted fish; it would soon seem like a feast. I would get up early before breakfast and go out to watch the sun's first rays bursting over the small hilltops and lighting up the sheep pens. We had escaped the fanfare for a short time. I told my disciples to rest, and I admit that it felt nice to stop, sit and wash off the dirt. I had my last bath there.

The teaching continued daily, but it didn't go exceptionally well. Now that my disciples had seen Lazarus raised, all they wanted were more miracles. They thought King David would rise next, ready to swing his slingshot and kill Pontius Pilate and hew down all the other Romans with his sword, and any Pharisees who stood in the way, too. I knew they'd get the right idea eventually, but I grew tired of their boasting and chomping at the bit. In just a little while, everything would be different.

LXXXII – Meeting with a Rich Young Man

Night: 20
Entry: 4

Mark 10:17-22

Context Summary

After leaving Ephraim, a young man with great wealth comes up to Jesus, calling him "Good teacher", to ask him what he has to do to get to heaven. Jesus first circumvents that question, then tells him to obey the commandments. The man confirms he has done so. So Jesus tells him he must give away all his possessions and come and follow, but the man walks away sadly. At this point, Jesus sums up the encounter for his disciples.

Key Verse

[18]"Why do you call me good?" Jesus answered. "No one is good—except God alone."

Night: 9
Entry: 2

Matthew 19:16-30

Key Verses

[23]Then Jesus said to his disciples, "Truly I tell you, it is hard for someone who is rich to enter the kingdom of heaven. . . ."
[25]When the disciples heard this, they were greatly astonished and asked, "Who then can be saved?"

We were not far from the Jordan River when this happened. It was a beautiful day, and most people were happy just to go about their business. The roads were busy, though not jam-packed, and a steady breeze blew down the valley, providing comfort. I looked over at the river and imagined the long lines of people who used to wait to see the Baptist, ready to repent and go under the water. Each time we passed that way, I could only think wistfully of what those people were doing now. Some of them now followed me, but only some. On this day, people hauled goods or followed the caravans as they kicked up clouds of dust, joining up with them, sticking to safety in numbers. My group was sizable, as well, and became artificially inflated this same way, with few of the joiners-on knowing the make-up of the party when they first intermixed with us.

They soon noticed me, however. That always caused a commotion. As people converged on me, the various other traveling parties became unavoidably intertwined, creating confusion and local moments of chaos. Word about me filtered quickly from one caravan to the other in such close quarters, and what little order was left went by the wayside. The news dispersed up and down the line: a prophet, a teacher, a healer. The excitement grew with each word! Each one of those caused elation, for they wanted to learn from teachers of Torah, or to have the presence of one they considered a prophet, a living symbol to them of God's provision in their lives.

And the healing bit? That's the one that really got them. Happy, excited runners fanned out to the small villages along the way, calling everybody, and other happy, excited runners (boys, mainly, either with too much energy or too many chores and happy to get out of them) scattered out to villages farther afield. Within hours, hundreds of families had streamed in, sometimes bearing their sick children or parents on donkeys or camels or on mats which they carried themselves.

I had compassion for them. I understood the irony of my position, though. They didn't care about it, the irony, that is. When they were healed, some of them (though at first it was usually only a small percentage) listened to the message that was the reason for the healing, pervaded it, was the complete underpinning of it. The rest of them celebrated, but went back to their lives. I get it, but they needed to understand that, without the message, there would have been no healing and—even more importantly—no reason to heal.

In the midst of that, others came, too. They came to ask me things. A well-to-do young man came, too. Most people in the crowd instinctively moved aside to let him pass, perhaps due to his better clothes. Like many, he needed to be challenged, uprooted from his complacency. So, I did that.

"Good teacher, what must I do to inherit eternal life?"

Now, I could talk for days on the subject, or complete it within a few seconds, really. Instead, I knew I needed to get to his innermost places. While there were occasions where something in the past or in the future was temporarily hidden from me in my humility, there were other times, other people, who were completely an open book to me. This man was one of the latter. I did not respond to his question with a question for information, but to engage him in a standard, rabbinic dialogue, to provoke his mind.

"Why do you call me good?"

I loved this young man, but he was so typical. By typical I mean that I saw (and still see) his kind frequently. He had knowledge (I like that), he had high morals (I like that, too). The knowledge and the laws he obeyed had been meant to drive one's heart to God. Though longing for God, the people were getting sublimated by religiosity. I don't mean everything about the "trappings" (or what have you) of a synagogue or church service—those are some of my favorite moments. No, I mean finding value in them and their very rote-ness, instead of finding the true value in the relationship with God expressed through them.

"You know the commandments," I told him, and he confirmed it loudly.

This man found value in his own morality, his own actions. He had heard of me and thought of me as rabbi and even prophet, and he approached me as such, looking for commendation, but I was more than he bargained for. I see it every time someone pushes against me by saying they are a "good person". As one who loves you, may I inform you truthfully: No, you're not. If you say you are a "good person" do you know you're saying you don't need a savior? That you don't need to repent? Can you be that good?

"One thing you lack," I said to him, and he waited breathlessly, elevating himself onto his toes and leaning toward me in anticipation. I smiled at him, and it was an honest one. How I wanted him to follow me!

This rich young man needed to be jolted out of his mindset, as cemented as it was. The cost to him—if he would humbly repent—would have been great, of course, but think of the reward! Think of the blessing I was trying to give him instead! I invited him into my inner circle; that was a rare offer. How many blessings might come of it, for him, for the world? Had he accepted, would you know him now as St. Eliathah? Would you have a few letters from him to churches in the New Testament? Would he gently instruct on the comparison of the riches of this world versus knowing one's savior? Would his humility lead others to Christ throughout all generations?

Yes, him I asked—as I ask some—to give up all his wealth. Him I asked—as I ask all—to trust fully what I tell them. There was a pathway for him, a tunnel I could look down, a possible future for him in which he followed, even haltingly at first, but it was only one path in the midst of many, many rejections.

See, I get it; people have their view of how they think the world works, and that becomes hardened like concrete over time (and it doesn't take that long, either). He had his view of what he needed to do; he thought it would be more than enough. I gave him a comparison point, and he walked away.

What was his fate? Suffice to say it's in God's hands and is no concern of yours. "It is hard," I said to my disciples, "for someone who is rich to enter the kingdom of heaven," and they were astonished, just as Matthew recollects. They believed exactly what they had been taught to believe (you might say "conditioned to believe"), that wealth was a sign of God's favor.

In some ways, it sure is. When it isn't is exactly the moment it crosses from wealth to power. That line is the thinnest in the world. Do you know where it lies? Do you know where you stand in relation to it?

Nothing is impossible for God, meaning no one is impossibly far away from salvation. The rich young man wanted easy actions, assurance and general approbation. He asked a question because that's what one did to a rabbi. It was a question filled with ulterior motives, however, and they were easy to discern. Why not rather start with a more heartfelt, honest question? One that even costs you something to ask, by exposing your fears and weaknesses, instead of from a position of power? "God, where am I in this world? Can I yet be saved?"

Good start.

LXXXIII – THE FATHER'S WILL

Night: 10
Entry: 1

Matthew 20:17-19

Key Verses

[17]Now Jesus was going up to Jerusalem. On the way, he took the Twelve aside and said to them, [18]"We are going up to Jerusalem, and the Son of Man will be delivered over to the chief priests and the teachers of the law. They will condemn him to death [19]and will hand him over to the Gentiles to be mocked and flogged and crucified. On the third day he will be raised to life!"

I'd told them this news before. It bore repeating, so I repeated it. It wasn't prophecy. I mean, it's not about telling the future. It's not about foreknowledge or predestination or any term like it. Believe it or not, I was talking to them about power and control.

This is a statement about God's power at work. There never was, nor ever will be, any more complete demonstration of God's power achieved perfectly in humble submission to His will than my life as the Son. That's why I call Him "Father", for it was His will. Maybe you don't get that these days. Sorrowfully, I know, many have no experience with a wise, loving father who can be obeyed out of love and respect. Worse, too many shrug their shoulders at the loss of this. My statements here say nothing respective to motherhood, for God has both masculine and feminine qualities (indeed, it's where humanity gets them in the first place; they are distinct and good and you're losing that, too, but there's only so many shoulder shrugs we all can handle in our relationship together).

Still, to be on display fully—or as fully as can be on earth—a family with both mother and father, each serving the other as God calls them, will end up raising humble children. In my view, that

221

makes the children strong, as well as godly. (If your first reaction was that humility would make children weak or would open them to abuse, I strongly recommend praying about your preconceptions of how your world is supposed to work; there's some real pain there, I know, and we'll leave the rest of that discussion for our time together.)

I was going to do my Father's will. He had given me all, so that's what I was going to give. As earthly fathers were once earthly sons, they've been designed to know each side of this relationship, like I do. So while your earthly fathers may be hard to obey, they're supposed to have your long-term best interests at heart (and not only at heart, but actively seeking God's will for the whole family). Sometimes they don't. Sometimes they're very bad. Sometimes their efforts are pure but they just get it wrong. They are supposed to be like my Father and show off their power. They're supposed to show off that power by remembering they were sons and showing the way by lying down, not standing up and over anyone in the family. Again, I'm not saying a mother can't do portions of this; it's not about the mothers this time. I'm only saying what I know is best. This is the pattern, and this is God's power structure.

You'll have to deal with it.

LXXXIV – THE GREATEST AND THE LEAST

Night: 10
Entry: 2

Matthew 20:20-28

Context Summary

The mother of the disciples James and John comes to Jesus and asks him to let her sons sit at his right and left hands in heaven. This request annoys the other ten disciples, so Jesus gets them all together to teach them some more, comparing greatness among them to how it looks in the rest of society.

Key Verse

[26]"Not so with you. Instead, whoever wants to become great among you must be your servant[.]"

Think about a triangle, a simple equilateral triangle, resting level on the ground. Now imagine that the triangle is crossed by many lines parallel to the bottom line, a sort-of 2-D pyramid; you've probably seen the thing. Now make entries for where people should be in any organization. For an army, here on earth, the Commander-in-Chief would be placed at the top. Right below would be all the generals, below them the officers down to the 2nd Lieutenants, below them the NCOs and at the bottom the privates.

Now replace those labels with God for the Commander-in-Chief, the apostles and pastors and leaders in the local churches all way the down to the people in the pews and anyone with the smallest desire to truly find God, even if they'd never think of going into one of those local churches.

Got the picture?

Good. Now turn it upside down.

Am I speaking in parables now? Is this a riddle? I'm telling my guys as clearly as I can: God's power structure is in opposition to this world's power structure.

It's not that there isn't a king. It's not that there isn't a throne. There is. It's nice. It doesn't look like an earthly throne or anything, but that's beside the point. God's power structure manifestly meant leaving that for the depths of the earth.

How many people ever serve willingly? I'm pleased and buoyed that it's actually more than you probably think; the willingness portion is just not done frequently enough by those who sometimes serve. When you serve, do you regret it? When you give a sandwich to a hungry person, does it displease you? Is this not the Spirit of God working in you? Keep on doing so, therefore, for you are closer than you think to really knowing me. Only don't mistake the work for the reason.

Do you hear the passion in my voice? They did, the disciples, the Twelve. They were very subdued for a while after this. Bickering like boys just moments earlier, now they muttered apologies to each other and averted their eyes. Such little faith! Yet, I was so very proud of them. I could literally see their full potential and their faith being nurtured, like a seed underground about to burst in prepared soil.

I needed their potential. It's no different today. Not at all. You've heard the same. Full potential is still in view. And still about one in twelve would happily betray me.

LXXXV – ZACCHAEUS WAS A WEE LITTLE MAN

Night: 30
Entry: 2

Luke 19:1-10

Context Summary

As Jesus is on his way back to Jerusalem, he and his disciples pass through the town of Jericho. A crowd gathers, and one man climbs into a sycamore tree to get a better view of Jesus as he approaches.

Key Verse

[5]When Jesus reached the spot, he looked up and said to him, "Zacchaeus, come down immediately. I must stay at your house today."

Good old Zacchaeus! It's funny to think that this day's miracles would eventually result—some 1900 years later—in a rather comical Sunday School song. This day was very nearly riotous, but not with laughter. We had actually come to a point between the "old town" and the "new town" of Jericho. The roads were already getting packed with pilgrims progressing toward Jerusalem, all hot and dusty, loud and sweaty, men and women, carts and camels, all clamorous and congested.

My party was rather large, even for the crowds. It attracted attention. People assumed, as they do, that someone important was at the forefront—they meant a ruler or a rich tradesman, maybe a Sadducee. Many were delighted when they heard it was me.

"Yeshua! Son of David!" they would cry up and down. And, "Teacher! Teacher!" Even a scattering of, "Save us! Save us now!" Cheers and whoops and much hand-raising from dozens of wide-smiling faces, always with children running to and fro. Yet I could look around and see hardly any hearts of faith, hardly anyone pursuing the things of God.

Not that everything had to be solemn and serious all the time, that there can't be laughter along the way. My disciples and I joked around all the time. However, my time for joking was ending, for my time on earth was ending. I looked around and saw plenty of people pursuing the worries of the day, assuming they would reach the end of them. What God had given, life and choices had nearly extinguished.

Many people called out my name that day, joyfully or seriously, but some mockingly. As I said, my time was ending. What could I give that would make a difference to them? The thought exhausted me.

Then, in low, thick branches rustling nearby, I saw him. My eyes were instantly drawn to him, vibrant orange robes easily discernible through the early green leaves. He was around fifty, balding, losing his once-sharp eyesight and his physical vigor. Another nearly hopeless wreck. I knew him immediately. He was rich, oh yes, but he was miserable.

I had run into a younger rich man not long past (*see chapter LXXXII*), also miserable (after half the years), but unwilling to gamble on me. That one had approached with a question and had wanted a pat on the back, thinking if a prophet of God (so he termed me) endorsed him, he would be happy. Zacchaeus was wise enough to know he needed more. An "endorsement" from me (so to speak) was not what he was after. Getting it, however, would let him know that God was big enough to stoop down to look upon a sinner.

Ironic that I had to look up into that sycamore tree.

When I chose him to stay at his house—another irony, as I was usually invited into a house—the rest of the local populace howled in fury and nearly started a riot. The extolling chants died on their lips as the locals immediately spread the story of who was in that tree; so they were furious with me.

When I told them that, "Today salvation has come to this house," they should at least have caught the pun on my name, since it means "God's salvation". Maybe they just despised puns? Understandable, I suppose. Maybe it was because this "endorsement" of choosing Zacchaeus was interpreted by the locals as propping up Roman rule, since Zacchaeus had long collected money for the Romans? I couldn't care less about that interpretation. Was it because Zacchaeus wasn't condoned by the Pharisees? That was who people relied on to give them the news. It was easy for them to go along with what was broadcast so out in the open to them. Or maybe, just maybe, they were apoplectic that I wasn't turning out to be their kind of "messiah", the kind who would have gotten Zacchaeus down from his tree only to string him back up in it.

That's the safe kind of "messiah", not me.

LXXXVI – BACK IN BETHANY

Night: 22
Entry: 1

Mark 14:3-9

Context Summary

Jesus is just outside of Jerusalem, having dinner at the house of a man known only as Simon the Leper. Bethany, the home of Lazarus and his sisters, Martha and Mary, is still abuzz with the shocking miracle of the raising of Lazarus from the dead. At the dinner, Mary anoints Jesus' head by pouring perfume over it. The people deride her, while Jesus defends her.

Key Verses

⁶"Leave her alone," said Jesus. "Why are you bothering her? She has done a beautiful thing to me. . . . ⁸She did what she could. She poured perfume on my body beforehand to prepare for my burial."

First of all, let me say this: Even in that culture, this was kind of weird, though not unprecedented (something similar had happened to me once before, where the perfume went on my feet). (*See chapter XXXVI.*) However, it was also a beautiful thing. Mary, Lazarus' sister who had so recently seen such a great miracle, had a heart of gold. She was intuitive, and took every opportunity she had to be with me. She had heard me talk about my upcoming death, and she had listened better than my other disciples had. She was a disciple—she wanted to be like me—she just wasn't one of the Twelve. The perfume jar was all the inheritance she personally had from her parents; it was to have been her dowry, but she willingly gave it away. It was brave of her. I was so proud.

I mean, this was a big dinner. I hadn't eaten all day. Simon's house was the biggest in Bethany (and, by the way, he hadn't been an actual leper for a while, thanks to yours truly, but I guess sometimes a nickname sticks). Many people had come from Jerusalem; it wasn't far. For most people, it was a festive atmosphere, like a wedding. I was happy, but filled with a welling trepidation, too.

Mary felt it. She sensed my discomfiture. She lived less than 100 yards away and went and got her prized possession. When she broke the jar, weeping the whole time, many people cried out loudly, others dropped dishes which shattered and surprised still others, and loud exclamations seemed to echo throughout the house. Soon the surprise turned to disdain, the contempt of a crowd against a single sinner. I'm sad they yelled at her. She was like one of the prophets of old. Of course I defended her, willingly so before my real burial.

LXXXVII – The Triumphal Entry

Night: 30
Entry: 3

Luke 19:28-37

Context Summary

Jesus enters Jerusalem on what is now known as Palm Sunday. The disciples are sent to find a donkey's colt for Jesus to ride on the way into the city. As Jesus rides, the rest of his party cry out as they go, while many in the crowd spread their cloaks and palm branches on the road.

Key Verse

[37]When he came near the place where the road goes down the Mount of Olives, the whole crowd of disciples began joyfully to praise God in loud voices for all the miracles they had seen[.]

Night: 21
Entry: 1

Mark 11:1-11

Key Verse

[11]Jesus entered Jerusalem and went into the temple courts. He looked around at everything, but since it was already late, he went out to Bethany with the Twelve.

The Big Plunge.

That's what I thought at this time, plodding sedately down the hill toward Jerusalem for the start of Passover week. There's a spot, early on, where we could see the city before it disappeared behind the rocks again. When I looked on it from afar—the first time I had seen it from that vantage in a while—glimpsing the temple and the ramparts and the many crowded buildings and even one of the gates, I saw it for its true potential, a home and a yearning for all hearts.

My own heart beat strongly in my chest. While content to be on my way, I was also—truth be told—scared. I knew what lay ahead, and I had never felt grievous, physical pain before. I would be pleased with a little distraction from that foreboding. Happily, there was more going on here: I was riding a new donkey! (*He gave me a silly "two thumbs up" gesture, but quickly settled back and continued with his recounting.*)

You may not get that, but that was kind of the ancient Jewish "Air Force One" of the time. I'm not kidding. The old Jewish kings had ridden donkeys and each had had their own private one; it was symbolic. Everyone beside and behind me was excited. By riding this young donkey into the city this way, I was proclaiming my kingship after all, in historical manner. My disciples had been waiting for an open announcement, now it was here in a way they only thought they understood (since I had actually been proclaiming it all along). So, they were ecstatic. There would be revelry and jubilation in Jerusalem, just like for every Passover, only this would be unique. Instead of a crowd being cheered, I alone would be, though still so many would misunderstand or make wrong assumptions. As my followers shouted praises and we got to the city gates, the story spread and the whole crowd joined in. The Romans also didn't understand the significance as they looked on from the sidelines. They expected merely a boisterous, Jewish crowd, and they had one. The mass of people thundered and shook the city, but it felt like a stillness to me.

Was this a moment of "calm before the storm", or were we "in the eye of the hurricane"? The afternoon had certainly been full. I had waited at Bethany for my disciples to return with my ride (the donkey's colt) since breakfast. We had come in toward Jerusalem from Jericho, treading on the paths of history. Soon it would be lunchtime, but I would go without. Time was fleeting. I had missed meals during my ministry aplenty, but now I would need to expend a lot of energy. I would miss more than one meal a day until Thursday, and it would cost me. I had no need to save up, though; I was going to give everything, all I had. By Friday morning, I would already be physically exhausted.

My disciples worried me, as I waited for them. This donkey had been prepared ahead of time—way ahead of time—and still they were late. If they could almost mess up something completely foolproof, how could I entrust them with preaching the good news to the poor in spirit? They would screw up that preaching here and there, no doubt, no doubt. They would not be perfect. That, at least, was guaranteed. Some seeds too were guaranteed to fall on good soil, if only through probabilities, but how many? At this time, the future was still not fully disclosed to me; I had humbled my divine omniscience, muting it somewhat. That present time could lead two-thousand years later to only a tiny minority of believers. As I saw my disciples finally coming back from Bethphage, I was okay with this risk. They smiled awkwardly at me as they approached, sheepishly pointing at one another, and tried to explain about a water trough and one of their sandals.

We were late. It was all right, though. We came down the valley and entered Jerusalem. It's called the "Triumphal Entry" and "Palm Sunday" and that's all well and good. I had been feted as part of a group in years past, and was finally feted alone.

As I looked around at the temple and the familiar landmarks of Jerusalem, I knew that my best work was ahead of me that week. If only that tiny minority came to be in the future—your present— they would at least be ever-faithful. I would do the work, just for them, just for you, if need be.

My heart was open to God the Father: I was there to seek and save the lost in order to bring God glory. It would all go wrong— well, in this world's view. Though I had been telling everyone around me about how good it would be to wait for the final appearance of the kingdom, I'm afraid they all still misunderstood, thinking the kind of kingdom they wanted was about to happen.

In many ways, it's the reason the crowds went from shouting "Hosanna!" on Sunday to "Crucify!" on Friday.

LXXXVIII – Stones Thrown Down

Night: 21
Entry: 3

Mark 13:1-2

Key Verses

[1]As Jesus was leaving the temple, one of his disciples said to him, "Look, Teacher! What massive stones! What magnificent buildings!"
[2]"Do you see all these great buildings?" replied Jesus. "Not one stone here will be left on another; every one will be thrown down."

This was not a happy day or a fond memory for me. Though I had just gotten there, it was beginning to feel overly long, this week that we were spending in and around Jerusalem, the last week of my life before my crucifixion. Time crawled, like a work-week in which every day was elongated by overtime (but without overtime pay).

Finally the sun began to set. Looking up, light reflected brilliantly off the temple and eyes had to be shielded. Moments later, angles altered, light and shadow played across the blocks and columns and gilding, brilliant against the deep blue of the sky. My disciples oohed and aahed as they chattered about the day that had just drained me. Laughter under their breaths permeated all their talk. James tugged at my sleeve to gain my attention, to point out the obvious. "Look, Teacher!" The others laughed more and with hand motions encouraged me to agree with them all, their intent subtle, but clear.

Yes, they were right, in a way. The temple and the complex buildings were magnificent.

I sighed before I answered them, though. I had grown up loving the temple, but it was a beloved old thing, choked with the dust of sin and perversion. Nothing was kept sacrosanct. I knew it all had to come down, not to start again, but to convince all the people there that it was time to move on to something more, that, in essence, the temple itself would be elsewhere. I don't mean "move on" the way you use it, leaving something behind; we were quickly moving on toward completion, toward something never yet seen on earth. That's what I saw when I looked at the buildings, and I told them so.

Simon, Andrew and the others were unable to fathom just what I meant. I saw it as a necessary event, the Romans destroying the temple in 70 AD. I shuddered at the thought of it, though. I knew I would lose some people there.

At any point in suggesting that an event where thousands died horrifically, mostly women and children and the elderly, some of you simply cease believing in my goodness (and therefore my divinity). You end up thinking you have a kinder, more loving heart than God, saying you would have stopped it, and therefore assume He is a product of a political movement or mythology, designed ultimately to control you through religious means.

I want to pat your cheeks and look at you sadly when you think like that.

That's basically what I did here to my followers. As with many today, they still didn't get it. But what was standing in their way? Hindsight is the process of things becoming clearer, if one is allowed enough time. Do you know why they wanted to draw my attention to the big buildings? They wanted me to predict when I'd kill all the Romans and kick out all the Gentiles and make the place off-limits to anyone but themselves and people just like them.

It's ironic what I saw when I looked at the stones, isn't it?

LXXXIX – Encouragement

Night: 12
Entry: 1

Matthew 24:1-8ff

Context Summary

Leaving the city for the day after he has told the disciples that the temple and all its buildings will be toppled completely, Jesus takes another question from them.

Key Verse

³As Jesus was sitting on the Mount of Olives, the disciples came to him privately. "Tell us," they said, "when will this happen, and what will be the sign of your coming and of the end of the age?"

It's not like spoiling the end of a movie. This will have to be lived out; that's unavoidable. Why tell the Pharisees they're in danger of hell? Because they're in danger of hell. They could do otherwise. The time is coming, but one's desire and reaction are still up in the air.

It's hard for a person to change. It's mainly due to pride. To let God's Spirit mold you takes a certain amount of surrendering of your pride. My disciples were no different. As I sat on that placid hillside those many years ago, looking out over olive trees not yet ripe, Matthew tells you what they asked, and he tells you what I said. You don't need a different answer. But what Matthew doesn't tell you is that I waited a long time before I gave my answer.

Sometimes I would answer the disciples almost as soon as they had asked their questions, but this time I closed my eyes and thought. It wasn't because of not knowing what to say, though there is a certain difficulty to that. Truth can be known, truth from God, for God wants to be known. Human language can accommodate this to a high degree; it is certainly and easily able to explain all that is needed to know Him. There are some areas where we will continue to struggle to come up with the right words, the full and complete meaning. Theologians have spent millions of hours unpacking these things; this is brave, this is good, but it remains incomplete. Parables remain some of the closest expressions of the spiritual reality ever, though even they fall short. With that said, I didn't pause because it was a difficult topic.

No, it was because I just wanted to think about each of my followers for a moment, and also to continue enjoying the slight breeze, for it was quite warm out. When I opened my eyes, I looked each of my disciples in the eye, to hold their attention and give them some kind of love and encouragement. Simon and Andrew, James and John, those two pairs usually near each other as they were again, heads erect and eyes looking forthrightly at me, with easily discernible thoughts behind them of wanting to appear ready for my orders to move out and take control. Philip and Nathanael, good friends for once muted and introspective, their arms wrapped tightly about their knees as they sat cross-legged. Thomas, Matthew and the other James, looking at me with serene smiles, so unaware of challenges ahead of them. Thaddeus, Simon the Zealot and Judas Iscariot completed the circle around me, each with a troubled look on his face, each trying to picture what power was coming next.

Couldn't I just gather them up and hold them? Yes, they needed love and encouragement (even Judas), would need it for the days ahead. They didn't recognize it at the time (that it was encouragement, I mean), but they would later. That's often the case.

XC – The Parable of the Foolish and the Wise

Night: 12
Entry: 2

Matthew 25:1-13

Key Verses

[1]"At that time the kingdom of heaven will be like ten virgins who took their lamps and went out to meet the bridegroom. [2]Five of them were foolish and five were wise."

A ll I wanted to say here was that if I could get that kind of ratio on wise vs. foolish in real life, I'd take it. Think whatever you want about that. Truth from God makes you grow. Continue. (*He said this last word to me.*)

XCI – THE PARABLE OF THE TALENTS

Night: 12
Entry: 3

Matthew 25:14-30

Context Summary

As Jesus is teaching his disciples, he tells them the Parable of the Talents, where a rich man goes on a journey and he gives one servant ten "bags of gold" (in Greek a "talent", an amount equaling 20 years' wages), another five bags, and a third one bag, to look after. The first two servants double their master's money, but the third one buries it, giving it back to his master when he returns. The rich man is angry with his third servant and wonders why he couldn't earn any profit on what he had been given.

Key Verses

[24]"Then the man who had received one bag of gold came. 'Master,' he said, 'I knew that you are a hard man, harvesting where you have not sown and gathering where you have not scattered seed. [25]So I was afraid and went out and hid your gold in the ground. See, here is what belongs to you.'"

I've mentioned that Nazareth didn't have that many rich people when I was growing up, not as many as seem to be around based solely on the parables I told. No, in Nazareth you'd mostly call us "working class" or "blue collar". Some of you would just call us "hicks". Anyway, the richest man was a farmer turned landlord, but there was another, a rather old man named Jacob, who was rich or nearly rich—by which I mean rich for Nazareth and nearly rich for the bigger town of Sepphoris. He was really quite poor relative to the merchants and Sadducees of Jerusalem, but back then we thought old man Jacob had it all.

Anyway, this old man had a servant name Nicolerius. I liked him. He was young, not much older than my schoolmates and me. We'd see him after school in the village as he ran errands. Many times, he'd stop and join in a game with the kids. He wasn't what you'd call the brightest bulb, but he took time out with us. I've always thought that if you're not that smart, it's good to be nice. In many ways it's preferable.

Well, anyway, he was sent on an errand once that involved him transporting a goodly amount of old man Jacob's money to a businessman in Sepphoris. Nicolerius tried, he really tried. Before he got to the correct merchant's house, he ran into a con man. The story went around that it didn't take long to separate the fool from his money (and although the phrase was not coined there and then, it could have been).

Old man Jacob—who after that was a lot less "nearly rich" than he had been—was quite disappointed. He didn't beat Nicolerius or anything, which a lot of people would have done. He merely sighed and made this motion with his hands (today you would shrug your shoulders) and said, "Well, okay. I'll go along with you next time."

A lot of tongues wagged at that in Nazareth, but it made me tear up. I guess I always appreciate sincere effort, too.

XCII – A Response to Pharisees

Night: 31
Entry: 1

Luke 20:1-8

Context Summary

Jesus is in the temple courts teaching people when he is interrupted by Pharisees who demand an answer from him. Jesus says he will give them an answer if they can answer a simple question from him first.

Key Verses

²"Tell us by what authority you are doing these things," they said. "Who gave you this authority?"
³He replied, "I will also ask you a question. Tell me: ⁴John's baptism—was it from heaven, or of human origin?"

I tell you, I had some good lines in my day, but my response to these members of the Sanhedrin was one of my best, one of my favorites. Oh, how I loved nailing them sarcastically like this. It felt so, so good!

See, I could handle their mockery and abuse, but they were so very hard on my children, my followers. Any of them could have been my children, could have followed me, but if you get the first thing wrong, the rest gets exponentially more difficult. Looking at them, all I saw was hatred for me, but I also saw that most of it was borne out of fear. What would happen if I told them I loved them? Truly, they wouldn't have believed me. They didn't want the kind of God I was showing them, so much like so many people today, both those who are part of my church and those who aren't in my church, those unwilling to come into it to even listen.

Okay, fine. They didn't want to be a part of what I was doing. But to try and stop children from hearing about it, that got me angry. It still gets me angry when it happens.

Oh, you should have seen their twitchy faces, bulbous and apoplectic. First sternness, a façade to cover their fear. They sent their tallest members to try and physically intimidate me; some even stood on benches looking down on me sitting on the floor. "Tell us! Tell us!" they chanted harshly. Please.

Theirs was a power-over-people method, one they so clearly demonstrated. It's an inviting approach for human rulers because it looks like it works. You can get a lot accomplished using it, and it's easy to justify (especially so because it seems like the normal working order of the world). All uses of it are not abusive, but to even suggest that that's how heaven works is nonsensical, at best. My way is the power-under-people way, a lift and boon to those in need, but a stumbling block to rulers and wanna-bes. How they stumbled, ha ha!

When I asked them whether John's baptism was of human origin or from heaven, all their eyes widened (the eyes of the cleverer ones did, anyway). Stepping down from the benches, gathering quickly, spitting sharp, desperate oaths under their breaths they discussed it, but it didn't take them long. They knew they were trapped in their own game. So they tried to evade.

"We don't know where it was from."

Out came my coup-de-grace: "Neither will I tell you by what authority I am doing these things," and out came their pure apoplexy. Maybe, just maybe, that frustration would lead them to repent and seek God.

It was their only hope.

XCIII – CONTENDING WITH PHARISEES

Night: 10
Entry: 3

Matthew 21:33-46

Context Summary

Jesus tells a parable about tenant farmers who beat and kill each of the servants that the landowner sends. Eventually the landowner sends his own son, thinking the farmers will accept him, but the tenants also kill the son, inviting severe retribution.

Key Verse

[45]When the chief priests and the Pharisees heard Jesus' parables, they knew he was talking about them.

Following me—I mean, following my meaning—has never been about having knowledge or intellectual ability. Not following me—I mean, not becoming one of my followers—has never been about having a lack of those smarts. No, for both, it has always been an issue of the heart, of soft- or hard-heartedness.

In the temple courts that day, as soon as I had entered the city and gone up to the temple complex, they came at me. "Who gave you this authority?" they kept asking. "Tell us! Tell us!" Crowds gathered. Had I wanted to flee it would have been difficult, but even without an exit I never felt trapped. I answered them and silenced them; then it was time to really speak out.

The Twelve stood mainly behind me, while the Pharisees and their allies stood blocking my way to the temple itself, cowed but still demanding in their words, their tone, even their posture. Many other pilgrims gathered round, forming a ring like curious children at a schoolyard fight. They whispered excitedly to each other about Jesus the prophet. With a hard edge to my words I told the Pharisees pretty plainly that they were going to hell, and their faces filled with fear and anger.

These men to whom I addressed my biting words and parables were men I loved and, ultimately in most cases, they were men I rejected (because they first rejected me). Looking upon them that day, knowing I was only days away from torment and death (at their very conniving), there was a mixture in me of sadness and anger. The anger was righteous. I don't regret showing it. I knew they were angry, too, but merely because I had poked at their pride and threatened their power-base. I could feel their rage. I matched it with passion. What else could reach them? This had a shot. There is a time and a place for such passion, and this was it.

They had been in charge of something good and wonderful and holy, but they had fostered the confines of their religion and turned it into their god. It looks like God to people like them, and to people on the outside looking in, but in the end, it isn't. Over and over I've seen it happen. Repent! Repent!

I could deal with them being confused that God had moved in an unexpected way (unexpected by them), and I had no problem with them loving their culture. Their ancestors had been called long ago to prepare for these exact days, though. Now people they had controlled were listening to my message; there were people having their lives changed, and what is their reaction? I didn't look on them with hatred, but the irony was the heaviest the world had ever seen!

See, they were actually doing many things right. My people had come out of exile five hundred years earlier more committed to God than when they had gone into it. Out of it had developed these spiritual guides, the Pharisees, whose very name meant the "separated ones", those set apart and wholly devoted to the things of God. That devotion had helped prepare the world for me! Now, at the last, they disbelieved. I spoke against them in the hope they would turn, search their hearts and search the Scriptures. I contend that God had not moved in such an unexpected way, at all.

XCIV – Springing a Trap

Night: 11
Entry: 1

Matthew 22:15-22

Key Verses

[15]Then the Pharisees went out and laid plans to trap him in his words. .
. . [17]"Tell us then, what is your opinion? Is it right to pay the imperial tax
to Caesar or not?"

What would they have done today? I would have been all over Twitter! All my words would have been captured, all my life would have been filmed. Some of you would heartily cheer this thought, proclaiming that you all would finally have full and complete words from me, and no one could twist them.

Oh, really? There will always be those who work to twist my words (for, along with more recording devices these days, you also have more editing devices).

Why didn't I come to earth later, for the first time, when Facebook and web-cameras had been developed, or at least video-tape or film? Why two thousand years ago? I imagine some would ask the opposite question, why did I not come on the scene much sooner in history?

Well, I said I wouldn't speak much of my pre-incarnate life, but I will say this: I waited with baited breath (metaphorically speaking). I wanted to come to earth as soon as possible. There were certain developments in the world that had to happen before I could appear. Otherwise, the time would not be ripe.

God gave you wonderful freedom. In your freedom, you had the chance to develop sooner or overly late. It would happen, though. The conditions needed would be met.

The Spirit whispered to the world, encouraging, inspiring, trying to get you on track as a helping hand, giving an idea even (to those who weren't prophets), then sitting back and waiting to see what would be done with various gifts. God is creative, and therefore people are, too.

What things were needed? Well, just to keep my words I'll say that not cell-phones, cameras or even Victrolas were needed. No, just good, human brains used to memorizing lots of data, parchment (or papyrus, really) and ink. That was the bare minimum to record my words. Then they needed to be disseminated. I needed more than just a few willing hearts. Books were being developed. Professional scribes were in every city, able to copy letters and writings, quickly and accurately. A decently large section of the earth was linked together (I'm talking about the Roman Empire, which joined three continents), all connected with established roads and sea lanes and a common language. A major sea-port had even been finished shortly before my birth nearby in Caesarea, to ensure that connection with Judea (and would be available to my followers only long enough to make sure they had a foothold in this "empire").

I'll explain some of this more fully at a later time (*see chapter CIV*), but no, my words would not be lost to this world. My words would be kept and proclaimed throughout the earth. That wouldn't have happened had I come any earlier, nor been more effective had I waited until the digital age. Why? Because my words have power, God's power, and they need to be heard.

Now I was in Jerusalem for the final time, for the culmination. No more purposeful but peripatetic wandering, gathering followers like a wave, seeing them disperse like the rolling surf on a shore only to build new momentum out at sea again. This was the full swell of people that could be gathered in the city for the final Passover of my earthly life. It would become known as Passion Week. The change was coming, as tension built up and built up toward it. Everyone went around sweating and it wasn't the heat. The people who knew they needed a savior were being shoved aside, my poor little children, shoved aside by the great temporal powers scheming. Final plans were being laid, politics was being played and displayed. I had only days left.

"Is it right to pay the imperial tax to Caesar or not?" the spokesperson said, while the others nearly chanted behind him, "Tell us! Tell us!"

What did I see? A hardening of battle lines as they came to test me. I was nearly ready for the fight. And as for my words being used for entrapment against me? Please! "Show me the coin!" I said to the Pharisees.

What does one do when they're setting traps but spring them? I will always risk the trap for my children.

XCV – THE GOD OF THE LIVING

Night: 11
Entry: 2

Matthew 22:23-33

Context Summary

The Sadducees—a highly political ruling group in Judea, wealthy and powerful, but not as widespread as the Pharisees—ask Jesus a hypothetical, to try and trap him, about a woman who had married seven brothers in succession, each of whom dies: Whose wife would she be in the resurrection? They felt certain there was no reference to a resurrection in the first five books of the Bible—the only ones they accepted—but Jesus quotes Exodus 3:6 ("I am the God of Abraham, the God of Isaac, and the God of Jacob.") to repudiate them.

Key Verse

²³That same day the Sadducees, who say there is no resurrection, came to him with a question.

Night: 31
Entry: 2

Luke 20: 27-40

Key Verse

³⁸"He is not the God of the dead, but of the living, for to him all are alive."

D o you know how many people have a question for me? (*Here he gave me a meaningful glance.*) Would you believe everyone? Do you think I mind the questions? I ask a lot of them myself. Really, I was raised to ask questions, though not necessarily because of confusion or ignorance.

No, we asked questions both to gain and explain. That's how we did it in bet sefer. Our rabbi (while we had one; after he left there was no one to take his place), he asked us questions. In response, we asked him questions, as well, phrased in a manner to show our understanding of the material.

I had a classmate named Matthias who did not like school at all. He would ask back the most sarcastic questions as answer to the rabbi. Rabbi Ben Shimon had great patience. The two of them together made me laugh.

"Matthias, why did God establish kings upon the earth?"

The question-answer probably should have been along the lines of: "Rabbi, how was order to be ensured in Gentile lands?" or something like that. Instead, Matthias said, "Rabbi, have you ever seen a king?"

Sometimes, Matthias' return was more than just needling or an expression of his boredom (he needed to move, a kinesthetic-learner, and the rabbi demanded stillness), but actually had great depth and sometimes vast subtlety.

"Matthias, why did God establish the sun and the moon in their places?"

"Rabbi, why does the school-day take so long?"

Matthias would later say to me that sarcasm was his one, true gift. I liked that. Many of those who asked me a question were serious, somber, needful, at their furthest end of hope. What they needed was compassion; what they sometimes got was a miracle. At other times, they got a challenge they were not expecting. Of course, there were others who truly wanted nothing from me (except perhaps for me to go away), nor, in that capacity, did they deserve my compassion.

I didn't know any Sadducees growing up in Nazareth. They weren't as prolific as Pharisees, and they were rich, much richer than anyone in town, even in Sepphoris. Whether it was their garb of full robes, multi-colored and embroidered with jewels of all sorts, staves with rings of gold embedded in them, or their practiced haughtiness, they were easily recognizable, a class people readily hated and secretly envied (and instinctively obeyed). Like everyone in Nazareth, I certainly knew of them. The high priest was almost always a Sadducee, having enough money to buy the position off of the Romans. "Career politicians" you would call them today. They had wealth, power and condescension for anyone who wasn't enlightened enough to be one of them.

People today think things are so different from when I walked the earth. They are in many mundane ways, of course, but not always the ways you think, nor in many substantive ways.

"Now then," the Sadducees said, "at the resurrection, whose wife will she be of the seven, since all of them were married to her?"

"You are in error," I said to start my response, still sitting, ringed by them but looking past them to the many faces of the crowds beyond, "because you do not know the Scriptures or the power of God."

Oh, the Sadducees got my sarcastic response (full of truth and grace, besides). They furrowed their brows and clenched their fists and the people gasped and clapped behind them. What should these leaders have done as I answered them? Trust me, I've seen every type of response possible. People have fallen on their knees in humility and others have socked me in the face.

It's not that I mind the latter (I'll take a punch any day instead of indifference). No, it's that people decide the world is exactly what they want it to be like, whether they think they have proof of that or not, when what they need is one simple bit of knowledge to make sense of everything. The Sadducees heard it that day.

"He is not the God of the dead but of the living."

Think of every question anybody has ever asked God about someone close to them who has died, wondering why healing didn't come, or justice wasn't served or where was God anyway? I assure you what I told the Sadducees that day is true. "Why did that person have to die now?" you ask. That person who was so important to you isn't dead, that's why. Clearly, I don't mean some form of reincarnation. Nor is that person staying with you in spirit, trying to communicate with you and comfort you. That's not it, either. It's important to remember: There is a beginning to your life; just no ending.

Look, I'm not trying to put a bow on your deep and complex feelings and call it all happy and say there is no suffering. You're not mistaken there; we go through true suffering. I know the truth of reality and still felt the same things you feel when I saw hurting people or I lost someone close to me. It's not for you to know now all the whys and why nots. It would fry your brain. I choose at times to move miraculously and at other times to let a fallen world or sinful choices work their course. The great miracle is usually truth presented and the opportunity not to reject it, to surrender and embrace the offer of a savior.

I wanted to convince the Sadducees to start there: Don't reject me. It was such a beautiful day out when they turned their backs on me, too. One of those days when you don't have a care in the world. Except that that's just a saying for a temporary feeling. What lasts longer in people is prideful vengeance.

I had angered the Pharisees, now I had earned the wrath of their normal opponents the Sadducees. Two political groups of polar opposites had found common cause. It's as if I had united Democrats and Republicans in America together . . . against me. Both were powerful. I stood no earthly chance.

XCVI – THE KINGDOM OF GOD

Night: 21
Entry: 2

Mark 12:28-34

Context Summary

A teacher of the law comes to Jesus and asks him which is the greatest commandment of God. The teacher likes Jesus' response, and agrees with him.

Key Verse

[34]When Jesus saw that he had answered wisely, he said to him, "You are not far from the kingdom of God." And from then on no one dared to ask him any more questions.

It was a pun. Get it? I stood only a pace from this man, looked him square in the eyes and told him this. I raised my eyebrows and let my pupils dilate some, emphasizing the dual meaning. Good pun, I thought. You are not far. . . .

Look, this was a good man, so to speak. His name was Shenumiel, and this was the first time we had spoken, but I had seen him around, not only in Jerusalem where we were right then, but also out in the Judean countryside and by the Jordan River. With bright eyes and an ever-present smile—it remained whether he spoke or listened—he showed his keen intellect by his roving eyes which alit everywhere, but never lingered, taking in each person as a hummingbird takes in nectar. He identified as a Pharisee, but he was low on their totem pole, being more independently-minded than most, and had been baptized by John quite early on, before John had become fully disenchanted with that group and desisted baptizing any more of them. Shenumiel had a good heart, but would he take the next step, a leap of faith? He needed to say that there has to be more than keeping the commandments, more than knowing and even living as one who loves his God and his neighbor. Would he admit he needed a savior? It's the ultimate question for every human being, religious or not.

Some say I should have put it more openly to this man. Trust me—he had heard me enough. I said it openly to the Pharisees. They understood me. I say it openly to all. Would this "good" man respond? Plenty of sinners had. Would he? Did he? I know the answer.

XCVII – FINAL CALL

Night: 11
Entry: 3

Matthew 23:13-36

Context Summary

Jesus speaks out against the religious leaders, calling them hypocrites, snakes, murderers and more.

Key Verse

[13]"Woe to you, teachers of the law and Pharisees, you hypocrites! You shut the door of the kingdom of heaven in people's faces. You yourselves do not enter, nor will you let those enter who are trying to."

I love people. All of my words and actions demonstrate this. I say, "Blessed are the meek," and I say, "Woe to you, hypocrites!" I am the same Jesus saying both of those things. Both show my love.

I want people to follow me. I want them to do this even when they don't fully know what that means. Understanding will come. I wanted more people who were being shut out by the Pharisees to follow me, but I was even here making a play for the Pharisees themselves, one final call to them, even as I risked pushing them to react with extremity. Do you know how many teachers of the law and Pharisees will follow me because of these hard words in this section? Of the group of forty-two that was listening to me that day: exactly one. That one would take a while yet, too.

I was angry with this group, and had been growing increasingly more irate with them all week. During Passover, with so many thousands of people flocking to Jerusalem to get close to God, the Pharisees showed off their full might. I couldn't turn around but see another display of them trampling the poor in spirit. One last attempt at trying to break the powerbrokers, to win them over. It was time to call it as I saw it. This would be a push to the breaking point, either in breaking their pride and winning them over, or forcing their hand to take me down. You snakes! You brood of vipers! The door's going to be slammed in your faces!

Now, I don't count what I said as rhetoric, as hyperbole, as even shouting or lambasting, and certainly not as hateful speech or lacking in diversity. Different words by a different speaker in a different context might be those things. Same as similar words not spoken by me. It's not carte blanche to shout down an opponent. It's about a calculated call to righteousness, leaving the safety of many to fly after a few. It's horrible marketing strategy, isn't it?

If I had merely hinted that there was a chance they weren't being as kind as they possibly could have been, how many would have turned and followed me? It would have been zero. I would have lost many of the ones who turned to me earlier after they had been shut out by the Pharisees, as well.

Does speaking the truth and going after just one sound like it's worthwhile? Don't tell me the odds (and not because you don't really know them, either). It has nothing to do with gambling and everything to do with people's misunderstanding of what is worthwhile. I do this even with the end-game approaching. Don't tell me that the people you look down upon (and you do) are unworthy. I'm the one who'll leave the ninety-nine! If you don't know what that means, you've missed a parable.

Go, if you must, you Pharisees. Go and plot and scheme to take me out. This is my final warning to this group, my final plea. After this, I will voluntarily place myself in their power.

I'm sure they'll be kind.

XCVIII – Washing the Disciples' Feet

Night: 37
Entry: 1

John 13:1-11

Context Summary

Jesus and his disciples have gathered to share what will come to be called the Last Supper. He gets up, removes his outer garments and begins to wash the feet of his disciples.

Key Verse

[6]He came to Simon Peter, who said to him, "Lord, are you going to wash my feet?"

This, I have to tell you, was one of my sorest trials. It wasn't, of course, the complete and real torture and brutality of the Romans on Good Friday that was coming, nor was it the burden and ache of the long fast in the wilderness, nor yet of the steady, persistent, malignant offer to declare myself a worldly king and forego the cross as came all during my ministry days. Yet a trial it was.

Here's the scene: We're in the Upper Room in Jerusalem, ready to celebrate the Passover meal. The room had been prepared for me and my disciples; my public ministry was over. I've told my final parable to the people of Judea, I've confronted the powers that be openly for the last time. My disciples are still wondering which of them is the greatest, and they're still expecting me to begin an armed uprising. Would it come after the Passover meal? The tension in the air around me is thick. A mixture of light and shadows stream in from a low, setting sun over walls and buildings, with burning oil lamps adding their perfume and smoke and flickering movement. The Twelve arrayed in haphazard order at tables are already low, their feet exposed and outstretched away from them. I strip down to next to nothing and—let's be clear—I go around, the backs of the disciples bending, the necks arching to see me in astonishment, and I wash the feet of five of them. Then I come to Simon and he says, "Lord, are you going to wash my feet?" (*He paused and cast a huge sigh before resuming.*)

The devastating sarcastic responses that piled up behind my tongue are almost too many to list. "No, Simon Peter, I'm soliciting magazine subscriptions. What do you think, Pete? Yeah, I'm gonna wash your feet!"

Now, I get it; it's kind of a weird thing in the 21st century, but many of you wear sandals (and most of you rightly avoid the black socks with them). If you walked all day at the beach in them, your feet would need washing, too. In my day, the chore of washing people's feet was assigned to the lowest servant or member of the household. Or the humblest. Simon Peter understood that it could be the former, but still wasn't grasping that I was the latter. This visible demonstration shocked him, and it would stay in the forefront of his mind forever.

I didn't mind touching their feet (though, honestly, they were pretty nasty as far as feet are concerned; a lot of corns, in-grown toe-nails, blisters, scabs, et cetera). I really should have healed them as I went, I suppose, but there were deeper lessons at stake.

XCIX – JUDAS

Night: 37
Entry: 2

John 13:21-30

Context Summary

Jesus has just finished washing the feet of his disciples and encouraging them to treat each other similarly.

Key Verse

²¹After he had said this, Jesus was troubled in spirit and testified, "Very truly I tell you, one of you is going to betray me."

Spoiler alert: It was Judas. Okay, I've of course noted this, as did the Gospel writers, early and somewhat often. It wasn't bitterness, per se, as much as it was a stark warning: Never have more than eleven friends, for that twelfth one betrays you!

No, of course that's not the lesson to be learned, even though people will be false. For John especially, he felt he should have seen the warning signs in Judas earlier. I don't think that was possible, but that's certainly how John felt.

Why did Judas betray me? It's not as simple as saying he was predestined to do so. No, at that moment, when I said that one of them would betray me, all of my disciples feared that God had predestined them; that somehow, they each would choose to betray me and there was nothing they could do about it. That was rather a terrifying thought for them. It brought doubt, not faith. It could be a rather terrifying thought for anybody.

I chose the Twelve. I even chose Judas. He had great spiritual potential in him. Had it gone another way, there might be many men walking about named after him (like in my day when it was a common name). "Hey Jude" might've been written centuries earlier, and been an entirely different song.

Really though, I still get upset thinking about this. After the fact, John and the other disciples hated the guy, though that faded as they matured. Their hatred came only partially out of love for me, for the remainder came out of their fear that it could've been them. When they realized they needn't have feared that, they started to heal. Even many decades later, when John wrote this, his vision of Judas was colored, though he got my words right. The betrayer and the betrayal having grown close and crystalized truly troubled me. "Deeply troubled" would perhaps be a better translation in verse 21.

Why spend so much time and so many tears over a false friend? It's not worth it, am I right?

Only, I say it is. Each relationship I have is vitally important to me. I don't want fewer of them, I want more of them, and deeper. I rejoiced at first getting to know Judas. He believed God was going to do big things during his lifetime. He could feel it in his spirit that God was on the move, believed deeply that this was different than years past. He called it the "consolation of Israel" (which was a mighty fine phrase for him, though not, of course, original to the man). He was strong, too, having had a tough life spent laboring hard and traveling long distances frequently. His mother had died when he was young and his father was stern, taking corporal punishment to heart in a way Joseph never did to my brothers. Through all that, he kept on the lookout for the Messiah. He went, like so many others, to see John the Baptist, but unlike many, he took the prophet's words at face value, that one greater than he was coming. He believed it was me, though he long wondered about what shape I was taking, why I didn't fight like the Jewish kings of old. Even John the Baptist himself had wondered at what kind of Messiah I was turning out to be.

I first saw him—Judas, I mean—when he came to hear me preach, just outside Capernaum. Everyone could tell he was not from around those parts. He wore a red sash never seen on locals and spoke with an accent that betrayed his heritage from the southern towns of Judea. He kept licking his lips as he sat in this expectant position, leaning forward, eager to hear. His heart was troubled and constantly in flux, that much was plain. There was definitely something to fear in him, but I thought that if I had taken on fishermen and tax collectors and wags, this man could have a place among them.

In his future was the betrayal. It was solid, and yet at the same time, it could have gone differently, especially after the deed had happened. In his deepest grief, he despaired when he could have had hope renewed. Had he lasted to Sunday, it could have ended differently. When he first joined our group, he was hard-working and could laugh almost as much as Nathanael, though that part faded quickly. For my part, he was always my friend. Sadly, he didn't last to Sunday.

People walk away for all sorts of reasons. Their choices choke their faith—or what could become full-blown faith—and feed their fear. In the end, I tell them to go, if that's what they really want.

C – Reclining at the Table

Night: 31
Entry: 3

Luke 22:14-16ff

Context Summary

Jesus is still in the Upper Room with his disciples during the Last Supper where they eat and observe the traditions of the Passover.

Key Verse

[14]When the hour came, Jesus and his apostles reclined at the table.

I eagerly anticipated this meal, and for multiple reasons. The savory smell of the roasted lamb both made my mouth water and my stomach turn to ash. I was so hungry. I had barely eaten all day—just a small, quick breakfast of cold lentils on old bread—and hadn't been eating well all week, either. My body craved food, but I couldn't help thinking about the sacrificed lamb set before us, about what it represented right then and what it would soon represent in respect of me. This meal had been on the edge of my thoughts for many months and had finally arrived. Do you look forward to Thanksgiving dinner? I know the standard joke about all the relatives you're not supposed to be able to stand, and how true that is for some of you and not true for most of you. I mean the dinner, though. Your aunt may be obnoxious but isn't her stuffing delicious? Something like that.

All around the table were the faces I knew best in this world. I could know them divinely, but knowing people well, face-to-face, in a purely human way, is also a beautiful intimacy.

Just as certain modern-day meals have their traditions (like grilling out and lighting sparklers on the 4th of July in America), the Seder—the Passover meal—is filled with them. We called it "Order", and I like that term. There is a beautiful connotation to that word and a twisted one, but I like the beautiful one, and I think it does a good job expressing tradition, referring not just to the meal but the entire celebration service around it. The customs of the meal were for my family, my whole Jewish family, but filled with my own story, as well, which also pointed toward the inclusion of my entire family, humanity. The bread and the wine corresponded to me personally in many ways; the sacrificial lamb, of course, too. Still, it was the Passover, the same as it had been for so many years.

All this was going to change. The material in the meal mattered little compared with the function. That is, the "what" was far less important than the "why". For reasons far beyond simple hunger I wanted to savor my very last "Order" service even as I transformed it, bringing to my friends (and thence to the world) a covenant, a promise: my offer, followed by your response. Though it went unrecorded in the Gospels, we did all the regular aspects of the Passover meal all of us had done each year of our lives. John, being the youngest of the Twelve, asked the Four Questions, not expecting anything unusual. (*I looked at him here with what must have been a blank stare, not knowing what he meant. From out of his robe he pulled out a "Jews for Jesus" pamphlet explaining the Passover meal. Very helpful. See "Seder" in the Glossary.*) The parts with the cup and the bread are rightly remembered and recorded, for I changed them, but something else happened when John asked the first question, something none of my disciples recognized.

John asked that first, standard question, "Why is this night different from all other nights?" and I, who was to respond, paused. Some of the boys eventually started forming and muttering the first few words of the required response, as if trying to spark my memory, as if they were embarrassed I had forgotten the words. I hadn't forgotten them, of course. It was a pregnant pause (I have an innate sense of the dramatic). I looked around the room and simply wanted to be with my friends. My whole life I've been tempted—I said no again and did not freeze time, but went ahead and gave the required response. I felt weak-kneed and slowly leaned back down.

As I reclined, I looked around the room. I could see that my friends were not yet able to comprehend how this night truly was different. Exchanging glances one with another, they frowned or (when I caught their eyes) quickly smiled in a somewhat embarrassed manner before turning away and returning to their hushed conversations with each other. I knew they didn't like my haggard, emaciated visage, or my wide-eyed stares that nearly pierced them.

I wondered: Would they fall away? Judas had already left me, in spirit. The betrayal and heartbreak and self-loathing in his heart were as clear as day to me. As we took our first taste of bitter herbs, I turned and looked with difficulty at every face, catching every painful detail.

Simon's face was blank, still lost in mere tradition. Philip was closest to crying, remembering his family's bondage. Thomas was stalwart. And Judas himself? A bundle of nerves. I saw him spit out the herbs and try to hide them up his sleeve.

CI – The New Covenant

Night: 13
Entry: 1

Matthew 26:20-30

Key Verses

[27]Then he took a cup, and when he had given thanks, he gave it to them, saying, "Drink from it, all of you. [28]This is my blood of the covenant, which is poured out for many for the forgiveness of sins."

This was like a going away party, like an ending, like the last thing one gets to do with friends before a seismic shift in life, a move, a marriage, a graduation. So, now it's called my Last Supper, but we were celebrating the Passover, having the Seder meal. Never had it been more intense, especially the blessing over the cup and the bread.

This is how God chooses to relate to people. It's an ancient custom, the covenant. In the Ancient Near East, the rites of the covenant were understood. It was basic contract law between two parties, but also sacred and holy and enduring, a cutting and dividing as much as a bringing together—both at once. As to the basic part, one party states what they will do, then the other party responds. There could be much more involved than that, of course, but this was its simplified terms, and they were all that mattered.

Do you understand my offer? It was clear to my disciples, but the years and miles in between when covenants were the mode and your current culture have eroded some of that meaning. The potency is still there, still able to be understood, still true—never truer—and is still a contract between us, or at least is still an offered one.

Oh, one other thing to consider before we get to this covenant. It was obvious to everyone in my culture of the time that if one said "all" in one instance (as in "Drink from it, all of you") and "many" in the next ("poured out for many"), context dictated that these two terms were actually synonymous. It was an idiom. What I mean is that when I said my blood was poured out for "many" for the forgiveness of sins, it does mean all, or at least potentially all.

"Potential". That's the key word here, although unspoken, not "many", not even "all". There's the potential I see in people for their lives, and there's each person's potential repentance in response to my offer. That means there's also each person's potential lack of repentance, too. The crucial pivot point therefore is my new covenant.

"Take and eat," I said, and the room hushed immediately.

I offer you my sacrifice for your sins because they are too big for you to pay and yet live. It will cost me everything, but this is the plan and I am willing to do it. I want to do it. The covenant—the bread and the wine in the meal, my body and blood, broken and poured out in the sacrifice—is my offer to pay for your sins, to change you. That's the covenantal offer.

"Drink from it, all of you." I held out the cup for them.

It's offered to you, too. The potential is your response. A covenant requires one. My disciples responded. The people who came for healings gave some sort of acknowledgment. Even the disciples who turned away proclaimed their answer, though I didn't like it. I will hear more responses over the next twenty-four hours, then many more after Sunday comes. Eventually I will hear yours, also.

In the room, with night descending fully and candles bouncing shadows across the wall, the hardness of the bread, dry and crackly, remained in mind and in bits in our mouths, now ready for the cup. The wine itself was nothing memorable. The markets were choked—so to speak—with cheap stuff for all the pilgrims in town. Only a few coins for the purpose could be pried from Judas who kept our communal purse. It didn't even smell good as I raised it. I felt flooded with emotion; my body broken, my blood poured out, still metaphorical for just a while longer. I will do this for them, I will!

As they passed the cup around, each of them—all of them—cast their eyes to me solemnly before taking the cup with outstretched fingers, trying to be delicate. It was actually such a tender sight, seeing these workers—fishermen and laborers, tax-collectors and businessmen, young but gruff and wholly gauche for polite society—work diligently to hold something reverentially. A newborn amongst new fathers. They are serious about it, but feel their hands are too large and bulky. While they don't know how to do it correctly, they take it anyway. When the cup came to Simon, my body shuddered and my heart felt momentarily constricted.

Every human being will make a choice. I will know the slightest nod of true repentance and I will perceive the cleverest act of feigned holiness. People have their whole lives to respond. Some have come and listened, then followed, not fully making up their minds, yet eventually walked away. It's difficult to turn back again, but watch my friend Simon Peter through this and hold on to hope.

The new beginning is just waiting for the end.

CII – CROSSING THE KIDRON VALLEY TO GETHSEMANE

Night: 38
Entry: 1

John 18:1-11

Key Verse

[1]When he had finished praying, Jesus left with his disciples and crossed the Kidron Valley. On the other side there was a garden, and he and his disciples went into it.

Night: 13
Entry: 2

Matthew 26:31-35

Key Verse

[34]"Truly I tell you," Jesus answered, "this very night, before the rooster crows, you will disown me three times."

I said this part to Simon about disowning me three times while we exited the city, having finished the Passover meal, afterward to be remembered as the Last Supper. What do you think about that word "truly" in what I said to Simon Peter? Matthew wrote "amen" in Greek, of course. The meaning is nicely what is here in this translation. Truly? I suppose it's just a word to many people, maybe even most. It's hard for many cynics to converse with someone who quite simply only tells truths. I tell truth beyond stating facts. Not to quibble, but my truths are as factual as they get, but focusing on those (that is, only on facts) is a fairly modern trend (and kind of boring, too).

Cynics love to laugh, thinking they're the only smart ones in the conversation. Truth-tellers often appear dim. In my conversation with Simon, who appeared so frustrated in the moonlight, with a giant frown on his face and furrowed eyebrows, he says he'll be steadfast.

"Even if all fall away on account of you, I never will," he vowed. "Even if I have to die with you, I will never disown you."

He feels it strongly; he's having an emotional argument with me. That's not what I'm having with him; I'm just laying some truth on him (to use some modern parlance). I know he feels his current steadfastness keenly, but it's going to go away, rising and falling like the tides (only much, much faster). I need him to be as steadfast as he says he'll be, but I know he won't. Not this night. He will disown me three times.

I see ahead as the divine one above time. God can see all, what is to happen in all choices, all circumstances, all possibilities. Think about all the choices Simon Peter could make in the coming hours. You can read the Gospels and know he followed along when I was arrested, wanting to be near me, wanting to find out what was going to happen, that he would be confronted by servant girls and would be unable to confess to even those lowly ones of that time that he was my disciple. You know that happened, I knew it would happen, but of course Simon did not yet know he would do that.

As he approached the worst night of his life, he grew tense, and deep lines of worry creased his forehead. Had I not warned him, he might have felt so bad that he would have done what Judas Iscariot did after betraying me in taking his own life. One tiny thought saved him: That if I had known about it and not rejected him ahead of time, there was a chance I would still love him afterward.

Was there any chance he wouldn't have denied me? It's not really the appropriate question. As I said, God sees all possibilities. God sees all as potentially saved. Why would I encourage you to follow me if that weren't a possibility? There are all but an infinite amount of circumstances for each life, but the end results are much fewer than you'd calculate, if you put numbers to it. If you're going to go out and do a big action, good or bad, it rarely matters to the outcome whether you choose toast for breakfast or an English muffin. No matter what, certain people never turn from themselves; people you like, people you call good (people who call themselves good). It's too risky for them. I mean they won't take the risk (as if the risk is only on their side). It's as if they think they can't approach God with their need—won't admit that need—and say if there is the smallest chance for me to be saved I will take it with God, betting on themselves instead of counting on me.

I know all about risking everything. I'm about to give it all away, and I'm afraid. But I would do it for the smallest chance that one more will ask me to be their savior.

*   *   *

There was a lot of activity this night. Passover is held on the full moon, so though it was night, there was good light, for there were few clouds. We walked easily about the city, eleven of my disciples and I (for Judas had left us, to go fetch the soldiers to arrest me in about three hours). Though we had had a room for our meal, we were not sleeping there. We had been staying outside of the city. Each night we had returned to the empty oil presses on the Mount of Olives where we had encamped. The facility—not busy now until the olive oil harvest in the fall—easily housed us and its use had been generously donated by Simon the Leper (the former leper) from nearby Bethany.

My heart and my mind were full, overfull, racing with what was left to do. Everything up until that time had been preparation. I prepared my disciples, I prepared the people of Judea and Samaria and Galilee. At the same time, I had been prepared. I had faced trials and tests throughout my life just to meet this night. Even the meal I had just come from had had its effect on the preparation. For the spiritually attuned, there was definitely something in the air, telling them subconsciously something of import was near, though they mainly knew not what.

As we left the gate of the city and crossed the Kidron Valley, we had to run the gamut of the steaming and stinking overflow of lamb's blood, dribbling down from the temple, where thousands and thousands of the animals had been sacrificed for all the

Passover meals, running down into the stream to be borne away by water and time. We crossed the stream and headed up the Mount of Olives. On the southern side were the main burial grounds. Tremors ran through the earth as we walked over this hill, as if something would break apart those graves. I had walked here many times in my journeys to Jerusalem, and often in the past week. I liked familiar places, like many folks do, for they are comforting. We headed for the cultivated side, the garden, the olive grove, with the "Gethsemane" (that was the word for the oil press facility where we slept), and my remaining eleven disciples thought only of their sleeping mats, for the day was over for them.

They were wrong about that in more ways than one. One of them they knew, but were conveniently forgetting, for we called that night "Leyl Shimerim", the Night of Watching. My family had watched back in Egypt when the Angel of Death had passed over the homes with the bloodstained lintels and visited wrath upon those without the mark of sacrifice. This night they were supposed to stay awake willingly, in remembrance of that earlier night.

The facility, the "Gethsemane", was a solid structure built into the side of the hill. We had plenty of room there, and my disciples immediately spread out and started taking off their cloaks and heading for their mats. I told them they could sit there while I went out to the garden in front of the facility to find a place to pray, a gentle reminder to them of their duty.

"Sounds good," Simon Peter said and yawned, quickly able to displace the fear of my prediction of disowning me that night, still forgetting Leyl Shimerim. Maybe he thought if he just went to sleep now he couldn't disown me three times before the rooster crowed, but his half-formed thought wasn't even remotely correct. There was no getting out of this.

"Come on," I said to Simon, James and John, and took them out into the chilly night, giving them the other reason why their day was not yet over. They followed obediently, but wrapped their cloaks closely about them. We all needed to pray and to watch.

Each night during that week I had spent time in that olive grove praying. I like olive trees very much. The olive trees on the hill can live for thousands of years and have no rings dating them. All my disciples knew this place well. Yet I chose to pray there this night specifically because it was known; known to me and known to be used by me. My betrayer would find me there, and knowing I'd be betrayed I went there. I couldn't escape that and wasn't trying to escape it at all.

The familiarity of the place brought some comfort. I felt both perfectly in control and highly distraught, at the same time. In the garden, I faced agony, contemplating being truly alone and without God for the first and only time, a paradox in human understanding, God apart from God. At the same time, I also contemplated the last cup I had to drink.

So I watched, waiting for my betrayer. It kind of ticked me off that my own disciples—having been told exactly what would happen—fell asleep.

CIII – SON-SHIP

Night: 22
Entry: 2

Mark 14:32-42

<u>Key Verses</u>

³⁵Going a little farther, he fell to the ground and prayed that if possible the hour might pass from him. ³⁶"*Abba*, Father," he said, "everything is possible for you. Take this cup from me. Yet not what I will, but what you will."

W as it possible? Could I have avoided that cup, that cup that meant torture and death? At that moment, I felt scared, nearly petrified. Shaking and sweating like I had the flu, grinding my teeth, I knelt on bare rock and thought I would sink into it, unable to escape the jarring pain. Everything was so strained! My hands felt so heavy as I raised them to heaven, my ears throbbed with my own heartbeat, as loud as the roar of a crowd. Why can't my friends stay awake! I am one step away from death! Take this away from me! Take this away! Then, in a moment both sublime and transcendent, at the end of my prayer, a calmness and resoluteness slowly filled my heart and mind until I felt swallowed whole by it. I bowed to God's will.

From the very beginning, the cross was the end of my road. I had always said it was the reason I had come. At that moment of prayer, in asking, had I truly wanted an escape? Would I have taken another path? Allowed the world to spin without my suffering?

At that moment . . . I honestly don't know. I didn't have to know because no other way was offered. No other way offered because I lived out being the Son. The Son is obedient, even to the point of death. That's what Son-ship is. We share that, in small part, as humans. Sons are meant to, and can be, obedient, just as fathers are supposed to have the will, a plan, for their sons.

Sin twists this. It's why you always have been able to send your sons to war and other destructive endeavors. Mothers and daughters share in godly attributes, too, of course, and in amazing ways similar to this (and in more amazing ways different from this), but this night is why I was the Son of God very specifically.

And I had a cup to drink.

I thought about from where I had come, and I mean just that evening, not Bethlehem and Nazareth and Capernaum or even about heaven, but from the Upper Room in Jerusalem, having just come from eating the Passover meal, my Last Supper.

Traditionally in this meal there are four cups. But there is a hidden cup. Today in Jewish homes it is called Elijah's cup, and it sounds pleasant, expectant, hopeful. That cup was symbolic in my day of the cup of God's wrath for the world's sin. The rabbis all asked one another, did that cup belong on the table with the cups of blessing?

It was an intense question for them, but one of the mind and sometimes even the heart. In the end, it was just a cup! Not one of them could drink it, nor had they ever seriously contemplated doing so. A cup of God's wrath was not laughed at by them, but neither had they ever looked into the depths of it.

I intended to drink that cup by dying on the cross. The tipping point approached quickly.

You remember Friday as "Good", and rightly so because of the completed act of my sacrifice, but in many respects—and the one that really matters—"Good Friday" begins here, after sundown as we Jews tracked days. Once I said "yes" to God's plan and started drinking that cup planned for me, nothing would shake me, nothing could turn me from my path, not punches or curses, whips or thorns, nails or the physical cross; not even aloneness without the Father, God apart from God, the very worst. Everyone bet against me, from Satan to my best friends, from my enemies to the tumultuous crowds.

It had to be, because you had to know I'd do it just for you. Is that possible, that someone would die for you, to save you? Is it?

CIV – Scriptures Fulfilled

Night: 13
Entry: 3

Matthew 26:47-56

Context Summary

Jesus is in the Garden of Gethsemane at night. Judas Iscariot comes to have Jesus arrested. Jesus states that he could call upon an army of angels to stop him if he wanted.

Key Verse

[54]"But how then would the Scriptures be fulfilled that say it must happen in this way?"

Judas entered the Garden of Gethsemane then. Behind him a crowd, the thugs and lackeys of the Sanhedrin, armed with weapons that would make a Roman centurion laugh but an unarmed civilian tremble. Simon and James and John arrayed themselves behind me, wide awake now, gasping at their former brother Judas as comprehension dawned on them. There were no words for it, really.

For a long moment, Judas hid his eyes by looking at his feet or turning to make sure he had his full crowd. As the tension built in the grove, filled with the light from flames and the steady mumbling of the wicked and the clanking of the metallic bits of their weapons, he seemed to steel himself for his final move. "Greetings, Rabbi!" he shouted, killing the murmuring as he opened his arms wide. Yet still he wouldn't—or couldn't—move.

"Do what you came for, friend."

My friend. He had shared the meal but had left on his own to gather this group to arrest me, henchmen on loan from the religious authorities. One infamous kiss and immediately swords flashed and it was almost what many of my disciples had wanted for so long: a bloody coup instituting something human-ordained and small and short-lived. I stopped it and asked this question about the fulfillment of the Scriptures. How would they be fulfilled?

What plans can be found in the mind of God? I knew what had to be done, but how to get there? What influence did God use to bring about all this? The prophets had had a vision, certainly. That was a gift, and they had written it down to share it. But how would the Scriptures then be fulfilled? Yes, at that moment, that dreadful moment, I reasserted that I would choose to follow through with the Plan—and I mean that with a capital "P" as the Plan from before time—to sacrifice my life.

What I mean is, what would it take to get to this point?

I want to take a step back from the emotional intensity of my arrest and trials, to show you what was also in my mind throughout this night. Across thousands of years, people had lived their lives, making decisions and changing the course of history. My people were called and were set apart to fulfill a purpose: to get the world ready for my church and the Gospel message.

Much could have gone wrong; much did go wrong. God allowed this freedom, proving his sovereignty. The Spirit whispered to people throughout history, to encourage them to follow, to move, to develop things, to allow the world to be ready for me and not to go too far astray, or if astray to get back on track. It wasn't part of the Plan to have it handed to you. God wanted you—humanity—as part of this process. I waited patiently, though (as I've said) with baited breath.

I needed, at minimum, a number of baseline earthly conditions met in order to come as the Messiah and launch the Gospel message of salvation. I've mentioned some of these already, but allow me to enumerate them, though still in a rather simplistic way. I needed:

1. A large, homogenized empire. In this case, the Roman Empire. It wasn't world-wide, it didn't need to be quite that. It needed to be large enough and include Judea. This was the first empire that had done it, though others had come close. In addition,

this empire needed to have a capital punishment that used trees or poles somehow. Hello, crucifixion. The way they would kill me had to show that I had taken on God's curse upon myself, and every Jew knew crucifixion showed that without a doubt.

2. A common language that would be understood by most of the inhabitants throughout this empire. In the Roman Empire, that language was Koine Greek. It was a second language for us Jews, but most all of us learned it.

3. Established trading routes throughout the empire. Wherever the Romans went, they built roads or established ports. It made the empire smaller, meaning it made all parts accessible to their governing bodies. That made all parts of it accessible to my followers, too (heh heh heh). Along with this, as a launching point, the roads had to pass Jerusalem (and they did) and there had to be a major port within reasonable distance. Herod the Great kindly built Caesarea Martima, and many early missionary journeys began there, until it was no longer needed by the 70s. (*I'm pretty sure he meant the decade of 70 AD, when the Romans destroyed that city.*)

4. At least a partial dispersal of my people throughout this empire. For over two-hundred years the Spirit of God had been inspiring Pharisees (yes, those guys) to go out and proselytize, though they didn't suspect the ultimate purpose. The Scriptures said that all nations would eventually worship the One True God, so they decided they would try and make that happen. They went throughout the Mediterranean world and established their enclaves and built their synagogues and preached. Throughout the empire, wherever they did this, some Gentiles would be curious and some would be furious. This was the fuse that when lit would spread like a wildfire. The Gospel would go to these synagogues where both Jews and the curious Gentiles would hear the message, my message of salvation. Some would accept it and some would not. The curious Gentiles would help

establish the message further, while the furious would just get more furious. In a way, they would do their part, too, helping to cement the faith of those who knew they needed me more than they wanted to escape their friends' fury.

5. The ability to disseminate written communication quickly and effectively. My followers would need many documents copied and passed around, including all the books and letters that would become my New Testament. Professional scribes were in every city so that any of my people who had one of these texts could get it copied and send it on, while keeping a copy for themselves, all very quickly and efficiently (though, truth be told, not without some human error involved, but none that made any important theological changes; even so, and this is a side-bar, you actually have access today to the best Bible ever).

6. My people to develop the rabbinic methods of community. This meant primarily that the Jewish people had to expect that a rabbi would call out disciples to live in community together. The expectation was key for the formation of my church (and should be key for its continuation; any assembly claiming to be mine that isn't a community has some serious problems). The underlying assumption of disciples was not simply to follow their rabbi, but to become like their rabbi. That's actually what I mean by "follow" and having "followers"; it is active and changing and life-long, not passive or just for a summer.

7. This last one is a bit harder to explain as it's not such a physical construct as the others. The Roman Empire embraced both the "West" and the "East". There were not just cultural divides (which were major and important), but there were also "thought divides". Hebraic thought and Greek thought were not just different philosophies, like two political parties. No, they were different ways of embracing reality and reacting to it. Generally speaking—I mean this as extremely basic for the purposes of illustration—in the West (especially of that time), a truth must

be one thing or another, where paradox was to be abjured because contradiction couldn't stand and therefore had to be wrong. Sequential logic, like a syllogism, was essential. For example, if upon reading the Gospels one became convinced of my humanity, a "western" thinker would process the information as: Men are mortal, Jesus is a man, therefore Jesus is . . . and either get stuck there unable to contemplate my divinity, or embrace the end of their concocted logic and disavow my divinity. Not to say that there isn't some value in sequential logic. I can make great use of it, but it can engender a lack of trust in God. In the East (especially what you call the "Near East"), these concepts were to be taken on together; the logic wasn't sequential so much as stacked. Jewish thinkers often call this "thinking with two hands", taking two concepts that seem opposed to hold them together. Their very togetherness helps explain the reality of what is being described. My message would go out with my followers—out into this empire because I was willing to go to my death—and they would write the remaining Scriptures, as well. All but one of those writers would be Jewish, with a background in the East. Most of them would end up preaching to people in the West. It was important to expose both cultural sides to each other, to have them in such close proximity that they needed to co-exist and learn from each other. The strength of the western thought was to see the individual sides, while the strength of the eastern was of holding them together. There's value in the chronological progression and contemplation, and value in the bringing of seeming opposites together. There was purpose to it, do you understand? The purpose was not to make one thing partially the other and so weaken them both, nor to subsume one with the other, but to use both together to help explain the spiritual realities. Need (1) led to fulfilling need (7). With modern language translation, communication, media and travel options, humans have the ability to take care of the first five needs; number (6) is about a personal commitment that is forever necessary, though the rabbinic witness is no longer indispensable. Need (7) is the only one that really still exists as a need today the same as it did back then.

Simply put, God used willing humans to get to this day in order to fulfill what had previously been said. All that work over all those days; I wasn't going to ruin it by letting swords continue to fly. Let them arrest me, in the dark as my disciples flee, with as few witnesses as possible (yeah sure, that's what you do when you know you're in the right). Let's get this show on the road.

CV – AT THE HIGH PRIEST'S HOUSE

Night: 31
Entry: 4

Luke 22:54-71

Context Summary

Jesus is arrested and brought before Caiaphas, the high priest. He and his cohorts question Jesus, accuse him of blasphemy and begin to abuse him.

Key Verses

[70]They all asked, "Are you then the Son of God?"
He replied, "You say that I am."
[71]Then they said, "Why do we need any more testimony? We have heard it from his own lips."

My betrayer came and sold me out to the guards. They handled me roughly. Binding my hands behind my back with a leather strap, they led me with numerous shoves out of the garden. I stumbled and fell to my knees three separate times, each an ironic prayerful pose, each time hastily hauled back on to my feet and shoved forward again. Down the hill, back into the city. My friends were nowhere in sight.

The guards took me to the high priest's house, leading me from the lower courtyard entrance, where a fire blazed and servants sat up and stared, up a flight of stone steps into the upper courtyard. Waiting there in full garb was the high priest, standing out from his lackeys in his blue robe with onyx stones, high white turban above a banded gold crown, and the wrapping around his midsection, the ephod and breastplate of his office. The scowl completed the ensemble, I thought, despite my pain. The guards presented me like hunting dogs dropping fowl at their master's feet, forcing me to kneel. There the high priest and those with him questioned me. Intent on hearing blasphemy, they kept going until they decided they had heard it.

"If you are the Messiah, tell us."

When people have power and are feeling secure, that's when you see their darkest sides. There were many in the nation of Israel that trusted the high priest to bring them closer to God. Of course, he looked down on them. Had he really believed in God, he might have asked me the same questions he did, not sarcastically, but in order to learn: "Are you the Son of God? Are you?"

In some ways, I understood the irony. They had been wounded by my sarcasm and couldn't wait for some petty revenge by unleashing some of their own. They actually enjoyed that more than the feeling of superiority they received as they ordered their men to beat me. All in all, I must say my own comments were wittier. The real difference was, of course, that I knew the truth, having brought it from heaven, whereas they were stuck in traditions that were not proper containers for the truth. They were empty because of lack of faith in God, Whom they couldn't recognize, and filled with faith in what they could see and hear and touch: themselves and their own rulings.

"We have heard it from his own lips."

Yes, they could have asked their questions sincerely, trying to learn. That probably would have been accompanied by fewer punches and kicks. If the Scriptures prophesied a Messiah, though, why should they be so surprised to see him?

What gets me laughing nowadays is skeptics who say I never claimed to be God, when the truth is that's just what these men were waiting for me to claim in order to go ahead with their scheme for my execution. My answer to them, in Aramaic, was a bit clearer perhaps than the English, but it's an answer you can take to the bank. Or you can hit me, either one.

CVI – PROPHESY

Night: 13
Entry: 4

Matthew 26:57-68

Context Summary

Jesus is still at the high priest's house, while Simon Peter has followed, and is in the lower courtyard.

Key Verses

[67]Then they spit in his face and struck him with their fists. Others slapped him [68]and said, "Prophesy to us, Messiah. Who hit you?"

There were many things going on almost simultaneously here, before the council, the Sanhedrin. They hit me, insulted me and questioned me ferociously. In the lower courtyard, where even more people had gathered since I had been brought in, I caught glimpses of Simon. He had fled the garden at first, but he had to know what was going on, he had to be close. At the same time he was scared, so when the people there questioned him, he denied knowing me. That hurt me more than the fists to my jaw, even the ones that knocked out teeth. "I don't know him," my good friend said of me, three times even. Heartache is the worst.

I knew he would be stronger for it, eventually, for denying me so vociferously. If he could survive the biggest waves of guilt and not kill himself on Saturday, he would understand that I still loved him, that I had always loved him and I always would. While he had been fortified by the meal and my final prayers, at that moment I really didn't know what his response would be.

I couldn't keep much attention on Simon, though, for in the upper courtyard, things were getting heated. The leaders had what they wanted. With a nod from the high priest, the guards hauled me up from my prostrate position and quickly started hitting me, taunting me with their cries of "Prophesy!" and "Who hit you?"

The ones who hit me were named Samuel, Levi and two Jonathans. One of the ones who slapped me was, ironically, a Judas (though not an uncommon name in my culture up until then, as you might be aware). I thought about telling them; I mean, actually saying which one did each individual body blow. I wonder what they would have done then? Probably they would have doubled-down on the abuse. I'm not normally passive-aggressive like that, even though I can be chillingly sarcastic when the situation calls for it.

Telling them wasn't part of God's plan, of course (which is why I don't really know how they would have responded; this far into the plan there were basically no variables, so it's not something that can be expressed). I was willing to risk everything and give my life, except to do the one thing that might get them to change their course of action and end up preserving my life. Healing the sick wasn't it; they had seen it. Raising the dead wasn't it; they had heard about Lazarus, at least, and had likely even seen him. Crying out to them that they were in error and were literally opposing God . . . also not it (though ironically, as happens with some frequency, their very opposition to God was ultimately used by God for His glory). Probably answering their sarcastic question wouldn't have cut it, either, don't you think?

No one in power at this time would have let me go. No one. Their power was corrupt and evil, though they used language around it that was couched in godly forms. The corruption had completely penetrated their hearts, and they were slaves to it. Not of their own free will nor under the influence of the devil would they have let me go. All of history bent toward this moment. So they hit me, men who knew how to punish, to torment, to bring pain.

And it hurt.

It's not some weird form of bragging; it hurt, it hurt a lot. Each time a fist landed on my face, bright flashes of light completely encompassed my vision without any thudding sound at all, a bit of synesthesia. Nonetheless I staggered under the blows and the massive waves of pain, but they forced me back up to receive more. They told each other not to disfigure me, though, so they switched to body blows, and the first one knocked the wind out of me. Gasping and flailing my arms about, I struggled immediately to breathe. Two of them grabbed my arms and held me up while the others pummeled me and I thought of going under the water with John the Baptist holding down my head.

But it wasn't the prophet. They had let me slip down as I struggled in and out of consciousness. No, not the hand of the Baptist, but one of the temple guards hauled me back up to my feet again by my hair, happy to yank some of it out by its roots. Laughing at me and spitting on me to show their contempt, they commanded me again to prophesy, though they didn't really want a word out of me. It was just as well. I was in too much pain to tell them anything, and it was only going to get worse.

CVII – PONTIUS PILATE: TRUTH

Night: 38
Entry: 2

John 18:33-38

Key Verse

[38]"What is truth?" retorted Pilate. With this he went out again to the Jews gathered there and said, "I find no basis for a charge against him."

The scene moved from the high priest, the Jewish power and authority, to the Romans, the true temporal power of that time. The mouthpiece of Caesar in Judea was Pontius Pilate.

Poor Pontius. A classic Roman, with the distinctive aquiline nose, imperious manners and hard intellect of his kind. Interested in power and control, he remained ceaselessly petrified that he presided over the one province where he could lose it all at any given moment. His first duty, he felt, was to Roman law, but it was actually to maintaining his rule.

We are all burdened with the choices set before us. Before me was the choice to go to the cross, or to skip over it, go right to the end. The latter would have looked like victory in this world. Had I simply been a character in a movie, there would have been enough pain and challenge for any normal story arc, enough plot changes to show the audience things were serious (though there was no character development, truth be told); we could now skip to the happy denouement: a king upon his throne.

Mine was a heavy choice, and I'm glad I made the right one, made it in the garden before being arrested. People have argued to me that I couldn't have made my choice—or had it go through—without Judas betraying, the Sanhedrin conspiring and Pilate playing at base politics.

Perhaps.

While it could have been—and would have been—others, the true choice is not there, not in what they did to put nails in me (though it was worthy of damnation in and of itself). No, it's what happened later: They all could have repented. It would only be three more days before they could hear a new story (well, I had been telling it already to my disciples—and some of it publicly—but the tenses at least would shift).

Judas could have held on to what I had told him, that I had to be killed so I could be raised. That he was my friend. Could he have heard: "It wasn't just your sin, Judas, but everyone's that put me there"?

You can't bluff me. Pilate blithely turned away from my teaching on truth. He could've said, "The truth will set me free," without irony, but there is no random truth that does that. Only one truth. There is no cosmic balance, no yin and yang equality on truth and lies. One is solitary and the other is legion. I am the way and the truth and the life. "What is truth?" Truth is right before you, right now.

CVIII – PONTIUS PILATE: POWER

Night: 38
Entry: 3

John 19:6-16

Key Verse

[11a]Jesus answered, "You would have no power over me if it were not given to you from above."

Pilate was what you would call "superstitious". He had been raised on stories of gods visiting the earth in human guise, though not fully human at all. Something even slightly similar coming out of the "problematic Jews" (as he called them) frightened him tremendously. He automatically thought I was more than I appeared to his eyes. When he heard from his wife about a dream of me that the Holy Spirit had sent her, he was sure I was more. An urbane Roman he may have been, but they believed in the spiritual world. They had it mostly wrong, which I was charging my followers with correcting, but they at least respected that it was a part of their lives.

Pilate wanted no part of me. When he came at last with intense questions about my origins, his voice echoing off the stone and marble, sounding as if we were within the confines of a cavern, he was baffled and even more convinced I was no ordinary human when I countered him. He was not used to a prisoner standing up to him, especially one looking so physically weak, who had already been beaten multiple times. I nursed my pain, felt the weight of the coming cross and stayed at peace by focusing on the outcome.

It is difficult to describe what it was like in this moment—difficult because of the ever-present language barrier; human language is limited primarily to human experience, and obviously no one had ever been fully God and fully human before. This moment was naturally beyond the scope of normal human experience. Suffice to say, I was in a known outcome. It was sure. It would happen, and was the most frightening thing to ever happen in the universe.

Pontius Pilate could look around at the Roman edifices, see his guards, plumed helms on the ones nearby for ceremony, while gruffer ones were always just around the corner, ready to fight or (more frequently) simply to inflict punishment. What would Pilate say he saw? Not the dust of two millennia later, certainly, but the eternal glory of Rome with its strong right hand.

He had his choices and every choice he was willing to make put him there at that moment. Three times he said he found me innocent (he wasn't stupid), but in the end, he bowed down to his own god. I guess you'd call that god "politics", though it has not just temporal power but also demonic spiritual power intertwined with it.

I almost pitied him. I would have been merciful to him later on, had he wanted it, which he decidedly did not (okay, maybe he was stupid).

CIX – SIMON OF CYRENE

Night: 22
Entry: 3

Mark 15:16-26

Context Summary

Pontius Pilate listens to the crowd shouting for him to crucify Jesus, and he hands Jesus over to the Roman guards. The soldiers mock Jesus, putting a crown of thorns on his head, among other things, and then beat him repeatedly before taking him out toward the place where he would be crucified.

Key Verse

[21]A certain man from Cyrene, Simon, the father of Alexander and Rufus, was passing by on his way in from the country, and they forced him to carry the cross.

A kindness and a cruelty, here at the pause before the final reckoning. How often they come together. Poor Simon of Cyrene, dragged onto the scene by the soldiers, just his unlucky turn. He had to carry the "patibulum", the top of the "T" of the cross to the place in front of the hill called Golgotha, at the old quarry where the "stipes", the perpendicular posts, stood. It wasn't a huge weight, perhaps, except in my weakened condition, so I was grateful. I nearly did not make it to Golgotha.

Things had happened so quickly, too quickly for me to even catch my breath. From Pilate's tiled chambers, down stairs with arched windows, flashing light and shadow in rapid succession. Suddenly I'm encircled by a whole cohort of soldiers, "stripped and whipped" as they called it. Then after draping me with purple cloth which stuck to my bloody back, laughing at me (since purple was the color of royalty for them), they jammed a twisted thorny branch on my head as a crown. No gentleness in their anointing; a dozen large, thick thorns impaled my forehead and drew heavy flows of blood. "All hail the king!" they shouted, then swung their clubs and staves.

"Get it," the centurion eventually ordered, and two rushed out to bring back the wood. The centurion showed his most businesslike face to his subordinates, but his constant licking of his lips and darting of his eyes betrayed his nerves; he heard the roar of the crowd outside which engulfed the city and his mind calculated exit strategies, none of them pleasant. With a quick jab of his finger in my direction, the others ripped off the royal robe, an excruciating moment as it had stuck to my nearly skinless back, then they stretched out my arms and loaded me down with the thick beam to which I would soon be nailed. "Get going!" the centurion shouted, his eyes resting on me briefly before shifting back to business.

Soldiers, of course, know how to be brutal, especially Romans in occupied territory. They did their job well, but all in all had an easy time of it. I was so weak from a week of one-a-day meals and mostly sleepless nights, combined with multiple beatings, I could barely hold the cross. I had lost a lot of blood already, and was nearly disfigured.

Some prisoners died in the beatings, others on the way out to the crucifixion posts. They didn't like it to happen on the way, the soldiers. They'd have to stand around in the streets, exposed and outnumbered, waiting for an officer. They just wanted to keep the procession going, which is why they grabbed a man from the crowd.

I wanted to catch Simon of Cyrene's eyes and mouth a "thank you", but between his agitation and my beaten face, I couldn't communicate with him. His legs shook in fear and he bent low to escape expected blows from the soldiers that I'm glad were reserved for me. Walking ahead of me two paces, I could just make out his bloodied back (my own marked him, transferred from the cross to him) Even unburdened, my gait remained barely a shuffle, my breathing ragged. What were my thoughts at this time, you might wonder, as the crucifixion approached?

I had used the idiom of "carrying one's cross" in my sermons. People understood that phrase, horrible as it was. It was like saying to the French during their revolution, "Carry one's guillotine," or to a more modern audience, "Carry one's electric chair." Sounds worse to your ears than "cross", doesn't it? That's how people in that day reacted to it when I said it originally. It made them blanch or turn away in disgust. How could I say such things? Truly, some who had heard those things were in the streets as I passed, thinking I had gotten my "just desserts". I had said it back then knowing I'd lead the way, though.

While I wasn't physically carrying my cross anymore—thanks to Simon of Cyrene—the spiritual weight was about to crush me. Of what was I thinking? As the crucifixion approached closer with each shuffling gait, the faces of billions streamed through my mind, including yours.

CX – CRUCIFIED

Night: 38
Entry: 4

John 19:18

Context Summary

Jesus is led to Golgotha, a hill known as "the place of a Skull".

Key Verse

¹⁸There they crucified him, and with him two others—one on each side and Jesus in the middle.

I was in so much pain already, one would think being crucified could not possibly add any more physical levels of suffering, yet it did. They took the patibulum from Simon of Cyrene and laid me on the ground. I was so happy not to stand anymore. New waves of pain tore through me as nails went through my wrists, at a bit of an angle so that the nail ended up covering some of the hand itself. In a daze, I was up, the patibulum hoisted by the soldiers onto the stipes, and they crossed my legs and drove a stake through them, pinning me there. As if in a dream I heard two other men scream near me. Then, a moment of silence.

Intellectually, I knew going into this what the pain levels would be, knew what it would do to a body, a brain, a nervous system; how from Thursday night onward I would go from hematidrosis to hypovolemic shock to dehydration to massive cramping to near asphyxiation and finally to heart failure from fluid build-up in the pericardium sac.

Heart failure, the final cause of death? In purely medical terms, yes. Spiritually it was another matter altogether.

Only the intense preparation I had gone through during my ministry, from baptism to my garden prayers, kept me going to the last, focused entirely on fulfilling God's plan to redeem lost people. They nailed me to the cross and hung me up. Was I now the Good Shepherd or the sacrificial Lamb? New waves of pain tore through me as my physical body started breaking down completely. Only with the greatest exertion I could muster kept me raising myself those four precious inches in order to breathe and take some pressure off the pain in my wrists and arms. The effort cost too much; it could not be long sustained.

People shouted insults at me, but the words became muffled and hard to decipher (the tone remained unmistakable, of course). I briefly wondered if I would be able to speak myself, and when I did, would anyone hear?

Then came worse than the physical pain. The weight of sin suddenly thrust itself upon me, the spiritual payment of the sacrifice that I had accepted. Murder and rape, lying and blasphemy, stealing and coveting, anger and rage. An unending parade of hell swept through and landed fully on me. From all over the world, from all across time. Tied into the physical punishment, the letting of blood, it throttled me and enveloped me like a death mask. I thought, "If only I could breathe!" Even then my world would have been one of darkness and pain.

Human beings are wonderfully creative; they take after their Father in a general way. Yet in this fallen world it does mean that creativity extends to methods of cruelty. Crucifixion was the height of this (I should say the "depth" of this), for it was simply horrendous, designed to be slow and tortuous, death by asphyxiation or any number of other final causes. The Gospel writers had seen this, knew it, and they refused to detail it. The crucified have to push upward from the twisted, nailed legs to raise one's chest up enough to get in a breath, but it eventually saps whatever few reserves of strength one has. When that's gone, you die. If death takes too long, the soldiers break your legs and it's over in minutes. They never needed to do that for me. My torture had been supreme. When my death came, they would stick me with a spear, and all the fluid from the heart sac would pour out.

As the Sanhedrin—the Pharisees and Sadducees—had found me guilty of blasphemy, their required punishment was stoning. Why not stone me, secretly, at night? Why go to the trouble of playing Pilate to get me crucified? Dead is dead, right?

Not when the method says more than even the result. I've explained this before, but it bears repeating: Crucifixion was the outward symbol of what I endured on the cross, God's curse. To my enemies, it signaled not just my death, but the defeat of my message. They had seen people come to me, listen to me, be turned by me. They rightly feared losing the masses. But who would listen to the teachings of one cursed by God? Who would follow him? Who would try and become like him?

Only a few fools, that's what they thought (and if anybody was upset about his death, why then they'd simply blame the Romans; they're the ones who killed him). They were more right than you know, and, of course, more wrong than their worst nightmares. See me on the cross, all bloody. Come, follow me! Oh, yes, only fools of this world can do it!

CXI – ON THE CROSS

Night: 32
Entry: 1

Luke 23:39-43

Context Summary

Jesus is dying on the cross. Many people mock him, including one of the two criminals crucified alongside him. The other one has a different response.

Key Verses

⁴²Then he said, "Jesus, remember me when you come into your kingdom."
⁴³Jesus answered him, "Truly I tell you, today you will be with me in paradise."

This. This is what I'm going for. I'm tearing up just remembering this moment. (*I can attest to that. I got up and brought him a box of tissues, though he just dabbed at his eyes with his sleeves.*)

Blackness was upon me, literally and figuratively. I'm up a little bit above the ground, my head about seven or eight feet above it, not quite looking people in the eyes (when I can open them), but close. The Romans wanted many people to see that someone was being executed—as a deterrent—but they also loved for people to be able to see exactly who was being crucified, to get up and spit on them, even. There was so much pain, but it bordered on shock and numbness.

I heard the man on the cross next to me. He, a man in his twenties named Simeon, was not what you would call a good man. No one—I mean no one—would pick him out as going to heaven. He had killed a man, robbed many and, shall we say, taken advantage of some women. He didn't like his lot in life, didn't like who he was, didn't even like his own friends. He didn't care that he deserved what he was getting, that it was fair punishment for the guilty. Struggling to breathe and shuddering under the weight of the cascading pain like all others crucified before him, Simeon first tried to retaliate against the people who stepped up to spit on him or throw something at him, but they were too quick for him, and everything coming out of his own mouth just fell against his own face and body. Every time he made an involuntary motion to try and dodge their abuse, the nails tore at him more, and his twisted face cried out in another wave of excruciating pain. Eventually, he just bowed his head and let them come at him, like they came after me. He was at the end, he knew it, but he didn't want to die. He just wanted and needed and so he cast his last coherent thought my way.

I barely heard his words; I was nearly gone, as well. The shock of utter aloneness, of no connection with the Father, overwhelmed my brain. Crushed by the weight of sin, your sin, my entire being erupted in pain and my heart plummeted in terrifying despair. My dry throat could barely make a sound, but I screamed in my mind until a sort of still, small voice cut through all of that like a clear, understated signal. The desperation in Simeon's voice—in his heart—punctured my own pain, albeit briefly. He needed, and so I offered. The very act gave me hope in that darkness that the weight of sin I bore was worthwhile. I ended this Passion Play with that great thought, even as God the Father turned away His eyes.

Some people watching cried, some for love of me, others simply at hatred of the Romans or empathy for another human life leaving earth. Others cursed or jeered, continuing to heap abuse on us. Many just shook their heads, desiring not to be around such things, claiming ignorance as their bliss and walking away.

How much better to be Simeon on his own cross.

CXII – THE END

Night: 14
Entry: 1

Matthew 27:45-56

Context Summary

Jesus dies on the cross.

Key Verse

⁴⁶About three in the afternoon Jesus cried out in a loud voice, "*Eli, Eli, lema sabachthani?*" (which means "My God, my God, why have you forsaken me?").

This was the low point. The lowest you have ever felt? I have felt it, too. I had compassion for you from the moment I walked on the earth, "veiled in flesh" (as Chuck Wesley called it) keeping me from being able to see heaven, despite how solidly I knew of its being. Wherever angels go (on earth, I mean), they remain spiritual beings only, and can still see heaven and hear God. For humans, it is a different and sometimes bitter experience. Though I knew it beforehand (intellectually, say), it was manifestly different upon incarnation than anything I had ever before known. I see why so many turn to so many different solutions to fill the hole in your heart; there are just so very many ways to feel hurt.

Then you come to your lowest point.

What will it be then? All bets are off; at your lowest point, it's time to get real.

You might say the situation is "life or death", but that phrase doesn't begin to describe it. There's terror, there's pain, even a sort of numbness that keeps one from thinking. At your lowest point, the one thing you feel above all others (whether you realize it or not) is separation from God, from the One Who truly loves you. I know. I know that feeling, that reality. This was my separation from God. The only difference from yours is: I went there intentionally.

Death came upon me. With one final cry, one last breath, my heart stopped. Utter blackness.

Friday. Saturday. To Sunday morning.

God's great plan entered its final phase. My body was stabbed by a Roman soldier. He thrust his pike deep into my chest cavity, creating a gaping, killing hole, except I felt nothing and knew nothing at the time. I was dead. They hauled down my corpse and gave it to some followers. Hastily prepared for burial as the Sabbath approached. Into a nearby tomb in a garden. Wrapped in a grave-cloth, laid out on a roughly hewn slab of rock, sealed up in darkness. That's how I died and was buried.

I died trusting what would happen to me, and I died hoping to get you to follow, crying out to me in that low moment of your own, even if it was, at first, in anger, fear or confusion.

CXIII – NEW BEGINNING

Night: 22
Entry: 4

Mark 16:1-8

Context Summary

Some women go to the tomb of Jesus early Sunday morning, in order to anoint his body with spices. They wonder who will roll away the stone put in front of the tomb, but when they arrive there, the stone has been moved and they see what looks like a young man in a white robe.

Key Verse

⁶"Don't be alarmed," he said. "You are looking for Jesus the Nazarene, who was crucified. He has risen! He is not here. See the place where they laid him."

I'm not going to dwell much on my time in the tomb. Being inside it is about being dead, and my story is about being alive. I've said what needs to be said about what transpired, and you can read the Gospels for the same: dead on the cross, taken down, moved quickly to a nearby tomb, a stone rolled in front of it, soldiers sent to guard it.

In the tomb early Sunday morning I was . . . I guess the word might be "restless". I can't describe for you in a way you could understand or with earthly languages what it was like to be dead and to rise. It's not like what people today call near-death-experiences. There wasn't a bright light and grandma's voice calling to me (not that Mary's mother wasn't a lovely woman). It was not that at all. I can only say it was a lot more.

It was more than a lack of oxygen followed by an ample supply of it. Rising up from the deep ocean is as apt a metaphor as possible. I was both active participant as well as passively worked upon. Air in you raises you slowly to the surface, while one propels oneself with steady kicks from flippers. It's not to say that either one would have gotten me to the surface alone, for that is not a thing. One could not happen without the other for they were working together and were both the same thing, all at once.

That may sound like a paradox, but spiritually speaking, it is a true statement. In fact, spiritual truth is often best explained in earthly language by what at first seems a paradox (that, or parables).

How else to explain to you that there is freedom and foreknowledge? Transcendence and immanence? Human and divine together? Father and Son and Holy Spirit and One God only? The already and the not yet?

I could go on.

I know some—many—will hear this or read this and yet doubt, even scoff. You're willing to believe me human, perhaps, but never more than that. Ironically, many people through the first couple of centuries after I had walked the earth were willing to believe me divine, but never human.

The Apostle Paul would later describe this life in comparison with the coming eternal spiritual life as looking through a "mirror dimly" (*1 Corinthians 13:12, but he quoted a different translation than mine*). We see in part and we know in part now, but then it will be face to face, and I will be able to describe it then, and many other things, as well. That's fine, for death and rising can only be explained in heavenly language and, really, must be experienced to be fully understood. And I have "Good News"—you will all get to experience this!

But after . . . the moment after resurrection. My eyes popped open and I gulped in air, gratefully and desperately, for not enough came through the linen covering my mouth. As I took several in succession, I thought that still it was nice. More air, and fresher, was needed, so I told the burial linen to come off (it fell in a heap), and I told the entrance stone to stand aside (it leapt three feet over). There were soldiers there, but that freaked them out, I tell you. I just needed the fresh air.

Now what? I wasn't going to hang around the tomb. What for? Tombs are for dead bodies or for mourners. I stood up, then bent over and picked up the burial linen. I had time so I folded it neatly and put it on the tomb-shelf, thinking back and smiling over memories of Mary folding garments, and sometimes helping my sisters when it became their chore and the garments were all bigger than they were. I patted the linen once, then quickly turned and went out, telling the stone to roll back as I went. Restless to begin my real ministry, for a short while still on earth, I ignored the dumb-struck soldiers and strolled through the garden.

I knew the women would be along later and would be worried about that stone, but I'd let the angels have some fun that morning, too. They were itching for something to do.

CXIV – WOMEN OF HOPE

Night: 39
Entry: 1

John 20:11-18

Context Summary

Mary Magdalene and the other women are upset to see the tomb empty, not knowing what it means. Jesus approaches them, but at first they don't realize it's him.

Key Verse

[15]He asked her, "Woman, why are you crying? Who is it you are looking for?"
Thinking he was the gardener, she said, "Sir, if you have carried him away, tell me where you have put him, and I will get him."

Night: 14
Entry: 2

Matthew 28: 8-10

Key Verse

[9]Suddenly Jesus met them. "Greetings," he said. They came to him, clasped his feet and worshiped him.

Into the tomb area came this small group, walking close together, their voices soft but carrying in the still morning air. None of them had slept well. Each had woken earlier than usual, eyes aching and muscles throbbing, each had found the others in the shared space where they were all staying. Gathering spices and ointments and cloths without any chatter, they left the house and stepped swiftly and silently out into the earliest fringes of dawn.

One of them attempted to speak but was hushed quickly by one of the others. All the sets of eyes darted back and forth along the quiet streets, half-borne fears of Roman sentries right around the corner disturbing their thoughts. Only the sight of the open gates, patrolled lazily, and a few early merchants and farmers passing through them, steeled their resolve to find the garden tomb just outside the city.

"Who will roll away the stone?" they asked each other once outside the gate, trying to cover up their sadness and fear.

They had no answer, but it did not slow their pace. Fear of the unknown within the city drove them on, even as the sun rose, until approaching the site they slowed to a crawl, huddling even closer together, gripping the cloths that held their supplies. They hated thinking of the tomb because it made my death solid, even more real than what they knew. I had died, though; they had witnessed it. That ran right up against their hope. I wish you could have seen them, so brave, so very, very brave.

Maybe they were helped along by having a task to do, but deep inside shone something bright in them. All their hope had been taken away on Friday, or so they thought, and still they came on Sunday, clinging to hope's remains. That meant there was faith there, able to revive hope that the world had nearly killed. Yes, they wouldn't let go of that hope that all the world laughs at. They knew I was dead and behind a stone they had no ability to move. Still they came, without a plan that included how to move that stone, for they wanted to perform one last act of service and love for me

They dared to believe the words I had said to the Twelve that had filtered down to them that after three days I would live again. Which of the Twelve had believed it as little even as these wonderful women?

They came and saw, Mary Magdalene and Mary the mother of James (I sure knew a lot of Marys, didn't I?), Salome and Joanna, though they came and went as they saw and felt such fearful things. I'll leave that to the Gospel writers, not to put in a coherent, step-by-step story, necessarily, for that wasn't needed, but simply to give you a feeling of that day from their point of view.

Think about just Mary Magdalene, who at one point ran ahead of the others. She was sweet. I mean her disposition. She clung to my words and I loved her like a daughter. Forget extra-biblical things you've heard about her. They don't matter. Whether true or not, I would have welcomed her into my group of disciples.

Many came like her, but few stayed. I went to the cross for the ones who stay, which is potentially everyone, but in reality, so many fewer. There needs to be more, and someday there will be.

Mary Magdalene was tall for women of her time. Like many women, she had married while very young a much older man. He had died soon after, leaving her childless but not penniless. She started following me after hearing me preach one day. The parables made her smile, they made her think, they made her question. When she wanted to tell me without words that she loved me and believed in me, she did what many do: She started paying for things. It was an extension of the role women had at that time of being in charge of the family's charitable offerings, but this now held much more joy for her than giving had before. I loved that about her, too. I knew there would be people like her, though she had her place for more reasons than that.

When I saw her that morning, I was happy and alive, one in Spirit with my Father, soon to return to Him. I found her crying and talking to me like I was the gardener. I kid you not, I really was perplexed why she was crying. Well, that's overstating things a tad. I had seen through human eyes and I knew what death looked like to her, so I had compassion for that limitation. I wanted to speak kindly to her, to all the women along that morning, but also to prod her along. It was time for a new, deeper level of understanding and faith. These wonderful women were ready, and they would be first!

Mary and the other women were in the garden in part out of devotion, but also for that hope borne out of hearing the Good News that knew instinctively that death was not the end. She was afraid, they were all afraid. Even after being told not to be afraid, they couldn't help it. Still, hope wins. That hope held her, held onto her. Mary Magdalene thought she'd be dragging me from some dump to bring my lifeless body back to a tomb. I got a kick out of that thought. So, I smiled and said her name, simply, "Mary."

She smiled back at me and, oh, what a smile. I always remember that first smile that I got. It's been repeated often, and even equaled, but never surpassed.

They all came up to me soon after and worshiped me, dropping their spices and ointments, kneeling and grabbing my feet and kissing the tops of them. Tears on top of tears, but these ones rejoicing, mixed with some shock and fear. The last still moment of the morning vanished, and it was perfect.

"Do not be afraid," I told them, and saw more wonderful smiles.

I want to tell you, I'm so glad I saw them first, hopeless and hopeful ones! They were last in so many ways, according to this world, so I rejoice that they were first to see me resurrected.

CXV – ON THE ROAD

Night: 32
Entry: 2

Luke 24:13-35

Context Summary

Two followers of Jesus walk from Jerusalem to their village of Emmaus, discussing all that has happened, including the reports from the women who went to Jesus' tomb and said he was alive.

Key Verses

[15]As they talked and discussed these things with each other, Jesus himself came up and walked along with them; [16]but they were kept from recognizing him.

What do you think of my activities on that first Easter so far? I spent some time in the garden, did a couple of minor chores, met some of my women followers and then decided to go for a walk. It was a good day, a great day even! It may sound like I was taking it easy, but I saw and did much from the early morning hours. I was the first resurrected one. This body wasn't like Lazarus or any of the others that I had raised earlier, revived but still to die again on earth. This was a new body, never before experienced, a new type of flesh I would give to all who believed in me. No beta version, this (you could possibly call it the alpha and omega version, if you wished), and it felt great!

When I met up with Cleopas and his wife Hannah, out of the city, on the road to their small village, I was ready to start truly amazing people. Why not start them off unable to recognize me? Their grief almost did that on its own. They were so sad and so perplexed, their eyes heavily painted with dark circles. Wanting to understand everything first, they went over all that they knew of me, from the start they had experienced to the finish they thought they had observed, speaking forthrightly and emphasizing each point with their hands. They remembered hearing me speak about resurrection, but had it happened? They wanted to believe, but they were afraid, and their hand-wringing palpably demonstrated their distress. Friday had dashed almost all their hopes.

Almost.

We got to their village, a small place at the top of a small hill, barely a dozen bright stone homes, all lined by short trees bursting with green. I was going to walk on and see who else I could meet, but they importuned with me to eat with them, so I altered my route to go with them to their home. It was great fun to break bread with them and remove myself straightaway. Technically, they were the hosts in their own home, and I was their guest. I took on the role of host, though, and took the bread, gave thanks and broke it. They recognized me then. It was in part because they were given a gift of faith, in part because they finally saw the wounds in my wrists as I lifted up the bread and my sleeves fell down, and in part because of the words I used which made them remember other things I had said earlier.

Then it was time for me to go. I mean, immediately. I had so much to do! There were a number of disciples to surprise.

CXVI – "Doubting" Thomas

Night: 39
Entry: 2

John 20:19-29

Context Summary

Jesus appears to his disciples after his resurrection.

Key Verse

²⁷Then he said to Thomas, "Put your finger here; see my hands. Reach out your hand and put it into my side. Stop doubting and believe."

I met up with ten of my Twelve. They were—as John rightly remembered—"overjoyed" at seeing me. Judas Iscariot was gone, of course, making them the Eleven. Another of them was on an errand, so I needed to come back and see them again. The remaining ten told Thomas I was alive, but he needed more. Indignantly he said, "Unless I see the nail marks in his hands and put my finger where the nails were, and my hand into his side, I will not believe."

Poor Thomas. Which of my disciples didn't have moments of doubt, before or even after the resurrection? Some of my female followers had the fewest doubts, perhaps, but Thomas did not have all that many more doubts than the majority of the Eleven remaining main disciples, all of whom questioned the first fearful yet joyous reports from the women of my resurrection.

Thomas was, like Simon Peter, impetuous. Taller and younger than Simon, had he not followed me he might've ended up a potter, for he was good with his hands and had had some training in it. He had been good in school, and was considered as a possible disciple by other rabbis. When I saw him and called him, he came straight away, his pointed chin coming at me like a dart. His impetuosity caused him problems, such as earning him a dubious nickname. Hopefully you can see the other side of him, the one where he charged into belief when he saw me, shouting (and rightly so): "My Lord and my God!"

Did you notice he said that without actually touching my hands and my side? I held my hands out to him, not to shame him, but to encourage him. Actually, it showed wonderful spiritual insight on his part, intertwined with his doubts. He actually had great hope— he thought we would all die together and go to heaven as a group. He was ready for a bigger vision, and I would make use of his growing faith to help establish my church.

His insight was that, having been resurrected, I would nonetheless still be wounded, perpetually so. It's a technical spiritual issue, really, having to do with the eternality of forgiveness. The wounds from the actual crucifixion process remain (wrists, feet, side), but everything else was healed and renewed. Improved, even. I won't bore you with the details. I will tell you that it no longer hurts and you won't be put off by it when you see me. (*I can attest to that; I've not been put off by it, and I usually get a little woozy at the sight of blood.*)

Yes, poor "Doubting" Thomas. He should be remembered for his best. "Confessing" Thomas? "Believing" Thomas? I doubt those catch on; just not snappy enough, I guess. Regardless, I'd love for more of you to have the faith of the "Doubter".

CXVII – SOMETIMES A BOUNTY

Night: 40
Entry: 1

John 21:1-14

Context Summary

Jesus appears to his disciples again, this time at the Sea of Galilee. Simon Peter is fishing with some of them, but they don't catch anything. Someone they don't yet recognize stands on the shore and calls to them about the fish.

Key Verse

[6]He said, "Throw your net on the right side of the boat and you will find some." When they did, they were unable to haul the net in because of the large number of fish.

This could make one think that these fishermen didn't know their business. As a living metaphor for being "fishers of men" (which makes for a great Sunday School song, by the way, though most Sunday School kids don't really get it), it didn't bode well for the future.

Okay, so I was messing with them there a little bit. I'm resurrected! I'm out meeting up with my disciples, here after they've been out fishing, catching nothing. They went fishing because they didn't know what else to do. They had seen me, but only for short times, and had gone back to Galilee awaiting more instructions. Their emotions were all over the place, though their faith was starting to grow as their hearts and minds were being stretched with the new reality God had shown them. Resurrection, and obviously not meant to just kick out the Romans.

So they went out fishing (and thinking). What was I doing there? Don't you want to say, "What are you going to do next, now that you're resurrected?" Like I'm going around doing magic tricks or something? Well, as the rising sun dappled the waters in between passing clouds, I kept the fish swimming away from wherever Simon and the others cast their nets, until they gathered at once in a place I directed, that's what I did. Of course, I was telling them all about dependence (the fishermen, not the fish), about humility, and they were finally starting to get it. This day I needed to get their attention again.

My full-time ministry on earth was ending, and so it was imperative that I finish preparing them. While I would be with them always in spirit and in truth, it was just plain going to be different. When they were rejoicing and in awe over their catch, and straining with the load, I thought about what lay ahead for them. It wasn't exactly like I had doubts or second-guesses; no, that's not what it was. I simply counted the cost of the path I had set out for them. It wasn't what you would call "pretty". It still isn't.

It would be a path fraught with earthly pain, yes. They would stumble on occasion and screw up. As they scrambled to reach me on shore, their faces beaming with joy, laughing and screaming, pointing at me and trying those awkward side-hugs with each other as they ran splashing through the water and onto the sand, I felt so delighted with them, so glad I had chosen them.

I told them to come and have a breakfast of some of the fish. They came and sat on their haunches or in the sand—James found a large rock on which to sit—while the fish cooked and everyone's stomach rumbled with the smell of the good food. As they ate, they looked over their catch, counting out the fish like bankers with cash, going over their figures three times to make sure they got the tally right, at 153.

After we finished our meal together, they kept wrestling with the number. To each of them, 153 meant something different, though special, and for a while they debated with each other about its significance. Some people still do. I admit numbers are important in the Scriptures, and are often full of meaning, but sometimes it's just an accurate count of fish, too.

What I wanted them to remember was that they would be "fishers of men" and at times, no people would listen to what they offered. Some days were good days, though, and there would be a bounty. I still had more business with them, with Simon Peter in particular. While overjoyed at seeing me from the boat, and unable to contain himself then, he had grown quiet and defensive. I knew him well enough to know that when he sat and drew in the sand with his finger, he felt uncomfortable.

CXVIII – SIMON PETER FORGIVEN

Night: 40
Entry: 2

John 21:15-19

Context Summary

After the large amount of fish are caught and hauled on shore, and after breakfast is eaten, Jesus talks with Simon Peter. Since he had denied Jesus three times before the crucifixion, Jesus asks him a question three times.

Key Verse

[17]The third time he said to him, "Simon son of John, do you love me?" Peter was hurt because Jesus asked him the third time, "Do you love me?" He said, "Lord, you know all things; you know that I love you." Jesus said, "Feed my sheep."

Life is hard. Of my closest friends I had doubters, deniers and betrayers. That's not the only impression I want you to have of them, but it is one of the impressions, and what they did pained me tremendously. They loved me, but they had hurt me, too.

On Simon's side, he had such a weight on his heart and mind. It is hard to come to grips with having hurt someone you love. How does one approach the other for forgiveness? That knee-jerk reaction of self-justification rears its head in humanity almost every time. After that, to actually embrace the forgiveness that is offered only comes by embracing humility.

The sun rose higher on our little beach gathering. Simon's clothes were nearly dry, while the fire had died down to embers. He kept doodling in the sand. Thomas and Nathanael still nibbled on the last of the bread and cooked fish; conversation had subsided. It was time.

"Simon son of John, do you love me more than these?"

He looked over at me sharply, his disheveled hair and red eyes betraying his long night, and answered swiftly, trying by the earnestness in his voice to gain that which he could not give, but could only take out of sheer need. "Yes, Lord, you know that I love you."

As I asked him each time if he loved me, I could see barriers and stones in the fields of his heart. Some were of pride, some of self-recrimination. Clearing those fields is hard work and doesn't usually happen in a day. Do you understand that it can be accomplished if we do this together?

"Simon son of John, do you love me?"

"Yes, Lord, you know that I love you." More fervor, along with some bitterness, the clear thought in his mind of me assuming he had lied or didn't mean it.

"Simon son of John, do you love me?" Tears flooded him now.

Please Simon, don't just hear the question, hear what it's pointing at, where it is leading. Surrender to the calling. Don't try and convince me you are sincere, not when your fervent denials from Good Friday still ring in your own ears! Don't you see it's not about that? Listen! "Feed my sheep."

Slowly he nodded. It was a start. Could I still use him to reach others who needed my love and forgiveness? That is certainly a common enough question. Doubts don't vacate easily. He did, of course, want to be forgiven; would he go further? Some people want the forgiveness but not the commissioning, not a job to do because of it.

Yes, I knew Simon Peter loved me. I knew all his faults, too. He thought it was a bad idea to use him (another common thought), and I could only agree. It was a bad idea, a terrible idea. Use a human? They're the most unreliable people I know! There's not a one of them that won't fail, doubt and at times even deny and betray. Use this particular one, after he had denied even knowing me, not once but three times? Worst idea since calling him in the first place!

Simon Peter—and all the Simons like him—would just have to get used to the fact of my forgiveness. I've given a covenantal promise and I await a response; I demand a response. I've also commissioned him to do a job. He could simply accept it and sit there and nod (a modest reaction), or he could find some "sheep" to feed (a more robust lifestyle change). The job-switch—from fisherman (literally) to shepherd (figuratively)—was the "bad" idea he would ultimately embrace.

CXIX – GOD WITH YOU

Night: 14
Entry: 3

Matthew 28:16-20

Context Summary

Jesus meets his disciples on a mountain in Galilee. There he commissions them to carry the Gospel message, leaving them with a final promise.

Key Verse

20b"And surely I am with you always, to the very end of the age."

Remember one of my names? Immanuel? It literally means "God with us". That is, God with you. I'm emphatic about this! That's why I decided to do this little side project and dictate these things. (*Here he gave me a little encouraging wink and the tiniest of nods. It felt great!*) I'm personally with my believers, and there's always the potential for more.

I had told my inner group, now the Eleven, to meet me back in Galilee. Climbing the low mountain in the morning, we left behind a sizable group, numbering in the hundreds. I felt I could have climbed all the way to heaven and I wouldn't have tired, but instead I stopped before the top, where there was a nice, level place, still grassy. It would be a good spot for a home, overlooking the land below, the surrounding hills, the lake in the distance. I sat and the Eleven crouched down, their hearts and minds overfull with so many memories of Galilee and my teaching flooding them. Out of their mouths flew wonderful praises: "Blessings to you our Lord and God!" they cried. While they worshiped me, Matthew and a couple of the others still processed all these things in their minds, in their spirits. They loved me, yes, but they still had questions. They took my commands to go and preach, but it would take time to surrender fully to me.

Possibly you might think I was disappointed, but nothing like it, actually. I loved them and trusted that that love had captured them and wouldn't let them go. All they needed was my Spirit, and perhaps a little bit of time. They would preach—and write—of me, the Word.

You have the Scriptures and, in many parts of the world today, it's available for free in many languages and in many different translations in English, in your pocket, everywhere you go. This work is not meant to replace that, or even to add to it. I know some of you have read this far, but will balk at reading more of the real deal, the Bible.

"It's a bunch of stories and myths."

"It isn't relevant to my life."

"People just use the Bible to oppress others."

Et cetera.

The first two of those statements that I've heard a lot are laughably untrue. The third, sadly, carries some weight, possibly how you think and possibly in ways different from how you think. If you need an apology for the latter before you'll consider any truth I'm presenting, then come speak with me privately. I'll do anything I can to win you over, except alter who I am (since I declare that it's you who needs changing). You don't need what I say here, though. You need the Bible, for that word is alive and active.

Though infused by the Spirit, it had to be written by humans and had to be a book for all time. The original audience knew more of the specifics and cultural references (even "in jokes" in places), but you have translations, commentaries and teachers. Plus, you've been given a brain! Use it! I'll risk offending you and seeing you walk away from God in order to get some of you to turn to me. I am the great risk-taker. I risked dying for nothing. Don't make it that I risked dying without getting you.

I will be with you.

CXX – THE OPENING

Night: 40
Entry: 3

John 21:25

<u>Key Verse</u>

[25]Jesus did many other things as well. If every one of them were written down, I suppose that even the whole world would not have room for the books that would be written.

What more can I say to wrap things up? These are, of course, just some of my memories and thoughts, just a few of the things I'd like people to know and ponder. After all that happened, I ascended from the Mount of Olives and will fully come back someday. In the meantime, my concern is you.

I'm not asking you to put your faith in me based solely upon these vignettes. No, go and read the Gospels themselves, if you haven't been doing that as we've been going along. It was a joy to sit here and hear them. In some ways, I shouldn't have interrupted David as often as I did, but then again, that was the purpose.

If you're disappointed I didn't address a question you have, well, you can keep on asking me. I don't mind questions, even the hard ones. They often start the most wonderful conversations. I answer every question, too, only understand that you don't always recognize the response, nor appreciate it (at least, not until later, if ever).

If you've read through this work this far, why don't we continue this as a conversation afterward? Some of you have some lovely things to say, and some of you have some harsh things to say. If all the lovely words or all the harsh words that are said to Jesus were written down . . . yes, not enough room for those books, either. So true; but also ironic. I too have things to say to you, some lovely and some harsh . . . or rather, you'll think them harsh at the onset, but only some of you will humble yourselves enough to change the header.

Do that, and I'll be proud to call you my brother or my sister for all of eternity. Truly!

Getting back to this last verse in John, the very last verse in the fourth Gospel. There shouldn't be any confusion about there being four Gospels. Four was barely enough to tell the story! They'll suffice as Scripture, though. I'm not adding to it with this work, far from it. I'm hoping to encourage you to go back to it, to consider it for the first time, maybe, to find new encouragement and faith because of it.

This particular book is written for you, for today. The Gospels were written to be part of a book for all time. Can you imagine how difficult that is? Take any book written even a hundred years ago and most of them, if in a recent edition, will have editorial notes attached to them, in order to make it discernible to you "modern readers". The Gospels were written nearly two thousand years ago. They had a specific purpose and were addressed to a specific audience; then they were added to the book for all time. The original purpose of the Gospels was not as a biography, and the audience was generally not a group of skeptics. So what is in there for you?

I know, I know. I've heard all the complaints. All of them. Over and over again. Some bunch of smarty-pants you guys are, thinking you can dismiss the Bible with one or two witty phrases or condescending curses. Go ahead. I can take it. I'm a big God. I'm the only God. And the Bible is the book prepared for you. This particular book is just one of those things I like to do from time to time, just for a generation, like *Pilgrim's Progress*. You can still read that today and get something out of it. Bit dull, to some. Guess what they'll think of this little tome in four hundred years (if it's ever read then)?

You can go ahead and think of the Bible in that same category. Bit dull. Nothing to it, though. I get it, Leviticus can be dry. You can't always understand the cultural themes that had to be wrapped into the original writings (and cultural themes had to be wrapped into the original writings because I used human beings to do the work). But you get thousands of years of teaching and commentary that could help you, if you wanted. The problem is, many of you don't want that help. Why not? If you've read this far, you're probably really ready to read the Bible, or really ready to have a good argument about it.

So what is it you don't like? You don't like that it says you're not supposed to have sex with that person with whom you presently engage in sex? Is that all?

I'm not being mean. I'm not being capricious. I see with the eyes of eternity. The "don'ts" don't outweigh the "dos". Why don't you try doing the "dos" and stopping the "don'ts"? It's hard. I know it is. I've felt the pressure of being human. I could walk blamelessly because I was also fully divine, and only because I was also fully divine. I don't expect perfection, even though that's the goal to shoot for! There is grace for you, there is forgiveness for you, but I've done my part now. All I can do is encourage you to do yours. I won't stop you from continuing to have sex with that person with whom you're not supposed to have sex. Even if you forget about the point of sin causing division, separating you from me and leading to a real, bad place, think about the blessing that I can't give unless you're trying. I mean this even after forgiveness. Over and above forgiveness. Do you want to be forgiven of your sins? Yes? Then it's done! Over and done with! But now what? Well, read the Bible and find out. Use your brain—that's why I gave it to you. Read this book again if it helps, but be encouraged to do the right thing. Why? So I can control you?

Have you been listening at all?

No, not so I can control you, but because you can't benefit in this life and spread the Gospel when you're not at least trying. Will you try? You can rely on grace while you do. I like effort more than anything. It's a picture to me of what's going on inside, in your heart and spirit. However, it's not usually the picture you might imagine. Effort, meaning your own effort by your own will and strength, will never work, not for salvation, not for spiritual growth. And the picture I get when you strive hardest is not of smiling at church, volunteering for a lot of things or even preaching a sermon, even a great one. We call those things wood, hay or stubble. Each one of those things can have a purpose, but they simply are not the gold or silver one intends them to be. Effort leads to desire, desire leads to surrender, surrender leads to the filling of the Spirit.

So, when there is sincere effort on your part, I appreciate it, and while you might look like a superstar to people on earth, the picture I see is one of struggle, of guilt, of rage, of frailty. Your self-effort always ends in failure. When you realize it is just the moment that your "effort" starts paying off.

When that effort leads to your proper response to my covenantal offer to be your Lord and your God, then you're ready to be filled by the Spirit. The effort becomes mine, all mine.

So, of course I like sincere effort. Why do you think I like Simon Peter and James and John? I even loved Judas, but he stopped trying. Simon Peter never stopped trying. It means he never stopped having failures, but he never stopped trying to follow. He figured out he had grace from me to cover all his failures. Why can't it cover yours? Do what I modeled out for you: Go somewhere by yourself and pray, then go back out to do ministry. We'll deal with all the issues as they come. Then, you'll wind up not just following me, but becoming more like me.

What else could it be keeping you away? You don't like: "There is no other name given under heaven by which you must be saved"? (*See Acts 4:12.*) You don't like the lack of diversity?

Tell me, do you get a lot of diversity when you put out a simple math question like: $2+2 = $ _____?

There are, technically speaking, an infinite number of answers that can be put into that blank, but the only one that is most obviously called for is "4". The kingdom of heaven is like a mathematical equation of the simplest sort. There's one answer to the question and a million wrong answers. Is that lack of diversity?

Yes, I know the mathematical types can put some strange responses in there and say it's correct, but I think Occam's Razor can apply here, that the simple answer was the one required in this example. See, this is why parables are only so good at explaining heaven. They don't work great with pure concrete thinkers and smart-alecks.

I know. I can be one.

But I have all sorts of different thought-patterns, not just my ancient Judaic one. I have all love languages in my psyche: I proclaim love in every way you could best understand it. Believe me when I say to you that you are important to me. I've pursued you to this point, and I may even pursue you to the end, but I will let you go now, if that's what you want, and I will also never let go if that's what you want instead. Your sins can be paid for, as long as you think you have sins that need to be paid for. You can have eternal life and you can have a changed life on earth, or not. I've opened up the way for you.

Who wouldn't want that?

Epilogue: The "Twenty" Questions I Asked Jesus and His Responses

To recap, Jesus told me he'd let me ask him twenty questions, though before I realized the game was on, I had asked five. At first, I felt like I had let down humanity, but then it made me laugh (as I now realize was his intention). Besides, I probably wouldn't have asked your question, anyway. My questions (and additional comments) are in italics. Jesus' responses follow.

<u>The first five:</u>

1. *Is this "Inspiration"?*

No, it's dictation.

2. *Those 20 questions... it sounds like a game. Do they have to be "yes or no" type questions?*

No.

3. *Why 20?*

It's a nice, round number. Seventeen questions left.

4. *Wait, did we start already?*

Yes, when you asked if this was inspiration.

5. *Can we go back to the beginning? Let me rephrase that! That's not a question!*

Too late. The answer is no. Down to fifteen.

<u>Here are the rest of the questions I asked him, along with his
responses:</u>

6.   Jesus, have you ever done this before?

Have I ever woken up somebody for forty straight nights and
talked to them? No, not in this way. I've inspired a lot of books
over the years. The Gospels were one thing, and inspired works of
art and science and literature and other disciplines is another. The
writing of the Gospels was different than this, as I say, although the
writers were chosen because they were ready to write them, like
you were ready to stay up with me.

7.   Do you ever regret coming down to earth?

You mean back then? No, I don't. Not for a minute. I still
have a lot of emotions over some of the things that happened.
They were just a few days out of all the days of history and were
with just a few people out of all the people on earth, but they still
resonate. With me, because I lived them, but with many other
people and whole societies because they were written about in the
Gospels. Do I regret it? David, as your grandmother would say
when she was otherwise speechless: "Mercy!"

8.   What's your favorite verse in the Bible?

Galatians 4:20. No, I'm kidding about that. I love the whole
thing, of course, but I'll pick out a verse for you. It would be a
cliché but not untrue to say John 3:16, but if you think about it
enough, you can understand all of God's love and purpose in the
very first verse, Genesis 1:1, so I'll lean on that one. "In the
beginning, God created the heavens and the earth."

9.   Is there anything you wish you had done differently?

For the things that matter, no. I did what I came to do. I started the community I wanted to start. I reached some people and missed out on many others. They walked away and I had to respect that.

For the rest, if I had to do it all over again, I'd probably get a dog. It would've been nice to take him out on walks, in the desert, through the villages, across the lake. That sort of thing.

10. Do all dogs go to heaven?

That's one of your twenty questions, is it?

I'm sorry, I kind of panicked after you mentioned a dog.

Trying to blame me again? I'm kidding, I understand. Listen, I'll tell you the same thing I tell all the dogs: Worry about the humans.

11. What was it like walking on water?

I've said this in other places, but human language and experience can't correctly express the human and divine together in me. Walking on water was no trickier for me than walking on sand. The feeling on the soles of your feet is different, that's about all. In the end, it's a miracle in the sense of course that it defies the natural order that God set up. However, what is that? I mean, if you believe that I died for your sins and rose again on Easter, what is the walking on water in comparison to that? Miracles like that were for a purpose, and that was to teach and to underscore the message that God was there to save you from your sins and give you His freedom. They were about God showing compassion vividly to His people. I wasn't out to prove I was better than anybody else. I didn't need to do that. Why is this particular miracle so difficult for so many people to believe?

12. You mention God a lot, and it sometimes sounds like He's different from you, or separate. Can you explain that?

Once again, it's a restriction on human languages and human minds to fully comprehend God's spiritual reality. It was understood by the writers of the New Testament that there is only one God. It was a baseline assumption they never questioned. They also became fully convinced of my divinity without ever challenging (or feeling the need to challenge) their belief in the one God (and rightly so). They received the Holy Spirit and never questioned that. What had been revealed to them and gifted to them they described in many ways in their writings, all of which were true, but none of which satisfied everybody. This is the limitation I mentioned.

As years passed, believers kept thinking about it and finally hit upon the word "Trinity" to describe God, and then struggled with how to explain that. I only was completely separate from the Father on the cross; the worst thing imaginable. Otherwise, the "separateness" you seem to experience is in reality the blessing that God has given you, to get to know Him as Father, Son and Holy Spirit, different Persons, different aspects of one God.

One of the true characteristics of God is that God is light. When you look at photons of light, what do you observe? Is it a particle? Is it a wave? It seems to be two things at once, truly but illogically. In some ways very apropos of God.

Here is an incomplete metaphor that many people have tried. Now, when they try it, it fails, but that's because it can only be incomplete. If you get that it will end up incomplete, that can help in understanding it. Anyway, you are a father, David. You have two children. They know you differently than any other people know you. You're also a son. You have a mother and a father, and they know you differently than anyone else does. You also have a wife, and so you're a husband. Your wife knows you in a way no one else does. So you are father, son and husband, yet you're the same person, you're just one David. You play your roles, and they also intermingle. Your children don't know you as son, and your parents don't know you as father, but they get to see those other aspects of you functioning, like when you get together for a family birthday party. At the same time, it's also like there are three people. There's you, there's your wife and there's also your child, and there's a separateness there, with a union as a family.

That doesn't do it, not by a long shot, as intended. It will have to do for this format, though, and it will remain a mystery. Besides, if I could make it not be a mystery, what would all those theologians do?

13. Is there going to be any "me-time" in heaven?

Really? Okay, it's fine if you want to ask that question. If you mean "me-time" in the manner of needing some alone time to feel like yourself again, then the answer is not going to please you, because all that I can say to you now is that heaven is eternal and there will and will not be "me-time" in heaven. I mean that in the aspect of both things happen at once, even though that's logically impossible. Maybe it's a nicer explanation for you to rest assured that God knows what your temperament is. You get a new body but you're still you, except sinless. Since God knows your temperament, when you're with God, you feel more whole, more complete, more satisfied than you ever have before, because you actually will be those things. The introverts and the extroverts each don't have to worry over when does the party end (but for different reasons). If you meant "me-time" meaning something selfish, this just won't cross your mind then.

14. You didn't know when you would be coming back again when you were first on earth, but I imagine you know now. Can you give me a hint?

Let's not cause any more problems than we need to, bud. No exact forecasting, sorry. I will re-emphasize only the same word I used back then: Soon.

15. Which church should I go to?

You sound like you wanted to ask, "Do I have to go to church?" Maybe that would be followed by, "Do I have to do this?" and, "Do I have to stop doing that?" I've found that when people ask those types of questions, they generally know the answers, don't like them and are looking for a way out of following through. Back in the day, this would make me very tired.

See, I'm not into petty things; I'm into important things. What you have to realize is that most small things—I didn't say petty things—are important, as they are the tiny building blocks of the bigger things. Have I mentioned I'm looking for change? That change doesn't come from your own effort, so no amount of "doing the right behaviors" is ever going to be good enough to get into heaven. Right behaviors are good, but it isn't about that. It's not about claiming the forgiveness and just getting on with your life, either.

I want to be your God, your only God. I will forgive you and I will get you into heaven, but I want to change you on earth, too. That's going to happen as you and I have a relationship together, but it's also going to happen as you join with other believers. They'll help you grow, too. Most likely, they'll also probably drive you a bit crazy, even as you drive them a little crazy.

I hope you hear how I'm trying to say that. You're all supposed to be working on stuff, allowing my Spirit access into your innermost places. Again, that happens in prayer, in reading the Bible, in serving and in community with other believers.

If there's a church near you, check it out. There are a lot of good ones; I will see you there. If, however, you walk in and no one seems interested in what I've scoped out here, you should probably look for another one. There's a long, complicated history of how my few followers at the time of the first Easter became the disparate—but worldwide—church of Christ.

It's not my purpose here to raise up or put down any denomination, or to tell you which specific church to go to. I will help you figure that out, if you don't know, same as I will anything else that's bothering you. What you've learned during this time, you should be able to apply to knowing if you should go to church, if you have to do this, if you should stop doing that, et cetera.

I'm sorry that not everyone who claims to speak for me speaks for me. I'm sorry that not every local church will help you. Some of them are great and some need you to be a part of them, but some of them won't let me in at all. All churches have one, incurable problem: They're filled with people. Then again, that's why I love them.

16. Jesus, are we getting to know the real you?

Are you getting to know the real me? Are you getting to know the real you? I am. This is a good format, a nice format. I chose it, I'm not denigrating it. It is limited, however. The real me? Why do you think there is eternity before you if not to use that time to get to know the real me? I'm not hiding anything, it's just that there are limitations for you until you get to that eternity. I have many aspects to my personality for you to get to know.

I'm reminded, as you read the Gospels, of many wonderful things. Some of them would take longer than you have to explain, based on the culture of that time, my upbringing, the languages of the day, and on and on. I want to highlight some of that; more of the context is important for reading the Gospels, but is up to you to seek that out. If you want to understand George Washington better, do you not learn about the 18th Century and Colonial America?

Yet I am not that man, that Jewish man from 2,000 years ago. I am he and I am more than he. I have a Jewish mindset and I now also share other mindsets. I have chosen to come to you with this admixture, intentionally. Sometimes I address you (singular) and sometimes I am trying to address you (plural, or "all y'all" as my friends in the South say). Sometimes I question you ("all y'all") as a rabbi would and sometimes I tell you (singular) the way it is. There's been some repetition in this book in what I've been saying, and that's intentional. Maybe somebody will get it because of that.

17. So, are you saying you've changed?

Have I changed? Have I?

18. Jesus, is *everything a test?*

Are you asking me for a grade?

Look, to a certain degree, God could let the earth and all life on it go on without interference, like a wind-up toy. He could wind it up and set it down and watch it move unsteadily for a time and then peter out. That would be it, from creation to end, from birth to death. Did He not set the heavens in motion? Did He not create time and gravity as a function of creating the physical world itself? God could sit back, but He rested one day and look what happened. So, He gets involved. Often people need tests to move forward. Don't confuse the circumstances of the world and the results of your choices with the testing (for your good) of God. Sometimes the tests are easy, sometimes they are hard. Sometimes people think they have failed, only the test hasn't started yet. Other times bad things happen and people lose the test of faith thinking the result is the will of God. Wherein lies the testing from God against the fallen nature of the world? Wherein lies the plan of God for your life against the choices you end up making?

Let me tell you a quick parable: There was a certain woman running for political office. She was cheered wherever she went, and so felt that the office she sought would be hers. She would be the first woman to win it. When the time came for the election, she did not win. "Why didn't I win?" she asked her advisors. "The polls were favorable and the media coverage positive." The advisors offered many theories to explain the event, all involving her opponent or her opponent's supporters. None of these theories pleased the woman, so instead she rid herself of the advisors and got new advisors, but they told her all the same things. She told the world that the election had been a test and she had been kept from passing it. Finally, one night she cried out to God and blamed Him for the results. Later, she grew old and died.

Um. . . .

You people need more parables in your lives. It's not that hard. Don't try and get the literal facts out of the parable, forget about those. What does it say about God testing us? Where do you think the test was and was there a failure to pass the test? That's what you should be thinking about. Let's move on.

19. So, Jesus, what is it you really want me to learn?

Do you need to re-read this book already?

20. Okay, then, what is it you really want me to do?

Look, learning and doing are almost the same thing, or they're supposed to be. I don't see the purpose of holing up in a library somewhere and studying everything you can about God, while never seeing the light of day again for fear you might not get to a certain book. Nor do I see the purpose of trying to fight every battle offered up by the world while not studying the truth of Christ. It's not even about balance or moderation, even where those are important for you. It's about relationship, which is dynamic and in constant motion. God is the same in purpose and holiness and love, yet is new every morning. His ways are higher than your ways. I've come down and gotten low, lower than any human being could ever go, but that is a high purpose.

Do I want you to do certain things? Yes! Are they difficult things? Yes! Well, sometimes. It depends a lot on your attitude. Getting stretched by God does not always feel good, but those who engage with God in this never regret it. What do I want you to do? I want you to respond to the faith God gave you! Get on your knees and say something, anything! If you don't know what to say, start with that! "Jesus, I don't know what to say to you!" If you don't know if you have any faith, tell me that! Ask me to help you do this, and I promise I will. I won't promise you'll feel it, I promise, however, that it will be true. Tell me you need me, because you may not have heard or understood, but I need you, because I love you. I'm ready and willing and able to forgive you, so ask me!

Live a life of daily repentance! It keeps you humble and makes you strong. Decide to be open to more change from me. Yes, there will be more. There will be things to do and more things to do, and that will never stop. You'll get stuff wrong and feel like I'm not there, but that's just the world getting in the way. Find more people who believe in me, too, and join in a community together. For in my community there are no dictators and there are no doormats; there aren't supposed to be and someday there really will not be any.

For those who find themselves doormats now, I am the floor beneath. For the petty tyrants who have climbed up somewhere they shouldn't be, I am the one who will look up into whatever sycamore tree they are in to call them down.

My life is true life and is always moving, moving closer to God. Movement without an anchor would be a hot mess of whatever spiritual nonsense you're able to latch onto. I have given you my Spirit and I have given you my Bible.

What do I want you to do? Become my disciple.

GLOSSARY

Aramaic: The common language of the people of Judea. It was a language derived from Hebrew and Persian, amalgamated during the exile of the Jewish people in Babylon in the 6th century BC.

Bet sefer: School up to age twelve, filled with Torah memorization.

Beth midrash: School from age twelve to around mid-teens, applying Torah and oral interpretations to Torah.

Bethlehem: A small town a few miles south of Jerusalem where Jesus was born and spent his first few months.

Cana: A village in Galilee, the site of Jesus' first recorded miracle, the changing of water into wine.

Capernaum: A village on the northern shore of the Sea of Galilee. Jesus used it as his home base.

Ephraim: A small village north-northeast of Jerusalem. Jesus went there after raising Lazarus from the dead, in part to escape the crowds and in part to escape from Pharisees looking to kill him.

Festivals: Seven festivals, or "feasts", are listed in the Old Testament (Leviticus 23): **Passover** (combined with a weeklong Festival of Unleavened Bread), **Pentecost** (also called the Festival of Firstfruits), Festival of Weeks, Festival of Trumpets, The Day of Atonement, **Festival of Tabernacles** (or Booths). An eighth, the Festival of Lights (now known as Hanukkah), was added between the Old Testament and the New Testament. The bolded feasts are the three main ones that required the pilgrimage to Jerusalem.

Galilee: The region around the Sea of Galilee. The people were Jewish and spoke Aramaic. They went to Jerusalem to worship in the temple, but were sometimes looked down on for being provincial or having an accent.

Gospels: The first four books of the New Testament, named after their traditional authors: Matthew, Mark, Luke and John. The word "gospel" means "good news" and is a specific type of theological literature, not a biography.

Herod Antipas: One of Herod the Great's sons. He inherited a portion of his father's rule, becoming Tetrarch of Galilee. He built up Sepphoris, later on imprisoning and beheading John the Baptist.

Herod the Great: Appointed by the Romans to be king over Judea, he was brutal and ruthless, but also was the driving force behind the greatest building period in the region, including rebuilding the temple in Jerusalem, greatly extending the plaza or "temple mount" still in existence today. He was king when Jesus was born, dying in 4 BC.

Hypostatic union: Theological concept to describe the two natures of Christ in one person, the fully human and fully divine.

Immanence: Theological concept of God's closeness to humanity and the world, seen primarily in Jesus' humanity. See "Transcendence".

Jericho: A city of Judea east-northeast of Jerusalem. Jesus met Zacchaeus here on his way to Jerusalem.

Jerusalem: The capital and largest city of Judea. The temple was located on Mount Moriah inside the city.

John the Baptist: Forerunner of Jesus Christ, the first prophet of God in 400 years, since Malachi in the Old Testament period. He called people to repentance from their sins and baptized them in the Jordan River. When he baptized Jesus, Jesus' public ministry began.

Jordan River: A river running north to south, starting north of and flowing through the Sea of Galilee in the north to the Dead Sea in the south, a traditional eastern boundary for the Jews.

Judea: The region around Jerusalem. The people were Jewish and spoke Aramaic. This is the traditional territory of the Israelites.

Koine: The type of Greek written and spoken during the time of Jesus.

Law, Prophets, Writings: The whole Torah or Old Testament. This phrase was used by Jesus and people of his day to describe the scrolls of the sacred writings that comprised what is called the Old Testament. The "Law" was the Pentateuch, or the first five books of the Bible (Genesis, Exodus, Leviticus, Numbers, Deuteronomy), the "Prophets" included the historical writings (e.g. 1 & 2 Kings) as well as the prophetic books (Isaiah, Jeremiah, etc.), and the "Writings" comprised the Wisdom books like Psalms and Proverbs. See "Tanakh".

Messiah: The Hebrew word essentially means "the anointed", (as in one sent by God), and its theological meaning has deep roots. All through the Old Testament there is a growing notion of a Redeemer that God would send, especially in the prophetic books and Psalms.

Nazareth: A small village in Galilee where Jesus grew up. The local populace believed the Messiah would come from among them.

Passover: One of the major Festivals of the Jewish calendar, celebrated each spring during a full moon. Passover celebrated the work of God redeeming His people as recorded in Exodus 12, when God sent an avenging angel over Egypt, killing the firstborn in every household, but passing over the Israelite camp if they had the mark of lamb's blood on their doors.

Pharisee: A religious and political sect in Jewish life at the time of Jesus. The word literally means "separate".

Pontius Pilate: The Roman governor of Judea at the time of Jesus' crucifixion.

Rabbi: A Jewish term of respect applied to all teachers, it literally meant "master", but colloquially "teacher". It was ascribed specifically to those who called disciples to teach them the understanding of Scriptures and how to live them out.

Sadducee: A religious and political sect in Jewish life at the time of Jesus. This group was usually fairly small, but often wealthy and in the top positions of power. Theologically they only accepted the first five books of the Bible and did not believe in the possibility of resurrection. Jesus confronted them on this view by quoting Exodus 3:6.

Samaria: The territory on the outskirts of Judea and Galilee. The people were Samaritans, looked down on by the Jews of that day for being of mixed race, supposedly the descendants of Jews who did not go into exile to Babylon in the 6th century BC, but intermarried with other people who came into the land at that time.

Sanhedrin: The body of 70 which was the top religious governing body for the Jews. It was made up of Pharisees and Sadducees, with a high priest at the head who was chosen by the ruling Romans.

Sea of Galilee: A large freshwater lake 12-13 miles wide in places, located in the territory of Galilee. Jesus spent a lot of time on or by this body of water, often crossing it with his disciples.

Seder: From the Aramaic word for "Order". The traditional meal, or ritual feast, eaten at Passover with lamb, unleavened bread, ground bitter herbs and red wine, each symbolic or spiritually significant. Several questions are asked during the meal by the youngest son or member of the group, to be answered by the father or head of the group, in order to re-tell the history of the Israelites from their time in bondage in Egypt, basically: Why is this night different from all other nights? Why on this night do we eat only unleavened bread? Why on this night do we eat only bitter herbs, and why on this night do we dip the herbs twice? Why on this night do we eat only roasted meat? The Passover meal in Jesus' time is somewhat different from a modern Seder.

Sepphoris: A city near to Nazareth that Herod Antipas had made a regional capital and was having built up. Workers from around the area would have been busy for many years working on the buildings during Jesus' youth.

Synagogue: Literally "assembly". A small building used for a variety of community purposes, including a Sabbath service with Torah reading, but also school for the local children during the week.

Tanakh: The word is actually an acronym of the (English equivalent) letters "T", "N" and "K" which stands for "Torah", "Neviim" and "Ketuvim". Translated this is Law, Prophets and Writings. See Law, Prophets and Writings.

The Spirit/The Holy Spirit: God. God is described as having three natures in one essence, Father, Son and Holy Spirit. The Holy Spirit indwells a believer. He came to people on occasion, until the Day of Pentecost after Easter. Now, He resides in all Christians.

The temple: The most sacred site for Jews in ancient Jerusalem, built on the summit of Mount Moriah within the ancient city. The original temple had been built by King Solomon around 900 BC. It was destroyed by the Babylonians in 586 BC. The second temple was rebuilt by Jews returning from exile in Babylon, under the leadership of Ezra, Nehemiah and Zerubbabel. Herod the Great undertook a major renovation and expansion of the temple and the grounds (called the "temple mount"). This temple was destroyed by the Romans in 70 AD.

Torah: Literally "Teaching". Torah often stands for the Pentateuch, or the first five books of the Old Testament (Genesis, Exodus, Leviticus, Numbers, Deuteronomy), but in some contexts can also refer to the whole Old Testament. See "Law, Prophets and Writings".

Transcendence: Theological concept of God being holy, or above humanity and the world, seen especially in Jesus' divinity. See "Immanence".

Tzitzit: Four tassels of blue and white thread on a standard cloak worn by Jewish men (surviving in certain fashions to this day). The word can also be translated as "wings" (or even "rays") and was thought to refer to Malachi 4:2, that the Messiah would bring healing in his "wings".

Author's Afterword

The story of the writing of this book goes back more than twenty years. I was reading the Gospel of Luke. I had read it before; several times, at least. This time I was stopped cold as I read Luke 7:9. It's in the story of the centurion who had a servant who was sick (chapter XXXIII in this book). Jesus says he will come to the centurion's house to heal the servant. The centurion sends word to Jesus not to come, for he is not worthy of that. Just "say the word," the centurion says. The centurion has authority to make soldiers do what he says, and he believes Jesus has authority over the sickness, and the sickness will have to listen to Jesus.

In Luke 7:9, Jesus says that he has not found faith like this even in all of Israel. That's a stunning comment enough, but not what stopped me in my tracks. No, before Jesus says that, the Gospel writer says that Jesus "was amazed".

I sat still for a while thinking it over. How does one amaze Jesus? I really wanted an answer to that question, though it didn't seem to have one.

Eventually I started with a word study. The word "amazed" happens with some frequency in the Gospels, but usually the crowds are amazed at Jesus. How often was it Jesus who was the amazed one?

It turns out to be two times. The first at Luke 7:9 (Matthew 8:10 has the exact same story), and the second at Mark 6:6. Two times in Scripture Jesus is described as being "amazed".

In the Mark example, Jesus has returned to Nazareth, to his boyhood home (chapter XX). The people there doubted him, wondering how he could have gotten his powers and his teaching. It says that Jesus was amazed at their unbelief!

That thought was with me a long time. Amazed at belief once, amazed at unbelief the other time. There was a real pendulum swing between those two extremes. I really liked that about Jesus, being amazed at those two things. I feel that way, too, sometimes, when I see belief and also unbelief exhibited by people.

There was another story I thought about, too, in relation to Jesus being amazed at the centurion's faith. The Roman had had such an awesome statement, so out of the blue, I loved it! There was one other person in the Gospels who made me feel the same way, the Canaanite woman in Matthew 15, who begged Jesus to heal her daughter (chapter LVIII). Jesus tells her that she's outside the circle of people he was calling, saying it wasn't right to give the children's bread to the dogs, but she answers so spectacularly: "Even the dogs eat the crumbs that fall from their master's table." Wow! Jesus heals her daughter at that statement of faith.

I thought for sure when I reviewed that story that I would find that word there, "amazed". Jesus must have been amazed at that woman's faith. Her statement seemed on much the same level as the centurion's that I was "amazed" when that word wasn't there. Possibly Jesus had been amazed, but the Gospels don't say he was. What did it mean if he wasn't amazed at her faith (though he called it "great")?

I wasn't sure about any of these things. However, at some point in the years of pondering these (and other) questions about Jesus, I thought I would write a book about it, maybe not just this one issue of being amazed or not, but encompassing those questions and more, everything I had learned or thought was interesting about the Gospels, including what I found challenging and difficult.

It was early on in that process that the title came to me. I thought it would be a novel, all prose, pretty standard really (except for the main character, I guess). I first imagined Jesus writing his memoirs by himself (i.e. me writing in first person), during his time on earth, but writing in English and addressing an audience for today. I did about ten pages of this nonsense before I quickly realized two things:

1. The only known time he had to write something like that after his baptism is the 40 days in the wilderness immediately after it. He's in the past, writing to a future audience about the events of his life that will take place in his future. . . . How do I write tenses for that?

2. If he does the writing, no matter who I get to edit it, somebody in the grammar police (a group I have some love and respect for . . . or is it "for whom I have some love and respect"?) would cry foul over the Son of God's usage of a semi-colon. I mean, was it worth that discussion? They didn't even have semi-colons during his time on earth!

So I let it sit for a while. A long while. As I had questions or learned little things that I particularly liked, I would file them away in my head, thinking that it would go into that novel, *Memoirs of Jesus*, that I would write . . . someday.

Then I became morose. Someday became some decade. It seemed like I would never get more than those crummy ten pages written (which were unusable, anyway). I felt like I would be burying my one talent in the sand, and that I would never have the time to do what I wanted to do. A lot of pride and angst wrapped up in a very human, very typical ball.

Though I felt I was a writer not doing any writing, I had actually been doing something. I had been doing a daily Bible journal. I had started one in college, but had let it go for a number of years. Now, since shortly after the "ten pages of *Memoirs of Jesus* as a traditional novel" debacle, I had gotten back into that, into journaling, after a pastor had encouraged me (well, not me personally; he encouraged a large crowd attending church that day, but it worked . . . and I write that in case a pastor ever reads this and wonders if that kind of thing ever works; well, sometimes it does). A few years on and I had hundreds of pages written, but of course, they weren't what I always meant by "writing". They weren't pages going into a novel that could someday be published; therefore, to me they didn't count. More pride and angst, I guess, but there I was.

One day, as I sat explaining this to God in what had started out as a prayer but had turned into a selfish rant (and not for the first time, I admit), the Spirit hit me pretty hard. It wasn't a physical shock, but a major sensation, a jolt, that went through me. I understood a rebuke—one said with a certain amusement, maybe wryness. I told God I hadn't done any writing, and He told me to look at all the notebooks I had recently filled.

I rolled my eyes (I did, I actually rolled my eyes at God). "That's not what I meant," I whined, continuing my bout of supreme selfishness (one could say idiocy, too; one could say a lot of things there). "I want to have a book written." I heard no more from God right then; He wasn't going to write it for me. If He had, it would have been awkward trying to put my name on it.

It dawned on me soon after that day, though. *Memoirs of Jesus* could basically be in the format of my daily journal. I would just write it as if Jesus were saying it. If he said it to me, today, the tenses would be clear and I'm the moron who is too comma-happy! (Seriously, those were my biggest worries, which today seem as naïve to me as they probably do to you.)

For about five months I read through the Gospels, Matthew to Mark to Luke to John. I stopped once a day, every time it seemed like there would be a good topic, one I had learned about or thought about a lot, or simply wanted to explore. Yes, I was going to hit Luke 7:9, I was definitely going to hit Luke 7:9 . . . but something happened on the way to the manger (or some biblical input for that phrase). Luke 7:9 wasn't nearly as important to the whole project as I had imagined it would be. It was merely one in a long string of amazing things about Jesus that I wanted to explore.

No, Jesus did not in fact visit me physically for 40 straight nights. In this respect, this book is still a novel (though not a very traditional one, I suppose). It's also a type of Gospel commentary. I call it "speculative commentary". My only starting point was that everything I read in the Gospels is true. I do feel that I was prepared to write it and, at least in part, inspired to write it.

I'm not a theologian, I'm not a biblical scholar. I must rely on others for the meaning of the Greek and the Aramaic. Others are studying about Jewish culture from Jesus' day. So much is coming to light, it's amazing . . . and also amazing that so much has been missed or forgotten over the years. I wanted to highlight some of these things, and in light of them to encourage you to read the Gospels (whether again or for the first time), and by extension the whole New Testament, and by extension the whole Bible.

Whether you agree with exactly how I presented Jesus in this book or not, I hope it can be part of how you think about him, a tool to be used, perhaps, if and when you do read the Bible. *Memoirs of Jesus* is not an end point, and if it isn't a starting point, either, then maybe it at least can be part of the discussion. For my fellow Christian, may you be encouraged, even if we differ on some finer points of theology. For the Seeker, may you humbly trust in Jesus to be who he said he is. For the Skeptic, thank you for reading; I hope this has given you something to think about.

Had I pursued those ten crummy pages years ago and forced them to go on for another 200-300 pages, then *Memoirs of Jesus* would be very different; not just in form, but in content. Had I waited another decade—or even just a year—to think over and redo what you have here before publishing it, the form would probably be similar, but small and possibly large pieces of content would not be the same. What I mean is, I hope in a year from writing this I will have learned more about who Jesus is and been more transformed by him, affecting all aspects of my life (not limited to my writing). Other pieces—though known already—will be more emphasized in my life than they are now, others correspondingly less. All these things would of necessity impact what I wrote. At some point, however, the proverbial pen must be set down.

Before it was set down finally, I had help along the way. God's help I felt clearly, but God likes using human beings, and so some were willingly useful in this project (and some helped without even knowing my name). All writers who look into this subject—whether writing anything from a commentary to a novel—stand on the shoulders of many teachers, preachers, scholars, commentators (and other "ordinary" people) who have come before them. I felt that acutely, and so some of the concepts in this book benefited tremendously from them. Some of the ideas are original. The presentation and any errors associated with all of them are mine alone.

I would like to thank some pastors and teachers who have had a bigger influence on me than most. I have learned a great deal from my own pastor, Scott Wade of Coon Rapids Evangelical Free Church. I'm mostly or completely unknown to this next group, but I am particularly grateful to them: Dr. Robert Utley of Bible Lessons International (*freebiblecommentary.org*), Ray Vander Laan of That the World May Know Ministries, David Johnson of Church of the Open Door (retired), Bob Merritt of Eagle Brook Church (retired) and Steven Furtick of Elevation Church. Other writers and speakers whose words, research and (perhaps wholly unbeknownst to them) encouragement through their own books and talks include: Lois Tverberg (especially her wonderful book *Walking in the Dust of Rabbi Jesus*), Amer Olson of Jews for Jesus (for his inspiring description of the Passover), Thomas Bradford (*torahclass.com*) and Dr. Ron Mosely (for his very helpful book *Yeshua: A Guide to the Real Jesus and the Original Church*). *Eyewitness to Jesus: Amazing New Manuscript Evidence About the Origin of the Gospels* by Carsten Peter Thiede and Matthew D'Ancona was an early stimulant to the project, as well.

The internet is wondrous for amateur researchers, and numerous articles, maps, photos, essays, blogs, commentaries, etc., were consulted over minor matters (actually, whenever I started making the metaphorical molehills somewhat larger in my mind). No single site outside of those associated with the aforementioned teachers was heavily used. With regard to the medical aspects of Jesus' crucifixion, numerous theories abound. Many agree in most respects (though I found an old article from Dr. C. Truman Davis the most convincing, and used it as more of a guide than any other). Parlaying pieces of a few versions together and forming them with my own thoughts, I arrived at what is presented within this book. A similar concept was employed for a number of chapters. For anyone who has posted something in one area or another, please accept this general but heartfelt thank you for the available material over which I could ponder.

A few good, respected friends read early drafts of this book and offered support and their own wisdom and insight for me to use. My thanks go out to Derek Sutermeister, Julie Kurtz and Ray Jarosik. Derek was part of a small group/men's Bible study, along with good friends Scott Leake and Jason Brandvold, who heard the first presentation of *Memoirs of Jesus* back in 2017 and received it enthusiastically.

There are many other people to thank for many reasons, most of which neither of us can remember, but the vignettes that ended up being in this book that were influenced by and built up over the years from little nuggets of ideas or conversations between us are a testament of my thanks.

To my wife, Beth, thank you every day for your love and support. You trusted me with this project, knowing how much it meant to me. Joshua and Emily, you were each a great source of encouragement; I love you.

Finally, thank you to Jesus, God's salvation. I thank you for your Spirit throughout the writing and editing of this book.

In humble appreciation of so many kind services over the years, for her faith, support, devotion and friendship, I dedicate this book to Julie Kurtz, the wonderful wife of my cousin Charlie. Thank you for all you do.

ABOUT THE AUTHOR

David Kurtz is a lifelong Midwesterner, currently residing in Coon Rapids, MN, along with his wife Beth, daughter Emily and son Joshua. He published his first novel *War and Peace in Dodge* in 2018. He is also the editor of *Dear Phil: Letters to a Brother, 2013-2017*. Visit him at www.newbrevet.com or contact him via email at newbrevet@gmail.com.

New Brevet books are published on Amazon.com KDP. Go there to find books by David Kurtz.